TRACY KORN

ANIMUS FERRUM
PUBLISHING

AQUA | Book One

Cover Design Copyright © 2015 by James Korn

Photography by J.Korn Photographics

www.jkornphoto.com

ISBN 978-0-692-49790-6
www.TheElementsSeries.com

Library of Congress Control Number: 2016906134

Edited by Ryan Bachtel, Rachel Carpenter, and Jim McClain

Summary: Only the best can begin career training at Gaia Sur, the elite academy on the ocean floor, but when Jazz begins receiving cryptic messages from past Gaia cadets coming from within the earth's core, she and her friends discover that the road to everything they've ever wanted now leads somewhere they never wanted to go.

First Trade Paperback Edition
Printed in the United States of America

For Laura and Michael.

A ship in the harbor is safe, but that's not what ships are built for.
~ John Augustus Shedd

CHAPTER 1
The Fear of Success

This morning is like every morning that has come before, and I am the only one who cares that it could be the last.

It's May, and through the shuttle window this time of year, it's just bright enough outside to see the relay dome for Gaia Sur, the only way anyone ever gets out of Seaboard North. It sits about half-a-mile out from shore in the Atlantic Ocean, though the school itself is miles below.

In a few minutes, the sunlight will wrap over the smooth, metallic surface of the dome and make it shine like a fallen star until it sinks into the rising tide, leaving only the blinking red buoy light by the time we arrive at the interviews today. I've watched this happen for the last twelve years of preliminary school, but this time, right now, could be the last, and it feels like I never saw it coming.

My twin brother, Jax, sits next to me on the shuttle leaning his head back on the seat with his eyes closed like he does every morning, but I thought he might look out the window today. Tomorrow, we'll either leave our mother and Nann, our little sister, and take a submarine to Gaia, or learn that we'll never be able to. I don't know which I think is worse.

Jax says *it's what we've been working toward all these years*, but now that it's finally here, the reality of possibly leaving and never coming back is paralyzing. I know everything will be taken care of here between the stipends that Jax and I will earn if we get into Gaia, plus my father's security package, so I just tell myself that if we can't have him, at least the hydrogen plant gave us that. Not everyone is so lucky.

No one except the seniors will be in school today, which means Nann and our mother will be able to distract themselves with going to the marketplace, cooking, and then decorating for the port festival tonight instead of worrying about how Jax and I are scoring. Both my mother and father sat for the interview when they were 18 too, but the only thing they ever said about it was that it's long. That's all anyone ever says about it.

"Will you *stop* bouncing?" Jax opens his brown eyes in a squint against the reflecting sun and elbows me in the ribs as our shuttle pulls away from the station and heads for the tunnel tube.

"Ow!" I say, stopping my knee abruptly and glaring at him, then turning my gaze back through my small circular window to watch our mother, Nann, and all the other parents and siblings getting smaller as they wave.

"Jazz!" Jax hisses.

"What?"

"You're making my teeth rattle," he says, pushing a hand through his dark brown curls, which are too tight to actually be in his eyes, so he's evidently trying to show me how exasperated he is.

"Sorry," I say, managing to roll my eyes right into the bright overhead lights that flicker on as we enter the

tunnel.

"Stop worrying about the interview. We've had twelve years of preparation for this, and we're ranked third and fourth in the class. If you want to worry about someone, worry about *this* guy..." Jax pushes the back of a light brown head of wavy hair in the seat in front of us.

"Let's go then, Ripley!" the boy is out of his seat and pushing back at Jax, both of them laughing and squashing me into the window with their flailing ape appendages.

"Hey, I'm sitting here!" I yell at Jax and the other half of the idiot equation, Arco Hart, who is ranked tenth in our class. He smiles an apology at me, but all I can do is shake my head and look out the window, which is pointless because there's nothing to see but steel and shadows in the tunnel on the way to the school.

"She's just wound up about the interview," Jax says, and I swallow hard to keep from rounding on him.

"Why are *you* worried?" Arco asks, his face falling when I turn to him.

"Because *I'm* the only one who—what? Why are you looking at me like that?" I press my lips together and scowl at him, then taste the blood in my mouth.

"Here, take this," Arco says, slipping out of the aisle and back into the dark blue covered seat in front of us, then reaching over the top of it with the handkerchief he's just fished from his pocket. I touch my fingers to my now throbbing lip and pull them back to see the bright red smear, then look up at the handkerchief he's offering and raise an eyebrow at him. "Come on, it's clean," he smiles again, so I take the cloth.

"Must have happened in the jostle. Sorry, Jazz," Jax says, wincing. "Make sure you press on it." I narrow my eyes at him and feel guilt well up in my chest about the whole situation, which makes no sense at all. Why should *I* feel guilty about getting hit in the mouth by a couple of orangutans? "I'll get a cold pack," Jax says after looking at Arco, then grips the steel pole at the end of our seat to hoist himself upward and toward the front of the shuttle where the medi-droid is stationed. *Why doesn't he just press the call button?* I think, and shake my head, even more annoyed. When I look back to Arco, I find him staring down at me with hang dog hazel eyes as he props his chin on his forearms over the top of the seat.

"It's fine. It's just a busted lip," I mumble through his handkerchief.

"I'm really sorry."

"I'll live," I say, but he doesn't look any less pathetic.

"Why are you so worried about the interview?"

"That's not what's bothering me," I answer, pulling the cloth away to see if the bleeding has stopped.

"Then what is it?"

I debate telling him because I don't even really know myself, but then it comes spilling out like a bucket of frogs.

"Aren't you worried about not coming back?" I ask. He looks at me, expressionless for a second, and I get the feeling whatever he says next won't be the whole truth.

"Jazz, it's not like we'll never talk to our families again. There are still port-calls."

"But that's only virtuo, and only for six days each year."

He waits another beat before responding. "They'll be OK if we get in—*when* we get in. Isn't that the most important thing?" he asks, fighting to maintain his smile, and now I *know* he's worried too.

This is the part no one wants to talk about. The fear of failure is easy, asking what if we don't make it, what if we have to stay in the overcrowded Seaboard stacks forever with nothing to do and no chance of making something of ourselves? But the fear of *success?* What's the danger in getting everything we've ever worked for...everything we've ever wanted? What's the danger in sacrificing everything we've ever known *just* so we can protect it? But no one else thinks like this.

None of it makes any sense, so I just look through the window into the tunnel and watch nothing race by.

***

The last of the cold pack disintegrates as the shuttle pulls into the school station, and the hydraulic steel doors slide open a few feet up the aisle. As we approach, I see teachers lining each side of the school foyer through the window—five women on one side, five men on the other.

"What's happening in there?" I ask Jax, but he just shakes his head as he peers over my shoulder.

"I don't know."

"Are we supposed to go in now? No one is moving," Arco says, then leans over the seat in front of him to talk to someone else just as we hear the school intercom.

"YOU MAY EXIT THE SHUTTLE IN THE ORDER

YOUR NAME IS CALLED."

My knee starts bouncing again, and I will it to stop.

"FRAYA CLEARMORE," the intercom voice says.

"Fraya is ranked first in the class, so this can't be bad, can it?" I whisper to Jax.

"ELLIS RAJ."

"He's number two, which means we're probably next. It has to be a rank thing," Jax says, looking at me reassuringly. I hear my heart drumming in my ears, then notice Jax's knee bouncing.

"JAZWYN RIPLEY."

The guilt I'd felt in my chest earlier is replaced now with a heavy sheet of ice that makes it hard to breathe. I stand and shuffle past Jax, his expression telling me he will be right behind me.

"JAXON RIPLEY," the intercom voice continues. "QUINN STALLWORT, AVIS LING."

When I step off the shuttle onto the concrete platform, everything is in slow motion. The seamless gray walls of the docking bay move past like in a dream until they flow into the brushed metal benches lining the building and then into the arching steel entryway of the foyer with the school icon, the shiny chrome letters *SBN* embossed on the inside of the globe at its peak. Through the window that wraps around the building, I see our teachers standing along opposite walls, all of them dressed in the same style, but differently colored tunics and pants. Ms. Wren is standing along the left wall wearing all sky blue, which stands out against her dark skin. Some of her long black braids have blue beads at the ends, which click together when she walks through the door smiling at me, her high cheekbones and delicately angled features like an ancient Egyptian queen's. She doesn't say anything, but her soft expression makes me feel like there's nothing to be afraid of.

"Ms. Wre—" I start, and she stiffens, shaking her head back and forth just barely, and just once. My stomach churns with the uncertainty, and my head feels like someone has left a screen on an empty feed, the static noise seeming to get louder as we walk through the foyer doors and stand against the wall. After a few minutes, the anxious feeling causes a nervous smile to pull at my lips, which stops in place with the searing pain and tinny taste of blood suddenly on my tongue again. I suck my bottom lip into my mouth and hold it there with my top teeth as Jax walks in with the others, each teacher approaching a student to stand together like Ms. Wren did with me.

Jax's dark, heavy brows are knit together, and he contorts his face into something that I'm sure he thinks is reassuring when he sees my expression. I'm exactly one minute and 18 seconds younger than him, but that's all he needs to feel like the protective big brother. We all have enough to worry about without him adding me to his list, though, so I point to my lip and shrug it off. His brows relax, and in knowing he feels better, so do I.

"CONGRATULATIONS, TOP 10 SENIORS!" our principal says over the announcement speaker. "AT THIS TIME, PLEASE FOLLOW YOUR INSTRUCTORS."

"Why are we—" I start to whisper what I'm sure everyone is thinking to Ms. Wren, but her quick gray eyes stop me. She shakes her head at me slowly, deliberately, and I know I can't ask her anything else right now.

I look over to Jax on the other side of the room and find him mouthing the word *breathe* to me, but that's not helping to melt the spreading freeze I feel. I try to smile at him and remember my lip just in time, raising my eyebrows and nodding instead to assure him that I'm fine, even though I'm not. I find Arco right behind him, whose eyes are bright and smiling, and for just that second, I do feel better...warmer until he disappears down the shadowy algorithms hallway towering in the wake of Mr. Hmong's balding head, and the ice slides over my chest again.

CHAPTER 2
Threshold

I look back at our silver, bullet nose shuttle and see that no one else has disembarked yet. *Why isn't anyone else getting off? Why isn't anyone talking?* I think, over-whelmed with questions that I can't answer. Maybe I'm just picking up on everyone else's anxiety. Ms. Wren said that can happen sometimes, especially in a closed space like this foyer or the shuttle. Maybe that's really what is making me uneasy about the prospect of going to Gaia. *So, I need to calm down. I need to take a deep breath,* I think as I start to follow Ms. Wren. It's not like they're going to kill us. Ms. Wren could not look at me and smile if they were going to kill us. That I know for sure.

The sound of our footsteps echoes behind us in the communications corridor, and it's so palpable that I keep turning around to make sure no one else is there. They've turned all the holograms off, and until we pass the occa-sional steel water pooler, the long stretch of obsidian walls, doors, and floor make me feel like I've fallen through a hole in the earth beneath the daybreak blue of the ceiling.

Ms. Wren's eyes flash almost imperceptibly, but I notice. She holds my gaze for a second too long...she *wants* me to notice, so I watch her face more closely. She's using all the cues we discussed in the body language unit last week: eye contact, nodding, the way she's angling her head forward to draw me in. I don't understand everything from Empathy class, but I feel reassured now —as long as I don't ask any questions.

There is still no one else in the communications corridor with us when we stop at a room I've never been inside before. I've always thought it was a closet for the maintenance droids, but when Ms. Wren opens the door, it's much bigger—about the size of an office with a round metal table, two matching chairs, and a white, lidded box in the middle of the table. There are no windows in this room, which is strange since all the rooms in this wing have windows, and the walls are a milky white, which is also strange since all rooms in the communication corridor are blue. On the opposite wall there is one door, but I have no idea where it could lead. Ms. Wren takes my hand and leads me to the little table to sit down after she puts the tote on the floor.

"We don't have a lot of time, Jazwyn, so I can't explain everything, but you're all right. You and the others are able to interview first because you're in the top ten, isn't that wonderful? You don't have to wait here all day." She smiles her normal, bright smile at me now, which turns her cheeks into little apples, and I smile back at her as widely as I can without splitting my lip open again. "Oh no, what happened there?" she asks.

"Just an accident on the shuttle. My brother and Arco were wrestling," I answer. She smirks and nods, knowing them both well. "Ms. Wren, why did we have to be quiet back there?"

"Today, the commons areas are amplified to secure the

interviews just like every year, so even students on the shuttle can hear whatever might be said. Can you imagine how upset the rest of your classmates would be if they knew you were all interviewing first when they'll be here for hours waiting their turn?" Ms. Wren asks. "That's why we wait until we're behind closed doors to tell you why you were called off separately. You'll need to tell anyone who asks that you're not permitted to discuss the reasoning. Part of your Gaia acceptance, or the security of your topside career track depend on you not sharing the details of this interview with anyone outside your cohort, even years from now."

I look down at the table to figure out how to ask her about this, then meet her eyes again. "No disrespect intended, Ms. Wren, but wouldn't it be motivation for everyone to try harder if they knew the top ten didn't have to wait all day?" I ask.

"Of course, which is why we're not allowed to tell you. Competition like that would divide your focus—Gaia wants the top 10 to be motivated to achieve solely by the prospect of getting into Gaia. As for sharing the details of your interview with those beyond your cohort, it would only cause anxiety. Everyone's interview is different."

"But—" I narrow my eyes in confusion as she pushes her braids behind her shoulder and brings her chair around to mine, then looks at me soberly.

"Jazwyn, listen, this isn't important right now," she says, glancing at the watch that has slipped around to the inside of her wrist, her tone softer but her pace quicker. "Just know that some competition is good, but the wrong kind of competition here could skew the data. Anyway, I'm supposed to tell you that your natural ability is communication, you must know this by now. You understood that everything was going to be OK from the look I gave you in the corridor, didn't you? Just like we talked about in the body language unit—and you knew how to tell me you understood by using the same tools."

"I did understand, but I don't understand how, or why it matters. Why does Gaia care about me understanding a look?"

"I'm sorry, we're almost out of time. It will all make sense to you soon, but you have to get ready for the interview. The rest of the students from the shuttles will be heading to their sorting rooms now, so I need to help the other communication candidates."

"But if you're leaving, which teachers are interviewing me?" I ask.

"Your interviewers are not teachers—they're from Gaia," Ms. Wren says proudly after a pause. I feel the blood drain from my face and my mouth fall open. "It's OK, you don't have to know anything specific. You can't actually prepare for this interview, remember? They know you're ranked third, and they also know your predisposition for understanding people...for making yourself understood. That's what matters to them. Trust your instincts. You have to get dressed now. They're through that door, so just go in when you're ready."

She gets up and puts the tote on the table, then pulls out a long sleeved dusty blue tunic, a matching pair of linen pants, blue socks, and finally, blue slipper-shoes.

"Why do I have to change my clothes?" I ask.

"It will help you—blue helps communication, just like these classrooms. Here..." she smiles and sets the clothes and shoes next to me on the table, but doesn't sit again. I stand instead, and she hugs me.

"I'm so proud of you, Jazz," she says into my hair, hers smelling of rosewater. "Make a difference down there. Make things better." She squeezes me hard, and I feel my throat start to tighten. It hits me again, the feeling that this might be another last thing—the last time I ever see her, see this school and my friends.

"Thank you, Ms. Wren, I—" is all I can choke out. There's so much more I want to say to her, but the words won't come through. She holds me at arm's length then and smiles her perfect, bright smile.

"It's all right, Jazz, I know. Now clean up, and don't try to be anything you're not. Your best asset is being exactly who you are. Just remember that." I only nod because I'm afraid to open my mouth and have nothing come out, stuck behind the barricade in my chest. "All right, get dressed," she says, then squeezes my shoulders and cups my face in her hands before she turns to go.

When she leaves, the room is silent again. Deafeningly silent. I swallow hard and blow out a heavy breath as I look over my shoulder at the door behind me. The interviewers from Gaia are waiting for me on the other side right now, and I can't even imagine what they will look like. I've never met anyone from Gaia in person except for maybe the State representatives over the years who have come to tell us about Gaia and the homestead initiative, about what it's like to live on the seafloor with clean air and opportunities. They didn't look much different from any of Liddick's or Ellis's friends from the elites in Skyboard North. *This will be OK,* I think. *I'll just be myself.*

I kick off my shoes and swap out my gray pants for the blue ones. They're thin, but warm, and the tunic is soft against my skin, much softer than my old woven shirt. I've never felt clothes like this before—maybe they're from Gaia. Everything is supposed to be better there, isn't it? But despite the clothes being soft and warm and beautiful, the same sense of dread I've had for months— the same feeling that I had on the shuttle and just now with Ms. Wren—creeps over me again. *What if I'm not ready for this to end and for something new to begin?* I think, but then I realize I have a more important question: how do I hide this feeling before I meet the interviewers?

CHAPTER 3
The Interview

I open the door, and window light floods the room, temporarily blinding me as my eyes adjust. I raise my hand to shadow them, and a woman's sharp, cheerful voice greets me from somewhere.

"Hello, Miss Ripley. We've heard wonderful things about you."

My vision starts to acclimate, and I see three people seated at a table. In another second, I'm able to see that the one speaking on the left has short, copper red hair that slashes past her ears and narrow green eyes, which don't show evidence of her too wide and too bright smile. The dark haired, bearded man next to her is also smiling in the same exaggerated, perfect way, and so is the blonde woman sitting on his other side. Even though they're smiling, I feel my stomach start to churn, and I don't know if it's the starkness of this completely white, empty room that makes everything so intimidating, or if it's because all three of these interviewers are dressed in white military uniforms that seem to glow in the bright light. Their hands are folded in front of them before me, but they seem like they're a layer away.

"Hello," I manage, and swallow to stabilize my voice.

"Why don't you have a seat?" The man in the center gestures to the single chair behind the small table across from theirs, and I walk toward it. Their smiles relax as the blonde woman on the right sets a small metal cone in the center of their table.

"Jazwyn, this is called a holographic capture; it will record our interview. Will that be all right with you?" she asks. I don't know why they would want to record this, but I can't see anything wrong with it either, so I agree. She presses a button on the device, and a blue light floods slowly from the top, then rises up and out. There's a strong hum as the umbrella of light falls down and eventually encapsulates us, but the closer it gets to the ground, the quieter the hum becomes until it's gone.

"It says here that people call you Jazz—could I call you Jazz?" The blonde woman asks after looking down at her tablet, and I nod. "My name is Ms. Plume. I'm the careers and placement officer for Gaia Sur. With me today is Mr. Styx, our admissions officer, and Ms. Rheen, our school's chancellor. We have been looking forward to meeting you," she says, folding her hands in front of her again. She seems too delicate—too wide-eyed, like a painting from a different era than the others, who are more boldly lined and more sharply edged.

"Thank you. It's nice to meet you too," I say, and decide it's a good idea to fold my hands like they do so they can't see them shaking.

"Jazz, we'd like to start by congratulating you on your class status. You've obviously worked very hard to be third out of 458 students," Ms. Rheen says, leaning forward on her forearms and tapping her teeth with her long red fingernail, the cut of her hair shifting on her cheekbone as her bright green eyes flicker. "Could you explain your motivation to us?"

All at once my brain starts trying on possible answers. I can't tell them that living in the cramped stacks of the Seaboard North quadrant is a ticket to nothing but day-to-day survival for a family, or that we can't even breathe the sulfured air for too long without getting dizzy. I can't look like I'm trying to escape. These people were probably born in the underwater homesteads, so they wouldn't appreciate my situation, and I don't want their pity.

"My family has always encouraged hard work," I say instead, which sounds safe.

"And you live with your..." Mr. Styx punches something into his tablet, "...mother and two siblings; is that correct?" he asks, angling his head to the other side as he fixes his steel blue eyes on me.

"Yes," I answer, wondering if there has ever been another person who looked more out of place in a military uniform. His eyebrows have yet to relax from their indignant furrow, and it makes him look like he should be on a pulpit telling people how everything is their fault, or behind a podium telling them that nothing is.

"Your file says that your mother runs one of the covered greenbeds in your quadrant; that could be a comfortable apprenticeship. How fortunate that you have a fallback if you're not admitted to Gaia," Ms. Rheen says, tilting her chin down and looking at me from under a slash of eyebrows. That look paired with her condescending tone spark inside me, and I feel my teeth pressing together to contain it.

"Yes, I'm very lucky," I say, biting off the protest still

knocking at the back of my teeth.

"Now your father, he was *incinerated* in an accident when you were 13 years old—an explosion at the hydrogen plant?" Mr. Styx continues reading from his tablet like he's reading the latest cinestar gossip, then looks up at me intently. This question hits me in the stomach, and the heated indignation I'd been feeling turns cold.

Ms. Rheen crinkles her eyes and pinches her red lips so tightly that the corners of her mouth turn down. I think this is supposed to be a smile, but her eyes are hard and anticipatory. I look over to Ms. Plume and then back at Mr. Styx, but only Ms. Plume, with her raised eyebrows and small smile, seems to sympathize with the impact this has on me. I take a deep breath, which helps, and I feel a little of the indignation restore itself. *I've worked my whole life to be in here right now, I think. If they're waiting for me to crack, they can get used to disappointment.*

"From what I can remember," I say, looking directly at Ms. Rheen. She forces a smile and angles her head, blinks purposefully, then leans forward on her elbows, resting her chin over the bridge of her interlaced fingers.

"Would you say that you are close to your brother?" she asks, narrowing her mossy eyes.

"I suppose. We get along and fight like all siblings," I reply, suddenly feeling compelled to play everything down under her scrutinous eye, to mute all my feelings about everyone and everything and appear as neutral as possible. *Follow your instincts...trust yourself...*Ms Wren's words echo in my head.

"But he's ranked fourth; do you feel a sense of competition with your brother?" Mr. Styx asks me this question with an edge in his voice, but he doesn't twist his expression like Ms. Rheen; he only raises his neat, dark eyebrows and leans forward in his chair. I feel my heart pounding against my ribs and take another deep breath. *Calm down. Don't let them intimidate you,* I think.

"Not really. We both just want to do our best," I say, to which Mr. Styx nods, expressionless, and types something into his tablet.

"Jazz, tell us what you've heard about Gaia. Why would you like to begin career studies there?" Ms. Plume's wide blue eyes are kind, and her voice is soft, which almost makes me feel safe here. Almost.

"We've all heard about the amazing opportunities at Gaia from the State representatives, and we've heard about the successes of past graduates," I say, but they all just blink at me in the hollow silence, seeming to want me to say more, so I do. "I get the impression that people there are...professionals, and I want to be a professional too." I don't consciously choose the word *professional.* It slips in after a brief pause because it's the first word that comes to mind when I think about the State presentations we've all seen about getting into Gaia and then being able to live in the homesteads, and about their infobit broadcasts on our neural channels, both of which make it seem like there is nothing beyond reach there. A person can study anything, can *be* anything, and everyone is supposedly treated with respect no matter if they were from Skyboard North or the Fringe quadrant before they were admitted.

This belief must be exactly what they need to see in my response because they all genuinely smile at me now, and I feel a dull warmth of relief spreading in my stomach. Mr. Styx arches one tailored eyebrow at me and lowers his chin. He leans into the table, stroking his short beard into a point with his fingers, and speaks in a hushed voice.

"People are indeed professionals, Jazz. I imagine it's taxing for someone like you with your obvious talents to be surrounded by so many others who have no interest in bettering themselves," he says, leaning back and brushing something from his white jacket lapels with two of his fingers. Ms. Rheen leans over and whispers something conspiratorially, then turns her gaze on me.

"They simply don't want to put in the work, and maybe they just aren't *capable* of it because they've been conditioned by their culture that mediocrity is acceptable. But not you and your brother, Jazz. You understand the value of bettering yourself, don't you," Ms. Rheen says, ending the sentence as a statement rather than a question. I take a deep, quiet breath and try to smile at them in agreement. At this point, it's clear that the less I say, the less likely I am to change their minds about whatever lofty assumptions they're making about me, but for the record, I want to tell them all to get back in their boat. Do they really think I consider myself better than everyone in the stacks? That everyone in Gaia is better too? They'd never last a day in Seaboard North.

Ms. Plume clears her throat and interrupts the euphemism game Mr. Styx and Ms. Rheen appear to be playing. "Jazz, we just have a few more questions," Ms. Plume says. "Are you aware that if you are chosen to complete the remainder of your studies at Gaia, you may not return here to Seaboard North except in virtuo port-call transmission, and that this may only occur six times per year unless you receive special permission in the event of a death in your family?" She says this as if she wants to have it out as quickly as possible.

"Yes, I know," I respond, but what I don't know is why they insist on this, what's the problem with coming home? And before I can stop myself from asking these questions, the adrenaline from that last round has them sliding out of my mouth, which I immediately regret when I see Mr. Styx and Ms. Rheen exchange pensive, knowing glances. They breathe in quickly through their noses, and Ms. Plume looks down at the table, at the other two, and then at me. Her blonde brows draw together as she leans in. I need to get myself together. I don't know why entirely, but something in her expression tells me I can't appear to challenge things now.

"We know you've likely heard rumors, Jazz, which is one reason we like to conduct these interviews with prospective students...to dispel any fear or confusion. You understand the intensity of our four-year study program is such that students can't afford the time it would take for extended physical shore leave, not to mention the biological stress frequent topside trips could cause. Gaia Sur *is* nearly 5,000 meters under water, after all. But once studies are completed, and if students would like to return at that time, we do offer many career options that would accommodate that, at least periodically. We try to avoid displacing others who do not have the option of relocating to the ocean floor."

Ms. Plume's eyes widen a little with her last words as she presses her lips together and angles her chin down. This is the look Ms. Wren gave me earlier to get me to stop talking and just go with things—this body language, this way of talking without talking, she's giving me a lifeline. I understand now, I understand that she's my ally. I take a deep breath and make myself smile as genuinely as possible before I speak again.

"That makes sense. Thank you for explaining," I say confidently, as if this is exactly what I've been waiting to hear. Mr. Styx and Ms. Rheen seem to relax again, and Ms. Plume exhales quietly.

"Wonderful," Ms. Rheen says, looking at her tablet, then to Mr. Styx and Ms. Plume, then back at me. "Then there's just one more thing."

She gets up from her seat behind the table and walks over to me with something in her hand. Her thin, red lips twist into a smile as her heels echo in the large, hollow room, the downbeat to the growing pounding in my chest.

"Wait...um..." I stumble, unsure of what to say, but feeling compelled to protest—to say *something* as I fight the urge to stand and run out the door.

"May I have your wrist?" she asks, needling her jaded eyes at me, and even up close, she really does seem to glow. My heart hammers, and I jerk my gaze from Ms. Rheen's and look to Ms. Plume because I'd felt a rapport with her just now, because I think she will help me even though I don't know why I need help, but she only nods her head at me with a crushed smile between her lips.

I have to slow this whole thing down, I think, but I can't. *All right, then just breathe through it,* I think again, despite every feeling in my body to the contrary. *She can't hurt me, especially not here or now because everyone is expecting me to come home today...at least for a while.*

I look back into Ms. Rheen's eyes, which are large and anticipatory, like a cat about to bite the head off some pitiful thing it has just caught in its claws. I feel her icy, red-tipped fingers wrap around my forearm and lift it enough to close a wide metal bracelet around my wrist. I try to resist, but it all happens too fast. The seam between each of the ends seals in a flash of green light and a sliding hydraulic sound. The brushed cuff is cool and surprisingly weightless on my arm as I stare at it, then look back up to find Ms. Rheen smiling down at me, backlit by the intense, bright light.

"Welcome to Gaia, Jazwyn Ripley."

Her words hang in the air before me as she makes her way back to her seat, and the blue cast of the recording holograph dissipates.

"This bracelet now contains your medical history and your campus admittance information. You will not be able to remove it yourself, so please don't attempt it," Mr. Styx continues.

I try to think of something to say, some question to ask, but I can't seem to put any words together. There should be more to this whole process, shouldn't there?

For years all we've heard is how long and exhausting these interviews are, and while this one has been a little intimidating, it was nothing like what I've heard.

"Congratulations," Ms. Plume says with a gentle smile.

"We're told that the North quadrant shuttle will be waiting for you and the other nine at the foyer shortly. Please report to the West Shore launching station at 6:00 a.m. tomorrow morning," Mr. Styx says. "We'll be sending a vessel to take you and your peers to the relay station, where you will then take the submarine to Gaia Sur, so please be prompt. You will not need to bring anything with you," he concludes, then gets to his feet. "You're dismissed now, Jazz. It's been a pleasure."

They smile at me again with those impossibly white teeth, and offer me their hands one by one, which are all as cold as Ms. Rheen's. Mr. Styx releases my hand last and extends his arm to show me to the door that leads to the room where I spoke with Ms. Wren. I walk through it to my old clothes that are folded on the small table where I'd left them, and when their door closes behind me, I tie my woven shirt into a makeshift sling bag so I can stuff my things into it, then make my way to the corridor.

CHAPTER 4
Arco's Confession

All the doors are still closed as I head to the foyer. I don't think I've ever seen the school this still before, which makes the sound of my name whisper-yelled from somewhere behind me that much more startling.

"*Jazz!* Wait up," I hear, then turn abruptly and smile in relief as I see Arco approach. He's wearing new clothes too, a dark green shirt, a matching pair of linen pants, and shoes like mine, but then I notice that his jaw is clenched and his eyes are wild. He pushes messy waves of hair from his face and starts jogging up the hallway toward me, then seizes my arm and pulls us forward.

"What's wrong with you? Stop pulling me," I say, trying to wrench my arm free while maneuvering to avoid tripping over my own feet, which are turning over double time to keep up with his long strides.

"Just walk faster. I'll explain in a minute," he whispers. I've only seen him this intense one other time—when he almost got into a fight with Liddick Wright in the cafeteria over Arco's older sister, Arwyn. I never found out the whole story, but knowing Liddick, it probably wasn't wholesome. Arwyn is about 26 now, the same age as Liddick's oldest brother, Lyden, and working as a Molecular Coder on one of the space stations. It's one of the most prestigious jobs anyone can get, but also one of the most time consuming. Arco knows this, but he's still been unpredictably moody ever since her port-calls stopped coming four years ago.

We stop at the end of the communications hallway and turn down the corridor that leads to the courtyard behind the school. At the end of the hall, he steers me through the door, securing it behind us.

"Arco, *what the—*" I stumble onto the cobblestone and almost fall into the cactus garden, which is flooded with hazy sunlight that ricochets off the granite stepping stones and makes me squint.

"You're OK? Did they tell you?" he asks, looking me up and down, his face flushed with exertion.

"I'm fine, and tell me what? What's wrong with you?" I ask, pulling my arm out of his grip. "Why are you acting like a riot drone?"

"Did they tell you if you got in? You had to get in," he says, trying to regulate his breath without much success.

"Yes, see?" I say, raising my bracelet cuff, then suddenly feel my stomach drop as I realize why he might be so upset. "Arco, didn't you get in?" I look for his wrist, which is concealed behind his head. He brings it forward and shows me his bracelet.

"I did, yeah," he says, his face relaxing a little. "Sorry, I just needed to find you. Your interview was OK?" He lets out a long exhale and moves his hands to his hips, then takes measured breaths.

"Arco, yes—just some weird questions, what's *wrong* with you?" I ask again, rubbing my arm where he'd gripped it. He scrubs his hands over his face and then motions to a bench under one of the flowering trees for us to sit down, which we don't actually do before he starts talking.

"They said not to talk about it, but they can't hear us out here," he says as we cross to the bench. "There were these three people from Gaia in there, a man and two women. They asked me a few questions and then told me to go into this blue light field—" he starts, and I raise an eyebrow.

"I had that. They said it just recorded the interview," I interrupt, unsure why this would make him so frazzled.

"They said it would do that too, but for me, its main job was running a sequencing game—you know, probabilities. I had to make choices..." he trails off, shaking his head and pressing the heels of his palms into his eyes as if to stop himself from seeing something. "Sorry, I just needed to find you," he says again, this time the words sounding strangled through his tightening throat. I watch the muscles in his jaw flex and relax as he exhales, takes another long, deep breath through his nose, then slowly lets it out again. The adrenaline rush that had him so wound up must be wearing off now.

"Why do you keep saying that? Here, sit down," I say, the frustration and confusion I felt with him just a second ago now turning into concern. He drops his hands and sits under the tree on the stone bench behind us, which faces the honor wall that encircles the courtyard. The bronze faces of the last 80 years of Gaia's cadets from our quadrant line rows and rows of the wall, and I've never felt comfortable out here with them all staring at me like this. It's like they're watching me from somewhere inside those panels without making a sound, like they're just following me with their eyes. "Are you OK?" I ask Arco, my own anxiety starting to rise.

"Yeah, sorry," he says, leaning into his hands and pushing them up through his light brown hair with a quick shake before he sits up again.

"You said there were two women and a man? I had the same in my room. One of the women had this reddish hair and wild dragon lady nails. I didn't like—" I'm cut off by Arco's sudden, wide eyed look. "What?" I ask, confused.

"Ms. Rheen, with reddish hair and dragon lady nails...she was in my room too. And a tall guy with dark hair who looked like a polly running for State—*Styx*.. Mr. Styx?" My stomach drops again like it has been cut loose from the rest of my insides.

"And a blonde woman named Ms. Plume..." I mumble, watching his eyebrows crash together.

"The careers officer?" we say together.

"But how could they have been in your room and my room at the same time?" I ask.

"I don't know. What did they do in your room?" Arco asks, sitting up even straighter now.

"Nothing really, they just asked me some questions, and Ms. Rheen seemed to want to provoke me into something, but I'm not really sure what," I answer.

"Like she was forcing you to make choices?"

"Sort of, like she wanted me to say something so she could lower the hammer on me, I think. I didn't understand, but Ms. Wren's last bit of advice to me before she left was to pay attention to how I felt, and I felt like they were trying to suck me in, so I just tried the best I could to stay neutral with everything I said."

"Rheen did that to me too, but I didn't stay neutral. I made things worse."

"What do you mean? What did she say to you?"

Arco looks away from me into the stone water fountain globe in front of us before he answers.

"Nothing really, she just listed the probabilities if..." he trails off, turning his face back to the cobblestone under our feet. "Anyway, like I said, there were just these scenarios where I had to predict outcomes, and others I had to try to prevent before they happened." He swallows and then stands again, walking toward the fountain and gripping the railing. "You were in them, and I had to choose between getting you out, or Jax, or Fraya, everyone like that at the same time...and I couldn't get everyone. I told her that, yelled it at her, but she just kept telling me to *confirm my choice, or to authorize the termination* of the ones I didn't choose."

Arco's voice slips in and out on the last words, and then he is quiet and still. I'm frozen in my skin, but also feel like something inside me is ripping down the middle. I feel compelled to go to him, but also like if I do, I'll only make things worse. So, I wait. When he turns to face me again, the flush has returned to his cheeks and he's clenching his jaw. He seems terrified and angry all at once, and I don't know how to help him.

"Arco, it's OK—just try to forget it for now. It wasn't real. You can tell me later if you want, but for now just forget it," I say from the bench, trying to sound calming even though now I'm feeling tense too. In the same breath as my last word, he seems to have made a decision about something and closes the distance between us in two long strides. He sits next to me again and grabs my shoulders with both hands to fix me in place.

"Listen to me, Jazz—I don't know what they were trying to prove with these interviews, or head games, or whatever they were in there, and I don't know what's going to happen when we get to Gaia, but I know I will not let anything happen to you. That sounds random, but you're just going to have to let me say it, OK? I have to know you understand I won't let anything happen to you. Do you understand that?" His fingers press into my shoulders, but all I can do is stare at him and abruptly close my mouth once I realize it's open. "Jazz? Are you listening to me?"

"*OK*—I mean yes," I say, nodding. "I know you won't let anything happen...*thank you?*" I add awkwardly, not intending it to sound like a question, but it does.

He lets go of my shoulders and chuckles, then interlaces his fingers behind his neck and takes a deep breath before heading to the door.

"All right, let's go find everyone else. Remember not to talk about any of this in the corridors, OK?" I nod again, and we make our way down to the foyer. I take one more look over my shoulder at the bronzed metal faces on the honor wall before we do, and a shudder runs up my back until it stops in a pinch at the hollow behind my jaw.

When we arrive back at the foyer, Jax is there dressed

in dark gray and sitting next to Fraya, who is a deep red and looks like she's just been pulled back from a cliff edge. Jax looks rattled too, but not as much as Fraya. He has his arm around her, tucking her long auburn hair behind her ear with the other hand, but it doesn't seem to help her shaking. It feels like someone died in here.

"Are you all OK?" I say, crossing over to them and sitting next to Fraya. "What's wrong?"

"It'll be all right," Jax looks at Arco and then at me. "How are you?"

"I'm fine. I don't think my interview was as...intense as everyone else's seems to have been," I answer, remembering we can't talk about it in here when Arco sends me a warning look. He snuffs out a muffled laugh, which I think is kind of rude until I realize he's just seen number eight, Liddick Wright enter the foyer. He's dressed in black and is pushing a hand through his wavy, sun-bleached hair as he smiles ear to ear.

"We should go," Arco says before Liddick comes into earshot.

"Don't you want to wait for everyone?" I ask, curious to see if their interviews were anything like Fraya's.

"We can wait for them on the shuttle. It's not going anywhere before all 10 of us are back," Arco says, gripping Jax's shoulder. "Get her aboard. We're coming."

As we start walking, I see number seven, Sarin Nu come into view right behind Liddick in the mouth of the WAR corridor, which stands for *World Affairs and Relationships*. She's dressed in purple, which looks nice with her tanned complexion, and when I see her laughing next to Liddick, she even seems pretty despite her black hair being pulled into the tightest spinster bun I've ever seen her wear. She sees number nine, Myra Toll smiling as she approaches, and Sarin's rare, happy expression gives way to her normal pinched face scowl. Fortunately, she has no effect on Myra, whose earth brown clothes offset her strawberry blonde curls and make her look even more like sunshine next to Sarin.

I turn my gaze from the others to Jax, hoping that his interview was more like theirs and mine than Fraya's and Arco's. His arm is still around Fraya as they approach the shuttle, and once we're on board, Jax shows her to a window seat and pulls her into him. He talks through her hair, and after a few minutes, whatever he's saying seems to help. Her convulsions give way to occasional hic-coughs of catching breath until she's still and calm, lean-ing against him with her eyes closed like this has been the most exhausting day of her life.

CHAPTER 5
The Others: Part One

It's only about a quarter of a mile walk to the Seaboard North quadrant gate when we get back to the station, and most of the others are already ahead of me. Fraya seems better thanks to Jax, who has been telling her stupid jokes since we got on the shuttle back at school.

The haze has lifted a little, and I'm glad because I don't want my last thoughts of this place to be of muted sunshine and thick air that tastes like the dust from the Tinkerer's metal grinding shops. The sound of laughter breaks the little bubble I'd been creating around myself as Sarin, Myra, and Liddick walk past me, and I slip away from Arco to catch up with them.

"Hey!" I call. Myra is the first to turn and smile at me.

"Hey, Jazz! I know you got in. Aren't you excited? Ouch, what happened to your lip?"

"Oh, that was just an accident on the shuttle this morning. I got in, did you?" I ask, and she beams.

"We did too!" she says, smiling so widely it almost looks painful. But her big blue eyes light up like the sun coming out of the clouds, and I already feel better than I have so far today. She just has that effect on people. "Aren't you excited?" she asks through a halted giggle.

"I don't know—I mean, yes, but not really," I answer, which sounds stupid when I hear it. "I have mixed feelings."

Sarin looks down her long, broomstick nose at me, and Liddick just smirks while Myra's eyes go wide.

"But why?" She drags the last word out in a whine.

"Because even getting into Gaia isn't good enough for Jazwyn," Sarin informs her, then looks back at me like I've just sneezed on her lunch before she struts ahead of us all. As much as I'd normally give anything for her to go away, this time I wanted her to stay so I could ask her about her interview. Liddick chuckles, throwing his arm over my shoulder.

"So, the interview was a drink of water, right?" He throws his other arm over Myra, so now we look like his pixies. I push his arm away and make some space between us.

"It wasn't like that for everyone, Liddick. Didn't you see Fraya crying her face off?"

"Didn't notice her. What was her problem?" he says, trying to swing his arm back over my shoulder, but I block it with a swing of my own.

"I don't know, I haven't been able to talk to her yet. Why were you two and Sarin so happy? What happened in your interviews?" I ask, but Myra's attention is captured by a butterfly dancing just in front of her, and she drifts ahead of us to try to get it to land on her hand.

"Cheddar for me. Some *tuhao* in the room named Styx asked most of my questions, and *crite* he was wearing slick digs, a white military jacket with a clipped collar. Two women were pressed out just like him from Gaia. I guess they all work there or something," he replies.

"So, you too, then? They were also in Arco's room, and

mine. All at the same time. How do you think they did that? And why did you leave so happy?" I ask.

"I don't know, I was happy because they were like, my people, you know? Maybe they were in everyone's room *in virtuo* like the cines."

"But they shook my hand. I touched them. They put these bracelets on us. They had to be there," I insist.

"True," he says with a shrug. "They were probably port-calling then—Dice McClain told me his manager made a deal with the State to let him use their port-call tech for premieres so he could sign autographs without actually having to leave the Skyboard hill as long as he'd also make an appearance at Gaia once a year," he says.

"But how could they do it at the same time in all those different rooms?"

"Who knows, Riptide? It's science. Anyway, did I tell you they're putting me on a field team after matriculation is over?"

"Stop calling me that. And what's matriculation?" I ask as Myra comes back from her butterfly adventure.

"It's a three-month learning period where we're not held responsible for mistakes in our programs," she says, squealing as another butterfly floats into her path.

"Wavy, right? It's all going to be a drink of water," Liddick says.

"You really jack in to too many virtuo-cines. Where did you even hear that expression?" I ask, wondering which cinestar he's going to say he's been lagging around with now.

"Oh, Sera Lim. We took down the infrastructure on

Scarborough 8 a few days ago and freed all the pilgrims they'd been holding captive in the core. Saved the universe from an intergalactic shatstorm," he says, cocking an eyebrow.

"Beacon Ship!? That cine isn't even out until next month—how did you get access? What's Sera like? Is that where you met Dice McClain too, or was that when you went into *Dionysus 2* last month?" Myra gawks at Liddick, abandoning her butterfly.

"How did I get access? Because I'm Liddick Wright, beautiful," he says like it's the right answer to every question in the world. Myra swoons, and I gag. "Dice was last month in *Dionysus,* and Sera? Well, she's a lot smaller in person than I thought she'd be. Dice is *stone* at G-ball—completely fierce. I'm still tired!" I roll my eyes and try not to roarf straight onto my own feet while watching Myra's reaction, which indicates she is now seconds away from total body combustion. I have to stop this.

"OK, Liddick, redirect. Your interview. You were saying something about a field team?"

"Yeah, something about me being a niche coach, I don't know. They said I was perfect to help fellow freshes adapt to the all-new."

Did he just say *freshes?* Please tell me that's not what they're going to call us.

"Myra, was yours like that too?" I ask, all but jumping in the air to snag her attention away from hero worshipping Liddick.

"Basically. I just had to file things, and they didn't ask

me to be a coach, but I am one of only five other freshes getting my own library database code right off the dock," she bubbles, still shimmering with excitement about Liddick's latest brush with fame and fortune. I mean, it's interesting and all, and it would be fun to meet cinestars and go on all the adventures, even if it is only virtual, but my family has more important things to spend our chits on than virtuo-cines—things like thread and fabric for the printers, and seeds for the greenbed, but Liddick doesn't need to worry about these things. His parents are our quadrant representatives to the Seaboard North council, which means they get a whole house instead of a habitat in one of the stacks complexes, plus a stipend. Not to mention the stipends from his two brothers who have already gone through Gaia—Liam, who graduated this past year and is already a rising star as a biodesigner for Skyboard North clientele, and his oldest brother, Lyden, whom he hasn't talked about since his port calls stopped coming from the technology complex he ran about four years ago. Add in both of their contributions, and Liddick's family is the richest in Seaboard North.

"Do they really call us *freshes* when we get there?" I ask Myra, hoping I've been mishearing.

"Just for three months," Myra says, playing with the elastic band at the end of the long reddish-blonde braid she's just finished. "After that, they said matriculation is over, and we're on a career path," she adds, and begins her sycophant question barrage at Liddick all over again. Why didn't the Gaia representatives tell me any of this about matriculation and being called *freshes*? It makes me wonder what else I don't know, both good and bad.

Maybe Liddick is right; maybe everyone is overreacting because none of the rest of us, except for maybe his best friend Ellis, has a lot of experience with virtuo-cines. But I guess if we turn into a bloat-headed chutz like Liddick, I'm glad we don't. I'll stick to flat-cines, thanks. Nothing wrong with being a bystander. Though, I must admit, I probably wouldn't say no to fighting alongside Sera Lim and liberating thousands of imprisoned pilgrims from the core of a planet. That could be fun.

Once we're through the quadrant gate, I let Liddick and Myra walk on without me. The day seems heavier now that the sun is starting to slip closer to the horizon, and I know this feeling of exhaustion must be the result of the constant struggle between my excitement for the new adventure of leaving home, and the knot in my stomach about not having a choice. I suppose I could turn down the scholarship and the stipend, but no one does that just to stay here in Seaboard North where the best thing you could hope to become is an apprentice, and that's if you're lucky. No one throws something like this away after working a lifetime for it, and I'm not going to be the first.

CHAPTER 6
Aftermath

I hear footfalls behind me, and turn to see Arco jogging. He is out of breath when he catches up to me, and his shirt is damp at the center of his chest. How long has he been jogging? I couldn't have gotten that far ahead of him.

"There you are," he says, panting.

"Where did you come from? I thought you were right behind me," I ask, looking around to see if anyone else is behind us.

"No, I decided to take a detour. I wasn't in any hurry… I'm still not," he says to the gravel between each of his steps as he slows down and catches his breath, then looks up at me.

There is a long, awkward pause between us as I try to decide if I really want to ask him about his interview again, but I feel pulled to do it, so maybe he wants to tell me.

"Arco, what really happened to you in there?" I ask, and when his eyes lock with mine, he lets out a long sigh.

"It's all strange and disconnected, but I guess the best way to say it is that in one of the scenarios, I had an opportunity, and I missed it," he says as he looks out on the waves that are crashing on the shore to our left. "They wanted to put me in charge because apparently, I *had the skills*," he says, curling his fingers into quotes at his waist around the last words.

"You didn't agree with them about that?" Arco has never been one to doubt himself, at least, I hadn't thought so.

"I didn't at the time. They put three of us at the controls of the sub—me and two others I didn't know—and something hit our ship. Water started rushing in, and they just kept yelling for me to do something. I could have, and I see that now. I know that I could have jumped in and hijacked the system override to seal off the gush, but I froze instead and left it up to someone else who wound up getting himself...electrocuted," Arco stops and swallows, then begins again, "...all because I didn't trust that I'd be fast enough with the codes." He picks up a flat stone from our path and tries to skip it sideways over the water as he talks, almost to himself now, and I wonder if he's forgotten I'm here. "It's worse, you know, to watch someone failing like that, to realize too late that you could have made the difference for everyone if you'd just had the guts."

He turns his profile completely away from me and faces the sea, then whips another stone overhead as hard as he can. It sails well past the first several breakers and drops into the water behind the lapping surf.

"It wasn't your fault, Arco. It was just a game. You must have known on some level that it was just a game," I say to the back of his head, his sandy brown hair catching the breeze from the water and whipping into a tangle.

"Maybe," he says, finally looking forward again, and I

feel a struggle inside myself like I'm losing my grip on a heavy package. I can only think to tell him that the Arco I know isn't afraid of anything, but then I realize that I don't really know this. I don't really know him beyond our childhood pranks because the last five years have been so isolating in preparing for today. Do I *really* know him any more? Do I even know *myself* any more? When is the last time I had an idea about anything other than information and protocols, or about mastering skills and presenting myself properly? Who are any of these people I've been with almost every day of my life so far?

To help us both, I try to think of the last moment I can remember feeling like I had an identity beyond my class rank, and finally, it surfaces.

"Do you remember the summer before we started secondary classes? We were 13 and sneaked away from the port festival with Ellis and the others so we could watch the shuttle relay surface by the dome to get ready to pick up Liam Wright the next morning?"

"You just had to go in the water after Liddick dared you," he shakes his head, chuffing out what is almost a laugh.

"Yeah, and I was in bed for two days with that jellyfish sting, remember? It felt like someone was burning my ankle off with a soldering iron!" He looks at me sideways and smirks. "Remember how I froze when it happened? And how you just splashed right in after me and pulled me out?"

His eyes hunt again for an answer he seems to have dropped in the sand, and as I try to remember the details of that day, how it all felt floods back. It was the first time I was ever really afraid, the first time I thought I could be hurt or lost. I don't think I'd ever felt so small before, and it crashed into me all at once. I was alone in the middle of the ocean. Looking back, I wonder if maybe that was the only way to prepare me for the loss of my father later that summer. I had to know what it was like to feel lost so I wouldn't freeze when it happened again, and maybe it happened to show me that no matter where I was, I could never be alone as long as I had friends like Arco Hart.

"That was a long time ago," he says.

"But you didn't freeze, and you could have. You could have waited for someone else to jump in, like Ellis or Liddick, but you didn't. And you won't if it's ever real again like that, so don't let their head games get to you. It wasn't your fault."

We walk on in silence listening to the gulls, to the water hitting the beach, and after a few minutes, he pulls his hand out of his pocket and rests it on my shoulder. He seems relaxed and casual again until his whole body goes rigid, but once I understand what he's doing, I also understand that it's too late for me to run.

"Let's see if I can still haul you up this hill while you're flailing and squealing," he says, and in one quick dive, sweeps up my legs and throws me over his shoulder. My breath is forced out in a *whoosh*, and I grasp the back of his shirt once I realize I'm suddenly upside-down.

"Put me down!" I yell into his shoulder blades as I try to kick free, but he wraps his long arm over my legs and pins me in place.

"You should probably hang on now," he says, and starts attempting to jog, the constant bouncing preventing me from getting enough air to produce much more than clipped protests. "You're a lot heavier than you were when we were 13, by the way," he laughs, and the rest of my rebuttals fall on deaf ears as I watch his footprints appear, then disappear into the distance as the tide rises and the gulls swoop at the shore.

CHAPTER 7
Coming Home

I know we're at our habitat complex a few minutes later when Arco's pace slows from a trot to a walk and I hear Jax and Fraya laughing.

"OK!" I shout, and he releases my legs. I slide off his shoulder, my feet hitting the ground with a thud that sends a shockwave through my teeth. I push the hair out of my face and punch Arco in the arm. He feigns a mortal wound, and I roll my eyes for what seems like the hundredth time today, then rub my pummeled ribs.

"I better go up and help my mom with the food for tonight. See you in a little while," Fraya smiles, letting her eyes linger on Jax an extra beat. "And thank you again for everything," she tells him, then stands on her tiptoes and kisses him quickly on the mouth before she turns to go inside. Jax's face explodes in a stupid smile as she walks away. Once she's gone, Arco pushes him off balance and makes some kind of accusation in the grunts and jeering language that only boys seem to speak before he collects himself and heads for the door.

"I should probably go in too," he says as he finishes laughing at Jax, then angles his head in a quick nod to me before starting inside. I feel a stab of disappointment that takes me by surprise, and when I realize it, my face and neck flood with heat. I push away the random and completely *wrong* implication that I somehow wanted Arco to say more to me or look longer at me in acknowledgement like Fraya did with Jax, and shake my head to dislodge the idea as a warm breeze comes off the water over us.

"This is my favorite time of year," Jax says as we head up the walkway, breaking the spell of my indignation.

"Even though we're leaving?" I ask, and feel a sudden stab of cold in my chest as I realize I don't know if he's leaving too. "Wait, you got in? You *got in*, right?" I reply, panicked and reaching for his arm in search of his bracelet cuff after the jolt of adrenaline hits my blood-stream. He steps ahead of me, then turns to face me with his hands behind his back as his face falls. *"Jax!* Tell me!"

"OK, listen…" he starts, walking backward from me, and my stomach drops. "You know mom and Nann will have dad's package and yours now, so one more would just be…virtuo-cine money for Nann," he says without changing his conciliatory tone, then whips his bracelet from behind his back with another wry grin.

"You got in!" I shout and jump up to hug him around the neck, then drop down and slap him in the chest. "You got in—crite, you chutz. Don't do that to me!" He throws his head back in a laugh, then skims his hand over the tips of saw grass that line the walkway up to our habitat.

"Did you see the infobit about the new releases next week?" I ask, wondering if he's thinking what I am.

*"The Willowers…*I almost forgot!" he says, a new smile reigniting the one that had just been on his face as we walk to the end of the hall. "Nann will implode when she sees that giant bird," he laughs.

The thing about being twins is that we can usually tell

how the other feels, and I know he would give just about anything to see Nann's face light up when she sees a bird bigger than she is standing right in front of her. When you're older, being inside a virtuo-cine story may be surreal, but when you're young, it's magical.

Jax opens the door with the retina scanner. The air inside is warm and smells like fresh bread, which makes my stomach clench as I realize we didn't eat lunch because we left before everyone else. Nann is backlit by the sun beaming through the small kitchen window as she carries a basket of cookies toward us, her brown pigtails bouncing with each step. Our mother follows behind her with a covered dish in hand and her blue apron untied in the back. When she sees us, all the blood rushes out of her face as she stops in her tracks trying to force a smile.

"Mom, it's OK," I blurt, feeling compelled to push back the worry crashing into me when I see her. Jax shoots me an expectant look. "Tell her," I say.

"We both got in. We're both going to Gaia." He waits for an explosion of excitement and celebration from her like I do, but aside from Nann jumping up and down and rushing to throw herself around his leg, the room remains quiet. Color washes back into my mother's face, and though a smile blooms, the confusing guilt from this morning clamps around my chest again. But this is good news, isn't it?

"I'm so proud of you both. I couldn't make my parents proud like this, but I always knew you would," she says, tears starting in her wide brown eyes. I walk over and put my arm around her.

"What are those?" Nann asks, pointing to our bracelets.

"They're like the medi-credit bracelet we put on to go to the clinic if there are no medi-droids available to come here. You know how we put those under the light and it tells the doctor all about you?" Jax kneels in front of her to explain while letting her touch the cuff, and she nods. "This does the same thing for us. It's a ticket to get on the shuttle sub tomorrow morning...you know, since we...*got...in...to...Gaia!*" he sing-songs this last part as he lifts Nann up into the air and swings her around, the basket of cookies now also in orbit around his head.

"Jax, the basket!" our mother says through a gasp as she reaches up, and Jax slows to a stop. "We're just on our way to help set up. Now you can come with us," she laughs after her initial alarm. It's a good sound to hear.

Jax settles Nann onto his shoulders where she balances the cookies on the top of his head, then leans over and feeds one to him. He ducks through the door holding her legs down tightly so she doesn't wobble with the shift in altitude as we all start toward the center of town for the festival. My chest tightens when I hear Nann giggle in front of me as Jax makes chomping monster noises. I'm going to miss so much of her life, and I'm reminded again of how frustrating it is that no one talks about this.

I think about asking my mother, who's walking at my side, but I finally know the answer the second I ask myself the question this time. People don't want to burden anyone else with the sadness. We all just maintain, pretend that everything is perfect...we've been accepted into Gaia and have therefore fulfilled our responsibilities as children. Our parents have fulfilled their responsibilities as parents. We have won, and that's the focus today.

I catch my mother's eyes, and this time I see pride in her smile. She's always been there for us, and in thinking about this, I understand the guilty feelings I've had today. It hasn't been easy on her own these last several years, but it never occurred to me that she would bear the weight of us not getting into Gaia on her own too.

She would blame herself, and so would others. She and everyone else would think that she failed us. No one talks about it, but everyone in our community thinks it's always the parents' fault when someone doesn't make the cut, even though so many don't, and no one wants to bring that kind of shame onto his or her family. That doesn't stop it from happening, but living in quadrants makes it more difficult to fail. I read that when we still had states, schools failed because they were too large and run by people too far away. The way it is now, you have to fear failure because everyone in the stacks knows you, knows your family, and you could lose more than just an opportunity for a better education if you don't do well. You could lose the respect of your whole community.

The only way to minimize the whispers if you don't get into Gaia is to graduate from secondary studies here at Seaboard, and then apply for an apprenticeship program in energy at the hydrogen plant like my father did, or in education, medicine, or agriculture like my mother did, but since most families keep to their own for apprenticeships, it's hard to break in. We were lucky that my grandparents ran the covered greenbed field that feeds our stack complex and three others, but if you can't get an apprenticeship, you wind up studying with the Fisher or the Tinkerer clan, which is looked down upon even though there are never enough people to catch fish or to fix and invent things. I've always wondered why we don't associate much at school with the few of them who are there, and why we don't interact anywhere with them outside of the marketplace where we meet to trade for goods once a week. They disappear into their boathouses near the shore, or into their factories on the edge of the quadrant, and we can forget the smell of the sea on their clothes and the grease stains on their faces. We can forget that were it not for one particular set of expectations, we would be no different from them at all.

CHAPTER 8
The Others: Part Two

The timbre of colliding shells strung from the rafters of the community center's covered walk fills the breeze as the sun peeks out from behind the clouds. Soon, it will sink into the horizon in a fever of orange and purple, and like so many other things today, I feel a pang in my chest knowing it will be the last time I will see it. Not just from the shoreline, but *ever* see it again. How have I prepared for something my entire life—even made conscious progress toward it—only for it to feel like I never saw it coming? Something from just beyond that horizon reaches under my ribs and squeezes until I can't take in a full breath, and after I exhale, I feel as hollow as the strings of shells surrounding me.

"Cadet!" The loud, sharp voice just behind my head jolts me out of my skin, and as I turn abruptly from the doorway, I find myself running straight into Jax's chest and looking up at his smirking, stupid face. Our little sister, Nann, has since disembarked his shoulders—no doubt having been assimilated by the swarm of other kids running all over the complex as their parents help set up—so I find no compelling reason not to punch him in the stomach. He grips my shoulders with wide eyes and starts to laugh.

"You're hilarious, Jaxon," I say, trying to keep my voice low. "Let me go," I tug back and forth, but he's not giving in.

"That depends on if you're done swinging," he cocks a dark eyebrow and tilts his grin down at me, enjoying every idiotic minute of being almost a foot taller.

"Yes, I'm done. Come on, it's going to start." I push past him and head toward the closest table where I see some of our friends sitting.

"What's wrong with you?" he says, at my side again.

"Nothing. I was just watching the sky," I say, picking up my pace so he falls back. Why am I the only one who seems to notice that there will be no more sunsets for any of us? What's the matter with everyone?

"Hey!" Jax catches up to me again and throws his arm over my shoulder. "You know, it's going to be all right. Stop thinking of what we're leaving and start thinking about what we're going to gain. Our family has a chance now, Jazz, and everything will be new. That's exciting, isn't it?" he asks, dodging two boys who dart into our path after a ball.

I can never hide anything from him, and I know he's right. I have to shake this mood. Feeling sorry for myself is not how I want to spend my last few hours topside, so I take in a long, deep breath and let it out fast as I walk over to start setting up the tables.

***

It's nearly 5:00 when Jax puts a hand on my shoulder and pulls me out of the flower arranging hypnosis I've evidently been in for a while now.

"Hey, come sit down because the sooner Paxton starts, the sooner we can eat," he says, pointing to a table where

Avis, Quinn, Fraya, Arco, and Ellis Raj are sitting. "That cookie wore off a long time ago."

I shake my head and smile a little at how easy things can be for him. Even though we're twins, sometimes I can't tell if I feel a decade older, or he just seems a decade younger. Either way, I wish I had his ability to let things go.

"Avis, what was your interview like?" I hear Quinn ask as I take a seat, and feel as if someone has just clapped right in front of my face as I look over to Fraya, who stiffens next to Jax.

"Mine?" he starts, trying to contain his laughter. "I nearly died of vertigo, but before that, they made me the weatherman," he says, bouncing his black eyebrows at us from under a wing of blue-tipped black hair.

"Who made you?" Quinn asks.

"The interviewers—the man and two women," he says, leaning in on his forearms.

"Rheen...and Plume?" I ask.

"And Styx?" Fraya asks, twisting the ends of her hair. Jax's arm tightens around her. Avis's brown eyes blink quickly before he looks from me to Fraya, and then back at me.

"They were in all our rooms," Arco says. "Nobody knows how. It had to be rigged port-call, a multi projection or something. What do you mean they made you the weatherman?" he asks in a curious tone, trying to downplay the tension.

"Yeah," Avis says, nodding slowly at Arco as if he's talking himself into this explanation. He nods once more, quickly this time in decision, and continues his story. "Anyway, I had to figure out how to kill a superstorm so this sub could surface in the first situation, and in the next one, I had to minimize fallout from multiple plates shifting under the seafloor all at once. I'm not stretching; they actually had me configure the order that the volcanoes blew. All that power, man," he splays his fingers in front of him like a maestro of volcano puppets. "Pelée, trigger, *POW!* Pinatubo, trigger, *POW!* Krakatoa, trigger...oh, but I do not recommend teleporting," he adds, looking up and turning his hands out in a stop gesture.

"Teleporting?" Ellis leans in and narrows his dark brown eyes in scrutiny, but then, they're almost always like that regardless of what anyone says or does.

"Yeah, teleport from the interview room to the control site and back. They said it was virtuo, but my stomach did not concur that it was a cine."

"What a sand dollar," Ellis says, shaking his head, his course black hair not budging a centimeter. "So, why did the volcano order matter?"

Avis's expression crumples as he quickly shakes his head. "Geophysics—what are you, a first year? CO2, you know? Too much in the atmosphere all at once, and the oceans can't absorb it fast enough to reset everything?" he says, scanning our faces before continuing. "Uh, some volcanoes produce more than others...ring a bell?" We all stare at him like he's just been talking backward. "Are you *serious?*" he says, his eyes widening in disbelief. "How did you people get into Gaia...OK, so too much

CO2 in the atmosphere—what do we breathe, class?" He folds his hands in front of him, flips his hair again, and blinks at the table.

"So, we suffocate," Jax states more than asks.

"Sure, unless we all drown first," Avis says as we all exchange silent glances. "Oh, I quit the human race. Volcanic Tsunamis, anyone?" He closes his eyes and shakes his head quickly from side to side again, then gets up and makes his way to the bathroom, mumbling something in Chinese.

"Did he just call us squid piles?" Arco laughs, triggering the rest of us.

"*Brains*. He called us squid brains," Quinn corrects. "Which is ironic considering squids are very intelligent creatures." There is silence for a beat as we all look at her. "What? They are," she adds, and we all laugh again.

"What about your interview, Quinn?" Ellis asks.

"The same interviewers were in my room, but the interview itself was a simple matter of evaluating supply and demand," she replies, sitting up straight in her chair.

"So, you had an economics test?" Ellis asks, raising an eyebrow and smirking, unimpressed.

"Something like that. Settlement *A* produces medi-droids, Settlement *B* requires medi-droids; decipher a fair exchange for said medi-droids if the established currency has been found worthless. Scenarios like these." Quinn brushes a strand of her short blonde hair from her nearly invisible eyebrow.

"What did you do?" I ask.

"A new currency had to be established. I simply evaluated what Settlement *A* could want from Settlement *B*, and then a trade could be facilitated."

"So, what did they *want?*" Jax asks a little too rigidly, his voice holding the impatience we all feel when she starts talking like a text-file.

"Entertainment," she says with a shrug as if it's the most obvious thing in the world.

"Oha Krishna," Ellis says, putting his face in his hands, then peeling up through them, leaving his fingers to cover his mouth. We all start laughing at his exasperation, and almost can't get ourselves together before Mr. Paxton, our head councilman, starts testing the microphone at the front of the room. His balding head is shiny even after he wipes it with a napkin, and there is a damp circle marring the center of his white linen tunic.

"Good evening, Seaboard North residents, and of course, Gaia cadets!" he says, and people begin to applaud. He takes a shaky sip from a glass at his podium and then continues. "What a beautiful evening we have here in the company of our friends and family. This is a bittersweet time indeed, but we come together each year like this to show our support for all our graduates, and for the ones who have helped them achieve their goals." The crowd applauds again, and I spot Liddick, who is seated in the third row back from Mr. Paxton facing me from the opposite wall. He meets my eyes in almost the same moment as Paxton continues. "As you all know, it has been four years since we last had cadets heading to Gaia, and this year, astoundingly, we have 12, the largest number we have ever had!" Mr. Paxton raises both of his meaty hands out to his sides, the sweat stains under his arms matching the one on his chest. The room roars with the cheers of everyone as the ten of us look around at each other to figure out who the other two from Seaboard North are.

"Who are the Tinkerers and Fishers at school?" I whisper to Jax, suddenly curious. He draws in his eyebrows to think, but then just shrugs.

"I don't remember their names," he says.

"Cadets, know that it's natural to worry for those who will not be traveling with you to Gaia, but also that your families will be wrapped in the warmth of our community. This is your time to pursue your dreams, to meet world leaders, to even become world leaders yourselves, but whether you join the field of medical research like Arwyn Hart and Liam Wright, or become part of the State's technical transport division like Lyden Wright, you will always be here in our hearts." The crowd applauds again, and I look over at Arco to see if the mention of his sister has had any effect on him. Fortunately, it doesn't look like it has. I look over again to check the same for Liddick, and find that his parents are beaming, but he's not there any more. "Let's recognize these fine young people at this time. Cadets, please come forward when I call your name."

Mr. Paxton calls the ten of us in order of our rank, Liddick rushing in from outside after his name is called twice. We make our way to the podium and arrange ourselves in a single line that faces the seated crowd, the small children sitting cross-legged at the feet of the adults in the front rows. When Mr. Paxton calls Arco's name, I hold my breath for the eleventh.

"For first dibs in line—Mainstream, Fisher or Tinkerer?" Jax bets me.

"Mainstream," I say, remembering that there are only five or six Tinkerers in our class this year and only two Fishers.

"Joss Tether!" Mr. Paxton says, and quiet gasps wash over the crowd. Jax nudges me, a wide smile spreading over his face in anticipation of being *that* much closer to eating.

"A Fisher?" I hear several people say in hushed voices, and admittedly, think it myself. The Fisher and Tinkerer clans are technically part of Seaboard North, but the Fishers live off the shore by the docks east of us, and the Tinkerers live on the inland side of us, just beyond the hydrogen plant in the old factories and stacks in the southwestern quadrant nearby. Past that is a forest that wraps farther westward toward The Badlands, which encompasses the city ruins and the expanse of sand beyond, but only The Fringe—societal deserters and cast-outs—live there. Skyboard mountain is in the far North-ern quadrant, but they have their own school, and no one except Liddick and Ellis ever really see anyone from there.

Joss stands up at the back of the room, and a broad, muscular man with long, platted, white hair grips his shoulders hard and smiles. This *has* to be his father. Joss hugs a tall, thin woman with a long dark braid, and after he pulls away to kiss the head of a small, dark headed girl, the woman with the braid wipes her eyes and puts her arm around her. This must be his mother and sister. Like his father, Joss looks like he's built out of boxes as he walks to the front of the room to stand with the rest of us, but the closer he gets, the rounder his arms and shoulders appear. He walks strangely, gliding more than stepping, and the flap of his sandals against the floor draws my eyes down. His legs are corded in tanned muscle with one of them dotted in shiny, evenly spaced dark scars over his upper shin and inner thigh, his nails white as the sand, and I notice the same is true of his fingernails. His forearms also have raised veins running up and disappearing into the crooks of his elbows, then starting again over his biceps. His orange tunic is belted in a knot around his hips while his rolled up linen pants skim just above his knees. He looks up at all of us and smiles one of the whitest smiles I've ever seen, especially for a Fisher, then takes his place next to Arco.

"And our twelfth selectee from Seaboard North...Vox Dyer!" Mr. Paxton says enthusiastically, but there are no gasps, no explosions of applause, just quiet, obligatory clapping.

"Fringe," Jax says under his breath to me, and it just won't register. I look out over the tables for Vox and for any other Badlanders who might be here with her, the hairs on the back of my neck standing on end when she gets close enough for me to see her eyes, which are so light green they're almost yellow, peering out from underneath dark burgundy hair. The charcoal tribal tattoos on her face and neck begin at the center point at her hairline with two inverted letter *V*s over a hollow diamond between her eyes, the bridge of her nose marked in deep arrows stacked inside each other. The etchings reappear in a long, narrow arrow under her bottom lip that runs over her chin, then branches into a column of arrows that travel downward along the length of her pale throat. They finally come to a diamond shaped maze starting at the divot in her collarbone and ending in the center of her chest. Her hair is braided into rows on the left and falls loose over her right shoulder as she makes her way to her place next to Joss, surrounded by the sound of tiny chiming bells and the chink of small chains rustling with each of her steps.

Her tan canvas skirt is frayed and uneven on the edge, but it's short enough that it shows her knees, which are scarred and freshly scratched, giving way to shins that are tattooed in the same arrow column pattern as her throat. Black sandal straps wrap her feet, and around each of her ankles, several bracelets are the source of the sound surrounding her. Her black tank top is torn in places and patched with the same canvas as her skirt, and I can't stop staring at the rivers of lines that mark her arms, which look like roads scrambling all over a map. She catches me gawking, and as she takes her place next to Joss, she locks those yellow eyes with mine and does not look away.

Heat rushes up my neck and over my cheeks, and I feel a wash of anger that I do not understand. I've never spoken to her before, and have really only ever seen her from afar a few times at school, but I immediately can't stand her. She reminds me of a snake tasting the air with its tongue in the way she moves, and in the second the thought enters my mind, I imagine her flitting hers at me. The shock of this snaps me out of whatever feelings of anger have just come over me, and I quickly look back out into the crowd.

"May I present your Gaia cadets! Let's give them a round of applause along with all of our graduates this year, and then follow them to the tables to enjoy this wonderful feast!" Mr. Paxton says a little too quickly to the gathered crowd, who all begin to cheer one last time.

CHAPTER 9
The Message

The last rays of sunlight glint off the serving spoons and blown glass bowls through the tall, mottled windows. It distorts and bends in bows, throwing flecks of color onto the floor and onto the white, concrete walls. Every family has brought something to share, and every table along the banquet wall is filled with salads, stews, oysters, fruits, lobsters, and someone has even brought a *marlin*. It must be six feet long and two feet wide, and I gasp at the sight of it laid out in the center of the main table. I've never seen one this big before, or this beautiful. The blues and greens of its skin catch the light and shimmer in the filtered, setting sun, and I'm drawn into its eye, which is as large as the palm of my hand even from several feet away. The black pupil seems fluid in the bluish gray, watery iris as I approach, and I'm suddenly angry to think how stupid it was that this fish never realized the bait was a trap...how stupid that something has survived the dangers of the ocean all the years of its life and never even saw the hook or the net coming. I feel heat rising in my cheeks, and notice that I'm *actually* angry at this dead fish, then roll my eyes as I realize that feeling like this is really the only stupid thing going on here.

"Beautiful," Liddick says over my shoulder, and I must still look angry because he flinches when I jerk around to face him.

"Stow it, Liddick," I say, then look back toward the food choices.

"I mean, I don't know about you, but I've only seen a blue spectrum like that on a fish in the rift—gorgeous, right? The horn isn't quite as long as the ones out *there*, but otherwise, quite a specimen," he says, nodding, then winking as I give him a sideways smirk and shake my head at him.

"Wait, wait…was that the virtuo-cine where you got the whole crew eaten by that Kraken squid? Or was it the one where you wound up sinking the boat and drowning everyone?"Arco says from the other side of Liddick as he reaches his long arms in front of him to fork some rainbow prawns onto his plate. I smile and take a few steps down the table—the pear slices and lobster suddenly appearing far more interesting than the rest of that conversation—and catch up to Jax to see what he thinks about Vox Dyer coming with us to Gaia. His plate is already three layers high with one of everything on the table, and I'm stunned that he's even been able to balance it all.

"You know you can come back up, right?" I say, marveling.

"Plan to!" he says around a mouthful of food, and I shake my head at him as I realize the Vox conversation clearly won't be happening until he doesn't have to choose between eating and talking. At that, I look around the room for her, but she's nowhere to be found.

As we make our way down the table, I notice that the marlin is even more beautiful close up with its smooth, iridescent lines from the tip of its spear to the end of its tail. Jax plunges the edge of a serving spatula into the pink flesh of its belly and carves a slice that's rimmed in the shimmering midnight blue and silver spectrum of its skin, and with a surgeon drone's precision, deposits it on top of the pile of food already on his plate. I pick up the spatula after Jax moves on, and the eye of the fish catches mine again.

I blink a few times to be sure, but the pupil slowly starts changing shape—the circle becomes an oval, then the oval becomes a circle again. I squeeze my eyes shut and then blink several more times to clear my vision. *I must be more exhausted than I thought*, I think, and the black disk of the pupil returns, still and locked in the frozen blue-gray layers of the marlin's eye. I shake my head, then pierce the meat with the tip of the spatula just as the gape of the marlin's mouth wrenches down at the corner. Its gills flare out in a long gasp, then start to quickly flap open and closed over and over again. I drop the spatula, and my heart begins to hammer in my chest as I try to say something, but realize in horror that only small crackles of sound actually come out of my mouth. The pupil begins undulating again as it darts left, then right, then down, up, and then directly at me.

"I never saw it coming..." it says in a low, singular male voice that becomes more shrill with each repeat. *"I never saw it coming! I never saw it coming!"*

Its tail fin lifts, then slaps the platter beneath it, and I drop my plate to catch the scream that now spills free. I back away from the table holding my hands over my mouth to stop any more sound, but it doesn't matter. Everyone in the line is staring at me, the marlin's eye looking again at the ceiling, cold and still, but the voice is still loud and clear in my head.

I never saw it coming! I never saw it coming!

"Jazz?" At the far end of the last table, Jax's eyes flash to mine, then shoot behind me as he starts nodding. I feel hands on my shoulders steering me away from the table toward the door and jerk around to see that it's Liddick.

"No, no...you did...you saw that. Did you hear it?" I say to him in one, heaving breath.

"It's gone now, Jazz. It's gone," he says to me in an oddly loud voice, and then to the people staring at us at the tables as we walk past, "Tunnel rat, just nipped at her under the table and then shot out the door..." he snaps his fingers for everyone, "...*eel*-quick." I suck in a breath to protest, but he pulls me into him hard and fast by my ribs, and the air is forced out of me. "Didn't even make a hole in your shoe, see? It's gone, let's just get some air, Jazz," he says too loudly, and pushes the wide screen doors open when we get to them. The rush of cool sea air hits me, and the hollow tinkling of the shells at the entry-way muffles behind me as the surf grows louder the closer we get to it. At the water's edge, I shake loose from his grip, which I realize has been holding me up as my knees buckle under me. I catch myself and round on him. "Wait, stop," he says, holding up his hand, then takes a quick step toward me and grips my shoulder. "We have exactly eight seconds before your brother and Hart get out here, so listen. I saw it too—the marlin. I heard it too."

"Then *wh*—"

"Because no one else did, Jazz, think. You were the only one who tweaked in there. If anyone else saw that don't you think they'd be screaming too?" he asks, and after a second to process, I nod. "So it's something else, and we can figure out what that is later tonight, but for now you have to tell them you saw a rat and go back in there so everyone can get through this night, do you understand?" he says, gripping both my shoulders now until I nod again.

"We need to talk about this," I insist, and now it's his turn to nod. He looks over his shoulder at the sound of the community center doors closing behind Arco, who is making his way toward us with Jax.

"Meet me in front of your complex at eleven, when the dome light changes to blue, all right? They're coming. Rub your leg or something." Liddick loosens his grip as I kick off my shoe and bend down, pretending to examine my foot. Jax reaches us first with Arco just a few steps behind.

"What was that? Nann won't get off her chair now," Jax says. Arco pushes past him and steps in front of Liddick, forcing him back. He's a few inches taller, but Liddick matches his broad, lean build and wouldn't have been so easily displaced if he didn't want to be. I straighten up and scrub my hands over my face, then take the deepest breath I can.

"Here, sip this," Arco says, holding a cup of something pink in front of me.

"I'm fine, it was just a rat. It bit my foot," I say, taking the cup. "Thanks."

"Bit you? Do you need the medi-droid?" Arco says, taking another step toward me trying to look for damage.

"No, it's fine. It didn't break through my shoe." I slide my foot back in and shake out the sand through the slats in the side.

"You wouldn't have tweaked like that over a tunnel rat. What really happened?" Jax says, looking up from under his dark, drawn brows from me to Liddick.

"It was a big, scrappy, black tunnel rat, chief. Crite, even I almost screamed," Liddick laughs. "Can we go eat now?"

"Yeah, let's go in. Everyone is waiting in there for us, and we just have tonight," I say, but Arco and Jax don't move. I try not to look them in the eye because I'm no good at hiding anything, especially from them. For the first time in my life, I wish I were more like Liddick, who can adapt to any situation.

Jax gives me a hard look, and I know that if I stay out here much longer, he'll figure out for sure there was no rat, so I just start walking back toward the door to the community center. Liddick falls in behind me, cutting off Arco and Jax. They both catch up in a few strides, and we all walk in together to find everyone talking and eating again. Only a few people look up at us as Jax and Arco maneuver to our table around people returning with plates of food to their own, and Arco takes hold of my elbow as Liddick leans in and whispers quickly to me.

"Ask Hart to get you a plate or something, and then go

sit with your brother. Stay away from the marlin." He starts walking in the opposite direction, then looks back over his shoulder to make sure I've heard. I nod. "Eleven," he mouths, and disappears into the crowd as Arco, Jax, and I sit down with Ellis, Avis, Quinn, and Fraya.

"I'll be right back," Arco says, and heads up to the food tables before I can ask him anything with everyone fawning all over me. He returns with a plate of pear slices and soup for me, but I'm not even hungry any more. Jax has somehow already managed to eat half the food on his plate, and as my mind settles back into reality, the thought of him exploding six kinds of fish all over everyone makes a bubble of laughter start in my stomach.

"Are you sure the rat didn't bite through your shoe? You look beached," Fraya says to me from across the table, her wide blue eyes scanning my face from under her mane of auburn hair.

"No, it didn't. I'm fine," I say, and force a smile. She smiles back, but her forehead wrinkles in concern.

"You are pretty pasty, though," Avis says, swallowing a bite of pie.

"Just hungry," I say, then feel ice in my veins as I see Vox Dyer's yellow eyes on me from across the room.

CHAPTER 10
Last Sunset

Everyone disperses just before the sun sets, all the hugs and congratulations well distributed, and we all begin walking along the beach to our complex, my mother and Jax a few steps ahead of me with Nann fast asleep in Jax's arms and Fraya at his side with her family. I look around for Vox again, having lost sight of her just minutes after I caught her staring at me at the table. I exhale and listen to the surf hitting the beach rhythmically, making me yawn, but I refuse to let my eyes close because I don't want to miss any of this last sunset. I wrap my arms around myself against the breeze and try to sort everything out—what it means to be leaving in the morning, and whatever that was back there with the fish...

"Hope that yawn doesn't mean you're planning to stand me up tonight," Liddick says, appearing at my shoulder. I jump, and a burst of adrenaline hits my bloodstream.

"Safe to say I'm awake now," I say, smiling. "Liddick, what was—" I start, but he interrupts me, angling his head back at Arco, who is right behind us listening to Avis yammer on about something with both of their families surrounding them.

"This is the last one of these we'll see," Liddick says, tilting his head toward the sunset once he realizes I understand. I take a deep breath, resigned to wait until later to talk about what happened back there.

"I've been trying to tell people that all day," I say.

"You know there's only one script today, Rip," he says, lowering his voice and eyes to the sand beneath our feet. "You know the world would come apart otherwise." He smiles to one side, and I sigh.

"I know."

We walk silently like this for several more yards watching the sun slide down the sky, and we eventually slow to a stop at the edge of the saw grass that lines the winding path to my complex as my mother, Jax, and Nann head inside.

"So, I'll see you in an hour?" I ask as we stand watching the horizon.

"If you can manage to stay awake." Liddick slips his hands into his pockets and shoots me a grin.

"I'll be there," I say, neither of us quite ready to tear our gaze from the setting sun.

***

Liddick leaves not long after Arco approaches with Avis and their families, and Arco lingers as the others go inside.

"Staying out here awhile?" he asks. "It's an early morning tomorrow."

"No, I'm coming in. Last night with everyone and all," I answer. He nods, then turns to head inside.

"See you in the morning then," he says with a half smile, then abruptly turns back around. "Jazz—" he starts, but then changes his mind about whatever he was going to say, opting instead just to raise his eyebrows and nod. "It really will be OK."

"I know. Thanks, Arco."

He nods one more time before heading through the door, and I watch him disappear up the flight of stairs that leads to his family's habitat. I turn back around just in time to see the last of the sun disappear into the water, the orange and pink sky fading to purple.

When I come in, my mother has already put Nann to bed. She hugs Jax and me through a yawn, and quietly tells us again how proud she is before heading to bed herself. She looks exhausted, and I wonder if she slept at all last night in anticipation of today. Jax has eaten so much that it doesn't take long for him to fall asleep, and I'm left with the sound of the waves for company as I stare out my bedroom window and wait for the dome light of Gaia to change from red, signifying high tide, to blue, the beginning of the water's recession. When we all head to the shuttle in the morning, we'll be able to see the whole brilliantly lit dome again instead of just that light, and it's hard to believe it was just this morning when I saw it last.

After I'm sure everyone is asleep, I slip out the door and head down to the shore in front of the complex. I look down the beach and see that it's dark, not even one of the fires that usually light the Fisher clan's docks is lit, and I wonder if they are all gathered somewhere for a separate, additional ceremony or sendoff for Joss, who will board the shuttle with the rest of us in the morning. The red light on the water dims for a second, then begins to glow again as blue, and I look around for Liddick. He is nowhere to be found until he is right behind me, and I nearly swallow my tongue on the gasp, having no idea where he came from.

"What are you, a selkie?" I ask, only halfway kidding that he's one of the Fisher's sneaky myths.

"Too blond for that," he smirks, and tries to skip a stone over the black water that we can only see in sparkles against the backdrop of the starry sky, which makes it look like we're floating in outer space. I pick up a stone and try to skip it, but it just hits the water with a plunk.

"Liddick, what happened tonight? How did that fish move and talk like that, and why are we the only ones who saw it?" I ask, feeling as if I've been holding my breath all day.

"*Slow down,* Riptide," he laughs, using the nickname he's called me since we were kids again, and throws another stone on the water. "Come on," he says, turning to walk toward the dune just up the beach.

"So start with one question then—why just us?" I ask as we walk.

His hands dive into his pockets as he looks down at the sand and takes a deep breath, then blows it out. The breeze coming off the water sweeps up in a gust and sends his wavy, sun-streaked hair off his forehead. He lifts his chin against the gale, and for a second, I get the impression he's actually trying to see which of them will back down first.

"It's not the first time I've heard something like that," he says. "And it's not the first time I've seen something come to life like that to tell it to me," he continues, still staring down the wind. In a few steps we reach the foot of the small dune and start climbing to the top.

"What? How long?" I ask between steps.

"It started happening about a year after Liam left for Gaia—whenever I'd jack into a virtuo-cine after that, I'd get something. At first, these random objects or people would tell me names, coordinates, phrases like 'don't go,' 'no more water,' just things that didn't make sense in the plot, but then I started to put it together," he says, extending his hand down to me from the top of the dune.

"Wait, that would have been years ago. This has been happening to you for *years*, and you've never said anything about it? I can't close my eyes and not see that fish all over again."

"Wouldn't have done any good to say anything—no one else ever saw or heard it," he says, sitting down and resting his forearms on his knees after he picks a long, narrow blade of saw grass. "So, I started trying to talk back to it, and when that didn't do anything, I started looking for some people who could help me figure out what it was."

"But you just said you wouldn't tell anyone because no one else could see or hear it," I say, bringing my knees up to my chest against the wind.

"Well, I figured out that if you pay someone enough, it doesn't matter if they believe you—they'll help you."

"It couldn't have been anyone around here who helped you—everyone else would have found out in a minute."

"No, it was at Skyboard, at least at first," he says, and I

nod, not surprised that he has connections as often as he's been up there the last several years. "I started talking to the cinematics crews, story-boarders mainly, and got some names that led to other names, and eventually found a guy who had the tech to help."

"What did he do?"

"Got me a frequency meter," he says. "That picked up the separate transmission waves and confirmed I wasn't losing my mind, and once I knew that..." he tosses the blade of saw grass and shrugs. "I was just angry. What kind of prank was someone playing, you know? I've made a lot of important friends, but I've made enemies too."

"So if it's someone's idea of a joke on you, why am I seeing and hearing it now too?"

"I never said that someone was playing a joke, Rip. It's just the possibility that made me angry enough to find out."

"Did you find out?"

"Yeah," he says, and looks down at the sand. "It's Liam."

"Liam? Why would he play a joke on you like that?"

"It's not a joke," he adds, turning to look at me now. "He's gone, Jazz."

"What do you mean *gone?* He just started as a biodesigner in Skyboard. See all those lights up there?" I say, pointing to the twinkling mountain in the distance.

"That's not my brother," he says, looking out onto the water toward a horizon that we can't see.

"Who then?"

"I don't know." He picks another piece of saw grass, then suddenly chuckles to himself. "Once he chased me up this dune when we were playing as kids. I fell and clipped a rock on the way down, gouged my eye right here," he says, pushing back his hair to reveal a thin white scar line running through his left eyebrow. "I was only nine and he was 13. It wouldn't stop bleeding, and pretty soon I got so scared I started tweaking and telling him I was going to bleed to death," he says around another laugh. "The only way he could get me to stop was to go pick up another rock and cut his *own* eyebrow in the same place," he adds, looking sideways at me, wide-eyed. "He just held his hair back with one hand and cut his eyebrow with the other; *can you believe that?* And then he just said, 'See, I'm not going to bleed to death, and neither are you, so let's just hold it together until we get home.'" Liddick tosses the other piece of shredded saw grass away, then continues, "So he pinched his eyebrow closed, and I pinched mine the way he showed me, and we walked home like that. The medi-droid came as soon as our mom sent for it, it sewed us both up, and we had this matching scar after that. It was like this thing for us, you know? *Just hold it together until we get home.*"

"Liddick..."

"Anyway, so the first time I saw him in person after we were told they stationed him in Skyboard last month, his scar was gone."

"But he's in biodesign now; he probably just fixed it."

"No, he wouldn't have fixed that scar," he says, looking back down to the sand, then shaking his head a second later as if he'd asked himself one more time if it could have been possible. "I don't know who that is, but it's not Liam. He wouldn't see me any more after that first time I went up—too busy, out on remote call—it all made sense then."

"Do you know where he really is?"

"Not yet. But I have people working on it."

"I just can't believe it," I say, stunned as I lean into him, shuddering a little at the sudden gust of wind. He puts his arm around me, and this heavy feeling I've had for days starts to feel a little lighter.

"I'll figure it out one way or another," he says in the face of another gust of wind, then turns to me over his shoulder and motions with his chin for us to walk. We get up and dust off, then head down the hill.

"You know, you never really told me about your interview," I call after him, and once we clear the foot of the hill without any new facial trauma, he starts talking again.

"I said they were like my people, Styx, Plume, and the dragon lady, but it's like they just wanted me to feel like that. They kept making these little comments about people not trying, about being comfortable in mediocrity, then asked me if I had any attachments, about my brothers, about what I thought about going to Gaia. I told them what they wanted to hear: that Seaboard North wasn't really my scene, and they seemed interested in that, especially that *sally* with the hair."

"Rheen?"

"That's her," he said, and raised his wrist. "We talked

about what *was* my scene—getting out in the world, seeing different places and meeting new people, doing something that changes how everyone thinks, you know? She cuffed this on me then, and that was it."

"That sounds just like my interview, but everyone else had some kind of situational test—everyone I've talked to anyway, except maybe Jax. I can't believe I haven't talked to him about his interview yet," I say, mainly to myself. "I'll have to ask him about his on the shuttle tomorrow."

"His was rough, and almost the same as Ellis's. Sarin's and Myra's were similar, too, just like yours and mine," Liddick says, bending down to scoop up another stone to throw. "I talked to him on the walk back from the shuttle. There was a hospital where some patients had lost limbs and were being fitted with repros that had been grown from their own cells. He had to mix their biotechnics so their bodies wouldn't reject them."

"If they were grown from their own cells, why would they need biotechnics?"

"That's what Jax and Ellis wanted to know too, but when they asked, the Gaia people just kept telling them to start mixing, showed them this timer and told them if they didn't have things configured before it counted out, everyone was going to die. Outer ring, no?"

"That's *split*. What did they do?" I ask, impatient for him to go on.

"They figured out how to mix it all, then had bracelets clapped on and were sent to the shuttle like the rest of us. Jax said they wouldn't answer any questions when he came out of it, even acted like they didn't hear him asking."

"He didn't tell me any of this." I say, a twinge pulling in my chest.

"No time with everyone else locked down the way they were. You saw Fraya."

"Do you know her story?" I ask, and he raises his eyebrows.

"Who do you think had to harvest the original cells, splice them to regrow, then reattach all the people-pieces they used in Jax's and Ellis's interviews?"

"*No*...they wouldn't. She's not a surgeon."

"Jax and Ellis aren't molecular programmers. Avis isn't a meteorologist. Hart's not a pilot."

I let this settle into my mind, and what bubbles up in response must be the root of why I've been feeling so displaced today—the missing piece of my highly anticipated and anti-climactic testing experience. I really wanted today to tell me, one way or another, something about who I am.

"What aren't *we*, Liddick?" I ask.

"I've been trying to figure that out all day," he says, veering from the shoreline to hike another small, nearby dune next to a boathouse that blocks the wind, and I follow. Near the top, he turns to me and offers a hand again. I take it, he pulls me up, and we sit close together on the narrow peak.

"Did Hart tell you about his interview?" Liddick asks.

"Some of it, but he was cagey. Something about running probabilities where he had to choose between saving some of us, and that because he waited too long to fix one of the systems, someone was electrocuted," I say, and Liddick nods. "He was really intense about it," I add, remembering him in the courtyard right afterward.

"You died every time, even when he managed to get to you," he says, leaning over to scoop up a handful of sand. "He was always too late."

"He told you this?" I ask.

"No, Ellis," he says. "Hart's not exactly my biggest fan," he chuckles, letting the sand fall through his fingers. "Not after that day in the cafeteria anyway."

I smile in agreement and pick up my own handful of sand. "What did you even say about Arwyn?" I ask, then shake my head. "No, actually, I don't want to know," I say, holding up one hand to him before he can explain.

"No, you don't," he laughs.

We sit in silence for a few more minutes, and I think about Arco's interview. No wonder he was so obsessive and erratic when he caught up with me afterward. I'd be the same way if every one of my attempts to save a friend wound up that way. It must have been awful for him to feel that no matter what he did, it still wasn't enough.

What I don't understand is why they would put him through something like that? Why put Fraya and Jax through it, but spare Liddick, me and a few of the others?

"Are you afraid of what will happen next?" I say over the sound of the surf in the distance before us. He doesn't say anything at first, just picks up more dune sand and lets it spill through his fingers.

"I guess a little. Not about leaving, though. There's nothing I'll really miss here. Well, breathing without technical support maybe; that's a little daunting," he forces a laugh, and I'm amazed that I hadn't even considered the environmental differences between here and Gaia in my obsession about leaving my family behind. Once again, the obvious sneaks up on me, and I add a new layer of anxiety to my feelings about tomorrow and whatever comes after.

"I didn't even remember that," I say, then shake my head in disbelief.

"Sorry, I meant it as a joke. They've been down there 80 years, Jazz. It's not going to be an issue."

"So, does that mean you're not really afraid after all?"

"I don't know. There's something I couldn't place about those interviewers. I got their vibe and all, could tell what they wanted to hear, but that's all there was to them. Like that interview—me in my interview—I was the only thing there. They were empty; does that make any sense?" he asks, looking over at me again. I stare at him for a second, a little shocked that he's articulated exactly how I felt about them too.

"It does. They just had this singular sense of superiority, except for Ms. Plume, but even she just put out this one-dimensional innocent feeling. It's been bothering me all day that not only could I have had such an easy interview with them, but also that I still feel like there was something missing, or something that I didn't do—information I didn't have that would help me decide how I did in there. I felt like I was just in a holding pattern, you know? Until now, that is. It helps not to be the only one," I say, and feel the weight that's been pressing on my chest finally start to give way.

"Yeah, it does," he says, his blue eyes catching the moonlight as his dark roots disappear under the night sky over his sun-bleached hair, which makes him look like he's only mostly here, like some kind of beach apparition. "Why didn't we work out, Riptide?" he asks, suddenly studying my face, and I manage to catch the surprised laugh before it comes out as a guffaw.

"Because we were 13, Liddick," I say, a few chuckles slipping through despite my efforts.

"So? Kids in some South American villages get married when they're 13 and have 10 of their own kids by the time they're our age."

"That's impossible," I say, picking my own piece of saw grass and shoving into him with my shoulder. "Besides, we're not kids in a South American village, are we?"

"So you're telling me that geography has ruined my life? *Geography?*" He raises his dark eyebrows, then looks toward the sky for the answer I'm not giving him. I laugh, and, he turns to me, still smiling. "Are you afraid?" he asks, passing me a little red saw grass flower and leaning into me. I'm surprised when the answer I've been fighting with all day finally comes out, and I let my head rest on his shoulder as I take the little flower from in between his fingers and twirl it in my own.

"I think I just feel wary now, not as afraid as I thought I was before," I say as the side of his head touches mine. "What do you think the difference is between those two things? Why would it feel more secure when we still don't really know *anything?"*

"We do, though," he says, his chin raised against the sea. "We know there's something off about all this—we can see it coming," he nods like he finally believes it. "That's the difference."

CHAPTER 11
Embarking

The silver relay shuttle has already arrived when we get to the dock this morning. It looks almost like the one we take to school, except the rounded walls are windows from the midline up. People from the quadrant and the fringe line the beach to say goodbye to the 12 of us, and when I see Liddick, the smudges under his eyes tell me he hasn't slept much either. I dreamed of the marlin, and then had to convince myself that it *actually* happened—that my dream was a product of that reality. Liddick must have had a similar experience, and then I remember that he's been having similar experiences for years.

In the distance, against the sunrise, Vox stands near the shore with her sandals in her hand. She's standing perfectly still with her back to the crowd of people surrounding the rest of us. If she does have anyone at home, no one has come to see her off. I scan the beach hopefully for someone with tattoos like hers, someone who could possibly be here looking for her, but I don't find anyone.

"Jazz, will you port-call me?" Nann asks, pushing wind-tossed strands of long dark hair out of her wide brown eyes as she pulls on my shirt and bounces on her toes. I look down at her little face, and the reality of everything arrives like a rainstorm that has been brewing —finally, but suddenly.

"You know I will. We can go to the virtuo-cines together and you can introduce me to some of the cinestars. Would you like that?" Her face lights up, and my mother smiles at me. I've learned to cover and deflect, to protect them all; she taught me that, and in her light brown eyes I can see her acknowledge it. She smiles, then hugs me.

"I'm so proud of you, Jazwyn. You're going to be so much more than I ever was."

This causes tears to start a slow burn in my eyes, and I blink them back to protest.

"Mom, you have three apprentices helping you run the greenbed, and probably three more for next year. You make a difference for so many people," I say. She smiles, her dark eyebrows drawing together before she hugs me again, and in the silence between us, we say everything we haven't and can't. When she lets me go, she peels Nann from Jax's leg while he feigns rescue.

"I still win! I still win! Interference!" she yells until Jax concedes whatever war they had begun.

"OK, OK, you still win."

"I told you I would. I'm not as ticklish as when I was nine."

"You were just nine last week, Nanobot," he says.

"I know! And that's why you could win then!" She punctuates the claim with her chin in the air, utterly victorious. He laughs and shakes his head, and then our mother hugs him for a long time before letting him go.

The shuttle bay doors open with the sound of hydraulics engaging, and we hear an announcement pour from the intercom.

"GAIA CADETS, PLEASE BEGIN BOARDING THE

RELAY SHUTTLE AT THIS TIME."

With a final hug for Nann and our mother, Jax wraps his arm around my shoulder, and we walk toward the bay doors.

"They're going to be OK," Jax says, keeping his eyes straight ahead, and I know he's saying this to himself as much as he is to me.

"I know," I reply, keeping my eyes forward as well. "We'll be OK too."

He squeezes my shoulder, and I lean my head against him all the way out to Gaia's relay dock, watching the shore of our home get smaller and smaller in the distance.

Two men in crisp, white uniforms with a navy stripe running down the sides of the pant legs stand just inside the relay doors, the dome surrounding them wide and gleaming with a submarine about twice the size of the shuttle locked in port behind it. They motion us forward and extend a hand toward our bracelets, scanning them with a wand that turns green at the tip before they let us pass.

"Welcome to Gaia Sur, cadet," they say to each of us as we're scanned in, but they do not look at us. Arco comes up behind us as we walk with the others through the corridor of the dome, which opens into another corridor that ends in a narrow, downward staircase that makes everything look like it just drops off from this angle. The walls are seamless and white, and the soft fog of light bouncing off them makes this seem even more like a dream.

"This is really the submarine,"Arco says from behind me. I turn to see that his eyes are bloodshot and raise my eyebrows in inquiry, but have to look away before I can get his answer when Jax pushes against my shoulder.

"Steps," he says, as I'm about to topple into him. We can only walk two by two down the stairwell, which opens at the bottom into a galley with shiny metal tables built into the left side and narrow steel cabinets behind them. A kitchen area is on the right with a double wide chiller against the back wall and another long metal table in front of it. A small stretch of steel countertop along the same back wall as the chiller gives way to a double sink with more brushed metal cabinets above it. Situated in the middle of the long stretch of countertop on that back wall is a stovetop with a vent reaching down from the ceiling, and next to it is a slab of black marble with several buttons along the side. I swallow the gasp that almost escapes as I realize that this is a *matter board!* I shouldn't be surprised to see one here, this is Gaia—or at least, almost Gaia—after all, but I've always thought matter boards were just in science fiction cines.

The group in front of Jax and me has fanned out and slowed, and murmurs begin penetrating the air as I elbow Jax to get his attention.

"*Jax!* That's a matter board—do you think it works?"

"Those aren't real," he says, then looks over to the countertop where I'm pointing with my chin, and his mouth falls open.

"Why would they bother with a stovetop or chiller or anything if they have a matter board?" I ask, and he shakes his head.

"Always have a backup plan," Vox says, suddenly at my side, and I startle. Up close like this she's even more intimidating, and I instinctively take a step back. I tell myself to reply with some casual acknowledgment, but I lock up and can only stare back at her—at the slashes of charcoal colored etchings down the bridge of her nose, and then again at the yellow-green of her eyes, which peer from behind her razor's edge of dark burgundy hair.

"Does it really make anything, like in the cines?" Jax asks her, surprising me with how casual he sounds. She peels her cat eyes away from mine and looks up at him, quirking the side of her mouth into a grin.

"Let's see," she says, and starts walking over to the counter as the rest of us move through the room looking for someone to give us instructions. Panic and excitement flood my veins, and the tips of my fingers turn cold.

"No—I mean, *Vox...*" I start to call after her, but trip over my own words as I look around for a guard or one of the Gaia representatives from the interviews. I don't even see the men who scanned us in coming down the stairwell. Weren't they right behind us?

By the time I turn around, Vox is already behind the counter pressing a button that creates a soft green light under the marble. I look around in all directions to see if anyone has noticed her, and my stomach falls as I realize that almost everyone has. *"Vox, stop. You're going to get us in trouble,"* I whisper, but she just smirks at me and turns her attention back to the matter board. She looks back to Jax, her finger hovering over the button again.

"What do you want to make?" she asks, raising an eyebrow.

"Jax, tell her—" I start, but he is already answering.

"Ice cream cone."

"Jax!" I hiss, crushing his name between my teeth, which just makes him laugh.

"What? You said to tell her," he says, mocking me.

"I was going to say tell her to *stop.*"

"Come on, it's not like I asked for a parson fish," he replies, smiling as he sees Fraya standing a few feet away. Others laugh, knowing that parson fish don't exist outside of the cines, but then, neither did the matter board until now.

"What's a parson fish?" Vox asks, her smirk giving way to pursed inquiry.

"They walk straight up to you out of the water—one touch and you're on your knees, or whatever is left of your legs," Sarin says from the other side of the room. "So why don't you stop playing with things you don't know anything about, *Fringe.*"

Vox's eyes flash, igniting the spark of tension that was already in the room. Liddick, who is standing next to Sarin, chuckles over the low moan reactions as he crosses to the counter and holds up his hands to Vox like he's going to tell her a joke.

"So these fish were in the last Dice McClain cine, and...wait, what was your name again? Sorry, but I can't remember my own name looking into those eyes," he says, folding his hands over his heart. I would probably roarf if my own heart hadn't already jumped into my throat to block anything that might come back up. He takes a few steps toward her.

"Vox," she says, putting one hand on her hip and tracing the button with the finger of her other.

"Vox, that's it. *Voice,* from the ancient Latin..." he takes another step toward her, "and that your name means voice makes sense because, I mean, am I right, gentlemen?" He looks around at the boys in the room, then angles his head at Jax, making sure Vox sees him. "Hers is honey, right, Ripley?"

She returns her eyes to Jax, and the corner of her mouth hooks up again as Liddick takes another step toward her.

Jax squirms, "Uh, right. Honey." Vox raises an eyebrow at him. He looks over at Fraya, who covers a smile with her hand, then over to Arco in the stairwell, who shrugs and nods.

"Why don't you sit with us over here so everyone can get to know you," Liddick says, slipping around the counter and offering his hand. Instead of taking it, she stops him in his tracks with a narrowed yellow glare, and the blood drains from his face as she pushes the button with her command.

"Parson fish!"

CHAPTER 12
Parson Fish

Vox rips away from the matter board, and the electric blue stripe across its eyes and the muted orange underbelly take shape almost immediately as the green fins begin to twitch, sensing there is no water. They fold down and under like the petals of a wilting flower until they solidify into legs as the coconut sized body drops to a lower center of gravity and spreads out like a crab. After a few steps off the matter board, everyone begins screaming and scattering, knowing that it will only be seconds before the parson fish begins to skitter around the room in search of prey.

"It's real!" Myra yells, and climbs on top of a table behind us. Vox has disappeared in the frenzy, and I feel fingers gripping the sleeves of my jacket from behind me.

"Let's go! Let's go!" Jax shouts, pulling me backward toward the stairwell, but his grip is broken when I stumble and hit the cold metal floor.

"It's locked!" someone yells from the stairwell.

"They've already launched!"

People have started scrambling onto the tables and chairs when I see Arco struggling to get through the fray. He looks at me wide eyed and calls my name, then pushes through all the arms and legs enough to kick a chair in my direction, which slides several feet before it falls sideways and clatters against the ground. The parson fish notices and darts over to me.

"Jazz! Get up!" Arco calls, and I scramble to my feet now that the space around me has cleared, but Sarin has already climbed up onto the chair that Arco slid over to me. I freeze again like I froze in the ocean that day with the jellyfish, the day Arco didn't have to think and just acted. *There has to be something I can do, or somewhere else I can go to get away.* This thought pounds against unanswered doors in my head as I look around and find no options, only the horrified stares of my classmates, and suddenly everything slows down. Everything gets quiet. I will my legs to run, but they don't move. A numbness falls over my whole body like in a dream as I watch the parson fish flitting on its pointed claws toward me, and in the back of my mind I ask myself if this must be what it feels like when you're about to die. I thought it would be more terrifying. Instead, it's still and quiet even though I see people making screaming faces and throwing hands in my direction.

As the parson fish gets closer, I can see the iridescent electric blue strip of scales threading through its eyes like a bandit's mask hiding the green mottled splashes underneath them. It rounds on me when it finally gets close enough, then peels back its bright green lips to reveal two hooked fangs, and I hear my name again from behind me.

"Jazz!" The cracked, anguished sound of my brother's voice breaks my paralysis; *I can't stand here.* I think, looking behind me and seeing him pinned against the wall behind a table with others on top of it, and I try to run to

the other side of the room. The parson fish skirts in front of me, and the sight of that green lip curling back again sharpens my attention. This time, I am not so easily paralyzed. There is no room on the counter or the tables and chairs for me, so I try to calculate a safe way to kick it or to duck if it launches itself at me, and then I remember I am wearing a jacket—I can swat it away, or maybe I can just throw it over top and cover it long enough to step on it, but I don't know if its venom has to be injected, or if just the touch of it will disintegrate flesh and bone.

"Give me a pan or something!" I yell as I pull my arms out of my jacket and hold the cuffs together, ready to swing at the fish if it jumps or scurries at me. "Hurry up!" I yell again, without daring to take my eyes from it.

"Get off! Move!" I hear Arco's voice, and from the corner of my eye also see Jax trying to escape the pile of people in front of him.

"Stay back!" I yell to them both as the fish lunges at me, stopping itself at the serendipitous timing of my raised voice as my stomach flips.

With room to move now, I step sideways around to the counter so I have something at my back, and whip my jacket once at the fish to keep it at a distance, but it grabs on, and I don't realize it until I'm already retracting for another swing. I drop the jacket instantly and duck upon seeing its kelp colored lips curling to bare fangs that are flying right toward my head. The momentum of the initial pull sends the fish sliding a few feet behind me, and I run toward the stairwell where Avis and Fraya are frantically waving me over, having made room for me, but suddenly from behind, I hear the clatter of metal and a high pitched keening. I turn in the doorway and see the handle of an ice pick sticking out from the top of the parson fish, which is now twitching and flickering green around its eyes and mouth until it lies still on the ground. Joss stands at the other end of the room, his hand still suspended in front of him from having released the ice pick. He looks at me, then at the fish.

"Don't touch it. It still might be poisonous," he says in a steady tone, then exhales. I nod, feeling the icy current of adrenaline pulsing through my veins and behind my ears until everything sounds muffled and thick. People start getting down from the tables and countertops, and seconds later Jax is in front of me gripping my shoulders.

"Are you OK? *Are you OK?*" he says, scanning my face wildly. I nod, then nod again.

"Where is Vox?" Arco yells. "Where is that—"

"Arco!" I yell back at him. "It's fine. The fish is dead," I say as he takes a deep breath, but still scans the room furiously for her.

"What the hell is this place? Shouldn't there be a crew or something?" Jax shouts to the room, one hand still on my shoulder. We all look around for someone official, but see only the twelve of us—well, the eleven of us with Vox somehow gone. I move toward the stairwell doorway again to see if she's up there, but don't exactly want to lead Arco or anyone else to her if she is. I turn back to the galley and see Joss again, still standing in the same place, the ice pick running straight through the center of the very dead parson fish, its bluish blood now pooling underneath it.

"Thank you," I say to him. He blows out a breath, then smiles to one side and nods.

"Never thought I'd spear fish again after yesterday," he says, which breaks the tension in the room. Arco's eyes are still wild when I look over to him, and I really hope for Vox's sake that she stays out of sight for a while.

"Let's get out of here," I say, and motion to the door on the other side of the galley.

"It's locked," Liddick says, "we tried it when you were starring in *Girl vs. Gaia* back there."

"Stow it, Liddick," Jax says, taking a step in front of me.

"Level, Ripley. It's a joke," Liddick replies with his hands in the air, and Arco takes a few steps toward him.

"Please give me a reason to hit you," he says. Liddick raises an eyebrow at me and smirks as if to ask, *should I?* Arco grabs him by the shirt with both hands before Ellis and Jax pull him back, but Liddick just laughs and starts brushing off his shirt like Arco has somehow gotten it dirty.

"OK, everyone relax. Let's just figure out how to get out of here," I say, and look over to the matter board, which is still glowing. "The board is still on."

"Tell it to make a key for the door," Avis says to Myra, who is closest, and the people next to her nudge her forward.

"What do I do?" she asks, wiping her eyes.

"Push the first button and tell it to make a key for the

galley door," Ellis replies. She pushes the button, and the green light glows brighter as the hum starts up again.

"Why is it making that noise?" Her voice is shrill and full of panic as she looks around for an answer.

"It's just getting ready. When you hear the high whirring, tell it what to make," Ellis says. After another second, she leans down closer to it.

"Make a key for the galley door," she says, then scurries back. The key starts taking shape immediately, and in a second, the bright green light fades back to the baseline glow. She reaches for the key and drops it with a yelp.

"It's hot!"

"Hand me that towel," Liddick says to Quinn, who tosses it to him. He picks up the key near his feet with the towel and crosses to the locked galley door, then inserts the key into the lock. "It fits," he says, turning the handle. He opens the door, and through it we see our interviewers—Ms. Rheen, Mr. Styx, and Ms. Plume—all typing into their tablets.

CHAPTER 13
Bearings

Mr. Styx and Ms. Plume are seated at either side of Ms. Rheen, smiling as she stands and straightens her white uniform, then opens her hands to us before clasping them in front of her as she talks. "Well done, cadets! Welcome aboard. You'll forgive our abrupt greeting, but we needed to establish a few things about your personalities before assigning you roommates on the Gaia campus. If you'll follow us, we'll get you seated for departure now." I look behind me to Jax. His eyes are narrowed, suspicious, like mine. We are in for much more than we bargained for here, and based on the odd quiet of the group as we start to shuffle in the direction of the interviewers, everyone knows it. Arco begins crossing the room in measured strides as I see Liddick fall back. He shakes his head as his eyebrows dart together when he sees Arco; *no more drama...not right now,* his expression seems to say. And then, as startling as if one of the windows had burst, Sarin's voice shatters the silence.

"So, should we expect to be brought to the brink of homicide regularly at Gaia, or will this be the last time you sit back and watch us all nearly vaporized for your entertainment?" Her voice comes from somewhere behind us, causing the interviewers to stop walking and turn around. Mr. Styx and Ms. Plume smile, but Ms.

Rheen does not. She steps toward us all, and the students nearest to the front step aside.

"Miss Nu, is it?" Ms. Rheen says, sliding two of her red dragon lady nails across her forehead to tuck back wayward strands of fiery hair. Sarin doesn't say anything, but from my angle, her large brown eyes are narrowed, and she holds her chin defiantly in the air.

"Yes," Sarin replies, clasping her hands in front of her.

"Miss Nu," Ms. Rheen interlaces her fingers like a basket at her waist and talks to the floor while stepping even closer to Sarin, her eyes lighting, but not with anger. She seems...*impressed?* "Amusement was not the objective of this exercise," she says, now stopped just a step from Sarin's face and locking her eyes with hers. "We need to know what you're capable of...in any situation."

Sarin doesn't look away or step back, and in this minute I'm a little impressed. She's an iceberg.

"So you're saying we *can* expect more attempts on our lives as part of the curriculum?"

I am frozen where I stand, but strangely, the feeling of wanting to twist something to death comes over me, setting me back. Why doesn't she close her mouth before they bunk her with someone like Vox? I look up to see that Jax's jaw is clenched, and he meets my eyes with a warning. He can't think I'm going to step into this ring, can he?

Mr. Styx and Ms. Plume are not smiling any more. The silence in the room becomes a fog of unintelligible murmuring anticipating Ms. Rheen's response, and the tension is so unbearable that my ears begin ringing. I narrow my eyes to brace against the noise, then notice that across from me, Liddick's expression is strained just like Jax's.

"What? What's wrong?" Jax whispers next to me.

"The ringing."

"What ringing?"

"You can't hear it? The high-pitched..." I trail off because the sound is getting louder, too loud, and just before my hands fly up to cover my ears, I hear Liddick.

"Ms. Rheen!" he says sharply and abruptly, and the ringing breaks off. I almost collapse in relief, then feel Jax's arm move around my shoulder. "You mentioned that we'll have roommates?"

She looks in the direction of his voice, her lips wrestling each other into a smile as Jax whispers to me.

"What was that about? Do you still hear ringing?" I shut my eyes tightly a few times to clear my head, *"Jazz?"* Jax whispers again through my hair, and I turn to him shaking my head.

"Yes," Ms. Rheen replies on an exhale. "Your roommates are being arranged as we speak based on the data we have just uploaded." After a sweeping glance around the room, she speaks to all of us, raising her tendril like arms to her sides, "So, congratulations. Your matriculation period is officially underway." When she meets Sarin's eyes again, she presses her lips into a tight, thin line. Sarin lowers her chin to meet her eyes, but does not step back and does not look away. "If there are no more *pressing* concerns, Miss Nu, we will show you to your seats for the launch," Ms. Rheen says under a rigid brow, still looking at Sarin, whose eyes now travel to nothing in particular off to the side. "Good. This way then," Ms. Rheen says, turning to walk as the group filters in behind her. I start to make my way through the crowd to Liddick, but Jax grabs my arm as I start to pull ahead.

"Where are you going?" he says.

"I need to talk to Liddick. I'll be right back."

He releases my arm and I begin slipping in front of my classmates toward the far side of the group. About halfway to it I feel a hand on my shoulder, which stops me in my tracks.

"*Jazz*, are you all right?" Arco says, and I nod, searching for Liddick.

"I'm fine," I say, and try to walk on, but he doesn't let go.

"Wait, Jazz, I know I told you that I wouldn't let anything happen to you, and it almost did. And I—"

"Arco, *why* is this even..." I trail off, remembering his interview, and then struggle to keep the impatience out of my voice as I crane my neck around him, still looking for Liddick. "I mean, OK, never mind. Really, it's fine. I just have to go."

"Jazz, don't be like this," he says, causing a wave of guilt to crash into me as I pull away knowing that he's confused about my reaction, but I don't have time to explain right now.

"It's not that, I just have to go," I say over my shoulder, trying not to run into anyone's back before turning my attention again to the far side of the crowd. In a handful of maneuvers and strides, I finally fall in next to Liddick, who blows out a low whistle.

"Welcome aboard, right?" he says, rolling his eyes and returning his attention forward.

"What was that ringing? You heard it, I know you did. I saw your face."

"I heard it. And I don't know."

"Jax couldn't hear it."

"Neither could Sarin, or she wouldn't have been able to stonewall Rheen like that," he says, a smile spreading across his face until it gives way to a chuckle.

"Liddick, this isn't funny. I feel like it's just going to get worse here."

"Worse as in more orchestrated scenarios that can get us evaporated? Probably."

"I'm not kidding, Liddick."

"I'm serious!" He laughs again. "They don't need us, Jazz. They only need some of us."

"What is that supposed to mean?" I ask, trying to keep his pace as we make our way down a white-walled corridor that I'm starting to think lasts forever.

"It means just what I said. If we are all the top picks for the year, why would they be so reckless with us like that? You heard that noise they were obviously cranking up in our heads back there after Sarin's episode. Not to mention at the dinner, no one heard that marlin except for you and me. Don't you see that we're being singled out? We're the only ones they're testing—everyone else is expendable."

"But why would we be singled out?"

"Who knows, but it's pretty clear that's what they're doing—trying to map our behavior patterns. Rheen just said it herself, in not so many words."

"Even if that's true, how could they have anything to do with the marlin? That happened topside, and besides that, you said it was Liam. They weren't even around," I press.

"I don't know the extent of their involvement with that, but you didn't hear anything until they slapped that cuff on you, right?" he meets my eyes expectantly, and I nod.

"I agree that something is going on, but I don't think it's just about us," I say.

"Suit yourself, but watch your back," he says, palming his ear. As we turn the corner, I notice the ringing echoing in my own ears as he walks ahead, and I stop racing to keep up with him.

Why would they single us out for anything at all here? We're not even at Gaia yet. Maybe Liddick is just paranoid—tainted by all the virtuo-cine conspiracy plots he's been part of over the years. There was something subversive happening that started in the interviews for sure, but aren't all tests subversive? Don't they *all* ask you questions with no real intention of finding out if you know the answers so much as if you're smart enough to figure out the game? We've been training our whole lives for this, and they have to know that.

"Jazz," Arco says, catching up to me from behind and letting his hand fall on my shoulder again. His face is twisted into a grimace, and the wave of guilt I felt before returns.

"Arco, I'm *really* not mad at you, I promise. I just had

to ask Liddick something before I lost sight of him. I don't need you to protect me from anything," I blurt out all at once, trying to stave off whatever pledge of redemption he's about to offer.

"I know you don't. Sorry, it's just leftover from my interview I guess. I didn't expect it to linger around like this," he says, and I nod, relieved that he seems to be more like himself again.

"It's something about this place—I can't seem to get my bearings either," I say.

"Well, we *have* only been here half-an-hour so far, every minute of which we've spent trying not to get disintegrated," he says from behind a grin. "Maybe it will all fall into a groove once we're resettled."

"I hope so," I say, and stop with the group just outside a room with seats lining each wall. An orange light clicks on, and a hovering digital clock begins counting down in the doorway we've all just come through.

"Submersion will begin in three minutes," a female voice says from somewhere. "Please secure your deployment seats and fasten your belts as prompted by the monitor," it continues as a large screen materializes just under the ceiling at the back of the room, and we all make our way to a seat.

CHAPTER 14
Launching

When we're all seated, the same female voice comes through the speakers again after the initial sound of the hydraulics detaching from the land bridge. After a jar, we are moving. I feel a sharp pain in my wrist and jerk it back, but there is nothing around that could have stabbed me. I move the bracelet cuff and see a red pin-prick as others around me are also examining their wrists and complaining, looking around, and asking each other what just happened, but no one seems to know.

"Do not be alarmed. You have just received a pressurization stabilizer. The nanotechnics will regulate the amount of oxygen inside your body and adjust pressurization to match your surroundings at any given time," the voice says. In punctuation, Sarin throws up into a bag that flies out from the panel next to her chair.

"Nooo!" Avis shouts, then dissolves into pained chuckles while shielding his eyes from Sarin's *terrible* misfortune. I grin, but look away before I'm roarfing up vital organs myself as the announcement voice goes on.

"Nitrogen and helium levels will be adjusted in your body, which may produce temporary disorientation, nausea, pins and needles sensation in the extremities, irritability, and vomiting. Your vitals are monitored by sensors in your wrist cuffs. Note that your episodes of disquiet will be anticipated, and in the event you become sick, a receptacle will be dispatched automatically for your convenience. Enjoy your journey to Gaia Sur, cadets. We will arrive in two hours and 13 minutes."

When the voice stops, I hear a few other people getting sick, and try to look away. The smell of spearmint fills the air, and I imagine this is to help prevent a chain reaction. Jax sits next to me, and across from us sit Avis, Fraya, Ellis, Myra, Joss, and Sarin. I wonder where Vox is as I crane my neck around the room and find everyone else. *Is she even still aboard?*

"Nanotechnics!" Ellis jabs Avis in the arm in his excitement. "Stabilizers are just one class down from hemorovers." Avis raises an eyebrow under a wing of blue-edged black hair.

"Huh?"

"Blood bots. Crite, don't you read?" Ellis rolls his eyes.

"I don't read about blood bots. What are you talking about?" Avis answers, weaving in his seat and starting to look a little green.

Exasperated, Ellis sighs in disgust and begins sawing the air with his hands as he explains. "They repair your cells, change them. The State just released clinical trial results of a woman in a Gaia homestead who is 106 years old and looks 30—*feels* 30, and do you know why?" Ellis bounces his knees as my ears begin to pop. "Because all of her cells are 30, or at least, they've been repaired to that point." Avis looks on, chewing his lip as the hydraulics stop humming. We must be in the water now.

"So when an organ wears out, they synth it; what's new about that?" Avis asks.

"It's not just synthesizing organs that give out. Rovers create *A-sym patches*," Ellis adds. Sarin closes her eyes and leans her head against the back of her seat while Fraya and Avis stare blankly at Ellis. He shakes his head and continues. "OK, look, these nanotechnic cells read the compromised cells around them—cancers, viruses, damaged, whatever, then mask themselves to look the same so they can get close enough to—are you ready for this?" he says, holding his palms out. "They hunt down, then *consume* the cells that are compromised, and then, *then...*" he straightens his arms as if to hold off someone rushing him. "They extrapolate the DNA from what's left of the cells and use it to regenerate healthy new cells that then bridge the hole they've just made in the organ, bone, muscle...whatever, all by cannibalizing the corrupted ones! Isn't that *fierce?*" Ellis sucks in the breath he's been delaying with the deluge of information he's just spilled all over everyone. Avis raises his chin, juts out his lower lip, and nods his approval.

"Cannibalize?" Myra asks, raising her eyebrows. "So those things are inside of us right now? Little machines eating our blood cells? We're full of little machines right *now?"*

"I'm sure they're just helpers," Joss says, trying to comfort her.

"Right, they can't hurt us. They fix us, and anyway they didn't inject us with Rovers. The announcement said stabilizers. Those just read the air pressure in nasal cavities, lungs, eardrums, and basically adjust it to meet what's pressing in on us from outside," Ellis replies, rolling his eyes again at everyone else's general lack of understanding.

"That's disgusting," Sarin cuts in, her eyes open now. "How do we get them out of us?"

"Aren't you listening? They're *stabilizers*. Do you want your insides to implode down here?" Ellis asks, and Sarin goes a little green again.

"What?" Myra's eyes manage to open even wider at Ellis, but Joss says something into her ear, which seems to help.

"Nothing is imploding, don't worry," Ellis says to her, but she doesn't seem any more relaxed. "Sarin, they just put them in. They're not coming out. Done deal," he says as Sarin lowers her chin, narrowing her eyes at him.

"I mean how do we get them out *eventually,"* she speaks slowly and overly enunciates like Ellis needs time to reprocess the question. It's a good thing for her face that I'm strapped into this chair.

"Do you think we're going on vacation or something? We're probably never coming back, Sarin. Ever," I say, and notice that my hands are gripping the straps of my seatbelt.

"Mind your own business, chutz," she sneers again, this time at me, and the seatbelt edges bite into my palms.

"Why don't you tell me that again when we're not strapped down," I say, pressing into the restraints.

"Somebody's ready for a fight," Avis beams, the rising color in his cheeks now starting to push back the green. I clench my jaw and cut him a look. "Hey, innocent bystander here!" he says, holding up both of his hands. "It's just the nanites; they can cause irritability. Did *anyone* listen to the announcement?" Ellis helpfully reminds everyone as Sarin and I both glare at him. "I don't feel right," Fraya says, and lets her head fall back against her seat. My own head starts to spin, then feels heavy in the base of my skull. I lean back and close my eyes, waiting for the sensation to pass, but it doesn't. "And the bots are off to work," Ellis says. His voice is slower and quieter now. I open one eye to look at the people nearest to me, who are all leaning their heads back, all except one who is awake, yellow eyes wide open and staring at me... *Vox?*

***

I wake up to the female voice on the intercom, but can't make out what she's saying because my head not only seems heavy now, but also muffled. It feels like there's a weight on my chest when I try to breathe, and when I turn to look around, my eyes have to catch up with the motion. I rub them to try to wake up more, but it doesn't help.

"Don't bother with all that," Ellis says. "The lag feeling will go away once you get used to it. It's the pressurization. It's the same for breathing. Heavy, isn't it?"

"Why?" Myra asks. "Did she say we can unclip?"

"The air pressure in your lungs, nasal cavities, and ear canals has been adjusted to the same pressure at this depth. We'll probably all have headaches for the next few days," Ellis says.

"This trip just keeps getting better and better," Sarin

adds, and I don't even have the energy to roll my eyes at her.

Ms. Rheen, Mr. Styx, and Ms. Plume enter from the long corridor and smile at everyone.

"We trust you have had a pleasant trip. If you will please finish detaching from your seats and follow us, we will get you settled in," Ms. Rheen says, and I look around for Vox, but she's no longer there.

CHAPTER 15
Arrival

My legs feel like they are filled with sand as I try to shuffle out with the rest of our group. Vox has disappeared again, and I hope that means they either pulled her off the sub, or she's somewhere far ahead because I don't trust her behind us after that stunt with the matter board.

"You OK?" Jax says, now at my side.

"Yeah, just groggy," I answer, rubbing my eyes with my knuckles. "What do you think the malfunction is with Vox?" I ask. He shakes his head like he's just smelled something bad.

"She's just unstable. She can't be stupid, or she wouldn't be here."

"Liddick thinks she was trying to impress you."

"Me? Why?" he says, his dark brows shooting up.

"Because she's into you."

"I've barely talked to her!" he laughs.

"Must be all your animal magnetism shining through," I say, nudging him in the ribs with my shoulder.

"Well, *you know...*" he says, thumbing lapels he doesn't have as a grin spreads across his face. Fraya falls in behind us, and he straightens up. I sigh audibly as he narrows his eyes at me.

"You're such a reed," I whisper, and shake my head at him bending himself into a coil as he shoos me ahead.

The corridor spills into the galley, and my eyes go

straight to the matter board. The mess we left in here has been cleaned, but I can't stop scanning the group for Vox. I finally see her rivers of arm tattoos first, then the bold lines on her throat near the back of the room where she's walking by herself. Everyone gives her plenty of space, and I don't blame them. It won't be long before people at this new school know about her, and if the students at Gaia are anything like the rest of us, it's going to be a lonely life for Vox.

As if she hears this thought in my head, she looks up and scowls at me. The bridge of her tattooed nose wrinkling like a wolf about to snap, and I turn around as fast as I can. Crite, please don't order up some kind of nitrogen bomb or biotoxin in the eight seconds it's going to take us to get up these stairs and off this sub.

The top of the narrow stairwell is a wash of hazy white emanating from the banked lights near the molding around the ceiling. When we're all through the connecting corridor, we are directed to sit on a long, metallic bench that wraps along the edge of a softly lit gray room that bows out to the left before us. A cylindrical metal lectern faces the bench, and we stare down three hallways that branch out on the other side of it.

"Cadets! Welcome to Gaia. Please, take a seat," Ms. Rheen says coming through one of the hallways on the other side of the lectern in a blinding glare of white jumpsuit instead of her uniform, the short sheath of hair skimming her cheekbones in stark contrast as she raises her arms to us and takes a position behind the lectern.

The bench isn't cold like I expect when I run my hand

over the smooth seat and up the wall, which, at my touch, suddenly fades end to end to reveal a window that stretches the length of the room. My breath catches in my throat when I see that it's water on the other side, top to bottom and as far as forever. Strange tube-like fish startle, then begin floating in different directions in the diffused midnight blue light, the source of which seems to be coming from the building we're in. *Can I even call it a building? Are we in another vessel, or is this a fixed place?* I wonder.

While everyone filters in around me, more quickly now that I've somehow tripped the window covering, I look down and see perimeter lights on the ocean floor, which is several feet below us. Pillars of jagged rock form a small wall about 30 feet from the base of the structure we're in, and beyond that I see the outline of a tall column that stretches up and up, a continuous strip of seamless windows running the length of the building, which is dark in some places and translucent in others. I can't see with any detail into the translucent areas, only that there is light coming from inside. Beyond this the thickening haze of the water conceals the details of another column structure like the one in the foreground, and in the middle, a smaller cylindrical structure built up on long, thin beams, is also surrounded by lights. This must be a similar building to the one we are in now, based on what I can see outside of ours.

The noise level in the room rises with everyone at the window chattering, but then we hear the timber of a single bell toll. We turn and see Ms. Rheen smiling, waiting for our attention at the lectern. She's a tall, spindly woman now that I get a good look at her standing, especially next to the stocky, hawk-faced older woman also dressed in white with her black hair pulled into a Sarin-like bun who has now joined her. Ms. Rheen clears her throat a few times, and we start to quiet down.

"On behalf of the entire Gaia Sur staff, we welcome you to the matriculation wing of the campus. I'm sure that you are curious about the community here, the architecture, and of course, the security," Rheen says, sliding her long, slim, red-tipped fingers along the side of the lectern as she talks. "You and the other nearly 3,000 students on campus at any given time are the next phase of societal evolution. As your history tablets have told you, the Gaia Sur campuses, our homestead initiative, as well as the global relocation of government buildings to the ocean floor have been instrumental in combating the air quality and overcrowding issues faced by topside citizens in just the last 80 years."

"Combating it for *them,*" Vox says under her breath, and I glare at her.

"Please also know that you are completely safe here. Thanks to port-cloud technology, our buildings have been printed with Carboderm synthetics right onto the seafloor, and are therefore pressure sound. We have never lost a student to environmental hazards in our nearly eight decades of operation," Rheen adds. A few people exhale and begin to murmur, but Rheen doesn't pause long enough for it to get beyond that before motioning to the sharp faced older woman standing beside her. "This is Ms. Karo, our chief medical consult. At the conclusion of this welcome address, you will follow her to the medical bay for screening, processing, and if needed, inoculations. From there, you will be shown to your new facilities. Are there any questions?" She pauses, and I look around the room. No hands raise, which I can't believe. Why does anyone need to be *inoculated* down here? I put my hand in the air to find out. "Yes, Miss Ripley," Rheen says, and I'm not sure if it's a good thing or a bad thing that she knows my name.

"Why do we need to be inoculated? Can't these nano-things we were just given kill anything we contract?"

She gives me a long stare, long enough that I notice she hasn't blinked, and then draws in a breath before answering.

"I'm sure you will understand, Miss Ripley, that we must be diligent in maintaining equilibrium to the best of our ability here at Gaia. Foreign contaminants are a preventable threat, and we find it is more efficient to be proactive rather than reactive," she says, her tone flat and rehearsed as she drums her red nails gently on the side of the lectern.

"Are those our dorms?" Myra asks, twisting in her seat to look out the window.

"Yes. The tall structures you see outside are the dormitories, and the smaller structures in between these areas are the classrooms and the commons areas," she says, as more people begin taking seats along the wrapping bench. "We are located approximately 5,000 meters beneath the surface, just beyond the continental shelf—the edge of the Abyssal Plain. There are no regular shuttles from the Gaia campus to the surface, but as many of you are aware, you may schedule port-calls with your family and friends six times per year once your three-month matriculation period is complete. Now, if you will all please follow Ms. Karo to our med-bay."

Rheen steps out from behind the podium and extends an open palmed hand in the direction of Ms. Karo, whose face is expressionless as she turns and walks toward a lighted room just beyond the wall of windows and toward the hazy column of buildings that jut out from the ocean floor.

***

The med-bay is a deceptively small room with three beds along the wall closest to the entry on our right. A long metal table with a panel hovering next to it sits in the middle of the room, and next to this, a standalone white archway to the left.

"Please walk single file through the arch and stop when the light turns green," Ms. Karo says to Ellis, who is first in line. He passes through the arch, and stops as directed when it lights up. The green light travels in a beam from the floor up to his head and then back down again as a screen with a keyboard and several buttons appears in the air. Ms. Karo taps something into it, and as soon as she stops, a syringe extends from a section of the arch to connect with Ellis's arm.

"What's in that?" he asks as he flinches.

"Please remain still. These are standard medical nanotechnics and inoculations. You will feel a slightly cold sensation at the vaccine's point of entry," Ms. Karo purses her lips as he winces silently in the wake of compressed air being released and hydraulics pulling back the arm of the syringe. When the green light turns off, Ellis looks at Ms. Karo, who nods at him.

"Thank you. You may wait outside until you are escorted to your dorm," she says. Ellis exits, rubbing his upper arm.

"This shouldn't take too long," I say to Jax, who stands behind me. "And it doesn't look too painful."

"No, seems routine enough," he studies the scanning machine as Vox passes through the arch. The green light stops at her neck and turns red, and Ms. Karo taps at the floating panel. The robotic syringe deploys and injects something into Vox's arm with a small explosion of air. The light turns green again and finishes its pass downward, then back to the top of her head. She receives another injection just as Ellis had before Ms. Karo waves her on.

"Thank you. You may wait outside until you are escorted to your dorm," she says, and Vox turns to exit. Her eyes meet mine as if she's been searching for me, but I refuse to look away from that wolf-like face again. As she gets closer to me she narrows her eyes. I narrow mine back at her, but still, she doesn't turn away.

"Dog, what is wrong with you anyway?" Sarin's voice leaps over my shoulder and spins me around to see that she's standing just a few feet back. Vox's eyes rip away from mine and fix on Sarin.

"Did you just call me dog?" Vox's words are slow and

sharpened at the corners. She stops walking and squares off in front of Sarin.

"I did, but apparently I was wrong since dogs have excellent hearing. Haven't you caused enough trouble for one day? Just move on and stop eye-jacking everyone in line. In case you haven't noticed, you're not making friends here, *Fringe.*"

Sarin's voice is a needle threading through each word, fixing it in place. Vox's mouth smears to one side as she lowers her chin and looks up at Sarin from behind those arrows down the bridge of her nose. I can almost *hear* the growling.

"Move on," Jax says to her from behind me, and her expression changes from one where I half expect her to bare her teeth to one of shock. "No one wants any more trouble today; we're tired. Aren't you tired?"

We haven't been at Gaia long, so I am surprised to notice that I *am* actually tired. It must have something to do with the nanotechnics in our blood messing with the oxygen. That, or possibly almost being disintegrated by an animal that only exists in virtuo-reality cines, and let's not forget being knocked unconscious for a handful of hours while simultaneously being sucked into the belly of the ocean. I suppose that *will* put you on your butt.

Vox doesn't look at Sarin again before she makes her way to the door, and I hope this is the last I'll ever have to see of her. My scan comes through clean, no red flags for an extra injection of anything, and I breathe a sigh of relief. The injection actually doesn't hurt so much as it sends a cold blast through my arm, then a prickling sensation.

"Thank you, please step outside and receive your room assignment," Ms. Karo says through lips that wrinkle along the edges, and I turn to walk back through the door.

"Name, please?" A blue disc hovers in the air and speaks to me as I pass.

"What?" I say more in disbelief than actual inquiry.

"Please tell me your name, cadet," the disc says again.

"Oh, Jazwyn Ripley." I say, but can't believe I'm talking to a floating light circle. I reach out to touch it and am startled back when it suddenly speaks again.

"Your room is J-717. Please follow the blue arrow," it says in a pleasant enough sounding woman's voice as an arrow begins to take shape in front of the disk, then begins to move. I turn around to see Jax coming out of the med-bay, but when I stop to wait, the arrow does not. *Crite.*

"Jax! It won't wait—I have to go. I'll find you at…dinner?" I wave at him as it occurs to me I have no idea what the rest of the itinerary is for today. What if I don't see him at dinner? What if I don't ever see him *again?* He stops in front of the disc and tries to talk to both of us at the same time.

"Don't worry—uh, Ripley, Jaxon," he says, "I'll find you if you don't find me. Hurry up, your arrow is leaving!" He points down the hall to my left, and I smile at him one last time before running to catch up.

The hall it leads me down is narrow with long arched doorways made of opaque glass with dark blue carpeting. Room *J-311...J-313...* I can see shapes of people moving behind the doors, but not in enough detail to make out what they're doing, or even if they're male or female. The hall winds around and up, the floor ramping just slightly.

"Jazwyn Ripley," the arrow, or at least, the voice from inside the arrow, says as we approach the end of the hallway. "Your roommate for this quarter will be Vox Dyer."

My blood instantly turns to ice and stops cold in my veins. "What? No!" I say out loud, then, quickly turn around to make sure she isn't within earshot. The arrow doesn't stop to discuss my protest.

"Your aptitude scores are complimentary, indicating you will provide ample academic motivation for each other. Your compatibility scores fall within the acceptable limits. You may improve these scores further by talking about common interests," the arrow voice says as we approach the door. "Arrived, Jazwyn Ripley. Welcome to Gaia Sur," it says before it flickers, then completely fades away.

"Are you *split?* Hello?" I stop myself, realizing this is not a person, not to mention the arrow is now totally gone. I'm left standing just outside of an opaque, arched door like the others I've passed, and look for a knob or some way to get in. I reach for the archway to feel around for a button I should push, and halfway up the door, a blue light travels over my bracelet cuff until I hear a little bell ping. The door whooshes open, and inside, Vox is lying on a bed with her arms folded under her head on the left side of the room. She props up on her elbows and stares down her etched nose at me with her yellow eyes.

After I take a step inside, the door slips closed, and it's clear I can't avoid this any more.

"All right, well my name is Jazz," I say, and take a step toward the empty bed on the other side of the room, the head of which faces the wall nearest to me. The blanket on it is woolen gray, tucked in on all sides, and the pillow is almost a perfect rectangle with a white case. A small metal desk connects to the wall across from the foot of the bed, and a simple steel legged chair is tucked underneath it.

"I know who you are," she says, still watching me. I realize I have nothing to put into the half dresser that doubles as a nightstand next to the bed, but I assume I will at some point, and there doesn't seem to be a closet.

"Where are we supposed to put things?" I ask, and Vox's eyes dart under my bed.

"Shoes go in the footlocker under there. They gave us two pairs—they're inside."

"What about a closet?"

"Closet is by the desk. Wave your bracelet over the wall like you did with the window covering," she says, folding her arms behind her head, then turning her eyes back on me. Her pale legs stretch out toward the door, and from the side, I can see the ends of the same roadmap lines that are on her arms peeking out on her thighs from under her canvass skirt. "Hey…" she says, raising her wrist cuff, then looks at mine, which now has a blinking green circle of light in the middle. "Push it," she says.

I touch it, and a holograph screen about 12 inches tall appears, a 3-D disembodied face looking straight into mine, the corners of its green eyes crinkling into a smile.

CHAPTER 16
Playing with Buttons

The hologram version of Rheen starts to speak, her voice instantly on the *inside* of my head. I look to Vox, whose wolf eyes are already wide with expectation. Apparently, she's been waiting for this.

"Hello, Miss Ripley. This is a neural connect, and the way you will receive most transmissions specific to you here at Gaia Sur. Your bracelet cuff will not always project a hologram, but sound will always travel through a neural link that has been constructed in your inner ear by the nanotechnics in your recent injection. The process takes roughly ten minutes. If you can hear my voice, Miss Ripley, you are now biologically equipped to be a cadet at Gaia." My hands instinctively fly to my ears, and the realization that I have miniaturized robots in my blood—*in my ears*—hits me like a wave in the face. I sit on my bunk watching the hologram as Rheen continues. "Your afternoon meal will be served in the cafeteria in approximately 30 minutes. The guide arrow that brought you to your room will return in 20 minutes and will direct you to each of your destinations throughout orientation tomorrow. Your section color is blue, signifying that you are a first year cadet. Please intermingle only with others in your section color until matriculation is complete in three months. Welcome to Gaia Sur, Miss Ripley."

The hologram of Rheen's face smiles thinly before the

screen fades to nothing, and the audio stops. I look over at Vox, who has moved to her stomach, her bare feet swaying behind her like wheat in a field as she props her head up with her hand and drags her pinky nail over her bottom row of teeth.

"Bugs in our ears...how about that?" she says under an arched brow, which is quite possibly the worst thing she could have said to me at this moment.

"Thanks for that," I say, narrowing my eyes at her.

"I'm here to help," she says, rolling back onto her bed and throwing her arm over her eyes, her dark, knife's edge of hair in a wild fan all around the right side of her head and shoulders. A cold tingle crawls up the back of my neck, and the sight of her there and the sudden vibe like she's bored fills me with contempt. Before I know it, I've launched a barrage of words at her.

"Are you here to help, because it really hasn't seemed like it so far today. You know, with almost getting half of us vaporized within the first 10 minutes of boarding the sub."

She smiles underneath the forearm draped over her eyes, which makes me ball my fists at my sides. A tingle starts at the base of my skull, and I realize I'm shaking and short of breath, and wonder if I will *actually* hit her. It's almost a compulsion, like I have to hit her. I *hate* this girl, and I barely know her.

"Temper, temper," is all she says, but at least she finds the decency to look at me this time. I drill my teeth together, and I know if she says one more thing I will leap on top of her. "Sorry. I didn't know you had a problem with swarms of things swimming around inside your head," she laughs the words rather than says them as she leans forward on one elbow and flutters her fingers next to her ear with the other hand, then laughs again. The sight of her teeth opening so wide that I can see her long, narrow tongue slapping up and down behind them in guffaws sets me off. I hear nothing, see nothing, and want nothing else in this moment than to feel my fingers wrap around her long, ink-tracked neck and squeeze until I feel things break inside.

I launch myself at her, and within two strides am flat on my back, the ceiling black with white flecks and a furiously pulsing heat in my nose. For the second time in two days I taste blood in my mouth, this time running down the back of my throat. I turn my head to the side, caught in a gagging cough, and it's then that I feel the hot, wet deluge of blood pouring down over my lips and chin. My hands rush to my nose and are almost immediately filled with blood. Vox hasn't left her bed and is laughing, now, harder than ever.

"You should play with more buttons," she says, and presses a red one on the wall above her nightstand that turns green before she takes off her pillowcase and throws it to me. I press it to my nose, almost immediately saturating it.

"What was—?" I start, but cough on the blood pooling in my sinuses.

"Crite, sponge, pinch your nose shut," Vox's voice is full of equal parts amusement and disdain. I remember that this actually is what you're supposed to do for a bloody nose, and am even more quickly reminded that it's enough to give you tunnel vision if your nose is broken, which, my buckling knees tell me, mine, apparently, is. I sit down on my bed and wait for the world to stop spinning, blood streaming down my arm now and beating a steady tattoo on the floor. "You're a disaster," she says, punctuating with something that is mostly a chuckle. I look up at her and find her blurry, suddenly realizing that the burning in my eyes is not from the impact as I'd thought, but from tears, which I immediately wipe away with the heel of my free hand. I try to talk, to call her something, to threaten her, but my throat is closed too tightly to say a word.

"The bugs will have that fixed by morning. Should be fun at meal call, though." She lifts herself to her feet and pushes the white button next to the green one above her nightstand again, but it doesn't change color like the red button did. I look over my shoulder and see an identical set of buttons on my side of the room.

"May I help you, Miss Dyer?" the guide arrow's voice says.

"Biohazard clean up, and intermediary med kit—broken nose."

"Please stand by," says the arrow voice. Vox shakes her head at me after looking me up and down, the blood running in a heavy stream now and pooling between my feet. *How can a nose bleed this much?*

"I'd say you could tell everyone at dinner that they should see the other guy, but security screens are, well... *invisible.*" Vox smirks and winks at the same time as she stands and walks over to me. I wait to feel the urge to lunge at her again, but surprisingly, all the violence I felt seconds ago is gone. In fact, I'm almost...*happy*, comfortable. *What is happening?* I close my eyes, sure that this weird euphoria is the result of what is evidently, by now, a liter of blood loss.

"Medical reporting—entry in three...two...one..." I hear the arrow voice from outside the room just before our door opens suddenly. Vox steps back to her bed, and a floating metal sphere sends a sweeping blue light along the floor. It detects the blood, then positions itself in front of me. Another metal sphere extends from the top of this one, and the voice speaks again.

"Please place the soiled material in the receptacle, then, extend your hands in front of you, Miss Ripley," it says. I drop the pillowcase inside and immediately feel the blood rush over my lips again. "Please remain still, Miss Ripley, and look at the green light," the voice says again, and a blinking light appears in the first sphere. I look at it until a beam of what feels like cold water suddenly hits my forehead and begins traveling down my face. "Scanning..." I hear it say. As the freezing sensation passes over my nose, I notice the flowing wet and sticky warmth of the bleeding stops. "Isolating fracture... nano-restructuring already in progress. Elapsed time, sixteen hours, 17 minutes."

"See, good as new in the morning," Vox says from the other side of the room, but when I try to look at her, I discover that I can't break my eye contact with the light because my face, *my eyes*, are locked in place. "Remain calm, Miss Ripley. Sanitizing..." I can feel the pulse in my throat and chest pounding, but from the neck up, I feel nothing but cold. After another minute, the light releases me, and the sensation begins to return to my face. The pain is dull now, and I can't breathe through my nose at all. Both of the metallic spheres line up next to each other, and when I look at my hands, which feel dry now, I notice all of the blood is gone, my shirtsleeves and the floor are clean again, and it's like nothing happened here at all. "You have received a neural interruptor for pain while your internal nanotechnics repair your injury—a nasal bone fracture and slight cerebral contusion, Miss Ripley. Please avoid situations that require judicious consideration or prolonged concentration this evening," the sphere says, but the blinking light is gone. They both exit our room, and Vox calls after them.

"Hey, can I get another pillowcase!?" I feel pain in my left cheek as the corner of my mouth inadvertently turns up.

"What happened?" I ask. "What did I hit?" I look around the room, but nothing seems out of the ordinary until she pushes the green button, which turns red, and tiny silver threads weave themselves through the air in a crosshatched pattern, then almost immediately disappear between us. "Touch it," she says between attacks of residual laughter. There is nothing there to touch now, but I reach out and feel the pads of my fingers flatten against something cool and smooth, like a mirror or a window.

"So you did that on purpose—raising that screen when I wasn't looking, and then..." I realize I have no idea what she did to provoke me, not really. What did she say that was so irritating? I replay what I remember of the conversation in my head, but nothing comes to me except her lazy sarcasm, her indifference and boredom, and I can't understand why that was such a trigger. Yes, I was —am—upset with her about all the trouble she's caused today, but not enough to want to strangle her the way I did. "What did you do to me?" I say to her, both my giddiness and violence now gone.

"You're a receiver; I thought you were, but I had to be sure."

"A what?"

"Didn't your people tell you anything about yourself? At your interview?"

"I don't know...they said that my strengths are in communication I guess, so what? What's a receiver?"

She rolls her eyes and falls back onto her pillow, extending her hand in the air so her bracelet cuff slides up her arm. She lifts it back to her wrist with her other hand and lets it slide toward her again and again, her shirt having risen up on her stomach to reveal more inked map-like lines.

"I'm a transmitter. I emit, you receive." In a sudden, singular jolt she rolls to her side to face me and props up her head with her hand. "Didn't you feel stupidly happy right after wanting to tear my throat out a minute ago?" She smiles too sweetly at me and flutters her eyelashes. Oh, no way...does she *really* think she can control me?

"Is that what they told you, that you're some kind of puppet master?"

"They told me basically what they told you, but it's easy enough to figure out our strengths."

"I'm not your puppet," I say, a fever of adrenaline washing over me as Vox's eyes widen and her smile spreads.

"Of course not," she says, mockingly. "How's your nose, by the way?" She lowers her chin, grinning.

"You will never do that to me again," I say, fighting to keep down the heat I feel rising in my chest. "Did you hijack Sarin back there too? Did you make her pick a fight with Rheen? Or with you just now at the med-bay?"

Vox wraps one of her long braids around her finger and searches for something on the wall behind me.

"No, that could have been fun, though. Trust me, I tried. I thought it was working when she lipped off at the director. *That* was inspired. Is she always like that?" Vox's yellow eyes dart back to me, and she stops wrapping her hair around her finger. "Or is she just your average mean skag?" I nod and fight back a smile partly because it hurts to smile, and partly because I don't want to give her the satisfaction. "Thought so."

"So you think you can just program people—the receivers—and they act the way you want them to act?" I feel my steadiness returning, but it's not enough to keep the edge out of my voice.

"Not exactly. I have to sort of shoot a feeling at them, and if they're receptive—I mean, if they already have the start of that same feeling in themselves somewhere, it catches, like an ember that I just have to blow on then. Tricky work, really. *Exhausting."*

"Why can you do that? How?"

"Same reason you can pick up on what everyone else is putting out there, whether they know they are or not. We are what we are."

"So there are others who don't know? Others who are like you and me? But you do know. Is that why you pushed the button on the matter board? Why you started all that trouble? Were you trying to see who would pick up on your...*whatever* that was, your complete insanity?"

She works her mouth into a bent smile and furrows her brows. "Harsh. I prefer to call it excavating the ground I'm going to be walking on for the foreseeable future. Send out some impulsiveness, some rebellion... hey, a girl has to find out who the fighters are, who can be tapped for action if the need arises." She meets my eyes again and angles her head to the side. "You, for example. And that *Liddick.*" She raises her eyebrows and nods, a devilish smirk pulling at the corner of her mouth.

"I told you that will never happen again, and you didn't control me in the galley. I helped stop you because I wanted to—it was *my* choice."

"Like I said, I just put it out there. I don't make you act, only react. What's in you is in you."

"Where did you go after that anyway? After they got the door open?"

"I never left."

"Yes, you did. I know you did because I looked for you."

"Think what you want," she says, then meets my eyes again and winks. "I'll let you."

I narrow my eyes at her stupid smiling face, and the lights on our bracelet cuffs begin to blink. I push mine, and hear the arrow's voice behind a dull throbbing in my ears—it's time to go to the meal hall. We both get up to go to the door, and I stop short, catching the glowing red button in the corner of my eye.

"Do me a favor before we go," I say, angling my head until I can see the spiderweb crosshatching all the way to the doorway it bisects. I press my palm against the invisible wall floating in the middle of the room between us and cock an eyebrow at her. "Turn off the security screen."

CHAPTER 17
Food-Shaped Food

"What happened to your face?" Jax's eyes widen as he approaches me from the side, a thin, silver tray in hand. I look down at his food—differently colored geometric shapes—and instinctively wrinkle my nose while wincing at the jolt of pain it causes.

"What happened to your food?"

"I know. They say it tastes better than it looks. You'd think living *actually* in the sea they would be able to do better than this. Anyway, your face?"

We walk to the line so I can get a tray.

"The security screen in the rooms," I say. "Long story."

I look over my shoulder at Vox, who grins under her braids. Jax sees her reaction and nudges my arm.

"She did this to you? Have you even seen the cut across your nose?"

"No. I mean, yes, but it's not what you think. I have a cut?" I say, bringing my hand to my face to feel for it.

"What security screen? Like, for privacy?" he asks, and I shake my head.

"Invisible ones like a forcefield so you don't kill each other I guess. I don't know, maybe you can make it opaque or soundproof," I say, making a mental note to check. I begin to slide my tray along the rails and notice a panel of buttons, brown, green, red, and white. I look at Vox just off my shoulder who raises an eyebrow at me, then after another second, I push all three. The serving bar ahead of me starts to hum while a metallic cover rounds over the opening on our side, closing off the geometric food. Everyone in line stops and begins protesting.

"Nice work, Jazwyn," Sarin says, and thanks to her, everyone else in line turns around to stare at me. "And what happened to your face?" She sneers. Heat shoots up my neck and spreads over my cheeks, and I give Vox a sideways glare, knowing now that she set me up.

"Stow it, Sarin," Jax says. She begins what will no doubt be a typical biting reply, but is cut off by the metal shield completing its rotation and reopening the window to the food. Instead of geometrical food colored shapes, there are trays of fish, scallops, what look like sausages and even...*hamburgers?*

"Is that beef?" someone at the front of the line says, and the rest of the comments are lost in a deluge of celebration.

"That's ice cream!" Jax says.

"Bread!" someone up the line says.

I turn my head back to Vox, who smirks. "See what happens when you push buttons?" I smile back at her, and notice my face doesn't hurt quite as much. In seconds, robotic arms begin placing food on plates in response to the requests, and I let Jax slip in line in front of me.

"Ice cream," he says, but a red light begins to blink on his bracelet cuff. His face falls.

"What?" I ask.

"The neural voice thing said my tray was *at capacity*," he says, and I stifle a giggle at his crushed dream expression.

"Ice cream," I say, and a robotic arm places a big scoop in a small, clear dish in the corner of my tray. I nod for Jax to take it, and he beams, then shoots me a wink.

"We're over here," he says, pointing his chin in the direction of Fraya, Joss, Ellis, Avis, and Arco, then narrows his eyes at Vox as if to ward her off.

"She's OK," I say, and he raises an eyebrow at me. "Who's your roommate?"

"This giant, mute cloudy named Pitt," he replies. As we walk toward the table, I see Liddick sitting with Myra, Quinn, and several other Skyboard North cloudies I don't know. Sarin takes a seat at that table as we walk past and immediately begins her mouselike chittering to everyone at the table. They all look up at me, so I know it must be about the state of my face, which, despite feeling better, must not look better.

Liddick meets my eyes and starts to stand, but I shake my head to let him know everything is fine. He stops, and his eyes dart to Vox. I can see him putting pieces together, but I can't deal with that now, not with Arco and his impending overreaction 10 feet away and closing. As we approach our table, I prepare for the onslaught of questions that will inevitably begin the instant we sit down. *Talk about the technology in the room, the food,* the *arrow voice...*I remind myself.

"Jazz! What happened?" Fraya says, as if on cue.

"A little mishap with the security screen in our room,"

I say, sliding into a seat, but that doesn't seem to be a sufficient answer. "I ran into it before I knew it was there."

"Why was it there?" Arco says, immediately looking at Vox. I feel another tingling at the nape of my neck again along with the need to defend her even though Arco is completely right to suspect her, but then soon figure out that she's just trying to push me again. I shoot her a look, and she widens her eyes. "What did you do, Vox?" Arco says with heat in his voice, and I realize that my reaction to her pushing has made it look like I was outing her to the table.

"No," I say to Arco and everyone else, then look at Vox again and remember that I do have her to thank for eating actual food-shaped food right now instead of the bars on everyone else's tray. "It was just an accident." I don't know how much of this is actually how I feel and how much is the result of Vox's pushing, but we need to let this go before someone makes a scene. "So, was anyone else aware that those nano-technics they injected us with can also fix broken noses overnight?" I say, and spoon up a bite of broccoli.

"Your nose is *broken?*" Fraya says, then covers her mouth with her hand.

"Well, it was. Apparently, they're in there working on it right now. It already feels better, and I can breathe now." I say, forcing a wide smile until the pain kicks in again, but at least my lip is completely healed from yesterday morning's monkey-boy shuttle wrestling episode. I hadn't even noticed that until now.

"You'll probably breathe better than you ever have by the time they're finished," Ellis says between forkfuls of brown rectangle. "They'll restore everything to its original state, so if you've ever had any other injury to the area, even tissue inflammation that has accumulated over the years because of the topside atmosphere—it'll be gone now." He chews while everyone looks at each other, and the fleeting thought that maybe Vox did me another favor enters my mind, along with the tingling sensation in the back of my head. I reach up and rub it out, cutting her a sideways look as a warning. She pops a strawberry into her mouth and chews through a smile.

"Maybe I can break my leg and get a new knee from the little doctors," Joss laughs, pushing back his blonde hair as he takes a bite from the white circle on his plate.

"What's wrong with your knee?" Avis says from under a wing of blue bangs.

"When I was fourteen I was pulling in the nets. One of them got stuck on something, so I had to get out and pull it loose. Cut my ankle on a rock, and before I knew it a bay shark had come up and taken hold." He spoons up another bite of white circle.

"A shark bit your leg?" Vox pipes up in a clear, ringing voice.

"Almost lost it—bit down right there," he says, moving back in his seat and hiking up his pant leg to show us several dark, shiny scars along his shin, over his kneecap, and trailing off along his outer thigh. "My parents sent for a medi-droid, but the selkie said I'd lose it if she didn't treat it then and there."

"What's a selkie? A witch?" Vox asks, taking another bite of strawberry. Everyone at the table looks at her, and my stomach drops at the prospect of another situation.

"Not a witch," Joss says without any detectable chastisement, "just a healer. My gran says selkies used to be seals who took off their skins and hid them so they could walk around like people, but couldn't find them again, so they got stuck here."

"Seals," Avis says. "Like, the animal? How could a seal be a healer?"

"Suppose if they can take off their skin and put on a person suit, they might know a thing or two about fixing up boys who scrap with sharks," his dimples flash with a grin that ignites his hazel eyes, and his laugh is infectious. Soon, a warm feeling seems to spread over the table.

"So, does it still hurt?" Vox asks, lifting her glass to her lips, and I raise an eyebrow at her interest.

"Now and then, if a storm is coming, but I don't suppose I'll have to worry about that any more down here." He gives her an easy smile, then looks around the table in the same way before returning his eyes to his plate.

"Well, if you hadn't *harpooned* the parson fish, I'm sure it could have been of use," Vox says through a smirk that gives way to a smile, despite her efforts to look smug. I stare at her, feeling the heat spread over my own cheeks and the flutter starting in my chest. I take a breath when I realize these are *her* feelings—so that's how it works? There's nothing but the emotion when she's just radiating them, and the tingle at the nape of my neck when she's trying to push me one way or another.

Feeling like I finally have the upper hand, I smile a secret victory to myself and open my mouth to ask Joss what he thinks of Vox turning him into *Queequeg,* but she shoves a strawberry into my mouth before I can say a word. "See, you should thank me," she says, glaring at me sideways with her glowing reptile eyes. I smile as I bite down on the strawberry, content that I have harassment fodder for later.

Arco laughs under his breath, but not in amusement, and when I look over at him, I see him sending Vox a narrowed glare before he looks back at his plate, which he's only managed to rearrange in all this time he's been sitting here so quietly.

"Hey, what's wrong?" I ask, nudging his forearm on the table and swallowing the strawberry. He clips me a look and grabs up his tray to leave. *"Hey?"*

"What's his problem?" Jax asks me once he's gone. I shrug, then look over at Vox who is finishing off her drink. "Oh," he says, following my gaze and coming to terms with the fact that there are no more bites of food for him to scrape onto his silverware. "I'll talk to him." With a wink at Fraya, he gathers up his tray and goes after Arco.

"He's a bloated dead horse, isn't he?" Vox says around the last of the berries she has popped into her mouth as she watches Arco shove his tray through the receptacle slot at the front of the cafeteria before heading out the door.

"Eww," I say, taken off guard by the imagery before

reloading my sentence. "So why are you trying to start all this trouble here?" I ask, lowering my voice.

"Buttons," she says with a shrug. "I like pushing buttons."

CHAPTER 18
Tattoo Story

After lunch, I go back to my room to lie down, and amazingly, don't actually wake up again until the next morning, but when I do, my face is fixed, and there are navy blue jumpsuits that shimmer with small, scale-like texturing hanging at the foot of our beds.

The jumpsuit material is stretchy, but silky, even softer than the colored tunics and pants we were given at our interviews. It looks too small, like it would better fit Nann than me, and at that I feel a stab of pain in my chest. How have I not even thought of her and my mother before now? I remember Ms. Rheen saying we can't make any port-calls until our matriculation period is over in three months, but make a note to ask someone today about at least being able to send a message to let people at home know that we've arrived and that we're all right. In the back of my mind, though, I know they won't let us. My bracelet cuff blinks, and I press the light. *Breakfast in the cafeteria in 30 minutes, orientation to follow,* the arrow voice says in my head. I don't know if I'll ever get used to that.

I pull the jumpsuit over my base layer, and Vox is already up with her back to me stepping into her own. Her bold, charcoaled tattoo lines like the ones on her throat run up the back of her calves, but they stop at her knees, leaving the backs of her thighs and everything else unmarked until her shoulder blades. The lines fan out toward her arms from there, each side a different pattern of fine, meandering lines. I have two main thoughts as I watch her—that those lines must have taken forever to ink, and that she might just be the whitest person in the world.

"Yes, they hurt," she says abruptly without turning around as she pulls her jumpsuit over her shoulders, which breaks the spell I'm under. She turns to face me, and with the front of her suit still unfastened down the middle, I can see that her tattoos run the length of her sternum, where it turns into a twisting maze system over her heart. She smirks at me before flopping down on her bed again.

"Who did them?" I ask, and watch her begin to unbraid her hair.

"My mother did the clan ones. I did the rest."

"You did?" I ask.

"My mother was a mapper. It didn't take long to learn."

"Was?" I ask, then immediately wish I hadn't because a vice closes around my chest.

"Yeah, was," she answers, and I don't press her for more.

"So she was a Tinkerer, then. What's your father?"

"My father wasn't one," she uses the past tense again. I let it go, feeling ice in my chest now in addition to the compression as I watch her nimble fingers undo each braid before letting them fall in a series of wavy kinks around her right shoulder.

"So, all those lines are maps?" I ask. Vox pulls the suit down over her shoulder and collarbone, half her hair still in braids.

"These are the roads that lead up the mountain to Skyboard," she says.

"*You've* been to Skyboard?" I ask, feeling my eyes widen.

"Are you going to question everything I say?" she asks, and I feel my face get hot. "When I was 13. We all have to go at 13. The clan elders take you to the edge of the village and tell you to come back with cloud thistle, which only grows at the top of the mountain, or don't come back at all," she finishes, and after a second, it seems safe to ask her another question.

"But how did you get up there? It's all sealed off unless you have a bio-chip," I press, but she just stares at me with her standard smirk.

"You don't need a bio-chip if you can find the roads."

"There are no roads that go up there."

"There are always roads. If you can't find them, you just make them," she says, returning to her hair.

"How did you get past all the carnivorous plants they have around the perimeter, especially if you were just 13, and weren't you afraid of the cannib—" the word breaks off as I'm saying it as I look up at her, the reality of Vox's father's people, who have to be The Badlanders if her mother was a Tinkerer, dawning on me.

"The *cannibals?*" she asks, her fingers stopping in mid braid. She raises an eyebrow at me like she doesn't have all day for me to stop being so painfully stupid. I feel the ball of ice spreading in my chest again, and swallow hard to regain my composure.

"Yeah," I say, my voice barely a whisper. She laughs out loud and resumes unbraiding her hair.

"They don't eat family," she finally says, then looks at my expression and laughs even harder. So hard that her hands fall away from her hair and drape over her stomach.

"That's not funny. Are you one?" I ask, the combination of anxiety and anger at her constant games, at not being able to tell the difference, welling up inside me.

"Nn—no..." she finally sputters. "Do you even know how stupid you all are? *Oooh, look, she's from the tribe in the trees...she's from the clan in the caves...* Crite, cred-feds are so paranoid."

I narrow my eyes at her, unsure what she means, but it's evident she's not complimenting me.

"You're all sown and grown for Gaia. There's more to life," she answers through a handful of tapering chuckles, then starts shaking her fingers through her now completely unbraided hair. I feel my blood simmering just below the surface, but there's no way she's getting me to lunge at her again, only to discover she's a hologram or something after I bash my face into the wall behind her. I opt for the verbal throttle this time.

"More to living like what? Like drawing all over yourself and living under a rock? Or wait, you're saying there are no subterranean or forester cannibals in The Badlands, I forgot. It's all just made up, right?" I say. She laughs.

"I didn't say that. I just said I wasn't one of them. Who knows where they really are," she says, pulling her jumpsuit down over her right shoulder now, which is symmetrical to the left until the end of her collarbone where it breaks off into a different scraggle of fine lines. "These are roads through Seaboard North, back down again, and into The Badlands quadrant," she says, tracing over the lines she references.

"That's a *map* of The Badlands?" I ask getting up and walking over to her. "Can I see?" I ask, looking into her glowing animal eyes that never seem to blink. She pulls her arm out of the jumpsuit, and the lines stop just below the bend of her elbow.

"Why does it stop there?" I ask, pointing to the place about eight inches up from her wrist.

"Because that's as far as I got before I was caught."

My eyes snap back to hers. "Caught by what?"

She smirks at me again, and I feel a tickle in my throat like laughter bubbling up. She thinks my shock is funny?

"The *V*. The *Fringe*," she says, letting the empty sleeve flap to her side as she pulls her arm the rest of the way out, stretching the neck of the jumpsuit under it.

"Fringe live out that far?"

"They're not *your* Fringe—not my people. They're something else," she says, and I stare at her. The tickle in my throat is gone now and replaced with a lump from the pressure of my heartbeat, which feels like it's trying to claw its way out of me and run out the door. I try to swallow it down and take a deep breath. "These lines run past the old buildings where my people are, even past the tunnels underneath. Out past all that; that's where the *V* live."

"But it's just all briar and sand dunes out there," I say. "There's nowhere for anyone to live."

"They're underground. At least you cred-feds got that part right," she says, pulling her arm back into her suit.

"How did they catch you?" I ask, knowing I should let it go with how hard my heart is pounding in my ears now, but I have to know.

"I was scouting and fell in a sinkhole because I was stupid. I should have seen it coming," she says, and a chill runs up my spine. "It dropped into a room that fortunately wasn't too far under the surface, though," she says, pulling her arm back into her suit and zipping it. I blink a few times when I see the zipper disappear into the fabric once it's all the way up, then look down at my own, moving it up and down to make it...*absorb.*

"So you weren't really caught, it was just an accident?"

"Oh, no, it was a trap," she laughs. "They resealed the hole about 20 minutes after I fell into it. Then they lit some torch that I could only see through a reflection in the wall, but couldn't see out past it. Fifty pairs of eyes must have started staring through the slats of the walls then, and stayed there for the rest of the day. I didn't understand their mumbling language at first, but I figured out enough to know they didn't really want to hurt me, at least not just then."

"What did they want with you?" I ask, sitting straight up on the edge of her bed.

"Don't know. I didn't stick around to find out. All the

eyes disappeared once the sun went down, and I started digging stairs into the dirt wall with a few of my tools; just before dawn I broke through the surface and ran."

"And you were just 13?"

"No, I didn't map The Badlands until after that. I was 15," she says, turning away from me and then flipping onto her stomach.

I have so many questions, but my chest is already tight and it's hard to get a breath. She evidently doesn't want to talk about The Badlands any more.

"What about your neck and face," I ask, and can breathe a little easier. She puts her fingers through her unbraided hair to fluff it again over the foot of the bed, and it falls in an arc over the back of her neck when she flips it back up. Sitting this close to her, I can see that her tangle of tattoos runs up into the hair on the left side and over her left ear. She points to those.

"These are from the top of Skyboard North. The ones on my face and throat are the same as everyone else in my clan, like these," she flips onto her back and unzips her jumpsuit to the center of her chest again to show me the maze system, then raises her pant leg to reveal the markings of her shins and calves. "They're tradition. These are my lands," she gestures to the maze below the divot in her collarbone, then to her neck and face, and finally, her legs. "This is a map to Vishan; it's *in the stars,*" she says, rolling her eyes.

I feel the little tingle in the nape of my neck a second too late. "You've been…to the stars?" I say, feeling stupid the second I hear the words in my own voice.

"No, don't be stupid," she says, and I close my eyes in a long blink. *Why do I talk?* I have to get better at knowing which feelings are actually mine, and which ones she's just magnifying. "My father's people believe we're descended from the *people of the stars.* This is supposed to be our map back to where we came from. It's just stories they tell you so you don't lose your nerve and die when they set you out in the wild to mark your paths. They want you to feel like it's in your blood to travel long distances or something."

"Then why are the markings on your legs too? They make sense, as much as they can, I guess, at the top of your body. Closest to the stars…" I trail off, realizing it all just sounds even more ridiculous when I say it.

"They believe there are ways to get there by going down too," she says, closing her eyes and flicking up her brows as she shakes her head. "I don't know, they're just stupid old tales. I didn't ink these, so that's all I can really say about them," she finishes with a few more quick shakes of her head.

"How did you give yourself these others?" I ask, looking again at the intricate patterns that run down over her ear, and again along her collarbones before they disappear into her jumpsuit. They're different from the straight, bold, clean lines over her chin, throat, and nose. She nods.

"Mirror."

"In *Skyboard North?* Why not just use an imager?"

"I couldn't exactly be found with a program on me when I was supposed to be relying on my own abilities to get myself up there and home again, now could I?" she says, sitting up and leaning her back against the wall as she zips her jumpsuit and pulls her knees into her chest. "I don't know, could you?" I feel a stab of embarrassment as soon as I ask and realize with the cold tingle that it's her pushing *again*. I *have* to learn to outrun the impulse to act on it "All right, stop, it's a real question. I don't know your wild mapper girl rules," I say, and her eyebrows shoot up as a wide smile spreads over her face.

"Wild mapper girl rules?" she says, then starts slow motion nodding, her eyebrows climbing higher on her forehead like they're trying to beat each other to her hairline.

"Whatever. You just admitted that you're a mapper, and I think this morning more than proved you're wild. I refuse to verify if you're a girl, so I'm just giving you that one," I say, trying to maintain a serious expression, but in seconds, we're both laughing.

"All right, here are the rules then," she says after regaining her composure. "So if you're going to be a boundary scout, you turn 13, and at whatever time you were born that day, the elders set you at the outskirts of the village with no food, no water, no tools, nothing except your pick knife, and that's so you can mark your path," she holds up her arms at right angles and cocks her wrists out, presumably to show me her *paths*, which consist of the several intricately drawn lines and etchings I've seen from afar."When you come back, you have an inked path and the knowledge that you can carve out another one without anything to help you. After that first trip, you can bring supplies."

"What did you use for ink that first time if you couldn't bring supplies? Is this that trip?" I ask, pointing to the short line running from the edge of her collarbone to the top of her shoulder, which gives way to a blue line that looks like water, then starts again in a deeper black as it winds around and back up her shoulder.

"That's the Skyboard trip, yeah. I used char from a fire I made to start it out, that's why it's lighter than the rest, and some crushed plants for the water line right here,"she says, pointing to the bottom of her deltoid muscle. "I used squid ink that I...*borrowed* from one of the Fisher clan's docks for the rest of way up the mountain. That's what the elders used for these too," she says, waving her hand toward her throat and face like she's fanning herself. "Only they traded for their ink. Or, at least I think they did." She smiles, angling her head toward me, and I can't help looking at all her lines and imagining a 13-year-old girl using a pick knife, a knife that's more of a short skewer than it is a knife, to record all these roads on herself.

"So do you make maps for a job now? I mean, when you're not at school?"

"That was the plan, and scouting," she says, getting up and taking a pair of navy socks from the drawer, then pulling them on over her bone white feet, her ankle bracelets now in a pile on her nightstand. "My father took a group out to The Badlands Fringe after I came back and told them I'd fallen in a trap, and when they never returned, another group went out. We never saw any of them again, and the elders forbade any more mapping of the West," she says, readjusting her jumpsuit and falling back on the bed. "I could have found him, though. I could have found them all," she says.

"But instead you wound up here," I say, finishing her thought and not even realizing it until her eyes light on mine. She cocks one dark eyebrow at me and huffs a short laugh.

"Heh. I actually forgot you're a sponge," she says, lying back again on her bed and propping her feet against the wall behind me, making the legs of her jumpsuit fall up. I study her face as she looks at the ceiling, then at the door with her arms folded in support under her head, and suddenly I understand. *She never wanted to come here.*

"You're trying to get sent back, aren't you? You want them to kick you out?" I say in one breath. "It all makes sense now."

She meets my eyes long enough for me to be sure that I'm right, and our bracelet cuffs begin to blink. A 10-minute warning to report to the cafeteria plays in my head as a smile trickles over her face.

CHAPTER 19
Campus Tour

Everyone's trays are filled with food-shaped food this morning, brightly colored oranges, grapes, bananas, pastries, strips of smoked fish, and all of this in just the first bay of options. The next two bays are another wash of color before a sea of faces, some of them even smiling at Vox and me as we walk into the cafeteria. I scan the room for Jax and see him sitting against the far wall again with the same people from lunch yesterday, so after choosing our breakfast, Vox and I make our way over to them.

"So what happened to you last night? And wow, I thought you'd have a few black eyes this morning," Jax says, studying my face, and I'm surprised he commits his mouth to two full sentences when there is still food on his plate.

"Yeah, nanobots, or technics, something like that. I decided to take a nap, and before I knew it, it was morning," I smile, and brace for pain that never comes.

"Nanites," Ellis says, intrigued now and leaning over the table a little too closely to my face to study it, lifting a finger like he's going to poke my nose. I flinch backward. "They're amazing. It's like nothing ever happened. Did you know that this cartilage here..." he gestures to the tip of my nose as I flinch again, "...and the channel of blood vessels that connect it to the skeletal bridge are all brand new now? New, like the day you were born." He shakes his head, marveling, then sits down again. I exhale, relieved that he's no longer just three inches away.

"It's not right," Arco says without looking up. "They rewire us like we're their machines, like we're droids they can program." Almost everyone at the table looks at him, startled by his sudden vehemence.

"But she's all fixed—look," Avis says, then splits an orange, accidentally squirting Ellis in the face with juice.

"Ugh, really?" Ellis says, squinting and padding around the table for his napkin.

"That's what they want you to see, what they want you to believe," Arco says to Avis while throwing Ellis a napkin. "In the meantime, they can program whatever they want to tell us in our heads, rearrange anything they want." He looks up and around the table, flexing his wrist outwardly and gesturing with his empty fork. "No one else sees the potential problem with any of this?"

"Zone, Arc… it's just to keep the flow," Avis says, chewing. "Rheen said there are what, 3,000 students here? Not to mention all the homestead and industrial communities out there," he lifts his chin to the windows behind us. "It's hard enough to get medi-droids topside, but can you imagine down *here?"* He shakes his head and spears a piece of melon, then snaps it off the fork like some kind of blue-plumed tortoise.

"Sure, that's the reason." Arco shakes his head and looks back at his plate, stabbing at his eggs. I look over at Vox to see if she's behind his mood, but she just raises her brows at me like she's offended.

As if reading my mind like he tends to do, Jax throws the biggest green grape I've ever seen at Arco, which hits him in the chin and bounces off his hand onto his lap, then rolls onto the floor. Arco freezes in a long blink.

"What's your malfunction?" Jax asks, and Fraya nudges him for it. He turns to her, confused. "What?" he says, his shoulders jerking up as he looks at her.

"Nothing," Arco answers, hacking into his eggs again.

"So what's this about an orientation?" Fraya asks, breaking the tension in the air. "Did everyone get that feed this morning?"

"There aren't many of us, so it probably won't take long," Ellis says after finishing the last of his juice, then, looks around the room.

He's right. I look around and see only three other tables with people in blue jumpsuits like ours...Liddick's table, and two others with about ten students seated at each. No one else has tattoos like Vox, but one table in particular seats people who look like cinestars. Six boys and four girls, all of them athletic, long limbed, and oblivious to anyone else in the room.

"They're from the mountain," Vox whispers at my side, evidently following my stare.

"*Skyboard* really is here? I thought they were just automatically assigned an apprenticeship somewhere," I say.

"Well, maybe there's equality in the world after all," Avis says, grinning, then polishes off the last of his melon. Arco huffs out a cynical laugh as he chews.

"Ok, seriously, what?" Jax presses him, and he finally looks up. Now I notice that his eyes are bloodshot, the shadows below suggesting he didn't sleep much last night.

"See that one on the end? Dark blond hair?" We all look at once, and he sighs, lowering his forehead and pinching the bridge of his nose.

"Sorry," I say to Arco, "stop staring," I say to the table and shove my shoulder into Vox, who is vibrating with laughter. "So, what about him?"

"That's Tieg Spaulding. My roommate."

"Room—?" Jax coughs, then tries to enunciate the word. "Roommate?"

"They bunked you with a *cloudy?"* Avis blurts. "Did he even talk to you?"

"That's all he did—all night spouting about his father who's some kind of liaison to the pollies at the State, his mother, who's a language whatever-something, and about his six brothers who came through here already and are stationed all over the four seas doing diplomat-nano-surgeon-god-of-the-universe jobs. He's a droid. No one can talk that much in one sitting without program-ming."

I feel my eyebrows raise and my eyes widen at him as he makes another stab at his eggs, then fires them into his mouth. The table explodes in laughter, and he looks up, shocked. "What?" He rolls his eyes, then goes back to mutilating his food. Jax gets up and slaps him on the back while chuckling and shaking his head on his way over to the Skyboard table. Fraya follows him.

"What is he doing?" Vox asks me in a lowered voice.

"Clipping off Arco," I say through a sigh. In a few

minutes, Jax and Fraya head back to our table with Arco's roommate, Tieg, and a girl with straight blonde hair, which swishes over her shoulders as she walks. Coming along a few steps after them is a boy who looks like he could be related to Tieg, but his hair is black and his eyes are as intensely green as Tieg's are blue. He's also a little taller and thicker than Tieg, but otherwise similar. Ellis, who sits next to Arco, nudges his forearm, which causes Arco to spill eggs onto his lap. He sucks in a quick breath, ready to react, but has to swallow it as the cloudies walk up.

"Everybody, this is Dez Spaulding, Fraya's roommate," Jax says to our table, and as she smiles, I notice there are no spaces between her teeth. No individual teeth at all, just a solid white bar. "And this is Pitt Spaulding, my roommate." They all smile now, all of them flashing the same thinly sculpted wedge of spaceless teeth. I wonder if Arco wasn't kidding after all when he said Tieg was a droid, and I try not to stare.

"Spaulding?" Arco asks.

"We're triplets," Tieg answers, smiling to one side.

"Triplets? But you're all...*different,"* I say before I realize the tingling at the base of my skull, and immediately kick Vox under the table. Dez smiles and nods knowingly, then bites her bottom lip.

"Where we live, parents can...*tailor* the appearance of their kids, so, that's why Pitt and I look like opposite ends of the spectrum, and Tieg is somewhere in the middle. Lots of genes, three kids, variety, right?" she says with a nervous laugh, her eyes darting around the table as she chews her lip again. Is *she* actually worried about what *we'll* think? A *cloudy?* I look at them all more closely now as they stand side by side, and to my surprise, I really can see the dark to light spectrum she's talking about. Pitt's darker Mediterranean features and bright green eyes give way to Tieg's lighter skin tone and more sharply angled lines, whereas Dez is very fair with a heart shaped face, a long, graceful neck, and wide, innocent eyes that interchange the coloring of Tieg's: an icy blue with sapphire flecks where his are the reverse. The more I look at them, the more I can even see the similarities as well...how Pitt and Tieg have the same weighted gaze, the same deep pitch of their eyebrows, broad build, and imposing stature. "That's amazing," I say, and Dez's worried expression relaxes.

"Fraya tells me you've all grown up together shoreside?" she says, her smile widening now when she looks at me, and I can't help but stare into it like the solar eclipse the teachers specifically tell you to avoid. Just as that thought crosses my mind, I feel a stab in the side of my thigh closest to Vox and yelp at the same time I see her putting a fork back on her tray.

"Ow! I mean, yes, sorry...pinched myself on something," I recover in front of everyone, and promise myself I will throttle my psychopath roommate the second these statues leave. She could have just nudged me to get me to stop gawking.

"These smooth, moulded benches can be tricky like that," Tieg says, and drops a wink. Arco rolls his eyes, and I feel the delayed flush of embarrassment climbing up my cheeks. I try to cover it with my hand, letting it slip behind the back of my neck in a few uncoordinated gestures.

"They can," I say, trying to pull it together after my outburst. "So, Arco said you're from Skyboard?" I manage, and they all smile their strange wedge smiles again. I will myself not to stare this time. She nods, then looks around the cafeteria again, particularly toward the enormous window that travels the length of the room.

"Everything is all so unbelievable," she says, shaking her head.

"It's definitely not as predictable as we were expecting after watching all those years of advertisements," Pitt says, raising his dark, heavy eyebrows, his voice deeper and quieter than Tieg's, but just as articulate. As if waiting its turn in the conversation, I hear the arrow voice in my head:

Cadets, please prepare for orientation, which begins in five minutes. Your respective guides will arrive shortly.

***

All of our eyes dart to one another's as soon as the transmission ends, and I feel myself relax a little. No one, not even the perfect cloudies, has adjusted to these neural links yet.

Within minutes of the announcement, a tall, tanned girl wearing a green jumpsuit approaches our table. Her dark hair is woven in an intricate braid that starts behind one ear and spirals up and back until it winds around to a clip over her shoulder, then falls loose from there. She's fit and tall like the Skyboard students, and reminds me of a hummingbird the way her feet move so quickly over the ground, almost as if she's floating to us.

"And this must be our tour guide," Avis says, turning to see her beaming smile. When she's close enough, I notice that her teeth are normal rather than the flat, seamless bar of the Skyboard students, and for some reason, I'm relieved.

"You're all from Seaboard North?" she says in a voice that is much more assertive than I was expecting given her graceful build.

"And thereabouts," Vox says after a beat. The girl smiles in her direction.

"I'm Etta, and I'll be taking you to get set up with schedules," she says to the group. "I'm from Seaboard South on the Orlando coastline. This is my final year at Gaia before my apprenticeship begins at the State, and part of my job is to show you around, answer questions, that kind of thing...so, everyone ready to go?" she says as her eyebrows raise in an arc over her hazel eyes.

"Why didn't they just send another efficient arrow droid?" Vox smirks, apparently intent on making yet more friends. "And since when is anyone here interested in answering our questions?"

Etta smiles at her again and tilts her head sympathetically.

"Sorry about all that. Matriculation is always a little chaotic, but the administration has found that a little disorientation makes students pay more attention. When highly intelligent people are stressed, they want to talk and solve, focus on figuring things out, you know? Anyway, things tend to go more smoothly in the long run for everyone like this," she adds. "We should get going so we don't overlap with the other groups. This way, please," Etta says, gesturing for us to follow her.

We insert our trays into the receptacle as we walk to the edge of the cafeteria, the Skyboard students apparently coming with us. I shuffle past Vox and Ellis as we pass the rest of them waiting for their guide with Liddick at his table. I expect all their judgmental eyes to fall on us, but to my surprise, none of them do. I reach for Jax's arm to get his attention.

"Don't they have to go with their own group?" I whisper at his shoulder.

"They're in blue just like us," he says, tilting the side of his head to me, but not looking in my direction.

"What's with those teeth?" I say after looking over my shoulder to make sure the triplets aren't within earshot, and now Jax looks at me like I've asked him to help me remember my own name.

"Gene hybridizing, didn't you hear Dez?" he asks, his eyebrows arching."You know, parents can select the gen-"

"I know what it is," I say, biting off the words, "I just didn't think they'd pick something so obviously not normal to mutate. What's supposed to be the benefit of a solid wedge of teeth like that?"

"Pitt told me they can't get cavities or any other problems because of the lack of grooves and spaces," he says, shrugging his shoulders and returning his eyes forward, "something like that." I make a noise in my throat at this, still not entirely convinced that the wedge isn't just another cloudy aesthetic like those overly saturated eye colors. Jax laughs at my reaction, and I jerk my head toward him, surprised.

"What?"

"Come on, Jazz; if they gave you a bioprint with all the nose shapes and eye colors and every other genetic option in our family, do you really think you wouldn't pick the best of them if you could? I mean, why would you *want* to inherit those caterpillar eyebrows if you didn't have to?" He braces for the punch he knows is coming.

"You have the same eyebrows I do, mollusk."

"Yeah, but I don't have a tiny little head like you do."

He dodges the punch to his arm and laughs, and I notice the corridor we're now in is suddenly much narrower than most of the other hallways. *Where are we going?*

"That's different besides," I say. "No one in any of their families can possibly have naturally occurring wedged teeth like that with no grooves and no spaces anywhere. It's outer ring."

"Outer ring?" Jax laughs. "Where did you hear that? Anyway, who cares what's in their mouths?"

"It's just the principle of it," I say, and it's Jax's turn to roll his eyes as he shakes his head. "Vox is rubbing off on you," he says, bracing for another punch, but Etta stops our group just in time. I look around, wondering where in the building we must be. We didn't climb or go down, so we must be somewhere on the same level as the galley, med-bay, and my room. *How big is this place?*

The room we're in is round and nearly as big as the galley with student stations every few meters apart. Everything is smooth and the equipment looks too delicate to touch. Helmets hover over cylindrical stools with high, narrow backs and head rests in front of each flat metal work station, which sits just below plain gray panels on the wall. Jax and I exchange glances.

"And this is the Boundaries room," Etta says. "It holds 30 people comfortably, one at each station. The circles under each chair will light when you activate the unit, and this will produce a soundproof barrier. The same technology is in the Records room, which we'll also visit. You'll come here to the Boundaries room to link in for port-calls—which you'll actually get to sample today in visiting your advisors—and any work you're assigned to do remotely."

"Remotely?" Avis questions with raised eyebrows. "As in, not physically there?"

"Exactly, but you won't have remote assignments until you are upperclassmen."

"What kind of remote assignments?" Fraya says in a small voice.

"Some career paths require an immersion sequence before you're physically transported to the site. Cultural acclimation. Those of you who tested into State careers will have at least one remote assignment. If you're slotted for technical or biodiverse fields, you probably won't have to worry about it unless you're in Navigation."

"So, wait. How does any of this work? How do we know what we're supposed to be studying here?" Avis asks.

"You'll find out right now, in fact," Etta says, nodding to one of the stations. "You will all link into one of the units here and be transferred to the administration building at the State via port-call to meet virtually with your advisors. You must schedule any appointments with them through your bracelet cuffs, by swiping anywhere on it from left to right to call up your dashboard. Go ahead and try it out," she finishes, and I feel my heart race for a second at the prospect of being able to make a port-call after all, even though I wish it were to home.

I swipe my bracelet and a small 3-D screen projects in front of me with tabs that list calendars, classes, and contacts. *Whoa.*

"If you touch the calendar tab, you will be able to see your daily schedule, and the first name in each of your contacts now under my name is your advisor. Go ahead and pull that name up," Etta says, pausing to give us all a chance to do what she says. I pull up the list, and see Etta's 3-D picture beside her name as well as **CARIS PLUME —ADVISOR,** alongside another 3-D picture of the same blonde woman from my interview. "Go ahead and touch the name," Etta says, and I do.

When would you like to schedule an appointment with Ms. Plume, Miss Ripley? I hear the neural link voice say in my head, and instinctively look up at the others, who also suddenly look up and around the room.

"You should have heard the neural link ask you when you'd like to schedule an appointment. Your advisors and their proxies are expecting you, so you can answer by saying, 'in five minutes,' or you can just think it." Some of the others say the words out loud, but I just say them in my head.

Ms. Plume will be pleased to meet with you in five minutes, says the voice in my head, and the screen closes.

"All that's left to do now is choose a seat and place your palm on the work desk. This will activate the headpiece, and the neural link will prompt you from there. Your advising session will last about 30 minutes. You can ask your advisor any other questions about your classes, and if you need to reach me, just go into your contacts. Welcome to Gaia, everybody," she says as we all choose a station.

CHAPTER 20
Ms. Plume

The vibration in my head is the first thing I notice when I place my palm on the desktop, even though the thin helmet hasn't touched me yet. When it does, the confinement isn't as terrible as I imagined it might be.

Please close your eyes, says the neural link voice over a dull buzzing sound. I do, but instead of seeing darkness, I see a white film that dissipates until Ms. Plume appears behind a thin, glass desk. She's sitting in front of a picture window with palm trees and the ocean outside as she types onto a keyboard that isn't there.

"Jazz!" she says with a laugh in her voice. "It's nice to see you again. Welcome. Please sit down," she continues, her wide, white smile beaming. "I took the liberty of pulling up a shore view for our meeting today, but if you prefer to look out on a forest or something else, say the word," she says, gesturing to the window behind her.

"Oh, no, that's fine. Thank you," I say, taking a few steps forward, at least, it seems that I do. I reach out to touch the back of the chair in front of the glass desk, and am surprised to feel it's actually there—solid. It's smooth and cool, all brushed metal finish and seamless.

"Whoa..." I whisper.

"First virtual transfer?" Ms. Plume asks, her lips pulled wide in a smile that crinkles the corners of her blue eyes. "Feels real, doesn't it?"

"This is *actually* cold. I thought you could only process structures, maybe textures—solid, soft, liquid..." my voice trails off as I touch the underside of the desk. The pads of my fingers don't press in when I do, but I feel the pressure all the same. "And I'm still sitting in the Boundaries room, right? This is all in my head?" I ask. Ms. Plume's thin eyebrows shoot up as she smiles and nods.

"Technically, yes, but port-calls are a little different from virtuo-cines in that your *physical* makeup is simulated in a hologram, which then pulls Biotech's atoms in the port-cloud field of the atmosphere to match your hologram projection in 4-D—this is why others who are physically at your destination can actually feel your presence in say, a handshake or a hug. Then, like a virtuo-cine, your neural input is routed. What is the extent of your virtuo-cine experience, Jazz?" she asks, angling her head and interlacing her fingers on her desk as she leans forward in her chair.

"Well, just the school earth science versions. I've only seen the preview advertisements for the blockbuster virtuo-cines, and I'm familiar with Biotech's port-cloud field. It's the reason everything smells like sulfur back home," I answer, realizing my last comment was probably unnecessary when Ms. Plume's eyebrows twitch, but then I wonder if it also might sound more hostile than I mean because my voice feels loud over the buzzing still in my ears. "Should I still hear that buzz?" I ask.

"A buzz? Not really, perhaps it's something in the Boundaries room coming through. I wouldn't worry about it," she winks and nods before pushing a bowl of rose colored candy toward me that I hadn't noticed before, then swivels to her right to type, though I still don't see a keyboard. I reach for a piece of the candy and study the intricately carved letter G on it. "All right, let's get you sent as far away from here as possible," she says, and I look up suddenly, sure that I've misheard.

"Sorry, what did you say?" I ask, the small, round candy still between my fingers.

"Let's get you set up as soon as possible," she says, looking over at me and smiling as a 3-D picture of my face appears next to a block of text I can't make out. The buzzing in my ears grows louder as the image pixelates, then dissolves into an image of my *father's* face—his narrow, brown eyes and dark, curly hair like Jax's. I gasp and grip the arm of the chair before I nearly fall into it as the little round candy falls and bounces on the floor.

"I never saw it coming when I refused the stipend—" Ms. Plume says, only it's my father's deep voice I hear as she continues to type. I almost don't recognize it until I feel the sudden sinkhole in my chest, causing everything inside to fall through.

"Dad?" I say with the last of the breath I have, then struggle to summon another.

"I'm sorry?" Ms. Plume asks with her own voice again as the 3-D picture suddenly changes back into mine.

"N-nothing…" I say, shaking my head to clear it.

"All right, well it looks like we have you slotted for a diplomatic career, Jazz. That will be exciting for you!" she says, lifting her index finger to the text by my picture, then making small sounds of approval as she reads. The buzzing in my ears subsides briefly once my picture and Plume's own voice return, but dials up the second she speaks again. "Have you tried the candy yet? You can choose your flavor. What kind of *can*—candy do you *wa* —want it to be?" she asks without looking away from the screen, her image suddenly freezing, then jolting to a start again like a lagging flat-cine as her long, blonde curls slowly shrink upward into short, sun-bleached waves with dark brown roots. "If you're already there, pretend to be what they want you to be," Plume says in her own voice as she turns to me, but her delicate brows fade into thicker, darker versions with a thin, white scar through the left one.

"Liam?" I whisper, a ball of lead falling into my stomach.

I push back from the desk and stagger out of the chair, nearly falling as I back away. "Jazz?" Ms. Plume's face returns, and she folds her hands on the desk. "Are you all right? Please sit down again and just try to breathe—first transfers can be a little unsettling."

My heart is hammering against my ribs so hard I feel like it might break through, but when I press my hand to my chest to steady myself, I feel nothing.

"I don't have a heartbeat—*where's my heartbeat?!"* I say, hearing the hysteria in my voice.

"Just calm down, Jazz. Remember, this is a virtual transport. You can only feel what we've programmed, even though emotionally it may seem like a physical reaction. Here…" Ms. Plume punches something into her invisible keyboard, and suddenly, I feel my heart pounding underneath the palm of my hand, but not quickly enough. "Do you feel it now?" she asks, trying to smile.

I sit back in the chair, a layer away from everything. I've just seen my father, heard my father's voice, and now *Liam*, but Plume doesn't seem to know? Why can't she see what's happening? It has to be another message from Liam, like the marlin. But then, what about my *father?* I need to buy some time.

"I feel it now," I say, trying to steady my voice as the buzzing recedes again and my hands begin to shake— though, I don't see them shaking. I look around the room for another inconsistency like Liddick mentioned seeing in his virtuo-cines. Something that can help me understand what Liam and my father were trying to tell me, but all I see now are Ms. Plume's blue eyes narrowing with concern as she smiles gently and nods. I take a deep breath and let it out slowly, trying to focus.

"It can be an adjustment," she says, and then turns back to her screen. "Are you feeling well enough to learn your probable career field?" I study her face for a second before answering, wondering if she's going to glitch out again, but nothing happens. "Jazz, are you all right?"

I nod quickly at her. "I'm fine, sorry. Yes, I'm ready," I say, steeling myself, and she refreshes my 3-D image.

"All right then," she says with another wide smile as she references her screen. "It looks like you're on track to be a Diplomatic Liaison. The data compiled so far in your profile suggests that you are *a good judge of character... empathic tendencies...*" she reads, "...both of which are critical traits for this position. Of course, we won't have anything official until tomorrow afternoon when the rest of your profile generates, but for now, it looks like you will be part of a crew as one of three empathic advisors— in this role, you will also serve as first contact when a crew interacts with homesteaders or other civilians. Let's see about some classes for that," she says, and the low frequency buzzing increases in my ears.

She picks up a bracelet cuff from the window side of her desk and begins tapping something into the side of it with a slim, silver rod that ends in a fine point, but her hands and the bracelet cuff start flickering like the feed is breaking up as the buzz suddenly grows louder again.

"What's that?" I ask abruptly, watching the pixilation fade and reform. I move to the edge of my seat and brace my hands on the arms of the chair.

"I've just authorized your class schedule and your first training assignment. In approximately six months, you will be port-calling with an advisor to Arcadia Nine, a settlement much like Seaboard North on the Zealand coast, to negotiate the terms of three scholarship seats to Gaia. This will take effect the following matriculation cycle. You'll have recently completed your own cycle, so the requirements will be fresh in your mind."

"I'm…but I don't—" my mind stalls as her bracelet vanishes, then reappears. I wait for something to happen, a vision of Liam or my father, but nothing does.

"I know it sounds intimidating, but you have plenty of time to learn the field. Just consider this assignment an opportunity to escape," she says, pulling up another screen as the buzzing gets stronger.

"Wh—*what* did you say just now?"

"Just consider this assignment an opportunity to acclimate," she says, turning to flash a sincere smile as she puts the bracelet back on her desk. "There is no rush to know how to do it all," she continues, smiling to one side, and I steady myself for whatever is coming next. "You're more than capable, Jazwyn. Here, let me show you," she says, motioning to the projection area where my face was, but has now been replaced by a fuzzy image of Arco, Jax and I sitting together with me talking to them.

"What's happening?" I ask.

"That's your subconscious already beginning to work backward to align the steps you'll need to take to be successful on this mission to Arcadia Nine," Plume says, gesturing to the screen in front of her where code is generating next to the images. She points to the first few lines of it. "Here your mind has identified and outlined fears, the first one being speaking in front of others... there it is," she says, freezing the scrolling text and pointing to a specific line, which projects another 3-D image of Arco, Jax and me in mid sentence. "And there are the countermeasures for failure that you're producing threading into place...you see, right here...that's your data chain," she says, pointing to another line, then touching the thumb and index finger of each hand to the center of the screen and flicking them outward. The screen is larger now so I can see the whole exchange more clearly. "You're practicing. Isn't it wonderful?"

"Wait—" I manage to say over the buzz in my ears that now gives way to a distant, high-pitched squeal. "You can see me *thinking?*" I feel myself blinking repeatedly in disbelief. "But I'm not even thinking or planning any of that," I say, gritting my teeth against the noise that is starting to drill through the roof of my mouth.

"Indeed you are, you just don't realize it. Most of our thoughts are subconscious. Only a small percentage are conscious." She presses the pad of her thumb to her lips and shakes her head as she looks back at the screen.

The buzzing squeal in my ears finally breaks, and the image of me talking in front of Jax and Arco shifts into a scene with my father standing before a panel and Liam standing in front of him. Ms. Rheen and Mr. Styx are wearing white lab coats and standing over my father's shoulder. I glance at Ms. Plume to see if her reaction to the image has changed, but it hasn't. She's still seeing me talk in front of Arco and Jax. *How* is this possible if she can see my subconscious thoughts? The buzzing starts to fade, and I don't want the feed to break apart again, so I try to refocus on the image. I need to keep her talking.

"So that will be my job eventually? I'll travel to places and meet different cultures and negotiate things?" I say, willing the image of my father and Liam to stay.

The buzzing picks up, and the image shifts. Two men in white military uniforms like the guards who scanned us in at the relay dock bring Arco's sister, Arwyn, into the room with Lyden, Liddick's oldest brother. Both of them are struggling. Arwyn's guard puts her inside of a cube enclosure with clear walls and shuts the door. She immediately starts pounding against it as Lyden's guard loses his grip when Lyden elbows him in the stomach, and Arwyn's guard rushes over to help drag Lyden into the other enclosure, ripping Lyden's shirt open in the process. The guards cross the room to a panel of controls, and in minutes, water fills Lyden's clear walled room.

My father and Liam stand up and start gesturing wildly, but the guards approach them, and my father puts his arm across Liam's chest and steps in front of him, then holds his other hand up to the guard. He looks like he's trying to explain something calmly, but Rheen says something to Styx, who then gestures to the guard and he pulls a narrow, white stick from his belt and brings it to my father's neck. He doubles over as Liam lunges, but my father pushes his forearm into Liam's chest as he gets to his feet, keeping him at bay.

Arwyn stops pounding on her door and starts screaming something, then presses her hands against the wall adjoining Lyden's, who kicks the door of his enclosure as water starts filling his room, his wavy blond hair sticking to his forehead and cheek with the effort.

"All that said, basically. You'll be part of a crew, and you will most certainly log more transfer hours than actual physical travel, more so than in other career field. Go ahead and pull up your schedule," Plume says, and for a second I have no idea where I am. I stare at her, and she clears her throat in a nod at my bracelet cuff. "Just slide your thumb from left to right," she says, and the image before me flickers as the buzz begins to fade.

"But—" I say, panicking to think of another question that will keep her talking as I do what she says, all while trying to keep my eyes on the horror unfolding before me, which Plume still doesn't seem to realize is playing out. "Could you please explain all the classes to me?" I say, and her face falls just enough for me to register her exasperation, but she complies.

I turn my attention back to the screen and see Lyden starting to float in the water that's rising all around him, struggling for air when it reaches the top of the enclosure, his torn open shirt flying wide around him as a thin red line begins appearing down each side of his chest, thickening, and then moving like...*gills?* Arwyn continues screaming and crying, alternating between reaching up to Lyden against their adjoining wall and pounding on her clear door, pleading with the guards who stand by motionless.

Liam stands up then and shouts something to Ms. Rheen, who then nods to the guard next to Liam. He shoves the white stick into his shoulder, but then my father intervenes, putting his hand in front of Liam's controls and yelling something at the guard, then turning to say the same to Rheen and Styx. Rheen just nods again, and the guard brings the white stick to my father's neck, this time, holding it there until he passes out.

Liam lunges at the guard, who points the stick at him as a warning until Ms. Rheen waves him off, bringing forward a 3-D screen of Liam that shows Liddick walking into a virtuo-cine with Ellis. Liam pushes his hands through his hair, his face wrenched in pain, and quickly hits a combination of buttons. In seconds, flames encircle Arwyn's feet, catching her pants on fire. I can't keep my composure any more, and my hands fly to my mouth.

"No!" I yell, getting to my feet. Ms. Plume looks at me like she's trying to decide what language I'm speaking.

"Jazwyn? It won't be a long wet run tomorrow, but you *will* need these experiences as foundations for this career field," Ms. Plume says, looking at me, puzzled.

"What?" I say, completely confused, and when I look back at the image of Lyden, Arwyn, Liam, and my father, it dissipates into a list of my classes with the teacher's headshot next to each.

"Here, take another look at all the preparation you'll have before you ever get to the interface class," she says.

Blue: Empathy/Psychosomatic Systems - Luz Reynolt
Red: Biotransfer and Culture - Dame Mahgi
Green: Endurance and Survival 1 - Skellik Tark
Orange: Cross Curriculum Interface - Varies

"No!" I shout again, this time reaching for the screen that is no longer there. The buzzing is also gone—absolutely gone, not just flickering. "Bring it back! Can you bring back that screen? The subconscious thoughts screen, Ms. Plume, *please!"* I plead, but she just shakes her head in confusion again, concern in her eyes.

"Well, I *could*, but...I'm sorry, Jazwyn, I don't understand why you're suddenly so upset. Is this about going out with the crew for the initial ship training, or is it something with the subconscious image loop of you speaking in front of your peers that we pulled from several minutes ago?" Plume says, angling her head toward me. I tear my eyes away from the schedule floating in the air next to the animated teacher head shots, all of them smiling and talking to someone not pictured, and try to catch up to the moment.

"I...I don't know," I say, scrambling to think of something to say. "It was just..." I say, trailing off, blindsided by what I've just seen.

"It's all right, Jazwyn. This has been a long few days for you. Let's go ahead and stop for today—next time you visit, I'm sure it will be easier on your system," she says, but I'm numb to it all, my mind returning to the image of my father and Liam before a panel, of Arwyn screaming at the fire racing up her legs, and of Lyden struggling for air, then not struggling at all, but *breathing* with those flexing red lines along the sides of his chest until the images fall apart, and everything fades to white.

CHAPTER 21
Stabilize

It takes a minute for my vision to sharpen. Like just waking up from a night's sleep, my head is heavy and the muscles in my neck are stiff. How long have I been sitting here? Is it real time? I look around the room at the others and see Arco already looking at me quizzically, while several others are rubbing their eyes and stretching as they start coming out of their advisory sessions.

"Some of you have already discovered that you can just touch anywhere on either side of the helmet when you are ready to disconnect," Etta tells us, reappearing in the doorway. I lift my hands, which are inordinately heavy, to the helmet and take it off. I rub my eyes, then urgently scan the room for Liddick. When I spot him, he looks like he's just been thrown in a pool of freezing water, his eyes wide, his jaw set, and his chest heaving with effort. He nods at me, and I know he must have seen something strange too.

"We'll end this morning's tour in the Records room, and you'll be dismissed to lunch from there," Etta says, and once again I've forgotten where I am and what I'm supposed to be doing as we all filter out of the room. Liddick starts to walk toward me, then redirects when his eyes suddenly dart behind me. I turn and see Arco quickly closing the distance between us. Dez and Tieg filter in just ahead of me, so I have to slow down.

"You look like you just dodged a shuttle car," Arco says, scanning my face. I don't know what to tell him. I don't even know what I think about what I just saw in there, so I have to talk to Liddick. "Jazz, what's wrong?"

I shake my head and tell him the first thing that comes to mind. "I don't feel right," I say, which isn't a lie. I shield my eyes with my hand just to close them for a second, but immediately, I see those lines ripping down each side of Lyden's chest as he struggled in the water. My breath catches, and I open my eyes again.

"Hey, whoa…" Arco says, reaching for the hand I drop from my eyes. "You're shaking, and ice cold. Etta…I'm taking Jazz to the med-bay," he says. I shake my head.

"No, I'm fine. Just a little dizzy," I say, wishing I could just have five minutes of quiet to sort out the chaos in my mind. Etta stops, and everyone in the group looks at me.

"Jazz, are you OK?" Dez asks, turning around and looking into my eyes one at a time. Tieg angles his head downward as his brows draw together.

"You're really pale," he says. Dez puts her hand on my cheek, then moves her fingers to the side of my throat. I scan desperately for Liddick.

"Your heart is racing. I'll go with you to the med-bay," she says. Arco nods next to me and takes my elbow as Jax crosses over to me with Fraya at his side.

"You really don't look right," he says, and all the attention is just too much.

"I'm *fine!*" I blurt, and Dez takes a step back. "I'm sorry. I just need some air. I don't want to go to the med-bay."

"Maybe it would be a good idea to lie down," Etta says.

"The first transfer can play havoc with your system."

Oh, crite, fine, I think. If nothing else, it will be easier if I just go than if I stay here as the center of attention. I nod, and Dez loops her arm with mine as Arco's hand goes to the small of my back. I finally see Liddick looking back at me sympathetically and shaking his head. Jax stands in front of me and wraps his hand gently around the back of my neck, then brings his eyes level with mine.

"Don't roarf on anyone, OK?" he says seriously, then smiles as he grips Arco's shoulder.

"She'll be OK," Dez says, and we walk to the med-bay.

***

Ms. Karo is typing something into a floating green keyboard when we arrive. She looks me up and down, then raises an inky eyebrow.

"So what have we here?" she asks, turning in her stool.

"She came out of the port-call with her advisor like this," Arco says. "She was dizzy, and well...like this," he gestures to my face. If I look anything like Liddick did, no wonder he's been making such a fuss.

"I'm fine, really. Could I just lie down for a minute?" I say, hoping everyone will just go away so I can sort out what I saw back there.

"Let's have a look at you first," Ms. Karo says, standing up from her stool and gripping my arm firmly, then walking me over to the archway. "Step through," she says, almost pushing me as she punches something into the floating key panel next to it. "And stand right there."

A green light passes over my eyes and turns to red, then stops. It starts again, turning back to green, and scans the rest of my body without turning red again.

"What's wrong with her?" Arco asks.

"Just shock and disorientation," she says, reading the panel. "Happens with first transfers." Ms. Karo keys something else into her panel. The air syringe from our inoculations drops from a hydraulic arm, and I flinch. "Please be still. This will just help you relax."

The syringe stops at my arm and heat pushes through my shoulder after the sound of compressed air popping.

"What is that?" Arco asks, his voice slightly raised.

"Just a regulator—lie down here, Miss Ripley," Karo says as she directs me to one of the beds, which is sheeted in white linens against a brushed steel base and side table. "One of you may stay and set a comfortable tone, talk about your day, something neutral to help regulate her brainwaves. The nanites will take it from there."

"I'll stay," Arco says, looking to Dez, who nods.

"I'll come check on you if I don't see you by dinner," Dez says, pushing her blonde hair behind her shoulder. I smile at her, suddenly feeling heavy as I sit on the bed.

"Hey," Arco says, rushing over.

"You'll have about 20 minutes before she's out for a while," Ms. Karo adds as an afterthought, then crosses back to the other side of the med-bay to resume typing. Dez turns to leave, and the last thing I see is Arco's furled brows, his hazel eyes looking down on me before I close my eyelids, which are so heavy I can't stop them.

"So we're supposed to talk about something neutral... did your advisor tell you about your career field?" he asks as my head hits the pillow. I nod, but summoning the words is almost impossible. I open my mouth, and despite my efforts, nothing comes out. I *need* to tell him what happened. Someone has to know *exactly* what I saw in case... "Those things are probably hitting you now," he says. I try to force the words again, but still, nothing comes. "All right, well, my advisor was Ms. Plume, can you believe that? From the interview. She told me I'm going to be on some crew, maybe even as a pilot, which is a little disconcerting considering my interview back home and all the—er, sorry, I guess that's not neutral, is it?" he says through a chuckle, but he's sounds farther and farther away as the haze in my head gets thicker, and I know if I don't say something now, I may never be able to. What if it's all gone when I wake up? What if they know what I saw, and Ms. Karo gave me something to wipe everything? I *have* to tell him.

"It was…real," I say, pushing the words up from under the weight of the exhaustion bearing down on me.

"What was real?" Arco asks, but it feels like he's speaking from some disembodied, far away place.

"They put them in…containers. Lyden was fighting them…and Arwyn…"

"Arwyn?" Arco's fingers grip my hand. This helps pull me back, and I fight to open my eyes.

"She was screaming for them to stop. The water, and my father…Liam said just to pretend to be what they wanted us to be."

"Jazz—" I hear Arco's quick intake of breath and open my eyes just in time to see him looking frantically over his shoulder at Ms. Karo. I turn my head and see that

she's still typing, but suddenly I feel like I've been pulled into something thick and dark, which presses in on me from all sides. I don't have the energy to look back at him, but his hand is warm when it moves to the side of my face. He brings my eyes back to his, but they almost immediately close again. "Jazz, I don't know if you understand what you're saying right now, but—"

"Liddick," I manage to say. "Ask Liddick for the rest."

"Liddick? He was there? *Jazz?*" he asks, but I can't fight the heaviness, and Arco's voice fades like an echo until I don't hear anything any more.

CHAPTER 22
Questioning Liddick

Arco sits at her bedside a few moments more after she loses consciousness as he tries to put together the pieces she's just given him. *Had she seen these things? Was she just hallucinating under the influence of the stabilizers?* he wonders, and wrestles with himself to leave her side to find Wright and ask him about all this. If it's true, the code assembly he'd been working on would prove accurate—Arwyn really would be trapped somewhere, and there could be no more talking himself out of it.

"Ms. Karo, when did you say she'll wake up?" Arco asks over his shoulder, the sudden ache in his jaw with the words making him realize he's been clenching his teeth.

"By meal time at the latest; stop back then if you like," she says without turning around. Arco nods to himself, then looks down at Jazz's face, peaceful now, her dark brows relaxed instead of knotted, and her chestnut hair spilling over the pillow, the light catching its red undertones. The bow of her mouth opens just enough to make it look like she's reacting to something dumb that he's said again, and he waits for the smile that always comes afterward, but doesn't this time. He strokes his thumb along the edge of her bottom lip, wondering what it might be like to kiss her, wondering what she'd think of him wondering such a thing, and it makes him smile to imagine her rolling her eyes. She can't hide anything if he can just see her eyes, the same amber color as the tea the old Tinkerer woman back home reads when she's telling fortunes.

"Her color is coming back," he says, noticing the flush returning to her cheeks as his fingers brush her skin, and he feels a warmth spread in his chest at the idea she could be responding to his touch like that. She was ice cold when he'd touched her hand in the Boundaries room.

"Stabilizers are taking effect. She'll be fine after she sleeps it off," Karo says, again without turning around, and although Arco knows it would probably be all right to go and find Wright now, to ask him to fill in the missing pieces that might change everything, he can't seem to push off the side of her bed and take the first steps away from her to make it happen.

"You said she'll just sleep this off?" Arco asks, standing now, his hand still holding Jazz's, but at least he's standing.

"That's what I said," Karo sighs, punching something into the screen behind her, then opening the steel cabinet to her side and pulling down a small box of medicine bottles. Arco turns back to look at Jazz, who hasn't moved at all, then nods again, decided as he releases her hand and turns toward the steel framed door.

***

He remembers Etta mentioning that the group would be heading to the Records room as he and Dez walked with

Jazz toward the med-bay, so he calls up the arrow guide in his bracelet to reorient himself. After a few minutes following it, he approaches the threshold of a huge, spherical space, the far wall bowing out through seamless windows into the bluish black sea beyond. A hazy white light along the ceiling's perimeter pours down into the room over several small viewing booths that are similar to the Boundaries room stations, only without the strange helmets. A scattering of tables, chairs, and soft furniture are spread around the center of the room with metal stools sitting behind control panels, which sit directly in front of a concave, clear window that stands about six feet tall with a circular, white channeling platform directly under it. Arco had only seen these in cines before, but here they were, just like the matter board and the parson fish. He shakes his head trying not to think of all the nightmares that could actually be real now.

"And that's it for today. Don't worry if you don't remember how to use the interview stations. A tutorial that will walk you through everything will be uploaded to your bracelet dashboards, so don't be intimidated. It will all be second nature when the time comes to use any of this equipment," Etta says to the group, then smiles directly at Arco as everyone starts to disperse. "Lunch will be served in about an hour, so you're all free to go to the student center, or back to your rooms, whatever you want until then. Remember the neural links will give you a 10-minute warning, so don't be alarmed when you hear a voice in your head!" she calls after everyone with a chuckle, then starts making her way over to Arco as

Liddick spots him and angles his head over to a booth. Arco shakes his head and motions to another, the booth that he'd coded for a moment just like this.

"How is she?" Etta asks, startling him as he turns around.

"She's fine, sleeping. Ms. Karo gave her some kind of brainwave stabilizer. I think it was like a tranquilizer because it knocked her out."

"Sounds like a reset shot. This happens to lots of freshes. I'm sure she wasn't the first one down there today and won't be the last. She should be fine for next time, though. The nanites work like little vaccines, so they'll watch for the same biopattern if she starts down that road again and will adjust all her levels automatically."

"I thought they were supposed to do that automatically already," Arco replies, an edge in his voice. He didn't like the idea of billions of robots crawling around in their blood manipulating their systems—probably even spying on everything and feeding it into some giant mainframe. Things don't run the way they do here for 80 years without some kind of leash on the population.

"Well, they need to be exposed before they can learn, right? They're amazing, but they're not psychic," Etta says, smiling to one side. "Lunch is in an hour, so be expecting the neural link reminder. I'm in your contacts if you have any questions, OK?"

Arco nods, then turns his attention back to Liddick, who's waiting at the station Arco had identified. He crosses to him in a handful of strides, angling his chin toward the viewing window and the control panel just below it.

"Pull up the Abe Lincoln sim-corp," Arco asks Liddick, who puzzles briefly as he translates the abbreviation with the how-to instructions Etta has just given everyone about *simulated corporal* versions of someone from history. He keys in the instructions, and in seconds, the viewing window flickers until Abraham Lincoln appears.

"Good afternoon. What would you like to discuss today?" Lincoln says, thumbing his lapels.

"Tell us the story of your life," Arco replies, then keys in the button combination to mute the speaker while launching the privacy screen he'd installed.

"What did you just do?" Liddick asks, looking around for the source that has silenced all the ambient noise in the room.

"We're scrambled in here now because I coded this station earlier. See the blue outline?" he asks, looking up, then down. "They can't see it from the outside, but when that blue light turns on, I know they can't monitor us," Arco replies.

Liddick nods, impressed. "And how is he not reacting to us?"

"Because I just asked him for his life story, which will trigger the lecture mode instead of interview," Arco answers as Liddick's eyes widen.

"How do you know how to do all that already? We don't have these things topside—they don't even have them in Skyboard."

"Skyboard..." Arco shakes his head. "Guess they don't have everything there after all, then, do they? What a façade—just like this place."

Liddick narrows his eyes. "What do you mean *like this place?*" he asks, wondering what Hart knows.

"I tried to program this thing to pull up the staff file on Rheen, but guess what, it locked up. So then I sent the algorithm to pull the sim-corp stored data on her, all the cache, all the cross references, everything from her weird hair to what her friends and enemies say about her, anything that has ever been monitored that could be turned into a composite like this," he says, gesturing to the lecturing, muted Lincoln. "Should work just like it works for any other historical figure you queue up, right? Just punch in a name and get the computer's best guess of what the person is actually like, but all I got was a State promo feed on a loop." Arco spits it all out in one breath before shifting his weight away from Liddick, crossing his arms over his chest as the muscles in his jaw tighten again.

"She told you, didn't she?" Liddick says quietly, then takes a seat in one of the soft brown chairs.

"Parts of it. She told me you would tell me the rest," Arco squares his stance and turns to face Liddick. "Why do *you* know the rest?"

Liddick exhales, bracing his elbows on his knees and pushing his hands over his face.

"It's a long story, man," he starts.

"Last I checked we were going to be here awhile," Arco says, bringing his hands to his hips.

"A lot longer than we thought, that's for sure," Liddick says, meeting Arco's narrowed glare.

"What are you talking about? What happened in Jazz's advisor meeting?"

Liddick takes in a quick breath and straightens in his chair before dropping his gaze to answer, "We're never going home, Hart. There are no port calls. There's nothing but that," he says, jerking his chin at the bowed window and the endless water just beyond it.

"We've had people visit us on port-calls," Arco replies, but in the pit of his stomach, he remembers what the trace he ran on Arwyn's last port-call started to read.

"Those weren't from real people," Liddick says.

"Then what were they? What did you and Jazz see in your advising sessions?"Arco asks, his voice pulling tightly around the words.

"What did she tell you?" Liddick replies, his dark brows drawing together as they stare at each other for a few seconds, neither wanting to acquiesce. They were not friends, not for years, but each of them knew in the back of his mind that if they were going to make any progress at all, they would need to put the past aside and be allies, at least for now.

"She said she saw your brothers," Arco answers, looking toward the enormous expanse of dark water through the window across the room. "They were in trouble...and so was Arwyn. She said Liam told her to pretend to be what they wanted, whoever *they* is."

"What kind of trouble?" Liddick asks, now getting to his feet, his eyes sharpened on every blink, every twitch Arco makes.

"Something about a container that Lyden and Arwyn

were in. She said Lyden tried to fight someone, and then something about her father. Her *father,*" Arco enunciates the last word as if to convince himself.

"Did she see the water? The lines on Lyden?" Liddick asks, nearly breathless. Arco shakes his head.

"She didn't mention anything like that, but she was fading pretty fast with whatever Karo gave her. What did you see? What happened to Arwyn?"

Liddick takes in a deep breath, moving his hands to his hips as he looks down at the floor trying to find the right words to relay what he'd seen in there. Hart has a trigger, especially about his sister, and no one needs to see that go down right here in the middle of this fishbowl.

"She was all right at first—she was just locked in a clear room next to Lyden, then started yelling and fighting when they filled Lyden's room with water. Rheen and Styx came in to observe."

"*Rheen and Styx?*"Arco's eyes widen. "And what do you mean she was all right *at first?*"

"Rheen was supervising it all, and Styx just looked like he was consulting. They did something to Lyden, to his chest. He had these red lines that seemed to be..." Liddick forces himself to remember as he swallows and looks toward the dark sea pushing back at the window on the other side of the room, his brows and the set of his mouth fighting against the pressure to fold in on themselves. "They were like *gills.* They just appeared down either side of his chest when the water filled his room and he couldn't get any air. He was thrashing until he jerked a few times and then just stopped," he says, looking back up at Hart now and succumbing to the struggle with his composure, the same shock registering on his face as when he had first watched the scene. "I thought he was dead, but he wasn't. He pressed his hands to the glass wall trying to get Arwyn's attention—to let her know he was OK because she was wrecked—except he *wasn't* OK. He was a *fish*, Hart. A damn *fish!*"

Liddick's stomach knots, and he opts for the chair behind him again. He leans forward as he sits, resting his head on the fist he brings up to meet it, his blond hair falling forward and exposing the darker roots.

Arco is frozen where he stands. His initial impulse is to believe Wright because he can almost feel it tearing into him, but then, this is Liddick Wright, and he should probably tell him to go to hell—that this was nothing to spin about because something definitely happened in there with Jazz, and he needed to know what it was.

"I'm...sorry," Arco finally says, unable to reconcile more. "But maybe it was just some kind of projection, like a subconscious worry or something?" he grasps, although he knows it would be impossible for both Jazz and Liddick to see the same things if that were the case. Liddick looks up at him, seeing the effort, and at least appreciates that.

"I wish that were it, but we both know it's not," Liddick replies, taking a deep breath and blowing it out hard.

Arco steels himself. "The others, Arwyn...Liam and Jazz's father?" he says after several seconds, and Liddick doesn't answer for several more.

"Liam did the surgery. They made him put those things in Lyden because they said they'd kill me if he didn't do it, then they made him stay in there while they tested it all. He was the supervising physician. Jazz's father was the biocoder who mixed the hybridizing solutions so the gills would take."

"But her father is dead. The hydrogen plant accident..."

"That was never him, aren't you listening to me? I don't know what happened or how he got to that holding facility they were testing in, but it wasn't him at the plant that day, just like that biodesigner in Skyboard isn't Liam," Liddick says.

"And Arwyn?" Arco asks again, clenching his teeth in preparation. Liddick takes in another breath and looks up squarely at Arco.

"They'd made her fireproof, Hart," he says very quietly. Arco's chest tightens as the words squeeze out all his air.

"What?"

"Just like they made it so Lyden could breathe under water," Liddick continues, then pauses. "She's alive, but when they lit her on fire, only her clothes burned away in that container next to Lyden," Liddick's chest compresses and his throat closes up as he feels the news shoot through Hart, and he clenches his teeth against the emotional reverberation of it. "I'm sorry, man."

Arco bites down hard, sniffing back the tears that claw at the back of his throat, then swallows them down where they wrap around his heart like barbed wire pulling taut. He can't talk. He wants to scream, to hit something until it breaks into a hundred sharp, splintering pieces, but he can't do either closed up in this little cage with Wright. He begins to pace, one hand on his hip and the other wrapping around the back of his neck.

"Liam did that to her?" Arco finally manages to say, cutting a wild eye at Liddick.

"I don't know. If he did, it was because they made him, and they'd have gotten someone else if not him—probably someone not as good, and then she might be..." Liddick starts, then thinks better of the direction that's heading as he gets to his feet and takes a step toward Hart, "...they're alive, and the people we think are them aren't them. We have to focus on that," he says, trying to meet Hart's eyes, to get him to come back into himself before he does something stupid. "Hey, I *know*, all right. I know better than anyone what this is like. But we need to help them. They're reaching out to *us* to help them."

Arco stops pacing and crosses his arms over his chest as he looks at Liddick. He swallows again, then takes a deep breath and holds it for a second before letting it fall out of him. "I think you're actually right about that," he says, his voice thick as he looks again at the ground and clears his throat. Liddick watches him, feeling the swimming in his own stomach, and waits as Arco finishes wrestling with it. "I found an echo in the algorithm of the cuff mainframe the night we got here," Arco finally explains. "When they put the bracelet cuffs on us at the interview, they didn't tell us anything about them, not really. Didn't you think that was split?"

"I did, but there was a lot going on then," Liddick answers.

"Exactly. And they counted on that. What they didn't count on was you and Jazz hearing that marlin."

Liddick's air rushes out, and his expression hardens against the punch he suddenly feels to his gut.

"Jazz told you that?" he asks, feeling each little claw of it climbing up his back. She wouldn't tell Hart about that night, not *him* of all people.

"No, she didn't tell me," Arco replies, shoving his hands into his pockets as he turns to face Lincoln, who is still silently lecturing. "I followed you that night you met up. I was worried about her when I could tell you were spinning about the rat...I didn't trust you."

Liddick takes a motivated step toward Hart, then stops himself. "I *saved* her that night, you chutz. Was I supposed to let her become the butt of every joke until Nann's port-festival? Did you really want people to remember her like that? For her little sister and her mother to remember her like that? No one else saw what we saw, Hart!" Liddick's throat flushes with color, and his teeth lock together with the effort to restrain himself.

"*Zone*, I get it...just sit back down," Arco says, looking from side to side and noticing that they're starting to draw stares from a few girls across the room. "But that's why I had to find out what was happening, all right? I couldn't hear you any more after you went up that dune, so I went home and started examining my cuff. I couldn't get it off—in fact, when I tried, it made itself smaller so it wouldn't even slide over my wrist. When I stopped, it went back to normal size. It's like it had a mind of its own—it could read what I was doing, so I knew then that it was more than just a scannable ticket for the shuttle with our medical and school records like they said."

Liddick feels his pulse slow and his breathing relax as Arco crosses to the chair in front of him. Liddick moves back into his own chair and scrubs his hands over his face. *To our corners,* then, he thinks, chastising himself for thinking Jazz would ever tell Hart what he told her that night. He'd never told that story about Liam to anyone before, and she had to know that too.

"How did you hack it?" Liddick asks, pushing the thoughts of Jazz aside.

"After my roommate went to sleep that first night, I managed to pull up the same screen we just saw in the advising session—it was accidental then. I somehow pushed the right place on the cuff, and once I was in, it was just a matter of coding a workaround to reboot the system and get to the mainframe."

"But how did you know how to do that? We've been here two days," Liddick asks.

"I don't know. I was awake almost the whole night tinkering with it, hacking into this interview station from it," Arco says, gesturing to Lincoln, "...the whole time wondering how the hell I knew what to do, what the symbols and numbers meant. I've always been pretty decent with patterns, coding, but not like this. They put that bracelet on me and something just clicked on."

"That's why Jazz could hear the marlin that night...

something must have been activated in some of us with these cuffs. Have you heard any of the others talking about the same thing happening to them?" Liddick asks. "Ellis has been Captain Nanite since the port festival," he says, rolling his eyes.

"I don't know, I haven't been paying a lot of attention with everything else going on."

"All right, but if it's the bracelets, Gaia had to know something like that would happen, so why would they store Liam's message on there for anyone to find?" Liddick asks, leaning in on his forearms.

"They didn't. It's not on the mainframe for anyone to find, it's just an echo." Liddick raises an eyebrow, and Arco exhales impatiently. "OK, look," he says, leaning toward Liddick and opening his hands, "when information is in a place, then deleted, it leaves an impression. Think of it like walking on the beach—you leave a footprint when your foot isn't there any more, right, and then the water comes along and washes that footprint away, but the microscopic abrasions to the individual grains of sand can't be washed away, at least not instantly. No one ever sees those because first of all, they're impossible to see with the naked eye, and second, all the grains are scattered into different directions, and your eye can't trace all the paths at the same time even if it *could* see the microscopic abrasions. But if someone could trace all the grains and then reassemble them with the exact original geometry, they could reconstruct your footprint," Arco says, looking at Liddick for some sign of comprehension.

"OK, I can see that, but what does that have to do with

Liam's message, or what Jazz and I just saw in there?"

"After I found out about what happened with the marlin, I wrote an algorithm to find the data signature—the footprint—for that phrase it said about *never seeing it coming*, then I put in the time stamp. It collected all those scattered grains of sand, and from that, I was able to reconstruct the footprint and trace where it came from. Wright, that wasn't a marlin talking to you, it was an echo from Liam. He left a data signature in the code."

"You traced it? *Where?*" Liddick says urgently. "I know it's from him—it's not the first time I've heard it, or something like it, but I can't get a lock on where it's coming from," he says, moving to the edge of his seat.

"I don't have exact coordinates yet, but the ping is coming from somewhere inside the core," Arco replies.

"Can you trace it again now that we're here? Can you find out exactly where they are?" Liddick asks.

"I don't know. Maybe if I had more time. Since the trace was cut, it would take at least a day just to get to the plot points where it left off. Not to mention I don't have automators here to help carry the ping camouflage, so add even more time because the ping will have to run in the background of the rest of the programs instead of invisibly on top of them. Did Jazz's dad say anything? If he did, I can rig a trace the same way as the marlin message. Like the grains of sand, remember?" Arco says.

"He did, but I didn't hear it. I saw him arguing with Rheen, but there wasn't any sound. When is Jazz coming out of the med-bay? Maybe she heard it," Liddick says.

"Karo said she'd wake up around meal time. We'll

need to tell her about all this," he says, sinking back into his chair wondering if he has ever been this tired in his entire *life*.

"After dinner then," Liddick says, sliding back from the edge of his seat as they both stare into the dark blue depths just a dozen feet away.

CHAPTER 23
Aligning

Everyone is surprisingly quiet as we finish dinner, or maybe it's just that I'm not really paying much attention to them as I watch Liddick a few tables down. My head still feels like it's pressed in a vice, but I notice Liddick making eye contact with Arco, who hasn't mentioned anything about what I told him—or at least, what I remember having told him since he came to pick me up from the med-bay—but they must have talked.

"You didn't eat much," Jax says, looking at my plate. "You look a hell of a lot better than you did, though."

"I feel better, still just a little tired," I say.

"That'll be gone by tomorrow," Ellis says around a mouthful of dessert. "Wave stabilizers are in the same family as the pressurization stabilizers they gave us, except their lifespan is finite whereas the pressurization stabilizers regenerate." Everyone stares at Ellis in silence as he stops his fork halfway to his mouth and meets everyone's eyes. "Seriously. One briefing. No one has read *one* of the briefings about nanites?" he asks, and everyone begins chuckling.

"On that note," I say, trying to keep the laugh out of my voice, "I think I'm going to take a walk before heading back to my room to sleep off the rest of these things."

"I'll go with you," Arco says, putting his hand on my shoulder after he picks up my tray along with his and stands. Out of the corner of my eye I see Liddick nodding to Jax, then, both of them falling into stride behind Arco and me. This can only mean that either Arco or Liddick must have said something to Jax about me seeing our father, and I can't decide if I'm happy I didn't have to tell him, or angry that I never had the chance.

Arco leads us to the Records room, though I'm not sure why he chooses this incredibly public place over some remote corner of the student center. He steers us toward the far corner of the room to what the tutorial I just watched called an *interview station,* which looks like it's already being used by someone.

"Someone is already on this one," I say to Arco as he takes a seat at the station. "And it's broken. There's no sound."

Arco presses buttons on the control panel, and a blue light falls all around us. I look around frantically to see if anyone is watching. "It's just a program so they can't monitor us. I launched it just before I came to get you so no one would take the station," Arco replies.

"You did this?" I ask, looking around at the light and the gesturing, silently speaking Lincoln. Arco nods as Liddick and Jax take a seat on the brown couch.

"No one can see it, and they can't hear us now either. Well, they can't hear us from the outside anyway, but now they can't monitor us either," Arco explains. Jax and I exchange surprised glances, but Liddick doesn't seem terribly impressed.

"You knew about this already?" I ask him, then look over at Arco. They both exchange glances, then look back at me.

"Jazz, do you remember what you told me when you were going under?" Arco asks as Jax leans forward in his seat.

"Mostly, you talked to Liddick, didn't you?" I ask.

"There might be some things you and Jax need to know about what you saw in the advisor session," he says, then passes the floor to Liddick, who explains everything about my father being some kind of Molecular Coder guru like Jax's advisor—who is also, apparently, Ms. Plume—said he was slotted to be, and then finishes the rest of the scenario from where my feed cut out with Lyden. By the time he's finished talking, Jax and I look at each other like we've both nearly drowned. "I know it's a lot to take in," Arco continues, "but there's more you need to know. After I uploaded the algorithm that traced the message from the marlin back to Liam—"

"What message from the marlin?" Jax interrupts. "The marlin from the port-festival?"

Arco and Liddick exchange glances again, and Arco sighs, crossing his arms over his chest as he looks at the ground. Liddick explains what really happened that night, how he covered for me because he didn't want to have people remember me as some tweaker, which I actually didn't consider until he explained it just now. He had me thinking it was to protect everyone else, but he was really protecting *me?* My chest aches with this realization just as I notice Jax, who sinks low in his seat and wraps his arms over himself, gripping his elbows.

"I knew it. I knew you wouldn't have acted like that

over a tunnel rat," he says, looking up at me through narrowing eyes. "You could have told me," he says, and the ache in my chest sharpens. I lean forward.

"Jax..."

"It wasn't her fault. I made the call. She wanted to tell everyone, but it wasn't the right time," Liddick says, though Jax's eyes just narrow even more. "Look, I'm sorry. We didn't even know what was really happening, so I made her promise to keep it between us until we could figure it out later that night."

"Then how did Arco know?" Jax asks, sitting up and bracing his elbows on his knees. I raise my eyebrows at this, surprised.

"Arco, how *did* you know?" I ask, and Jax's eyes soften.

Arco sighs. "I followed you that night because I was worried. I didn't believe the rat story either, and...I just didn't trust him," Arco says, darting a glance to Liddick, whose jaw flexes. "But I was wrong."

Liddick's face relaxes as his eyebrows quirk, surprised. He nods, then gets Arco back on track.

"So you traced the code back to Liam, and then..." Liddick says.

"And then I could only get so far before I had to kill it because we were getting ready to board the relay vessel. That's why I was late. I started to run something similar to trace my sister's last port-call when I figured out that Liam's was fake, but I ran out of time for that one too." He looks away and shakes his head. "The pings were coming back the same up until that point, though, and what I could eventually pull from Liam's looked like it was coming from somewhere in the core," Arco says, and my stomach hitches like I've just jumped from a high place.

"Wait, you traced that fish message to the core of the *earth?*" Jax asks, his expression contorting in disbelief. Arco pushes his hands into his pockets and nods.

"It's a long story, but that's what the algorithm reported. Jazz, can you remember anything specific that your father said? I may be able to trace it back like I did with Liam's message," Arco asks, turning to me.

"He could really be alive?" Jax asks, looking at me, astonished. I can hardly believe the possibility myself, but I saw his face. I heard his voice.

"He said, '*I never saw it coming when I refused the stipend,*'" I say, closing my eyes to hear his voice again. When I open them, Arco is keying something into his bracelet cuff.

"The stipend for what? For Gaia?" Jax asks. "But that would mean that he *turned down* Gaia at our age. Why would he do that?" Jax looks over to me, then his eyes widen in realization. "He wouldn't leave..."

"Mom..." we both say together.

"That's why she always felt so guilty...it wasn't because of her parents, it was because she blamed herself for his death at the hydrogen plant," I say.

"Because if he just would have gone to Gaia..." Jax says to no one in particular as it all becomes clear.

"But they took him anyway because the hydrogen plant accident happened after Liam left for Gaia in May, remember? The summer I got stung by the jellyfish.

There's no way he already could have been there with Liam, Rheen, and Styx then, so the person who died at the plant really *wasn't* him," I say, turning to Liddick. He nods, and all the pieces begin falling into place. "It's just like Liam and Skyboard, and they must still have them all if they're still sending these messages. They really did take them. Jax, he's alive…" I say, and for the first time it actually sinks in.

"Jazz, did he say anything else? What did he tell you about *pretending to be what they wanted?* The exact words, can you remember?" Arco asks.

"Liam said, '*If you're already there, pretend to be what they want you to be,*'" I say. "Those were his exact words."

"He has to mean here at Gaia. After what they made him do to Lyden…" Jax says, his voice trailing off as he looks at Liddick and winces. "They've all been warning us not to come—to turn Gaia down because they're experimenting on people somewhere. But *why?* And why *them?*" None of us know how to answer him, and he stands up, shaking his head. "This place isn't what we think it is. It's not what anyone thinks it is. We need to get the hell out of here."

He pushes his hands through his hair as Liddick speaks again.

"Can you start another trace? You said it takes at least a day to find where it left off, so we should start it again now, right?" Liddick asks Arco, who nods, folding his arms over his chest.

"Not counting the camouflage, if I hack the mainframe from the Boundaries room it might not take as long since it's a larger processor. It moves information faster. Then I can sweep for echoes of these new messages, which I can then start to restructure and then ghost ping. I just have to extend this monitor mask to the room over there so they can't watch us, but that won't take long."

"OK, do it. If you can ping those messages, I have an idea of where we can go from there. I just need to sort a few things out first," Liddick says as Arco types something into the Lincoln station. The blue light field turns green, and I shake my head, looking around us.

"It's extended now? Just like that?" I ask. "This is incredible."

Arco shrugs and raises his eyebrows with a smile. "All right, I'm going over to the Boundaries room. Meet me there in 20 minutes. If I can't get it uplinked by then, I'll have to go back through the side door with this bracelet cuff like I did the first time," he says, and we all nod.

"OK, kill the interview program and we'll meet you there," Liddick says, and Arco shuts down Mr. Lincoln and the privacy field.

***

We make our way across the commons area again and down the corridor that leads to the Boundaries room after giving Arco a head start. It's abandoned with the exception of a few people moving to and from the Records room.

"So you saw him. You actually heard him?" Jax whispers at my side. I look up at him and nod.

"He was just the same, Jax. Nothing had changed about him at all," I say. Jax's throat moves with his effort to swallow, the line of muscle in his jaw pulling with his small nod.

"So we'll go in and get them all out. We'll find a way to get them back," he says, nodding more intently now. I interlace my fingers with his.

"I know we will," I say, and he grips my hand in his.

Our moment of conviction jostles when we arrive at the Boundaries room, which is empty except for Arco and...*Vox?* I stop in my tracks when I see her sitting sideways on his lap in one of the chairs, her tattooed shins moving back and forth as they hang off the bend of her long, pale legs. I blink hard a few times. Her arms are wrapped around his neck, his around her waist, and she's moving in to kiss him. *What?*

Liddick starts laughing out loud next to me, but I suddenly feel sick, though I'm not sure why. I look over at Jax, whose eyes are wide as he releases my hand and covers his open mouth. I look back over at Arco and Vox while clearing my throat, and all the blood runs out of Arco's face when he sees us, quickly unseating Vox as he stands and pinches the bridge of his nose.

"I—OK, so this is—hang on," he says, his hands taking turns reaching and pushing at the air like he's trying to stop our thoughts before they fall out. "I'm not even sure how this started because I was talking, and then we were sitting, and then—"

Vox is smiling so widely that it has to hurt, and I don't need any more explanation than this. I wave my hands out in front of me to stop Arco's babbling.

"OK, just stow it. Did you manage to do what you

came here to do before she hijacked your face?" Color runs up his throat like hands reaching from under his collar and blotches his cheeks as he scrounges for words. Liddick still can't get his breath to regulate between hysterical convulsions, and nausea gives way to a fire in my chest.

"I...didn't actually get to that part. I started to tell her what we were doing because...uh," Arco stops mid sentence and looks quizzically off to the side as if the answer could be there trying to get his attention. "Actually, I don't know why I started to tell her, but she knows most of it, and she'll help us," Arco says, hopefully.

"Help us do what? Reproduce?" Liddick is able to get this out around another cascade of laughter, and Jax finally loses whatever composure he's been holding in place behind his hand. Liddick smiles at Vox once he gets control of himself, then lets a long, low whistle escape his lips as he winces and rubs his chest with his hand, "Hey, just kidding there, killer, take it easy..." he chuckles, and I look from him to her. Her eyes are narrowed, and I can see the muscles working in her jaw.

"Vox!" I start, but Liddick puts his other hand on my shoulder and squeezes reassuringly.

"She can't push me," he says, "don't worry."

"But you're grabbing your chest—" He turns to me and flashes a wide, white, Liddick caliber smile.

"Just being a gentleman. She's trying so hard, after all."

I look back at Vox, now three shades darker red than Arco, who looks completely confused.

"How?" Vox asks Liddick from under a fiery scowl. "I

pushed you in the galley."

"Well, no, but I wasn't going to bring that up."

"How?" Vox repeats through her teeth.

"Well," Liddick says, thinning his lips and extending a hand toward Vox. "I learned a long time ago that my father is like you—a pusher—and that my mother can pick up on people's feelings. Apparently, I got the best of both worlds, so I guess that somehow neutralizes it, I don't know," Liddick answers, raising his hands out to his sides and shrugging.

"She can't make you feel things—I mean, she can't manipulate your feelings, but you can feel her try?" I ask, wondering if it's possible to learn this trick. He smiles to one side and shakes his head apologetically at Vox, who is only slightly less red in the face now. Jax crosses his arms and returns his hand to his mouth to hold back his smile.

"What's going on?" Arco interrupts, then rounds on Vox. "You make people feel things?"

Finally, her anger gives way to a smirk. "I can't make anyone do anything they *really* don't want to do," she lifts her chin and tilts her head, eyeing Arco up and down as she trails her index finger down his chest. I feel a stab of anger and want to rush forward, but then notice his face contorting as he huffs out an exasperated breath and moves her hand away, taking a step back from her.

"Don't touch me," he says to her, then presses the heels of his hands against his eyes. "OK, so for the record," he starts, then shows us his palms as if to keep our thoughts at bay again as he meets my eyes, "I am not interested in

Vox like that. I don't know what just happened here," he says, turning to Vox, "but I know I'm *not* interested in you like that, *OK?"* He punctuates his words with an extended arm to keep her away. "I'm sorry, but I'm not, and I didn't want to do that. I mean, I don't know why I did that, but I guess it's probably because *you* did that?" He looks at her half pleading for an answer, and half to confirm what actually just transpired. The ridiculousness of the whole scene comes together, and the odd heat I've been feeling cools to a flutter of laughter that I can't keep inside. "This is funny to you?" He stops all at once and looks at me in disbelief, which triggers another giggle that I try to stifle like Jax is doing. "Oh, nice. That's great, Jazz. So Wright, since you're the *best of both worlds,* did you do that? Or was it you again?" Arco asks, looking from Liddick back to Vox as he gestures to me.

"Don't look at me, man," Liddick says, starting to choke on his laughter again. "You're doing a pretty good job of busting everyone up all by yourself."

"Crite, all right, can we all just get serious for a second here? We have work to do,"Arco says, his throat and cheeks flushing even more with color as he turns to the transmission station behind him.

Liddick casually throws his arm around me as we walk toward Arco and Vox inside the perimeter of the station, and after a few steps inside, I see the blue light of the privacy field that Arco extended from the Records room. As my laughter subsides, I start to feel warm again, comfortable while standing next to Liddick, and for an instant, I let my head rest against his shoulder. His arm tightens around me, and Arco looks up at me from the keypad, then does a double take, his mouth frozen in the middle of a word. He looks to Liddick and back again to me as the warm feeling drains away. At first I'm confused, and then I'm not. I push away from Liddick, realizing he's no better than Vox.

"Stop," I say, and cut him a sharp eye.

"What?" Liddick's dark brows arch in surprise as his eyes flit from me to Arco, then back again to me, genuinely confused until understanding spreads across his face. "Oh, you actually think—?" he starts defensively, even offended, but then lets the sentence fall apart. "You know what, think what you want..." he sends it off in an exasperated sigh and takes a step back from both of us, his hands in the air in front of him. "Hart, did you sweep for those message echoes or not?"

Arco blinks away his confusion and answers. "Yes, but like I said, with all the camouflage I have to add to the code, it's going to move a lot more slowly when we try to ping the origination."

"How will that work then? How do we get to everyone?" Jax asks, all traces of humor gone.

"Now that I have the sweep back—all those grains of sand—"Arco adds, nodding to Liddick, "I'll just need some time for the ghost ping to carry the piggy back code I wrote, which will jump off once it gets to the destination coordinates and trace any related signals, like if the source is mobile. After it sweeps for related signals, it will send back all the possible paths to the source signal like a breadcrumb trail. That's how I traced the marlin message back to somewhere in the core, but it fell apart before it reached the point of origination. With enough time, it will generate exact coordinates for multiple paths."

"How long will it take to set up the ping?" Liddick asks.

"Like I said, it would take a day just to get back to where it cut off before, but from there to finish it? I don't have any of my equipment here, so probably three weeks, maybe a month. It depends on how far away the source of the signals are."

"We don't have that kind of time. You didn't see what they were doing to them," Liddick says.

"Don't you think I want to get them out of there as much as you do? All my automators are at home, so the code has to carry the camouflage manually. It's the difference between gliding 10 miles, or walking 10 miles with a pack of lead strapped to your back. Camouflaging is the only way we're not getting caught pinging them," Arco says.

Liddick clenches his jaw and turns away, bringing his hands to his hips.

"So what happens once we find the exact location? We just go digging into the core? There are about three miles of water on top of us, in case no one has noticed. Did anyone bring a beach pail and shovel, because I didn't," Vox says from the seat of a transmission station at the corner of the room, a newly sharpened edge in her voice to replace the smarmy tone she had earlier.

"Arco had to pilot a vessel in his interview scenario," I

snap at her before I realize what I'm saying, and my stomach instantly drops when I meet his eyes. *Crite*, this is not something he wants to remember. "Well, you did, and you know that you can," I say, trying to help him to remember how he dove in to help me with that jellyfish as we'd discussed on the walk home after our interviews.

"I'll figure that part out," Arco says, shaking his head as if to dislodge the memory. Vox shrugs and goes back to fingering through buttons and levers.

"They put me in for Core Engineering," Jax says, "I don't know how yet, but I'm sure I can help code the system organics if we get into a ship."

"And you're going to be able to keep this from Fraya?" Liddick asks, turning abruptly to Jax, but Arco brings his hands together and takes a step toward Liddick, answering instead.

"If we're really going to do this—somehow put a crew together and follow the breadcrumbs to his father, my sister, and your brothers, we're going to need medical expertise aboard. If not for us, for them. Didn't you say they were slotting Fraya for biodesign?" Arco asks, now turning to Jax.

"Yeah," Jax says, absently rubbing the back of his hand with the other. "Yeah, she is, and if staying behind means they're going to make her do what Liam's having to do— even if there's only the smallest chance of that—I don't see how I can keep it from her. I just hope her job won't be harder than all ours put together."

CHAPTER 24
The Echo Explanation

Liddick and I look at Jax, then at each other, both of us remembering Fraya's meltdown after the interviews.

"You're kidding me, right? How long did it take you to calm her down after the interview, Ripley? And now you're going to let Hart put her on board?" Liddick says, throwing a hand out at Arco.

"We won't be over her shoulder screaming at her to harvest cells like they did in her interview, and if there's any chance something bent really is going on here, like I said, I don't want her staying behind in the middle of it on her own," Jax replies, and Liddick folds his arms around himself in thought, starts to speak, then stops himself. *"What?"* Jax asks.

"Nothing. All right. I said I'll help. I just need to get in touch with a friend of mine. Hart, how long until you can hack into these things again and get me an open topside channel that no one can monitor?" Liddick asks, holding up his bracelet cuff.

Arco shakes his head. "They don't work like that—it's just an uplink to Gaia's mainframe. They made the port-call system totally separate from the bracelet platform."

"So we just need to find a way to port-call now?" Jax asks. "That shouldn't be hard, right?"

"Except none of us is credentialed yet, and I can't even modify our profiles to make it look like we are because it would set off alarms everywhere we went: meals, med-bay, the endless algorithms wouldn't align any more. *Unless...*" Arco jolts. "Wait a minute, I can modify this breadcrumbs piggy back for uplink, and then you can just attach it to the next port-call someone makes. I have to find the outbound schedule," Arco says, shooing Vox away from the enclosed screen of the transmission station and typing furiously.

"How far will it reach once you get it modified?" Liddick asks.

"Anywhere there's a receiver hop," Arco says. "I just need to camouflage the ping and the code it's carrying. It's really going to slow down the host transfer, so I'll have to find one that's going somewhere close so they don't dig around in the splicing looking for the lag source. Where's your friend?"

"Skyboard East, in the hills," Liddick answers. Arco chuckles while panning through screens.

"Of course," he says. "Let me guess, your friend is Ravvy Pierce? No, wait...Kit Dillinger? *No, no...*Sera Lim!" he says, chuckling again as he stops on a screen and scrolls with a wave of his hand.

Liddick gives Arco a tolerant smile, which he doesn't look up to see.

"*Actually,* he's behind the scenes—literally—a story-boarder."

"How can a virtuo-cine storyboarder help us port-call?" Jax asks.

"That's just a front for his real trade."

Arco looks up at Liddick. "Which *is?*" he asks, leaning

on the last word.

"Port-carnate," Liddick finally says after another beat and a few darting glances at each of us. After a second of silence, Arco guffaws again.

"You *are* a spinner, and the worst ever," he says, his laughter slipping into percolations as he returns to his screen.

"That's illegal, not to mention a death sentence. No way, Liddick," I add, about to dismiss the whole idea, but then I see the corner of his mouth twitch, and I shake my head slowly at him. "You haven't..."

He nods back at me just as slowly as the twitch gives way to a grin.

"So you *see,*" he says, extending his arms out to his sides and turning a 360. "Obviously, it's not a death sentence."

Arco finally punches his ticket on the clue bus and stops laughing, then looks at Liddick soberly.

"You've gone? *Physically* transmitted?" Vox comes out of the corner and walks quickly over to the group of us. Liddick nods again, and Jax narrows his eyes.

"Several times. And none of my parts have fallen off," Liddick says, wiggling his fingers in front of him. Vox's burgundy eyebrow arches sharply, and I feel a tingling in the back of my neck as the smirk spreads over my face. I swallow hard, resisting the urge to make the obvious comment she's trying to push me to make, successful only because I concentrate on the image of smothering her to death with a pillow tonight. "Hey, anytime either of you ladies want to test my honesty on that one, you just let me know," Liddick continues, his smile deepening again as he tilts a nod in our direction with a wink. "Happy to oblige."

Did he hear her push that thought into my head?

"Get wrung," I say through a smirk of my own, "and I don't care. It's too dangerous. Promise you're not going to try it," I insist, then notice the digital time projection against the wall near the door to the Boundaries room. How is it already almost 9:00 p.m.?

"I didn't say I was going to do it, but I do need to get a message to my friend," he says, and turns his attention back to Arco, "So, can you get that open channel?"

"The log says the next transmission is in two days. I'll work on reconfiguring the piggy back for port-call uplink tomorrow after classes, maybe during if this Organic Systems class gives me any autonomy," Arco says. "I'm going to need the coordinates for your friend."

"You'll have to embed my initials in the outbound message because if his system flags a veiled code dig from *here* without it, it will just mirror all the port-carnate cache onto your system. That'll blow up your camouflage, and you'll have the security corps on the next sub down here to haul you to—"

"I know, I know, Lima." Arco waves a hand at Liddick without looking up from the log he's pulled up on the screen.

"Lima?" Vox asks.

"Prison for tech crime," I say. "Not a good place."

"The only thing worse than being surrounded by criminals is being surrounded by smart criminals," Arco says, and Liddick chuffs a laugh.

"So what makes this port-whatever transfer so bad that it's illegal?" Vox asks.

"Port-*carnate*—it's illegal because it would just be too damn great for the unwashed masses. Biotech Global owns the State. It wants everyone to think port-carnate is going to scramble their insides, or make them come back short an eye, or an earlobe and a lip will misidentify and switch places if they try it. Otherwise, people would teleport wherever they wanted to go. No more shuttles, no more subs, no more Biotech port-cloud, or Carbonetics Corporation's synthetic atoms to rain down and flesh out your port-call holograms. Big companies would lose big coin," Liddick explains, and I suddenly feel hollow in the realization that things are much more complicated than I ever thought they were. The world is so much larger, and so much worse.

"Let me get this straight. Your actual, physical body transports from one place to another, no hologram and paste job—just like that?" Vox asks.

"Just like that," Liddick nods.

"Does it hurt?" The question is abrupt and bubbles out on a giggle at the same time I think it. The blood rushes hot to my cheeks for what must be the tenth time today, and I glare shards at Vox as I violently rub the tickle from the nape of my neck. She shrugs. "Ask your own questions," I tell her. "Seriously, I'm going to smother you in your sleep tonight."

Liddick tries to swallow his snicker and almost succeeds. "It doesn't hurt, no. Just a little nauseating at first, like losing your equilibrium after sneezing too hard," he adds, looking at Vox, then at me again like I'm four years old and have just told him how many animal crackers I can fit in my underpants. I raise my eyebrows at him and tilt my head to the side. *"What?"* he says in answer. "It's cute when you get so...*menacing."*

"Menacing," Vox repeats, slowly nodding like a wide-eyed idiot.

Arco smiles begrudgingly and nods. "I hate to agree with him, but he's right."

"Traitor," I say to Arco, who laughs. I close my eyes and take in a long, deep breath through my nose just as the curfew warning mercifully sounds in my head.

CHAPTER 25
Is This Seat Taken?

Fraya and I wind up in line together for breakfast the next morning, both of us agreeing on portable food options since we're running late. I grab a protein bar and a handful of grapes that are greener than any I've ever seen topside, and Fraya does the same. Vox was still asleep when I came back from the hygiene room, but she has somehow beaten me to the table as we walk toward it. She's sitting next to Arco, grinning stupidly and hanging all over him, and I shake my head at her on the way to my seat.

"What's that look for?" Arco says, surprising me. Oh good, now he's defending her.

"Like you don't know," I reply and narrow my eyes at him, but this only seems to puzzle him more. I sit a few seats down from him next to Ellis, who is talking a mile a minute about something, his barrage of words pummeling back the angry questions that begin to surface inside me about seeing Arco and Vox like this. So what if they get together. In fact, *good!*

"Anyway," Jax interrupts Ellis's monologue, "I will never do that again…" he trails off with a subtle laugh in his voice, evidently trying to kill the conversation before the whole table hears what he, Ellis, and Avis were just discussing, but I realize this a beat too late.

"Do what again?" I ask, which somehow causes the

table to erupt in laughter. I scan everyone's faces for input, a headache already beginning thanks to lying awake most of the night with the visions from Plume's office.

"Your brother here assumed the hygiene room was like the one at Seaboard, and just let it all hang—ow!" Ellis's snickering turns into a yelp as Jax apparently kicks him under the table. He starts again, "Guess they don't do that here."

Jax throws a blackberry at Ellis, which explodes all over the hand he holds up to deflect it. He laughs and grabs a napkin to clean it off.

"Stow it," Jax says, fighting his own laughter again.

"That's all that happened? What's so funny?" Vox asks, but Jax sends me an icy look through the remnants of his grin and clenches his jaw, his eyes alight and all the humor fading. I point to Vox in protest, and all at once Avis starts rambling.

"So he's walking around without his towel, and one of the cloudies asks him where he went for splicing because he wanted one just like that!"

The words are barely able to outrun the deluge of snorting guffaws that follows, which turn into soundless convulsions that bring tears to his eyes. Jax clears his throat and swallows hard as he instantly flushes red. He reaches for his juice and downs it, refusing to make eye contact with anyone.

"See you in class," Jax mumbles as he stands up and steps out of the giggling like it's a bath, taking long, purposeful strides toward the door. I put all the pieces together now and understand why he was trying to let it drop. Fraya pulls her chin to her chest, then covers her mouth with her hand as she blushes and begins picking all her grapes from their stems with the other hand. I look over at Arco, pointing him in the direction of Jax with my chin. If I thought I could help, I'd go after him myself, but I know that because I'm a girl, not to mention his sister, I'd just make it worse. Arco is still chuckling, but shoves Avis out of his seat in Jax's direction.

"Go fix it before he finds a way to get even," he says, his laughter fading. Avis nods, having just caught his breath enough to excuse himself. As he walks away, Dez makes her way to our table and slides in next to Fraya, her sheet of blonde hair falling around her shoulder as she sits.

"Ready for *Organic Systems and Theory?*" she says in an overly dramatic voice.

"As ready as I'll ever be," Fraya answers, swallowing the last of her thick, green juice and pocketing her protein bar as she scoops the rest of the grapes into her hand. "See you at lunch, Jazz." She gets up and crosses the room to the door with Dez, and I watch them go, noticing how different they are—Fraya small and slight, Dez tall and athletic.

"Ready for all this?" Tieg says, having straddled the bench next to me. I startle and turn directly into his perfectly sculpted smile.

"Your sister just buzzed over here and asked almost the exact question to Fraya," I reply, collecting myself. I feel edgy this morning beyond being nervous about classes, so of course, I look over at Vox, who's chewing on a straw and staring at me from under whatever Arco is saying to the table. She threads her arm through his and smiles at me as I roll my eyes at her and turn my attention back to Tieg.

"I guess it's a triplets thing," Tieg says with a shrug. "You and Jax are twins, aren't you?"

I nod, willing myself to relax. Sibling annoyances. I can talk about that. "Jax will be the first to tell you he's older, which gives him the right to be in charge, but otherwise, yes."

"Pitt's the same way. He's first, then me, then Dez. Three minutes between Pitt and me, a minute and 43 seconds between Dez and me."

"There's a minute and 18 seconds between us," I say. "Does Pitt act like he's years older?"

"All the time," he says, twisting to lean his forearms on the table as he interlaces his fingers. He has strong hands for a cloudy—hands that look like they've done actual work with a few scarred knuckles and raised veins that run up into his forearms. I shake my head and try to refocus on the conversation. "So what's your first class?" he asks over Arco's sudden throat clearing mission.

I open my mouth to answer, but hear Vox's voice instead. "Empathy and Psychosomatic Systems. We're roommates by the way," she says in a gush, which feels like a bucket of cold water on everything. I tense as Tieg looks over my shoulder at her and nods, then looks back at me trying to disguise the smile on his face by looking down at the table.

"What she said," I say, shrugging and raising my eyebrows before taking a bite of my protein bar, which I discover tastes like peanut butter. I *hate* peanut butter.

"So they have you paired up for classes too, then," he says, bringing in his outside leg and sliding closer to me as he talks. Arco starts clearing his throat again, and Tieg looks up.

"Do you need some water, man?" Tieg asks, raising an eyebrow. I turn around and find Arco glaring.

"I'm good, thanks," he replies from under a scowl. Tieg nods slowly when I turn around, then looks back at me and pushes the corner of his mouth to one side.

"Anyway," he says with a final glance at Arco, "we're in Organic Systems Design and Theory, Pitt and Jax are both in *Chemical Structures and*...something, I forget the rest of it," he laughs, "so, it looks like they've paired up roommates by career field." He holds my eyes in place with his, the unnatural sapphire blue like some kind of gravity field pulling me in. I feel a prickle at the back of my neck at this thought along with the urge to tell him about his *gravity field eyes,* but focus on the disgusting glob of peanut butter I'm trying to swallow instead. I take a long drink of water before straddling my seat and turn my back completely to Vox. She's *not* going to push me into embarrassing myself.

Tieg's blond eyebrows flinch, surprised at my sudden move toward him, but he mirrors my position by sliding his outside knee back over the edge of the bench. We sit face to face like this, and a small dimple appears just off the corner of his cheek as he smiles. It's then that I notice the flecks of *ice blue* in his eyes, and how broad his chest and shoulders really are now that he almost completely overshadows me. I swallow again trying to figure out what to say next.

"I wish they had sports here, but I suppose that wouldn't be very practical. Did you play any at your school?" I ask, relatively confident that this doesn't sound too stupid. His smile widens. I guess his teeth aren't *that* strange.

"G-ball, mainly," he says, brushing a strand of loose hair behind my shoulder, "but I like everything. Did you pla—"

"We're going to be late, come on," Arco says to Tieg, abruptly standing. He crosses behind me and grabs Tieg's bicep, which makes him nearly fall off the bench. He catches himself immediately and gives me the rest of his smile as he stands.

"Will I see you at lunch?" he says to me on the cusp of a laugh.

"Everyone will be here at lunch, let's go," Arco answers him, the edge in his voice growing. I raise my eyebrows and nod, trying not to laugh. Tieg's eyes widen with a surprised grin as he shrugs under Arco's marshaling before they turn to leave. I watch him until he looks back at me over his shoulder, and then quickly turn away, my heart suddenly hammering in my chest. After a deep breath, I set my eyes on Vox.

"Can I please help you get kicked out of here somehow? Seriously, what do you need me to do? Can you just hijack a submarine, or maybe go play with that matter board again and create a transfer booth that will put you on the moon? Please?" I spill at her as soon as the boys are out of earshot.

"You like him," Vox says, popping a piece of orange into her mouth. I throw one of my grapes at her.

"Stow it. I do not. Let's go. We're going to be late too if we don't leave now. Room 30B," I say into my bracelet, and a glowing arrow appears at my shoulder.

CHAPTER 26
Empathy Class

The lecture hall isn't far, and we're there in a matter of minutes. Students in the same blue jumpsuit as ours scurry around like ants trying to find seats among the smooth, white amphitheater rows. I scan for anyone I know without luck until I hear my name called.

"Jazz!"

Myra Toll is waving her arms above her head, strawberry blonde hair flying everywhere as she jumps up and down, drawing stares. I look around to see if anyone notices she's calling to me. Vox, of course, is laughing.

"Stow it. Go away," I hiss at her, but she follows me toward Myra, holding my hand up in a weak wave so she stops the sideshow.

"Is she always like that?" Vox breathes into the back of my hair, which sends an uneasy chill down my spine.

"Will you get away from me?" I say over my shoulder. Vox holds up her palms and widens her eyes in mock fear, then takes a few steps back...right into Liddick.

"Ladies," he says, chuckling. "You'll do me the honor of sitting next to me, won't you, Vox?" he says to her, maneuvering so she is on the other side of him and he is in the seat next to me. I roll my eyes and turn back to Myra, who is suddenly about five inches from my face.

"Hi! How was breakfast?"she asks, taking a seat.

"A little stressful, actually," I say, darting a glance at

Vox. "I was late. How was yours? I didn't see what the prepared meal was because I was hurrying," I answer.

"It was some kind of porridge with toppings and spices. I tasted something called an *agate fruit*; it's from somewhere down south. Isn't it nice that they try to bring in something from everyone's culture to make everyone feel represented?" Myra's big blue eyes flit from me to Liddick, then pause, fascinated on Vox.

"They can keep that thick green sludge I saw," Vox says, leaning forward over her knees and jabbing herself into our conversation around Liddick.

"Oh, that's kelp puree. It's not half bad! Joss's people have that all the time. Remember Joss, the Fisher?" Myra continues over my shoulder to Vox, whose eyes light instantly and color washes over her face. *So it's still Joss she's into then, not Arco?* I think.

"On your recommendation, I'll make sure to try it tomorrow," Liddick says, beaming every watt of his smile at Myra until our instructor quiets everyone.

"Good morning," the woman now standing down at the front of the room says. "Welcome to Empathy and Psychosomatic Systems. My name is Luz Reynolt."

She's dressed in a jumpsuit like ours, but hers is light blue. Her auburn hair reminds me of Fraya's the way it falls in loose waves around her shoulders, and her smile both lights up the room and calms it.

"Wow, she's beautiful," Myra whispers.

"Some of you may not be aware, or have only recently been made aware of the many different cultures here at Gaia, and I hope you are excited to learn about the similarities and differences among the many wonderful backgrounds. I, myself, am a native, born and raised in our fourth homestead quadrant like others in this room. We also have topside cultures such as Seaboard North, South, East, and West, as well as Skyboard and inland communities within those borders represented here today," Ms. Reynolt says, scanning the room.

Pictures of landscapes begin appearing behind her from floor to ceiling against the bowed back wall—underwater homesteads made of different, odd shapes that look like blown glass with uniform window pockets near the tops. They're all connected by air tunnel tubes with a big domed building in the center of the ring of pods that all the air tunnels funnel into. The next slide is of the woods, of rough construction houses with no seams or riveting of any kind. People start murmuring again, and Vox suddenly raises her voice over everyone.

"They don't call us inland culture. They call us Fringe," she says, startling those around us into silence, then pushing up her sleeves. "And those are stone houses, you tuhao, not clay. Maybe if you'd left your mountain once in a while you'd know that," she adds over the row of chairs in front of us where one girl suddenly elbows another hard in the chest, stopping her giggling.

"Hey!" the girl gapes at the one who just jabbed her.

"I'm sorry! I'm—I don't know why I did that," the other girl says, scratching the back of her head, confused.

"Vox!" I hiss over Liddick's lap, somehow feeling responsible. Liddick puts his hand on my knee to stop me from saying anything else.

"Yes, that is the colloquial term indeed, and I believe there is a term for Skyboarders and Shorelanders as well?" Ms. Reynolt extends her hand to us, palm up. Is she actually asking us to call the names out?

"Cloudies," a blonde girl a few rows over says. I strain to see her teeth, but can't make out if they are barred or not, though her eyes nearly glow the same ice blue as Dez's. Low murmuring starts all around the room again.

"Cred-Feds," Liddick says above it all, surprising me. *What is cred-fed already?* I think, and in answer to the question I didn't actually ask, he looks at me and nods. "That's what they call us," he whispers like he heard me.

I just stare at him, wondering why, and who calls us that? Fringe?

He turns back toward Ms. Reynolt. "People think Shorelanders don't have to work for their credentials… that they're just given to us—that the tests are written specifically for us, so they're easy. People just don't know about the pressure we have to pass, or that it's why so many of us do. We have to," Liddick talks like he's practiced this speech…like he's trying to rally the room.

"Well said, thank you," Ms. Reynolt beams. "And what's your name?"

"Liddick Wright. And I apologize; I just thought the term may need some clarification."

I realize my mouth is open and quickly close it. He's *really* good. The feeling in the room has gone from the paranoia of petty gossip to tolerance, even compassion.

"Of course. I believe it did." Ms. Reynolt looks around at everyone. I follow her gaze and see that several students are nodding. "Why do we have labels for people?" she asks us. "What do categories provide for society?"

No one answers for a long time, and the murmuring starts again. The pictures on the back wall rotate through the familiar scenes of the shore and our box style habitat complexes, our covered greenbed with its clear walls and ceiling, which runs the length of almost five of our habitat buildings and is the height of at least a few stacks. Then we see the scenes of the wooden, sun-bleached wharf with docked fishing boats and small wooden cabins, and finally, it scrolls through the factory complex where the Tinkerers live, which never seemed this gray or dirty back home.

"Security," Vox spits out of nowhere. I tense, and Liddick's sudden grip on my knee makes me realize that his hand hasn't moved from before. His eyes fix on mine.

*Let her go...*I hear in my head and feel myself flinch. It's his voice in my ear, but he hasn't said a thing.

Liddick? I say in my mind, feeling a little stupid for doing it, but his eyes widen, and he nods to my surprise. I blink at him, my heartbeat suddenly racing.

After class. Reynolt is looking at us, he thinks, and I pull my eyes away from his to refocus on the teacher.

"Very interesting. Please tell us your name and where you're from," Ms. Reynolt asks Vox.

"Vox Dyer. Seaboard North, *Fringe.* My clan are boundary scouts," she says as she stands, then defiantly pushes her sleeves the rest of the way up to reveal some of the winding bramble of her tattoos. The murmuring begins all over again, and I hear the word *cannibal* more than once. My stomach lurches, and I brace for something cold to hit me.

"Wonderful. Could you please elaborate on your answer, Miss Dyer? You'd mentioned we assign labels to people for security?" Ms. Reynolt asks delicately over the murmuring, which then quiets.

"People are afraid of what they don't understand. Put a name on someone, come up with a set of rules that you think defines them, and you can understand them. Nothing more to fear. But the problem is you *still* don't understand, you just think you do." Vox bites off her last word, takes a seat again, and spreads her arms wide over the backs of the chairs on either side, one arm extending across the back of Liddick's chair so far that her fingertips brush my shoulder. Her profile is defiant, chin up and out, which seems to dare anyone to contradict her, especially with her clan tattoos outlining the chiseled bridge of her nose, then arrowing down her throat. I'm surprised to feel proud of her, and a little envious too.

The sleek granite edifices of Skyboard North peek out of the mountain face like they're from ancient Greece on the back wall projection, then give way to tree lined streets with variations of the same basic two-story, single construction house and large swimming pools. The picture shifts again to the stone houses Vox called out, this time flanked by ragged forest and old women giving tattoos to young teenagers.

"Beautifully said, Vox. What she is referring to is a concept of self-preservation—even self-defense, if you will—called *incorporating abstraction.*" Ms. Reynolt says, taking a step toward the group and folding her hands in front of her. I lean forward, feeling pulled, despite the unresolved confusion I now have about what just happened with Liddick, who is looking straight ahead when I glance at him. "The human mind craves structure, and context is the vehicle of structure. In everything from our relationships to simply getting directions from one place to another, we are constantly building maps to meaning," Ms. Reynolt continues, looking up at Vox and smiling as she guides a strand of winding hair off of her cheek. "This is why we seek out context so ferociously when we are uncertain of our standing—when we are immersed in the abstract," she continues walking, opening her hands to the group. "If we feel someone may be judging us negatively, we become obsessed with minutia in their tone or body language until we can either confirm or deny our fear. We do this because upon this platform, we can base our next steps. It is no different from when we realize that we have made a wrong turn, and then try to situate the place where we are among all other places to gain context. We must first set parameters like this in order to feel secure because we are not born comfortable in the abstract, and so, we spend our lives trying to define it. To make it concrete."

Ms. Reynolt then waves her hand behind her, and a graphic of Ms. Rheen and Mr. Styx standing with several other people all wearing the same white Gaia uniform in front of the State building appears in place of the slideshow of our different communities.

"Who are they?" Myra whispers, and I blink several

times to pull out of what Ms. Reynolt was just saying.

"I'm not sure, other teachers and chancellors?" I answer as this picture gives way to a man in a long robe with his hands extended over a large crowd of people.

"Understanding this principle is the first step in empathic interaction. You all have shown a natural inclination for empathy among your peers, in your interviews, and may have even started to feel strange new sensations since arriving here at Gaia where there is a higher concentration of energies like your own." She waves her hand at the picture of the man in the robe in the slideshow, and it gives way to another man in a suit and tie—President Roosevelt, I think, from when we still had presidents—standing at the base of the Statue of Liberty, *actually* at the base of it before it was underwater. "Those who can harness the abstract for others who find it difficult provide an invaluable resource—as Vox has illuminated; this resource is security. These people are thus associated with comfort. They are trusted, even loved." She waves her hand again, and the picture changes to a 3-D image of Spokesman Cole Daniels, our smarmy, silver haired head of State.

"Welcome to Gaia, cadets. I look forward to your contribution to our thriving community," he says before the picture turns back into a cine frame, the vacant gray eyes frozen over a cold smile.

"But what if someone provides false security?" A boy on the other side of the room asks. "What if someone bends the abstract into a concrete that fits his own agenda? Like the dictators throughout history?"

Ms. Reynolt waits a beat and scans the room for volunteers to answer. None appear, so she directly asks us. "Who has a comment about this? Is it possible to tell the difference between those who are altruistic and those with a subversive agenda?" Ms. Reynolt scans the room again, which has now fallen completely silent as others start to look around.

"No, " Liddick says into the void now hanging in the air. "We never see it coming."

CHAPTER 27
Biotransfer and Culture

I turn to Liddick when we're dismissed to figure out how we could both talk without talking back there, but Vox buzzes like a fly around him all the way up the stairs and into the hallway en route to our next class, Biotransfer and Culture. Apparently, they're both in my cohort, so we have all the same schedule. The people who run this place must be trying to get me to kill her.

She laughs suddenly and threads her arm through his as we walk, and I roll my eyes, too exhausted by her impossible flirting with *everyone* to bother asking Liddick anything right now. I start walking fast enough to surpass our blue arrow, so I just call up one of my own.

You know you're the only one for me, Riptide, I hear Liddick say in my head, and whip around before I realize it. His smirk spreads into a full blown smile when he realizes I've heard him, and seeing the bewildered look on Vox's face is too satisfying for me not to smile too. I shake my head and turn to continue walking toward our next class, leaving them behind. Can he hear everything I'm thinking? It must be some kind of channel that I don't know how to turn on.

Arrived, the neural link arrow says after a few more turns, pulling me back into the moment, then dissipates. This room is bigger than the last, but the amphitheater seating is the same. Down near the front of the class I see

Arco, and start making my way down to sit by him when I run into Sarin. Her face folds in on itself in a scowl before a thin smile peels over her mouth and crinkles the corners of her eyes.

"What are *you* doing in this class? I thought you were in some kind of humanitarian love and kisses career field," she says, sitting herself down in the middle of the row and stretching out her legs so I can't get through. Crite, how does she get her hair pulled *that* tightly into a bun and still be able to blink?

"I thought you were in an ice-blooded vampire fish career field, sucking the hope and humanity out of everyone you meet," I say, smiling back at her and throwing my leg over the row of seats in front of us, then stepping down into that aisle and making my way toward Arco again. "But it looks like we're both going to learn how to turn ourselves into particle dust in here, so maybe I'll do extra credit and figure out how to keep you that way. It's what we humanitarians do," I smile over my shoulder at her and send her an air kiss.

"Skag," she says to my back. I hold up my hand, fingertips all touching to form a hole without turning around before I unfold the theatre-style seat next to Arco, who looks from my hand gesture to me.

"Crawl in a hole and die, huh? Ouch," he says, laughing. "What was that all about?"

"It's *Sarin,"* I say, and he nods.

"Say no more. How was your first class?"

"Strange. I mean, good, but strange. I think this place is doing something to us," I say, and he turns in his seat to face me, then looks around to see if anyone else is listening.

"I know it is," he says like he can't get it out fast enough. "Ever since we arrived, whenever I get too cooked about something—which is most of the time we've been here—I see these number sequences running in the corner of my eye. When I try to look at them, they just move to another part of my vision. The only way I can see them is peripherally. And it's only when I want to punch someone."

"Wait, numbers? When you get angry? And that's never happened to you before, not even that night at the port festival before we left?"

He shakes his head. "Maybe the tight feelings started then, but not the numbers. Not physically seeing them anyway. Not like here. What's happening with you?"

"You won't believe it," I say, then his expression flattens.

"Jazwyn."

"OK, OK. You know about Vox pushing me, so there's that, but now I can hear Liddick in my head, and he can hear me—we can talk that way, but I don't know how to control it or anything else about it. He seems to, though."

"What?" he says, shaking his head as if the whole thing is a spiderweb he's just walked into, face first.

"I know. It just started today, just last period. Our teacher said something about noticing things like this since we're surrounded by people with like energies now or something. What's happening to us here?"

"I don't know. My teacher told us we'd be noticing

changes, though, too. How does Wright know how to control it if it just started today?"

"He seemed just as surprised as I did when it happened, but then he figured it out somehow I guess," I answer.

"He's coming in right now with Vox. Can you hear her in your head too?"

"No, not like him. With her it's just more of a feeling of compulsion to do something or say something. It feels like it's my own instinct until it's too late, but I've noticed this little prickle in the back of my head when she tries it, so I'm getting better at stopping myself before I say something stupid."

"Here they come," he says, raising his chin to the door. I look to see Vox's arm is still linked with Liddick's as he scans the room, then I turn back around.

Where are you? I hear Liddick's voice in my head and flinch.

"What?" Arco says, suddenly looking at me hard. "What happened? Can you hear him?" he asks. I nod and close my eyes. Let's see if I can control this too.

Down front by Arco, I think without turning around to face Liddick.

All right, I see you, his voice answers in my head.

This is a thing we can do now? Is it all of us in the diplomacy field? How do we control this? I ask him.

I don't know, but it looks like we are controlling it.

"What's happening?" Arco says. "Hey, they're coming down here."

"I know. I told him where we were."

"You told him in your head?" Arco asks, and I nod once more. He opens his mouth to say something, but then closes it again.

"How'd you get here so fast, Hart?" Tieg says, coming down the row of seats behind us and surprising us both. Arco takes in a long, resigned breath and exhales all at once when he jumps over the back of the chair next to me and sits down. "Nice to see you again, Jazz." I turn away from Arco and smile at him, suddenly feeling awkward. "So they're going to teach us how to turn ourselves into atoms in here and not die—should be a good class." Tieg smiles, and I will myself not to stare at his teeth.

"I thought we were in classes by career field," I say to both Tieg and Arco, realizing that we're intermixing. "Guess we'll find out what we have in common. Sarin is in here with us too, and Liddick, and Vox," I nod, turning around to see Liddick and Vox almost to us, Vox still on his arm.

"Are they a thing now?" Tieg asks, his eyebrow cocked. "Didn't figure him to go for the...exotic type."

"No, she's just trying to annoy me," I say, shaking my head as I watch them navigate the stairs.

"Oh, so...*you're* with—?" Tieg looks at me tentatively, and I splinter.

"No!" I say too loudly and too abruptly. He flinches, then chuckles. "Sorry, I just finished telling someone else the same thing about another person," I say, turning all the way around in my seat toward the front of the room and folding my arms over my chest, then dart a glance at Arco as he shifts in his seat and tilts his head toward me.

I've literally been here four seconds. Whatever you're tweaked about, it wasn't me, I hear Liddick in my head, and can't help but laugh. Without turning around again, I can tell they've just sat down behind us. Arco and Tieg exchange glances, and Liddick suddenly claps them both on the shoulder.

"Gentlemen! How was your first class today?"Arco shrugs his arm forward and out of Liddick's grip before turning his back and to face completely forward like me.

"Decent. Fraya, Jax, Ellis, Pitt, and Dez were in there. Organic Systems and Theory," he says, then turns to me. "Basically, it's biology, but with a sick twist."

"What do you mean a sick twist?" Vox says, overhearing. Arco turns around to face her, and I suddenly feel heat radiating over my face and throat as I wonder how she was able to push him into almost kissing her earlier. I thought she could only push receivers. *Is Arco like me?*

"They had screen after screen of what this toxin out there does to the body. It was one giant campaign for anyone thinking about sneaking off campus—*be prepared to be turned into a cauliflower* by all the poisonous spores at this depth,"Arco says inside air quotes, then shudders in his seat.

Everyone's faces contort at that image, and Vox blurts out exactly what we're all thinking, "Why would they put a school here?"

"The school was here first," Tieg answers. "They put filters on the moon pools in each hub about 30 years ago because the spores started infecting people. The pictures were severe. It's impolite to describe it in front of ladies, though," he says, angling his head toward me and smiling. Arco closes his eyes, then subtly shakes his head, and I can feel his complete exhaustion with his roommate.

"So we're sitting in the middle of some kind of poison pit?" Vox interjects from behind us again.

"At least we're water tight in here, and there's no way the spores can get in the moon pool or the craft docks with the filtration," Arco says, his eyes still closed and his head now resting on the back of his chair. "There hasn't been a case in 30 years, anyway."

"Why doesn't everyone know about this?" I ask. "It seems like something everyone should know."

"I'm sure they'll brief everyone at some point," Tieg replies, again with that unnerving smile, but I'm saved when Liddick pulls everyone's attention to the woman walking down the aisle toward us with a low whistle.

She doesn't look at us when she passes by, her straight black curtain of hair nearly skimming the floor behind her like a long veil, sweeping from side to side with each step. Her jumpsuit is like Ms. Reynolt's from the last class, except instead of blue, hers is   a deep red. When she turns to face the class, her round, green eyes, which are offset by the color of her jumpsuit, snare us all.

"Wow," I say under my breath.

"Welcome, everyone. My name is Dame Mahgi, and this is Biotransfer and Culture," she says in a short, precise cadence, her voice almost echoing like the resonance after a bell. "In this class, you will learn safe passage through our connected world. It is a physically demanding process, so you will all be required to eat, sleep, and train differently than your peers who will not be in career fields that require extensive travel and interaction with other cultures." She extends the palm of her hand out, and flecks of light begin to appear a few feet from her. More and more appear until they start to take shape—the shape of a man. He doesn't move for several seconds after the particles of light stop, but then he blinks and smiles. His hair is brown, smoothed into one continuous wave over his head, and he's taller than almost anyone I've ever seen. His jumpsuit is white with a red sash over his shoulder. The class fractures into mumbles and gasps as Dice McClain's smile broadens just before he salutes the room.

"Welcome to Gaia Sur, cadets!" he says in a booming voice, and at the sound of it, everyone explodes into applause and cheers. Dame Mahgi smiles softly and nods to the room after the cheers begin to die down.

"Many of you recognize this man as Dice McClain, star of your favorite virtuo-cines. But did you know that he is also a Gaia Sur graduate?" Dame Mahgi asks, which causes the class to start mumbling all over again. "He comes to us from Skyboard North via Biotech transfer, also called port-call."

Dice McClain holds up his hands and wiggles his fingers. "Safer than swimming," he says with a smile, and as I look more closely, I see that his teeth are exactly like Tieg's, and I can't believe my eyes. How have I never noticed that before?

"How did he materialize? The port-cloud is topside?"

someone asks.

"Biotech Global and the Carbonetics Corporation are long-time patrons of Gaia Sur, and have graciously donated both the port-cloud and the atom synthetics that make incoming port-calls like this possible," Dame Mahgi explains without hesitation.

"Jax is never going to believe this," I whisper into Arco's shoulder, and he nods.

"Let me begin today by putting some of your potential fears to rest: port-call is completely safe," Dame Mahgi continues, "but it requires complete concentration and discipline. You have all demonstrated adequate base levels of these abilities, and when you have achieved optimal levels, you will be allowed to make assisted transfers to remote, trial assignments. For many of you, this will only take a few short months."

"Did you see how he was frozen there for a second?" Arco asks, studying Dice McClain as he stands in place next to Dame Mahgi. I nod.

"Does it hurt?" a boy from a few rows over calls out, and several people laugh. His face blanches as he rubs the back of his head, and I look at Vox, who's grinning. Anyone who had an advisory session in the Boundaries room knows the answer to his question, so I'm wondering what this poor kid did to inspire her *revenge via stupid question* hijack.

"Yes," Dice McClain says with a smirk, which stows everyone's hilarity. "It hurts to stay landlocked once you realize you're capable of transferring. And all of you in this room are, or at least you will be when Dame Mahgi is done with you," he says, and turns to face our teacher. "Well, I'll leave you to getting them registered. Always a pleasure, professor," he reaches for her hand, then kisses it before straightening up and facing us all again in a salute that slowly fades into glittering flecks of light until every trace of him is gone.

CHAPTER 28
Debriefing

"Busy morning for everyone I see?" Arco says, slipping into a seat next to Jax at the lunch table and stealing a grape from his tray, and I slide in next to him.

"Look at this," Jax says, shoving a paper in my direction. "We get to work on that. *That,*" he drills his finger into the paper. "The *Leviathan,* can you believe it? Look at those lines. See how the front just slides into the wing area? Seamless! Arco's training to pilot it. I'm training to run it."

I look over at Arco, who shrugs, quirking his eyebrows and then smirking as he looks away.

"You didn't tell me you might pilot that," I say, surprised. He looks back to me and raises an eyebrow.

"Well, you didn't ask," he says, taking a bite of his sandwich and trying to chew as his smirk widens into a smile. He swallows, then points with his sandwich to Jax. "He's the real hero. I can't pilot anything if he doesn't make all the systems work in the belly."

"It has a belly?" Vox stops chewing to ask, trying not to look horrified.

"That's what we call the core—the engineering room," Jax says, "you know, where all the guts are? *Guts* are in your *belly.*" Everyone just blinks at him as he raises his eyebrows at the table just before his mouth drops open. "Oh, come on, it's a perfect metaphor!" Chuckles begin to bubble around the table, but quickly die down as Fraya walks up looking scattered.

"What happened to you?" Vox asks as everyone is still processing her ghostly appearance, and Jax gets to his feet to help her into the seat.

"We practiced hemofusion today," she says, and swallows several gulps of the juice Jax offers her.

"Do I even want to know what hemofusion is?" he asks, reaching for her hand. "You're freezing cold."

"It's just extracting red blood cells by using ionic fusion instead of vacuum needles like we had at our inoculations. It was just a little hard to watch, that's all."

"You pulled red blood cells out of someone's—what, *through* someone's skin? And they pulled them through yours?" Jax takes both her hands in his now and rubs back and forth to try and warm them.

"Well, we put them all back. It was just strange," she says, now leaning more into Jax with a sheepish smile. "They said we'd get used to it."

"What class is *that?*" Avis asks.

"My second class this morning, Cellular Design and Infrastructure. Also known as Biodesign."

"You need to eat something," Jax says, taking the uneaten half of his sandwich from his plate, then, thinking better of the strawberry jelly dripping off, reaches for the bowl of sliced peaches on his tray and gives it to her with his unused spoon. She takes a bite, and color slowly starts returning to her face.

"I'll get you some water," Avis says, maneuvering out of his seat with a flip of his blue-tipped hair.

"Why did they make you do that?" I ask.

"To show us what can be done I suppose—what they can do. It doesn't hurt, but to see—well, it's not really a lunch topic," she says, stopping, but when everyone insists, she continues. "Well, to see the blood welling up through the skin in this little circle over your vein, then streamlining into the tube is disturbing. I mean, there is an instrument, but it's just the receptacle. The area is protected by an ion field, but you can't see that, so it just looks like you've sprung a leak that's being magnetically syphoned into a tube a few inches from your arm."

"Avis is going to split when he hears this," Ellis says, his face contorted in an effort to imagine what Fraya is describing.

"That's what I tried to think about when it was my turn. I could imagine him coming apart for it..the technology, you know? And like I said, it didn't hurt, but I guess I'd prefer to see the needle. There's something about knowing, does that make sense? Suddenly bleeding and not being able to see why, that's the worst part," she says, tucking her hair behind her ear, which looks darker in this muted light. "I just need to see it coming."

Arco and I immediately exchange glances as Avis appears with the bottle of water.

"What?" I ask before I know it. Fraya's color has returned now that she's finished eating the peaches that Jax gave her, but I've suddenly lost my appetite.

"The needle—there wasn't one, so it just started bleeding. At least with a needle you can see what's coming and brace for it," she says, taking the bottle of water from

Avis. "Thanks."

Arco darts another glance in my direction, then changes the subject. "Are you still hungry?" he asks Fraya.

"I'll go get the rest of your lunch," Jax stands.

"Thanks, but you need my bracelet. I can go. I'm fine now."

"Well, I'll go with you," he says. "Be right back," Jax nods to the table and walks Fraya to the serving station.

Ellis begins chattering to Avis, whose eyes widen almost immediately. They remind me of monkeys hopping between tree branches when they get like this.

"Mind if I join you?" Tieg says as he approaches our table, his eyes scanning quickly, then landing on me.

"We would just love it, but those two seats are taken by Jax and Fraya, so I'm afraid you'll just have to sit by Jazz," Vox says, her eyes flickering at me as she pops a grape into her mouth and grins.

"Perfect," he answers and slides in next to me. I try to move over to make a little more room for him, but bump into Arco.

"Sorry," I say, raising my eyebrows at him. "Could you slide down a little, please?"

He lowers his eyelids and pulls whatever he's going to say into the corner of his mouth, opting then not to say it at all as he slides over a few inches.

"So what's your career field?" I ask.

"Astronavigation," he answers, tossing a cube of cheese into his mouth.

"Stars? Down here?" Vox asks, arching an eyebrow.

"I know, it sounds counterintuitive, doesn't it?" he says, pushing his dark blond hair off his forehead, the increased surface area making his blue eyes stand out even more. "It's fascinating, and the Leviathan ship is fierce."

"Isn't that the same ship Jax was just slobbering about?" Vox asks, then snags the paper he left behind. "Is it this?" she asks Tieg, holding up the paper.

"That's the one," he answers after he swallows.

"Wait, so Astronavigation...does that mean those are topside crafts too?" I ask.

"Not exactly. They call the field Astronavigation because the Leviathan systems can tell where the stars are all around, even on the other side of the world by sending signals through the seafloor," he nods to the table, acknowledging their skeptical looks. "I know—it sounds flayed, right?" he says, lacing with a laugh and popping another cube of cheese into his mouth.

"And you simply *must* explain how it does *that,*" Vox says, forcing her eyes wide and resting her chin in her hands, tapping her fingers on her cheekbones in mock anticipation. I glare at her as I fight the tickle in my stomach to laugh, then press my fingernail into the tingle at the back of my neck until it hurts.

"Well, it just scans, then it reads the feedback and reports the findings to the console for the pilot's interpretation," he says, nodding and picking up another cube of cheese. Ellis's eyebrows draw together as he opens his mouth to say something, but Vox cuts him off.

"Fascinating. And are there *thingies* that make it work?

Arco, you're a pilot, tell us about how the *thingies* help you interpret the stars," she says removing one of her hands to pick up a cherry tomato and toss it into her mouth without looking down at the plate, then returns her hand and blinks purposefully a few times. The tickle comes back, and I push it down again and clench my jaw. Why does she try to embarrass *everyone?* We've only been here a few days—no one knows how anything works yet.

"Vox, you know what—" I start, but Arco laughs and covers my hand with his.

"It's OK," he says, and sets down his glass of water before replying just as Jax and Fraya return to the table with her tray. "The vessel has these internal sonic graphing machines that shoot a pulse through the source material—so in this case, the ocean floor—in two beams. One keeps going, and the other ricochets off what it runs into and fires back information that basically turns into a picture."

"Like a capture," Ellis elaborates for the table.

"A *laser* capture," Avis corrects, and Ellis rolls his eyes.

"Right. Then it compiles that data and turns it into a 3-D image that the pilot can pull up on the screen. So, not only can you see where the stars are on the other side of the world, even through the seafloor, you get a picture of whatever is between you and those stars too," he says.

Ellis nods, apparently satisfied with Arco's explanation. Arco is apparently satisfied with his explanation too as he finishes off the last bite of his sandwich and smiles at Tieg, who just narrows his eyes in return.

"So you'll be learning to drive a vessel that can read

the stars in any direction...even through the earth's *core?"* Vox asks almost obnoxiously, then turns a loaded eye on me. At first I glare at her, but then it hits me. *My father and the others, of course,* I think. She sees the realization dawn on my face, then, pinches the bridge of her tattooed nose, and I suddenly feel like the stupidest person in the world for not making the connection earlier. I turn to look at Arco, who's expression has gone from smug to resolved.

"Has anyone seen Liddick?" he asks, and rises to go check in his tray.

CHAPTER 29
Endurance and Survival - Part One

After lunch, the guide arrow stops at the mouth of a set of steel double doors, the light placard on the side reading **Endurance and Survival 1 — Tark.** There's something different in the air here making it thicker, or warmer, or both, and I find myself standing for a minute before reaching for the handle to open the door, which is dense, and heavier than I anticipated.

"Is something wrong?" Tieg asks, coming out of nowhere at my shoulder and pulling the door the rest of the way open for me.

"Nothing, sorry. It just feels different here, doesn't it?"

"How so?"

"I don't know, just…"

"Harder to breathe," Vox says, now at my other shoulder. She crosses in front of me and takes Tieg's arm, escorting him down the stairs as he looks over his shoulder with wide eyes and smiles.

Inside, the air is even thicker—so thick I expect to be able to see the difference when I look across the room. There are no individual chairs like in the last class, only a long, arcing bench that runs around the perimeter of the room with little foot locker-sized spaces underneath, each about a foot apart. The floor in the middle is black and multileveled, and the ceiling is a labyrinth of thin cylinders, lenses, and nozzles with tubing attached. *What a wild room,* I think.

I bet we haven't seen the half of it, I hear Liddick's voice in my head, and jolt.

Can you just always listen to my thoughts or what? I answer.

You're the one transmitting. I only hear what you send out.

What do you mean what I send out? Vox said I'm a 'sponge.' I can't send anything out.

Well, you just did.

Where are you? I think, impatient to tell him about the Leviathan and what it can do.

"Sit by the door," Liddick says, instantly and from nowhere at my side, scaring about a year off my life.

"Crite, why does that keep happening to me?" I ask, feeling the adrenaline hit my bloodstream and my heart begin to pound in my chest.

"Because you're nervous. Everyone is nervous the first day of classes. It's in the air," he says, nodding matter-of-factly.

"If you know that then *why* did you sneak up on me?"

"Because I got to watch you jump," he replies with a smirk and a wink before walking toward the bench along the wall. I shake my head. "Come on. I've heard this teacher hooks the first person he sees for a demonstration, and we don't want that to be us."

I follow him to a seat near the door and start scanning the room for people I might know. Jax and Pitt are sitting directly across from us talking energetically about something, but Jax looks up almost immediately and waves, then gestures for me to look to my right. When I do, I see

Tieg and Arco about 10 feet away, still not acknowledging the other's presence, and Vox has disappeared into the sea of faces.

I don't have time to scan any more of the room for her before a circle of blue lights appears in the black floor down in front of us. The panels beneath the lights open like a flower from left to right, and a platform with a tall black man in a green jumpsuit rises up through the circle. I know this must be the instructor, Mr. Tark, and swallow hard, pressing as far into the wall behind me as I can.

Liddick looks over at me and raises an eyebrow, almost as imperceptibly as the new smirk fighting with the corner of his mouth.

Stow it, I think, not sure if he'll even hear it or not.

What a jelly.

You said we shouldn't get picked. I don't want to get picked.

That doesn't mean I'm a jelly.

Liddick's smirk breaks free, but he is quick to reset his face before turning his eyes to the platform.

"Cadets," Mr. Tark's voice is deep and quiet. "Welcome to Endurance and Survival. You are here today because your career paths involve travel, and you will need to know how to operate in the event you become stranded," he says in a slow, even tone as he looks around the room like he's choosing which one of us he's planning to eat. He stands with his chest pushed out and his hands clasped behind his back, his lanyard catching whatever breeze must be up there flicking it back and forth. He takes a few steps off the platform and taps something into a metal cuff he wears on his forearm. In seconds, the walls shift from the opaque gray with white trim to a frontage of beach that surrounds us, which gives way to a wide sky and rolling sea.

"Whoa," I say, not realizing it is out loud until I hear my own voice.

"This is our arena, our continent, our world. When you come to this class, you will not be practicing survival, you will be surviving," Tark continues, louder now over the sound of the waves crashing. It's all so real, even down to the smell of salt in the air. I feel my throat tighten at the memory of home, everything there now seeming like it happened in another lifetime.

The temperature cools with the breeze blowing in over the water...well, from what must be the tubing in the ceiling. I look up to find it so I can confirm my speculation, but those tubes and cylinders have been replaced by a wide open blue sky, a bright, blinding sun, and wispy swatches of white clouds. It's like we've been transplanted here, teleported. Has that *happened?* Are we still in this room? I'm still sitting on this bench, aren't I?

"Wh—!" the girl next to me jumps up and looks at where she's just been sitting to find that it's a rock, not a bench. I look across the room at where Jax and Pitt are sitting and find a sand dune. Everyone has been repositioned.

"Are we still in the room?" I ask Liddick, hoping his virtuo-cine expertise will pay off as we abruptly stand.

"I think so," he says, touching the rocks behind us. "The rocks are cool. Real rocks would have been baking in this sun all day."

I feel myself exhale in relief, but just as I do, everyone on Jax's side of the beach suddenly gasps as they look in our direction. Over my shoulder I see 10 large, angry looking men running toward us in the distance. The wall has disappeared completely, or expanded out to accommodate them coming at us from what must be a hundred feet away, but I don't understand why, or what has just happened. Why are they so angry?

Everyone gets to their feet at once, and as soon as they do, they start searching for their tablets, but everything has turned into sand under our feet. I stumble backward and am sure I will fall until Liddick grabs my upper arm and sets me right.

"What's happening?" I ask him. "Why do they look like they want to kill us?"

"I don't know, but we need to move," he says.

"Where? And why do we have to move? This isn't even real, right? The rocks were cold," I hear the panic in my voice, but I'm not sure why. I know this isn't real. I saw Tark call it up on his wrist control. I know I am not afraid, even though the hammering in my chest suggests otherwise.

Where are we supposed to go?

We didn't do anything...what's wrong with them?

I can almost hear the voices, almost believe they're actually my own thoughts, but they're not. They're not Liddick's either, and Vox can only push me to express something I'm already feeling...this experience is something new. People are beginning to cry, and some have started running down the beach only to be chased back by people running from that end too. Some try to jump into the water, but waves roll up and force them back. My heart feels like it is going to jump out of my chest now, and my lungs begin to burn. Tears well up in my eyes and blur my vision, and I realize I need to get control of the chaos. These are not my feelings, they are everyone else's—they have to be because despite the way my body is responding, I *am not* this terrified.

I close my eyes, take a deep breath, and replay the image of Mr. Tark tapping his arm panel. I replay the image of the walls falling away and this beach terrain appearing. My heartbeat slows down and the tears that threatened to choke me start subsiding, it's working... Relax, they're not real. *They're all part of a cine he brought up,* I say to myself.

I open my eyes, and some of my classmates have stopped scrambling. I turn around to face the oncoming drove, and see that Jax, Arco, Pitt, Joss, and Tieg have crossed to our side of the beach. Their faces are stern and their eyes are set on the approaching men.

"It's OK. It's going to be OK. It's a cine," I say to the people skittering around me. "Touch those rocks. They're cool. How could they be cool if they were sitting in this hot sun all day?" It comes out all at once, and I don't even know from where. All the panic I had been feeling—other people's fears—all of it is gone now, and I just feel compelled to get the truth out as fast as possible. I look over at Liddick and concentrate as hard as I can.

Are you pushing me? I think, *Are you making me say this stuff?*

He shakes his head. *You're doing it,* I hear, and he nods to our classmates behind us, who are now taking steps forward, calmly. *You're doing all of it.*

When the charging people are about 20 feet from us on all sides, they stop. I hear a few people in the class still sobbing, but everyone else seems to have regained their composure. If I did that, I don't know how. I was just trying to make myself and the few people near me feel better, but maybe that's all it takes?

In seconds, we're all pushed into the center of this growing circle of wild looking strangers. I still don't see Vox anywhere, but Jax has found Fraya, and rejoins Arco, Joss, Pitt, and Tieg just behind Liddick and me.

As the strangers get closer, they remind me of the Fringe back home, only instead of tattooed skin, theirs is decoratively scarred. Their clothing is a combination of leather and canvas, small bones, and woven fabrics, and they all still look angry.

"*Vahg!*" One of the larger men growls and points to me. "*Vahg ipsti!*" the man yells again and starts toward us. I jump, not recognizing the language as even one of the Tinkerer's dialects, and my heart pounds against my ribs again as Arco pulls my shoulder back, which makes me stumble right into Jax's chest. The man begins walking quickly toward us, but I wriggle out of Jax's grasp. Liddick catches my arm and pulls me back again. I tug, but his grip closes around me more tightly.

"Are you split? Where are you going?" he whispers.

"Let me go," I say, wrenching free and pushing my way back to the front, ducking between Arco and Tieg as I hold up my hand to say stop. This makes the man approach even faster, and I don't know why I step toward him, but I do.

"Jazz!" Arco yells as I rush past him. I wave him off, then show both of my hands to the oncoming man. It's suddenly very important to me that he sees them empty.

"See! You see? Nothing's there," I say, and he stops advancing. My mind races from thought to thought. I can't talk to this person. He won't understand anything.

*But I didn't do it...*I feel from somewhere deep, a need to protest, to defend myself, but...*what didn't I do?* I look back at Liddick, whose expression blanches.

I don't know either. Just breathe. They think we're hiding something. You feel that?

But it's more...not just hiding something; they think we've taken something, I respond.

"Ishti, wah!" the man juts out his chin and lowers his eyes to my jumpsuit pocket, which I pull inside-out to show him that it's as empty as my hands.

"Nothing, see?" He starts looking around at the others, his eyes darting, hunting, then takes several more steps toward me, but I know I can't back away even though every muscle in my body is pulling in that direction.

Letting my eyes drop from his is a mistake. The man pulls a long, sharpened stick from his belt and grabs my throat with one hand while sticking the tip of it just below my ear. I can feel the sharp, biting point pressing in and wonder how this can be a virtuo-cine...if that's actually what it is?

All of the other men brandish similar sticks and take a

few steps toward us as I suck in a breath, barely feeling the ground under my tiptoes. From the side, I see Jax spring forward with Arco, but I hold up one hand to them while holding onto the man's forearm with the other.

"Stop—*stop!* It's OK," I try to say, stretching my neck for air. "They think we've... taken something. Show your...hands...and get down."

The man's icy fingers loosen just a fraction, and I pull in as much of a breath as I can. I move my eyes back to his, and realize that we're so close that I can see the tiny balls of chalky powder and clay in his eyebrows that make up his pale coloring.

"Listen to her, she's right," Liddick says, moving toward me now as the first to follow through. "Everyone get down, show your hands." Most in our group comply immediately, and the strangers relax their stances and sticks just a little. "We just have to explain to them somehow, so everyone just be still—no sudden movements," Liddick continues.

The man doesn't release me, but he relaxes his grip on my throat when the last reluctant few drop to a knee, except for Jax and Arco, who are crouched like they're on a G-ball defensive line.

"It's OK, you especially. Stop looking like you want to fight and just trust me," I insist, and Jax finally, slowly takes a knee. "Show them your palms—empty hands."

"Do it," Liddick says to Arco and Jax, who begrudgingly follow suit.

"Ipsti. Vahg ipsti..." the leader, with his matted locks of

brown hair and diamond pattern scarred skin repeats, not as violently this time, but his hand is still around my throat, and I can still feel the needling of the stick in the soft tissue below my jawline.

"Nic ipsti, vahg stolis," a voice from somewhere behind me says, but I don't recognize the guttural tone until she comes into my line of sight.

"Vox?" I whisper.

She sends me a quick, warning glance and a subtle head shake. The man says something long and complicated to the others, sheaths his stick, then looks back at Vox and holds out five of his gold ringed fingers like he's expecting her to give him something.

"Nic, ya nori ipsti wahg," Vox replies, her tone cold and firm as she pulls up her pant leg to reveal her tattoos. She points to her face, and finally, unzips the front of her jumpsuit to show the network of tattoos on her sternum. The strangers gasp, then take a step backward and immediately lower their eyes. The leader finally lets me go, and I stumble backward as my feet connect with the ground. He raises the small shell around his neck to his lips and blows, creating a high-pitched tone, which seems to be the cue to retreat.

We all watch them go, and no one from our class breathes, let alone moves until the men are about 50 feet away. As soon as I can, I cross quickly to Vox in the general scramble of everyone murmuring about what just happened before either of us can be intercepted.

"Where were you, and why do you speak barbarian?" I ask, my throat tight and sharp on the inside.

"I had to listen to some of the others muttering in the back. They weren't saying enough for me to completely learn it, though."

"Learn what?" I ask, coughing as I see Jax, Fraya, and Arco moving toward me.

"Their language."

"You can do that after a few minutes? I thought it took you most of the night when you fell into that hole in The Badlands," I ask quickly before I have to answer a hundred questions for the others. She shrugs.

"I thought so too, but it was easier just now. I felt like all I had to do was listen."

"The nanites..." I say to the ground as I continue putting the pieces together, then look back at Vox. "What did they think we took?"

"They thought we were here stealing eggs or something. Or maybe it was stones?" she says, her eyebrows digging in as she thinks back, then abandons it. "I don't know. I just told them we weren't thieves. Oh, and that I was a god," she says through a crippled laugh, then swallows, and for the first time I see that she's breathing hard. She was afraid. "Then he said we had five minutes to prove it, or die," she continues, holding up her hands dramatically and rolling her eyes, and I smile at the realization that I am finally able to see through her masks. "And I just—what?" she stops abruptly, then quirks her eyebrows and makes her way past me to pick up a handful of sand rather than waiting for my reply. "This is surreal—touch it."

I follow her and move my hand under the sand, which

is cool like the rocks.

"Jazz! Are you all right?" Jax bounds into our space and squares my shoulders with his big gorilla hands.

"Let me see your throat," Fraya says, gently moving her fingers over my neck.

"I'm fine, I'm *fine*," I say as she takes a deep breath and hugs me once Jax lets me go. I catch Arco's expression over her shoulder, his eyebrows drawn together and up, and his jaw clenched so hard I can see the striations of the muscles under his cheekbones.

"I can't watch you like that again," he says so quietly I almost don't hear him, then nods once before backing out of the fray and making his way to the outer circle, out of earshot even if I did know how to respond.

"Are you sure you're OK?" Fraya asks, taking one more look at my throat.

"Yes, it's a little sore, but I'll live," I say, then move a step back. Ellis and Avis stumble over each other to give me some space, and I look around for Vox to finish my questions while everyone starts to dissipate. I turn around and find her crouched over what's become a small pile of sand as she scoops and spills it onto a tiny mountain.

"So it was your tattoos? That's why they thought you were a god?" I ask her.

"The scars," Liddick says as he walks up behind us with Tieg, Myra, and Joss as Jax and the others filter back and watch the men get smaller in the distance. He turns to face Vox once he's close enough and repeats himself. "It was their scars, wasn't it?"

She nods to the sand and gathers up another handful, "They wanted confirmation, deep down anyway. I could feel them wondering about my face, like a deference or a hope or something, so thought maybe whatever they believe in has markings too," she stands and looks out at the strangers, now specs against the horizon. "So, I showed them some. People are always searching for others from their tribe."

The sky begins to dissipate, and the sea beyond us fades to gray and white. Our benches return, and the sand gives way to solid flooring again as Mr. Tark comes into view on the platform, smiling.

CHAPTER 30
Endurance and Survival - Part Two

"Miss Ripley, Mr. Wright, and Miss Dyer...you three have been making quite a name for yourselves around here already," Mr. Tark says, surprised, and the hairs stand up along the back of my neck. Liddick laughs and turns to face the rest of the class.

"Thank you, thank you all... I don't know about the ladies, but I'll be signing autographs in the student center at the end of the day, if you insist," he says, a huge grin spreading over his face as chuckles erupt around the room. He looks over at me, and I know he's trying to take this bullet all by himself once I see Mr. Tark's golden eyes narrow, but not a chance.

"We've just been trying to do our best, Mr. Tark," I say a little too abruptly. The giggles die down, and Tark's eyes dart from Liddick to me, then back to Liddick before turning to look out over the group.

"Someone tell me what happened here," he asks, causing everyone to stare at us as we take our seats along the bench again. I start to feel hot now, and I don't dare move. After what seems like several minutes, Myra finally breaks the tension.

"Vox learned the strangers' language," she answers, smiling, "and Jazz did too, but in a different way."

"Explain," Tark presses her, folding his arms in front of him and curling a finger under his chin. "What was different about the way the two ladies worked this situation?"

"They weren't the only ones. Liddick knew what was going on too. It was all three of them," Avis adds, and I can't help but smirk when I feel Liddick's sincere lack of appreciation at being pulled back into this, despite how heroic he just tried to be.

"But how? How did they just know?" a wiry boy with neatly cut, red hair and an exasperated clip in his voice asks. Mumbles begin to ripple across the room, and everyone looks at us accusatorially. Tark sighs and presses his lips into a thin half smile as his hunting eyes drift to the upper corner of the room. I follow his gaze, but only see more pipes and tubing. "I'm glad you asked that question, Mr…?"

"Parker, from Seaboard South," the boy answers.

"Mr. Parker," Tark nods and squares his stance. "As you will soon discover, some of you are Empaths—You're either Projectors, Receivers, or the best of both worlds, Readers. Some of you are Coders, Navigators, and some of you simply have the misfortune of being hard to kill; that's why you're here. My job is to teach you how to cultivate these skills, how to adapt to situations, and how to overcome obstacles," he says, scanning the room again. People begin looking around at each other, and I feel the tension start to die down.

See? He just said we're not the only ones, Liddick says in my head, and I nod to him.

"Some of you probably feel completely out of your element," Tark continues, folding his hands behind his back again as he steps down from the platform and makes his way over to us. "Suddenly, things are happening to you here, and you feel out of control," he continues. Liddick doesn't move, but I can feel him bracing in the seat next to me as Tark walks past us, turning his head over his shoulder to keep us in his peripherals. "But you will need to transcend your environment."

Vox is several seats down, and I feel a sense of calm from her when I look over, though it's not right. I try to focus on her more, to study her face and see what this scrambled feeling I have about her is, but her expression reveals nothing, not even as Tark gets closer to her.

He has to be a pusher. Can you feel him trying to intimidate us? I think toward Liddick.

He can try, but he won't. Especially not her, he replies in my mind.

But she's afraid. She's projecting calm, but I can tell she's afraid.

I know. I can feel it too, but it doesn't matter as long as he doesn't know that.

"And some of you thought you knew what you were doing, but have discovered that you don't know the half of what you can do, and you won't unless we put you in situations that make your subconscious see the *need* to figure it out." Tark continues, stopping now in front of Vox's seat and seeming to speak directly to her. I watch her closely and can feel her calm eroding. It pushes against my ribs like it's trying to get out, but can't as she struggles against it, trying to pull it back into herself because she doesn't want to seem afraid. She straightens her back and tosses her dark red hair, lifting her chin in a gesture of casual defiance as a tolerant smile starts to make its way across her face. Her yellow eyes gleam against her pale skin, but there's no mistake, not after I felt her nerves back on the beach and again just now; she's terrified. I have to do something.

"But why?" I blurt, getting to my feet—the words having come out before I'd actually planned what to say or do next. He turns from Vox slowly, takes a measured breath, and settles into a smile as he tilts his head toward me. "Why are these abilities just coming out in us now if they're so natural? Why here?" I ask, even though I already heard the answer in Ms. Reynolt's class.

The room begins to stir again after my question, and I want to look away from Tark, to look at the floor, at anything, but just like the native man with the scars, I know that I can't risk breaking eye contact with him.

He must see right through me because his smile suddenly peels back into a menacing grin, revealing bright white teeth in sharp contrast to his dark skin. He laughs low in his throat, and I can't help but see him as a panther—everything about him from the way he walks, long, measured, and smooth steps, to the way he stares not at me, but into me, his golden eyes like Vox's, intense and unblinking.

"Why…" he says, taking a step toward me, then another. *I won't sit down, I won't look away,* I think as he slows down noticeably with each step until he's about four feet in front of me, then three, then two, then leaning in as if any minute he will pounce and rip my throat out. I feel like crossing my arms over myself, but I suddenly remember Ms. Wren's advice about body language being telling, and stop. I don't want him to think for one second that he intimidates me, so I try to stand as tall as I can, feeling my shoulders square as I put my hands on my hips like Ms. Wren explained. *Look bigger, and you'll feel bigger,* she'd said, and when I feel the small tickle at the base of my skull, I know that Vox is helping to stoke this particular ember. For once, I don't mind her pushing me. *He's testing you. Just wait him out. He's not going to do anything to you.* Liddick's voice is barely audible in my head because I can't spare any concentration to make it stronger. "Why are your abilities coming out now..." Tark repeats my question like he's trying to taste each word in his mouth.

I bite the side of my lip to keep my voice from trembling, then force an answer out. "Yes. Why are these abilities here all of a sudden, and why now?" I insist. Mr. Tark's eyes seem to flicker like two small flames, but then his toothy grin softens into a genuine smile. At once I feel a deluge of relief pour over me, and I let out the breath I'd been holding.

"Well done, Miss Ripley," he says very quietly, and in just that second his eyes transform from predatory to warm and kind. "And that's a very good question," he says to the group in a louder voice now, still low, but no longer with the intimidating reverberation it had.

What just happened? What was that? I think in an avalanche, hoping Liddick has answers.

I think someone else is watching us, he replies, and I look over to him. *Watching you.*

Tark turns on his heel to face the class while clasping his hands in front of him, then starts making long, slow strides.

"Why have some of you been able to feel what others are feeling ever since you arrived? Why have you been able to influence others, or to suddenly see numbers in your peripheral vision that enable you to do calculations and run scenarios in your head instantaneously? Why have you been able to sense the right direction and calculate perfect trajectories even though you have no point of outside reference, and why can you suddenly talk to each other without even saying a word?" he asks, his eyes scanning the room. "Gaia Sur is designed to bring out the best in all of you, to maximize your potential. Your latent abilities have only begun to develop now because you're surrounded by like minds, like sensitivities, and there is strength in numbers. If you have not experienced anything significant yet as the result of your nanite catalysts, you will. You're all here because your careers need you at your best, and like it or not, my job is to show you what that looks like."

CHAPTER 31
Cross Curriculum Interface

I leave *Endurance and Survival* with my teeth together, not out of anger, but stress, and move as quickly as I can through the crowd funneling out of the room. The final class of the day is *Cross Curriculum Interface,* and I don't think I can do it—not after this last class, at least not yet. I break away from the quickly moving current of students once we get to the student center and walk toward the window, then press my cheek against the cool, clear material that has to be something other than glass. I close my eyes, trying to listen to my breathing, another strategy Ms. Wren taught us. Remembering this about her makes me think of home, of my mother and Nann, and then of my father. It dawns on me that I never told Liddick about the Leviathan's capabilities like I'd so adamantly planned to just a few hours ago, and I shake my head in frustration. *What is happening to me? How could I forget to tell him something like that?* I wonder, and slowly let out the deep breath I'd taken in a few seconds prior.

I already know, Rip, stop beating yourself up. You were busy negotiating with beach Fringe, remember? Liddick's voice in my head makes me smile against the window, but I can't bring myself to open my eyes until I feel his hand on my shoulder turning me around.

"Liddick, that was—"

"I know. The Navigators or Coders can deal with that split show next time," he says, throwing an arm around my shoulder, which I don't shove off like I usually do when he tries to do this in public. "One more class, and then we're free," he says, raising his bracelet cuff to his chin. "Cross Curriculum Interface," he says, and a blue arrow guide appears.

"The Leviathan—" I start to say, but he waves me off.

"I know. And we'll see it firsthand in a minute from what I hear," he says as the guide arrow weaves us through a few more corridors, then stops in front of another amphitheater style classroom with a center stage, but everything in here is metal, a brushed nickel stage area, steel beams, even the rows of benches and the walls are a smooth metal finish. I look around at the mono-chromatic surroundings in search of the teacher, but everyone is wearing a blue jumpsuit.

This is the splittest room yet, I think toward Liddick as we enter, but he doesn't reply. "Isn't it?" I ask him aloud, and he looks at me, surprised.

"Isn't what?" he asks, confused.

"You didn't hear me?" I ask. He understands immediately and looks at me hard.

"No. Did you just hear me?"

"Just now?" I ask, and he nods. I shake my head. He pulls me back into the corridor several feet from the door and scans my face.

I'm going to contact my friend tonight with or without Hart's help, I hear him say in my head. When he sees that his message registers, his face relaxes.

How? I ask him, but he just shakes his head. *Not enough time to talk about it now, and the room is blocking us, so I'll explain later tonight,* he thinks. As if in punctuation to Liddick's sentence, a low bell sounds once, and then again to apparently signify the start of class, or maybe just the dramatic entrance of the teachers, who walk into the room in a single line from behind a metallic divider. We quickly walk back into the room and find a seat.

There are five teachers, including Dame Mahgi from the Biotransfer class, Ms. Reynolt from the Empathy class, Mr. Tark, and two more I don't know. The first isn't as tall or as athletic as the second, but he's fit, if a little wiry. He seems to be too young to have streaks of silver running through his thick black hair, which falls into his eyes as he nods at some students he seems to know. He pushes a hand through it, then hooks his thumbs on the pockets of his yellow jumpsuit. The other teacher is in red with green bars on his shoulders, very tall, and athletic, almost as athletic as Mr. Tark. His intense blue-eyes stand out in contrast with his short, closely cropped white hair, though his face is relatively young, maybe early 30s, with angular features like Tieg's.

"Who are the last two?" I ask Liddick, who just shakes his head.

"The one with the white hair is Dr. Denison, the Nav and Technics teacher," Avis says, suddenly leaning over my shoulder from nowhere like the ninja spider monkey he is. "Arco, Jax, Joss, Pitt, and what's his brother's name, Tiger or something? We all had Denison this morning in

Systems Navigation."

"He doesn't look old enough to be a doctor," I whisper back to Avis, who nods in agreement.

"I know, but he's 63!"

"NO—" I say, catching how loud I am, then sink into my seat. "No, he's not. There's no way."

"Nanotech, baby," Avis says, working his mouth into a satisfied smile and nodding as he leans back.

"Good afternoon. Please take your seats," Dr. Denison says, his voice leveled and warm. He takes a few steps away from the other teachers and puts his hands in the pockets of his red jumpsuit until most people are seated, then, begins talking again. "This class is called Cross Curriculum Interface. Its purpose is to teach you about your individual predispositions, as well as the biological enhancements currently at work to hone them. My name is Briggs Denison. I teach Systems Navigation, as well as Biodesign here at Gaia Sur. You may already recognize my colleagues, Dame Mahgi, our Biotransfer and Culture mentor, Luz Reynolt, our Empathy and Psychosomatic Systems mentor, Callum Stryker, our Encoding and Infra-structures mentor, and Skellik Tark, our Adaptations mentor. We would all like to welcome your cohort to campus," he says, and bows slightly at the waist to the room, the other teachers following his lead.

"If this is our whole first year group, the rest of us from Seaboard North must be in here somewhere—Fraya, Sarin, Myra…" I whisper to Liddick, who begins scan-ning. "Jax and Pitt are over there," I say, gesturing to the other side of the class, but I can't find anyone else in the sea of faces.

"You will be assigned a sub-cohort in here—a team made up of individuals who will each bring a diverse and necessary aspect to Gaian society, which is to say, the emerging global society, considering our sister campuses operate in much the same way." Denison continues, waving his hand to bring up a slideshow that takes up the whole back wall, floor to ceiling.

The first picture is of people our age sitting around a table in blue jumpsuits like ours, one of them talking and gesturing to something on the projected green lined, digital grid in the middle of the room, and the others looking transfixed. The next image is of a medical bay with two students performing an operation of some kind while another in their group has his eyes closed in concentration as he touches the temples of the unconscious patient. The next picture is of three students sitting in front of their own panel of levers and buttons and a huge window that peers out into darkness.

"Is that the Leviathan?" I ask Liddick, who shakes his head and shrugs.

"Whether your career fields involve extensive travel or not, you will all be skillfully prepared in cultural interaction. No one career field is an island unto itself. You will see how you are all connected, how it is necessary for you all to work together to perform certain duties, and how vital each one of you is to the successful operation of the machine that your unit will become," Denison says, clasping his hands in front of him as people begin to mumble and look around at each other. "Until graduation, your sub-cohorts will become pod teams of roughly 8-10 members, as your advisors may have already explained to you. You will serve a territory of roughly 700 homesteads or State residents within a 2,000-mile expanse, and if a crisis occurs, your pod may be mobilized to combine with other pods to deliver first responder care, or to open a line of dialogue with State liaisons, and much more. The teams are the grounds upon which the State began building Gaia nearly a hundred years ago, and they are what has kept our society thriving ever since."

"Is that permanent? All the traveling like that?" I ask Liddick again, and this time he looks at me under raised eyebrows.

"I've been here just as long as you, Riptide," he says, smiling to one side. I tilt my head toward him and exhale. The one time I actually count on him to know as much as he acts like he does.

"After graduation, you'll be placed into a career field that best utilizes your honed skill sets, the foundations of which you are coming to understand already. Rest assured, you are in no danger whatsoever from your newly realized abilities—they are part of your natural biology. Much of what you can now do has manifested because similar energies on campus have organically helped to stimulate the nanites in your systems, which in turn act as enhancers to help you learn how to hone your new skill sets. This is the way we prefer things to happen, but understand that the nanites have not created anything that was not already present within each of you. That said, if your proclivities have not yet broken through, don't worry, they will. Please access your student profiles and follow the prompts at this time to discover your official classifications." Denison raises his forearm to demonstrate, and a blue digitized 3-D screen appears in front of him. "As you can see, I am a Hybrid, Classification Coder and Navigator."

I look at Liddick, then think better of asking him anything else as he looks at me expectantly. I turn around to see what Avis thinks instead, but he is already pulling up his mainframe profile. A beam of blue light scans his eyes, and a huge smile spreads across his face as a small 3-D screen appears just above his bracelet.

"Hybrid, classification CN—Coder and Navigator. Wild!" he says, beaming.

"What does a Coder do again?" I ask him. He starts to answer, and Liddick cuts him off.

"They can predict outcomes mathematically—probabilities..." he says, smiling. I look at him and nod, trying not to laugh.

"Oh, you feel needed again?" I ask. He tilts his head toward me and arches a dark eyebrow.

"Jazz, what are you?" Avis asks, leaning over the back of my seat.

"I don't know, maybe an Empath?" I say, exchanging a glance with Liddick, then raise my wrist. Before I pull up my profile, I catch Vox staring at me from a few rows back, and it hits me. How did she know about Empaths?

"How did you know about this already? About...*Pushers*, and *Receivers*?" I call up to her while everyone is engrossed in their mainframe displays.

"Maybe I'm just good at getting into places I'm not supposed to be in, and hearing things I'm not supposed to hear," she says, fluttering her eyelashes. I shake my head at her non answer, too nervous about finding out my classification to press her further, then raise my bracelet cuff again and pull up my profile. The blue light scans my eyes, and for a second, I can't see anything. Almost immediately the screen flashes the word Hybrid —Classification ERd-C. I read the explanation below it— I'm…a *reader?* Wait, and a Coder? I touch the screen again to see if it will tell me more, but nothing happens.

"It says I'm a Hybrid…Reader and Coder; does that mean I can learn people's language like you did?" I raise my voice over the chatter to Vox, who is immobilized by the blue light in her eyes. When it stops, she squints hard, then reads her screen and smirks.

"Probably, since I'm a Hybrid, too—Reader and Navigator. We're nearly twins," she says, batting her eyelashes at me again.

"How did you talk to the Inlanders in the last class? Will you show me?" I ask her, ignoring her sarcasm.

"I don't know how I did it. I just listened and it was there, but I've pretty much been able to do that since I was a kid. It's not this place or their stupid nannies."

"Nanites," Avis insists, tossing his hair out of his eyes in exasperation.

"Whatever," she says, darting a glance at him.

"Remember that he said it just comes later for some… your subconscious wakes it up when you need it," Liddick says, still not having scanned in.

"What does yours say? Check it," I urge, and he does, reluctantly.

"Hybrid—Classification ERd and Coder," he says, nodding. "We're the same, Rip. So, we'll be figuring out how to do it together." He smiles coolly and drapes an arm over my shoulder as I shift back in my seat.

"Jax—" I say out loud to myself, and look up to see him trying to get my attention. He mouths the word Omnicoder to me and raises his fists in exultation, a huge grin spreading across his face. *What's an Omnicoder?* I wonder. He points to me and raises his eyebrows in a question.

"Hybrid—Reader and Coder," I mouth, and he shrugs his shoulders, confused. I repeat the words more slowly, and he shoves out his bottom lip, nodding like he's very impressed, albeit so awkwardly I can't help but laugh.

As if he's just remembered something, he starts looking around the room. I'm sure he's trying to find Fraya, and start to wonder again where Arco and the others are, but Dr. Denison calls everyone to order.

"And now..." he begins loudly, lowering his voice when everyone's chatter subsides, then starts over. "And now that you all know your classifications, let's break up into groups and see what you can do."

CHAPTER 32
Sorted

My head is spinning when our bracelet cuffs begin to pulse with colors that correspond to sections of the room. "Please make your way to your color," Dr. Denison says, walking with the teachers to the center of the floor. "Mine is blue," I say, looking up at Liddick. He holds up his bracelet, which is pulsing green. The realization that we're on separate teams hits us at the same time as I feel my stomach drop, then the echo of it from him, which is the strangest sensation ever. He opens his mouth to say something, but Avis slaps him on the back on his way down the steps to the other side of the room.

"You and me, Jazz," he says, holding up his blue light as he bounds down the stairs.

"Looks like you're up there," I say, tipping my head to the crowd gathering in the corner behind him under the green light, then feeling my chest collapse in on itself, "with Jax." Liddick turns around immediately to confirm, then looks back at me and sighs. These sub-groups are what Denison said will become our career teams, and I tense at the idea of never seeing my brother once we're at that level. It's bad enough to lose Liddick, the only person who has been able to help me navigate what's been happening the last few days. I almost started feeling normal again.

"Don't worry. We still have four years of training before they send us into the world, you know?"

"I know—I mean, I remember," I say, smiling a little when I see that Fraya's light is also green as she tugs on Jax's shirt from behind. Liddick turns around again and chuckles as Jax pick her up in a bear hug. A lighter feeling washes over me when I see this, and I catch myself scanning their crew again for Arco—where is he?

"Well, that just made his entire week. Looks like your crew is down there," Liddick says, then gestures behind me. I turn and see the blue light beaming down from the ceiling at the bottom of the amphitheater stairs, exactly on the opposite side of the room from the green, which is lofted along the far wall at the top of the stairs. A red light and a yellow light are on opposite walls from each other about halfway down each side of the room, and soon, most students are at their respective stations.

"Watch out for him," I say in all seriousness to Liddick before turning to head to the blue group. "Jax may be *the older one*, but he's more impulsive than I am."

"Watch out for *him*," Liddick replies with a smirk and a nod toward my group. I turn and find Arco staring up at us, and relief floods over me. I look back at Liddick shaking my head, completely losing the battle with the smile fighting its way across my face.

"It's not like that. We're just friends," I say, but it falls on deaf ears.

"Oh, it's like that. You just don't know it yet," he says, making me roll my eyes on my way down to my group.

I'm happy to see so many familiar faces as I approach: Pitt, Dez, and even Vox—who, while I may not be thrilled to see her in my group, is better off with me than with Jax. She would blindside him.

"Jazz!" Myra nearly knocks me over in a running hug.

"Hey!" I manage, immediately happy to see her.

"What's your class?" she asks, and I look at her, puzzled until I realize she's talking about my classification.

"Oh, Hybrid—Reader Empath and Coder. That feels so odd to say out loud...what about you?"

"Projector Empath, that's deep, isn't it? Now I'll have to be more aware of what waves I'm putting out there." Myra turns a little pink and wraps a long strawberry blonde twist of hair around her finger.

"You never put out anything but good waves, Myra. Don't even worry about it," I say, trying to keep my attention on her, but I can't seem to focus.

"Nice to see you again, Myra," Arco says, crossing over to us. She gives him a bear hug as well, which makes him laugh. It's been awhile since I've seen him genuinely laugh like that.

"Arco! What class are you?" she asks.

"Mutant, I think," he says with another chuckle as he looks at his bracelet again, which pulses blue. "Hybrid class CN, Coder and Navigator, Latency Receiver Empath," he reads, raising his eyebrows. "So, yeah. *Mutant.*"

"Latency?" I ask him, but he just shrugs it off.

"Don't ask me," he says through a smile. "Do you know everyone here yet?" he asks Myra, and I look around to see if there's anyone I don't at least recognize.

"No, but I'm making the rounds. Hey..." she says, leaning in more closely to me, "have you seen Joss? I want to introduce him to someone," she asks, angling her head toward Pitt.

I shake my head and raise an eyebrow at her, but then see him making his way toward our group. I almost didn't recognize him with his blond hair cut short now—when did that happen?

"Actually, he's right there," I answer, and her face lights up as she bounces over to Pitt and pulls him by the arm.

"Myra's making friends," I say, turning to Arco.

"Looks like she's making more than friends," he adds as she threads her arm through Pitt's and calls after Joss, who tries to look tolerant when Myra starts rambling. "Uh oh," Arco adds.

"What?"

"I just know that look."

"What look? Joss's tolerant look? Yeah, Myra can get on a tear when she's excited," I answer. Arco narrows his eyes, then shakes his head.

"So, Vox was right about you being an Empath, then. And you're sure that's what you are?" he asks, then turns away from Myra's introductions and faces me.

"That's what my bracelet says," I answer, raising an eyebrow at his odd question. "Vox said I could only receive, but I guess we're the same. None of what we can supposedly do seems to work in this room, though."

"What do you mean?" Arco asks.

"What the teacher was saying…being able to talk without talking? Liddick and I have gotten pretty good at that, but it won't work in this room. I can't seem to connect with anyone else like I can with him, so I don't know if it's a thing all Empaths can do, or just the two of us," I say. Arco's eyebrows dig together for an instant before he rolls his eyes, then shakes his head in dismissal. "What's that for?" I ask.

"You're the Empath, Jazz. You tell me," he says over his shoulder as he heads toward the rest of our group. "I said it didn't work in here!" I call after him, but he just shrugs and tosses up his hands to each side. I blow out a breath and turn to check one more time on Jax, who spies me and waves, a huge smile on his face as he drapes his arm over Fraya's shoulder. Liddick stands next to him leaning against the wall with his ankles crossed and his hands pushed into his pockets. He sends me a nod, and I smile back at him before taking those last few steps to close the gap between myself and my group.

Avis has managed to engage Pitt in some kind of debate as Myra and Dez stand off to the side. I wonder if she's an Empath like Myra and me, or if Pitt is, for that matter, and walk over to them.

"Pitt, right? And you're Dez?" I ask. They both smile, Dez more broadly than Pitt, and I make a conscious effort not to look at their wedge of teeth. That will just never be normal to me no matter how many times I see it.

"I'm sorry, I thought you had already met them," Myra says, her beaming face dimming a little.

"I did, but just for a second," I say, "it's OK."

"Right, and you're...Jazz?" Dez replies, her blonde hair spilling over her shoulder as she tilts her head to me.

"Right," I say, smiling back.

Pitt nods to Avis as he walks toward Arco, then turns

to Dez and me. "So they're going to teach us how to be superheroes or something now?" he asks, then grumbles and raises his eyebrows in disdain, which surprises me.

"You're going to be great, stop worrying," Myra says, her face lighting again.

"Why is Omnicoder such a stretch for you to believe? You've always been good at figuring out solutions to problems," Dez hooks her arm in her brother's, but he just huffs out an exhale through his nose like a horse. That's when it hits me that if he were an animal, he'd definitely be a huge, black horse with radioactive green eyes. A giggle bubbles up before I can catch it, and Dez, looking a little confused, but relieved, laughs too. Even Pitt's mouth quirks for a second before he squashes it.

It dawns on me that the odd horse thought must mean Vox is somewhere behind me, but since I don't feel the tingle at the back of my neck that I usually do when she tries to put a thought in my head, I can't help turning to confirm. She's actually several feet away talking with Joss, but then looks up at me and smiles to one side before excusing herself to come over. She only gets a few steps before she's stopped in her tracks by a sudden haze of light in front of her, which fades to reveal a group of people near the center of the floor—a group of our teachers, only, there are several of each of them. Four Dr. Denisons, four Reynolts, Mahgis, and Strykers, but still only one Tark. Once the light fades, a set of them approaches each color group.

Our whole group comes together to look at each other in the seconds we can manage to tear our eyes away from the spectacle of teachers all walking our way, and when our set reaches us, we are stone silent. Dr. Denison—or, *one* of the Dr. Denisons is the first to speak.

"Go ahead," he says, holding out his arm. "Touch it." But no one moves. "It's OK. It's real. *I'm* real. We all are." Myra lets go of Pitt's arm and moves toward Denison, extending her fingers to brush over his wrist, then pulls her hand back quickly.

"He is," she says, looking around at everyone. A few others follow her lead, but no one dares to utter anything more than a few gasps of realization.

"Each duplicate instructor is a temporary copy. We have short term, intermediate term, and long term options in cloning here at Gaia Sur. There are no permanent options as of yet, though this is a point of political contention at the State right now, as some of you may know. This set of teachers," he says, extending his arms to encompass the group standing next to him, "are clones. The other groups are clones as well, and we will all expire in approximately six hours—we're short term."

"That means you...*die?* Where are the real teachers? And what happens to all the memories and information when the clones expire?" Avis asks, his mouth wide with excitement. I close my eyes in a long blink at his abruptness, but that's Avis.

"The originals are monitoring all four groups from observation stations under the floor of this room, and our experiences and memories are all uploaded to the primes in real time via neural uplink. Regarding the expiration of clones, our matter simply breaks down into smaller and smaller synthetic carbon molecules until they dissipate back into the port-cloud," Denison answers. "I'm sure you all have several questions about this process, but for today, we are going to talk about you and your abilities. Each day you spend at Gaia will provide multiple opportunities to familiarize yourself with the array of technological advancements and differences from your home territories, and your bracelet cuffs can provide direct access to tutoring scenarios if you would like to expedite your learning. These scenarios are largely self-directed because we believe the process of organic discovery is less jarring for our new cohorts than direct instruction of *what's to come*," Denison concludes, air quoting the last several words.

"Watching your teachers replicate before your eyes isn't less jarring, let me tell you," Vox says, and I feel a pang of embarrassment.

"Actually, Miss Dyer—it is Miss Dyer?" he says, checking a digital reader on the inside of his palm. "Yes. The extended anticipation of such an event and the potential paranoia it might engender often wreaks greater havoc on the psyche than more abrupt introductions; however, periodic surprises help hone your senses, which is critical for the training you will be receiving here at Gaia Sur." Denison's face is calm, but his intense blue eyes are fixed on Vox, and she seems caught in the web of them.

"So all of those teachers will really disintegrate after this class?" Avis asks, gratefully, albeit tactlessly, shifting the subject back to the macabre, and I'm suddenly relieved that whatever abilities we have seem to be muted.

If the tension I've already been feeling so far in here were amplified, it would probably be overwhelming.

"Dissipate, but essentially, yes," Denison replies.

"Does it hurt them—er, you?" Myra asks in a thin, almost pleading voice.

"No, our consciousness shuts down first, so essentially, we fall asleep, and within about ten minutes, we just disappear," he answers. "Are there any other initial questions before we begin assigning you mentors?"

"This is what must have happened at our interviews," I whisper to Arco. "Styx, Rheen, and Plume were clones. That's how they could be with all of us at the same time."

He nods, but keeps his eyes on Denison.

"Miss Ripley?" Denison looks directly at me. "Do you have a question?" My heart leaps into my throat at the sound of my name, my attention rifling forward.

"No, I mean, not really—I mean, yes. Is that how we all had the same people in our interviews at the same time before we got here? Mr. Styx, and the others?" I ask, not so much afraid of the answer, but for some reason, afraid to ask the question.

"Indeed. What an astute observation," he says, and despite whatever Empath ability I supposedly have currently being suppressed, I get a distinctly vacant vibe from him when he answers me. "If that's all, Ms. Reynolt?" Denison takes a step back.

"I will be mentoring the pure Empaths and Hybrid Readers on board," she says with a broad smile, her green eyes twinkling.

"And I'll work with the Navigators," Dr. Denison says,

his short, white hair shifting with his shallow bow to the group. Then, for the first time, I hear Mr. Stryker speak. His voice is quiet, but steady, and his silver-streaked dark hair falls in messy waves at his collar.

"I'll be working with the Omnicoders and the Coder-Navigator Hybrids. I see that I know a few of you already," he says, his large, brown eyes smiling.

"Any remaining Empath Hybrids will work with me, no matter if you are Empath Coders or Empath Navigators," Dame Mahgi nods to our group with a brief smile. I nod in reply, but only because I'm not sure what else to do until Dr. Denison extends a hand to the door behind us, and I realize we're about to find out.

"If there is nothing else," he says to the group, "shall we board the Leviathan?"

CHAPTER 33
The Leviathan

Dr. Denison leads our group out a door just beyond the curtain backdrop of the room. I look up at Jax's group, which is also leaving, but they are exiting through the door where we all came in at the top of the stairs.

We walk through a small corridor with overhead lighting that doesn't seem to be coming from individual fixtures of any kind—it's just...light.

"He said our ship is the Leviathan you were talking about earlier," I say to Arco, stumbling after Avis bumps into me in his excitement to get to the ship.

"Sorry!" he calls over his shoulder, and zips to the front of the group. Arco nods.

"Those are the crew ships—here..." he says, trading his place along the wall with mine in the middle of the current of students heading down the corridor. "You're getting swept up." Arco is taller than most of the other students, save Jax and the cloudies, and looks over the top of our group, then behind us.

"Thanks," I say, feeling wary again. The suppression of the room we just left must be lifting, and I realize it's getting easier to decipher my own feelings from the ones I pick up from other people—this time, they're Arco's feelings of uncertainty. "What's wrong?" I ask.

"Nothing, just wondering where everyone else is... Jax's group, and the other two."

"They went out the door we came through at the beginning of class—at the top of the stairs."

"And the other groups?"

"They all went out a nearby door on each side of the room. It's just like the auditorium at school back home—doors at all the walls," I say. He nods in reluctant agreement and turns his eyes forward again.

"Well, if you don't think anything is wrong, nothing must be wrong. You're the Empath," he smiles, but it comes off as sulky patronizing.

"Arco...what is with your yo-yo mood already?" I ask, exhausted by it.

A blast of cold air hits us in the face and stops whatever he was going to say in response. As we filter through the doorway and onto the metal walkway that runs the perimeter of the space, I see a hangar bottom out below us.

"Whoa!" Myra says, rushing from Pitt's side toward the clear guard wall so quickly that her momentum brings her feet off the floor. Joss is quick to grab her waist before she accidentally flings herself over the edge, and I suck in the gasp just in time to let it out. I don't think I've ever seen anything so potentially dangerous neutralized in the same moment it actually happens like that before.

"Are you OK?" Joss asks, letting her go as Pitt closes the distance between them in a few strides.

"Yes, thank you. Sorry, I just got excited," she says wide-eyed with adrenaline, her face flushing as she brings both her hands up to cover her mouth. Pitt nods to Joss, then puts his arm around Myra and falls back into the crowd.

"Right, please do watch your step everyone—it's a long way down," Denison says to the group after clearing his throat. I look up at Arco and swallow hard as he blows out a breath before we turn our attention back to the deck below, where a fleet of about 15 smooth-lined, iridescent metallic ships with streamlined wing curvatures are lined up in three rows, five ships deep.

"They look just like Jax's picture," I say.

"These are the Leviathan," Dr. Denison says, his voice raised to accommodate the enormity of the space. A huge doorway holds back the dimly lit midnight blue water of the sea just beyond it at the opposite end of the hangar with small flashing lights that flicker in a line.

"How do you keep water from rushing in here when they enter and exit?" Dez asks, apparently studying the giant clear door too.

"The exterior port is clear, so it gives the illusion that the water comes right up to the mouth of this hangar. In actuality, the exterior door is roughly 300 feet from this. Once the vessels enter the primary gate from the outside, they will stop behind this door. That area in between the two doors is called the normalization chamber, where the outside water and any contaminants are removed."

"And then it just taxis through this door?" Myra asks, fully recovered from her scare now and nearly bouncing with excitement next to Pitt, his arm still around her waist.

"Correct. Leviathan ships have hover capabilities as well as propulsion, so once past the threshold, it will find its way to its position, then lock into the grid for an automatically guided landing."

"This place. This is where I started my interview," Arco whispers into my hair, which causes a sudden, strange flutter in my stomach as I remember how adamant he was when he told me about it. "That's not the ship, but this is the place."

"We're going to learn to fly these?" Vox asks abruptly, which makes me stop trying to figure out the flutter and refocus on Denison.

"*Pilot* them, yes, some of you will. Some will operate other areas. Omnicoders will run the organic core system and will need a Navigator/Coder Hybrid consult, plus an Empath Hybrid as consult. Which kind of Empath Hybrid isn't important, though, because the base group sensitivity and big picture perspective are common to all Empaths, and will be the component most required by the Omnicoders to run efficiently," Denison answers.

"So if I'm an Omnicoder..." Pitt begins, "do I pick my crew?"

"Yes," Denison replies, then turns his attention to the rest of us. "If you have Hybrid Empath, or Navigator/ Coder classification, and you are interested in being the consult for the core, make your preferences known to Mr. Spaulding before we go to ship's stations today. Let's head down," he says, and we begin moving down the length of the suspended walkway. Dez and Ellis scurry over to Pitt and Myra. I consider going, but then pull back. I want to see what's in this core before I go and sign away my life to it, and to Pitt being the eternal boss of me.

"Are you going to do it?" I say to Arco as we make our way through the doorway and down the steps to the floor of the hangar.

"I don't want to be a mechanic," he says. "Especially not on one of these."

"That's what the Omnicoder job is? A mechanic?"

"Not entirely, but that's a big part of the job. You're responsible for all the systems—life support, hydraulics, weapons defense, there are a lot of biotechnical interactions."

"Wait, these things are weaponized? Aren't we just going to homestead families here? Why would we need weapons to be door-to-door service representatives?" I ask, baffled. "And what kinds of weapons?"

"Lots," Arco replies. "Mostly debilitators, target lock sonar vices, a few other immobilizers. You never know what's out there when you're this deep."

We go through the door that leads to the hangar floor, and the ships are even bigger than they seemed when we were standing on the suspended walkway, which is now directly over us.

"They must be 20 feet tall," I say, tilting my head nearly all the way back to see the top.

"All aboard," Dr. Denison's clone—and I keep forgetting that he's a clone—says, pressing his hand against the side of the ship, which becomes outlined in blue light as it's scanned. A stairway lift emerges seamlessly from the wall of the vessel before extending to the floor, and we follow him into the ship.

Inside, the cockpit is rounded with smooth brushed metal panels just below the enormous window that stretches from one side of the nose to the other. Silver stools erupt like mushrooms from the floor in each of the three areas, one in the middle, and one on either side with buttons, levers, and components sprawling before each one.

"Mr. Hart, have a seat in the middle to demonstrate the customization, if you please," Dr. Denison asks, extending his palm to the chair. Arco takes a few steps up and onto the cockpit deck, then down again into the pocket of the center unit. When he sits, the chair silently expands around him, a back appearing and extending upward and sideways. Arms also appear with a button panel and controls at each end.

"It forms to him," Myra says, grinning like a kid witnessing a magic trick as Pitt slips his arm around her waist again and pulls her in. I'm not sure when *that* happened, but it certainly explains why a bubbling feeling has replaced the sharp icicle in my chest whenever Vox is in the same room with Joss and Myra. *She really does like him,* I think as I watch her scanning Joss from several feet away.

"These chairs will adjust to your bodies. They will also work in sync with your nanites to help monitor your blood pressure and other biological systems that could interfere with your ability to navigate this ship."

"So, they're panic proof?" Arco confirms, and from the smirk he doesn't completely commit to, I can tell he's only half kidding.

"As a manner of speaking, yes," Denison replies. "Now then, the results of your simulator trials are in, and with them, your Nav assignments. Mr. Tether, since you're a pure Navigator, the left rig is yours. Mr. Spaulding, have you chosen your Nav/Coder consult?"

"Ellis," Pitt says, and Denison nods to Ellis.

"All right, Mr. Raj, as consult, you'll assist the pilot when you're not in the core, but the latter will be your primary station. Mr. Ling, that will leave the right rig to you. Everyone, please join Mr. Hart in taking your seats."

Avis and Joss walk toward their new stations and sit in the chairs, which conform to them the way Arco's did.

"Wait, I'm staying here?" Arco asks.

"Indeed," Denison says, then, registering Arco's blanched expression, takes another look at his palm pad. He scrolls with his other hand, and nods. "Coder/Navigator hybrid, and even an Empath latency...you're more than qualified to be the pilot Mr. Hart, and your performance in the simulator this morning was enough for me. Please make yourself at home," he says as he crosses to Dez. Arco blinks, then meets my eyes.

"You can do it," I mouth to him after I feel a wave of panic push over me, and after a second, he nods.

"Miss Spaulding, you may have guessed by now that you're our medic?" Denison asks, checking his palm pad again, then looking up at her.

"Well, my advisor told me I was slotted for biodesign."

"That's indeed you, then, Miss Spaulding. Mr. Stryker and Dame Mahgi will show you all around the med-bay. Note that the core is also below, so you would be an ideal choice for Empath consult as well. Mr. Spaulding?" Denison says. Pitt nods in agreement, and Denison angles his head at Mr. Stryker.

"Let's show you around then," Stryker says to Pitt and Dez, then waves Ellis along as they all disappear down a short flight of steps to our rear.

"Miss Ripley, Miss. Dyer, as reader Empaths, your stations will be here and here," Denison says, scrolling on his palm pad again, then pointing to two seats on opposite sides of the back of the room, each with a panel of instruments and screens spread out behind it. "Miss Toll, as a pure Empath projector, your station will be here." He points to another seat with similar, but fewer screens and instruments that falls directly between Vox's station and mine. "Your primary duty on this vessel will be to assist Miss Dyer and Miss Ripley with homestead relations—liaison work, situation assessment, as well as keeping a pulse on ship morale. You will also assist Miss Spaulding in her medical duties, of which she will be informed shortly." Denison gestures to the stairs, and Myra's face lights up.

"I get to take care of people?" she asks, her eyes brightening.

"Should the need arise, yes. You will train with Miss Spaulding and Dame Mahgi beginning tomorrow, and will alternate with Ms. Reynolt the following day. Today, you'll work here with Ms. Reynolt," he says.

"And what are we supposed to do again?" Vox leans back on her elbows against the console behind her and kicks her legs straight out like she's sunbathing right there on the stool. I narrow my eyes wondering why she is still so belligerent in everything she does. There's no way she's getting out of here, so why doesn't she just give up trying?

"You and Miss Ripley will be the team advisors. You will assess all situations you encounter and collaborate on the best course of action, then, you will advise the navigation and engineering crews."

"And who's in charge?" Vox presses. I feel impatience rising in my blood and a prickling heat crawling up my neck. She starts to smirk at Denison, but he just looks back at her calmly. Is she actually trying to push the clone of our teacher? Can't she tell he's just...empty?

"Not you," he says, a smile pulling at the corner of his mouth as he arches a white eyebrow at her, his sudden wit commanding my attention. "Mr. Spaulding and Mr. Hart will collaborate much like you and Miss Ripley after you advise them, and the final decisions will be your pilot's."

"What?" Arco straightens in his chair. "Why only mine?" he asks, then seems to think better of it, but it's too late. Denison doesn't look surprised, in fact, he seems almost pleased, like he's been waiting all day for this.

"Well, Mr. Hart, because you never saw it coming."

CHAPTER 34
Ship Stations

"Sorry?" Arco asks, his face having gone white.

"Your absence of ego, Mr. Hart, is the quintessential trait of a pilot. Ambition is good, but not when lives are at stake. Your testing results across the board indicate optimal levels of selflessness under pressure, so naturally, you are the clear choice for team leader," Denison concludes. The blood that had drained from Arco's face slowly returns, flushing his neck and cheeks. He can't speak yet, but blinks several times, then swallows and begins to nod. He looks at me, and as if on cue, adrenaline rushes my veins like a deluge of water through a tunnel, and my heartbeat crashes against my ribs like it's trying to escape the flood.

"It's OK. You can do it," I mouth to him again. He nods quickly once more as if he's trying to convince himself, then looks back at Denison.

"Thank you," Arco replies to him, then sets his jaw.

"All right, well let's take this out for a spin then," he says to Arco. "Ms. Reynolt, I believe Miss Dyer, Miss Toll, and Miss Ripley are ready for you."

I completely forgot Ms. Reynolt was in the room, and turn abruptly to face her, wondering if she also felt the emotional earthquake that just happened in here. Her eyes dart back and forth between Vox and me, but her face is smiling and calm.

"Certainly. Ladies, allow me to explain your systems to you," she says, and extends her hands to my panel. "Vox, Myra, please join us."

Vox and Myra come over to my panel, and Myra looks like she has a thousand questions ready to ask all at once. I feel her uncertainty, the anxiety at war with her indomitable optimism, and it starts a knot in my stomach.

It's all right, Jazwyn, I hear Ms. Reynolt say in my head, just like Liddick. I startle, then look quickly over to her.

Can I talk to you? Can you hear me? I think in answer to her, and feel a jolt of surprise when she answers me.

Of course. All Reader Empath classifications can talk via telepathy, but only Readers, and only one at a time. I will work with you and Vox to hone this skill.

I look over at Vox, debating whether or not I want to test this, but I have to know. I take a deep breath and focus on her. *Can you hear me?* I think, but she doesn't respond, and I feel instantly stupid as I step toward my stool, then collapse onto it.

In seconds, it envelops around me like Arco's. The cool, smooth material isn't leather or any other kind of hide, but it's not cloth either. It warms against my skin, and feels more like a thick blanket than a chair pressing against me. I feel calm again, the sweat on my upper lip that I didn't know was there beginning to cool and dry. My heartbeat regulates, and my stomach stops churning. Ms. Reynolt steps out from behind my new seat and begins explaining the panel before us as Vox leans in right next to my face to look at all the instrumentation, a wildness in her eyes.

"So, we're basically supposed to watch how everyone feels on these things?" she asks too loudly, waving indirectly at the screen and raising an indignant eyebrow as she lets her chin fall.

Crite, can't you be civilized for five seconds? What's wrong with you? I think to myself, but then see a smile dawning on her face.

You're breathing on me, I hear her think in response as her eyes dart to mine before she straightens.

The laughter in me breaks like surf on the rocks and spills out as Myra looks over and smiles, a little confused, but smiles nonetheless. The warmth in my stomach begins to radiate up and out through my arms, the general sense of wellbeing spreading as I realize that being able to talk with Vox this way feels like another piece of the puzzle is falling into place.

"These screens are your lifeline to the outside," Ms. Reynolt says as she pulls her auburn curls off her neck and tucks them up in a twist that she somehow ties into a knot. "This one will send back electropsychic varian—"

"Electro-what?" Myra giggles, interrupting the explanation.

"Electropsychic *variances.* When you enter a room, you have no doubt experienced the air feeling tense, calm, happy, etc., right?" she asks, and we nod. "That's because of the electropsychic energy that all living creatures emit. It is why some of us can communicate with animals, and even plants."

"Plants?" I say, raising an eyebrow.

"Of course. Plants do not necessarily have consciousnesses, but they do emit emotive energy and can receive emotive energy."

"That's true," Vox adds, and we all turn to look at her. "Strangle bushes and copperhead vines, I've been caught in both of those before and had to persuade them to let me go."

"What?" I say in total disbelief. *"Persuade* them to let you go. You negotiated with plants?"

"Influenced them is more like it," she smirks.

"So it just occurred to you to try and push the plants. *Push* them?"

"Wait and see what wild ideas you get when some maniac foliage tries to eat you for lunch, Jazwyn. Then you can judge me," she says behind a cocked eyebrow and another loaded smirk. Myra's eyebrows shoot up as she covers her mouth to contain her laughter, and I roll my eyes and smile back at Vox, somehow feeling...in sync? I don't even know if that's the best way to describe no longer wanting to strangle her with her own hair, but considering the stress and anxiety I've associated with her since the port-festival, I'll take the peace for as long as it lasts.

"Type in anything you like, and a manipulative will appear. You can alter the manipulative by ionizing your fingertips on this, just run your fingers over it, then touch the image," Ms. Reynolt says, gesturing to a circular silver disk next to the keyboard button of my console. "And to evaluate external scenarios beyond the ship, for example, pulling into a port, the electropsychic readings will appear here. You will be able to read them up to three miles out. This will give you enough time to decipher, prepare, and advise countermeasures for any hostile pockets that you—" Ms. Reynolt stops abruptly at the sudden movement that jostles us all—the ship is leaving the dock.

I grip the armrests of my chair to stop myself from sliding out as Myra topples into Vox, and they both fall to the ground. Ms. Reynolt manages to get a grip on the back of my chair to steady herself before we all turn to look at the front of the ship. Arco is pulling back on a lever, and Denison is talking over his shoulder.

"Steady—it's all right. They can be sticky coming out, just keep it steady. Mr. Tether, we need more pull on your outside"

"But it's—"

"Just pull in, you're rowing a boat—just like rowing a boat, remember?" he coaches. "Mr. Hart, more hydraulics when you feel that left tug."

Arco doesn't acknowledge him, but seconds later, we start to straighten out. "Off as she goes, well done, Mr. Hart," Denison claps Arco's shoulder, and something small and warm explodes in my chest. "Mr. Ling, let's bring it around now so we don't rotate again."

"Aye, sir," Avis says, and lets his half moon control wheel drift slowly from him. The craft begins moving smoothly forward, and aside from a blinking red light about a hundred feet directly in front of us, it looks like we're facing the open sea.

"Take her out," Denison says, but we don't move. Arco looks up at him, hesitant. "Push on to the gate, son."

Myra and Vox have picked themselves up off the floor and returned to their own chairs while Ms. Reynolt has moved to a stowed seat that she's pulled out from the side wall. Dr. Denison lifts the inside of his wrist to his chin.

"What's the depth, Cal?" he says into the inside of the panel strapped to his forearm.

"We're cleared for 6,000 meters," Mr. Stryker's voice comes through the device, and I flinch. 6,000 meters? That's 1,000 meters beyond our sea shelf.

"Do we have those Stingrays ready to go?" Denison asks.

"Give me 10."

"What's a stingray? I mean, I know what a stingray is, but why are they getting them ready?" I ask Ms. Reynolt. She smiles, and I suddenly feel a little silly when I realize they're not talking about the animal.

"They're two-passenger vessels...looks like Dr. Denison wants to take you all on a little outing this afternoon."

"We're going outside the Leviathan? In the ocean? In our own little ships at 6,000 meters down?" I stammer, but she just smiles again.

"I understand your anxiety, Jazwyn, but you're perfectly safe. You may experience a bit of nausea as your nanites stabilize your oxygen levels, but it will pass. I find holding my breath at the onset helps give them a little head start with turning over the cells."

"But what about the ships? We don't know how to drive anything."

"No need to worry. Anyone can operate the Stingrays, besides, you'll either be in with one of the staff members at first, or with one of the Navigators."

Talking has taken my attention away from the fact that we've been inching forward this whole time, and had we not suddenly stopped again, I probably wouldn't have even noticed. We're at the exterior gate, and Denison, now sitting next to Arco in a smaller chair that extends from an arm at the base of the pilot's, waves Arco forward with one hand.

"Just push on, the gate will see you coming."

Arco inches us forward toward the red, blinking light that turns green when he's close enough, and the tall, clear window panel it's attached to slides open. Once we're inside and stopped behind the red center light of another panel, the one we've just cleared closes behind us.

"We're sealed in here?" I ask out loud, but to no one in particular.

"This is the normalization chamber," Ms. Reynolt says, and I hear a roar start all around us.

"What's *that?*" Myra's voice pitches.

"Water. In a second, the other panel will open, and we'll be able to jettison. Without this step, the force of the water rushing in would crush us against the back gate panel," Ms. Reynolt explains in a voice that could just as easily be reading a child's bedtime story. I swallow hard and try not to panic as the water level rises over the front windows of the ship. After a few more minutes, the red center light in front of us begins to flicker green.

"Push on," Denison says, but we still don't move. "Mr. Hart, as you've seen, it will clear as you approach."

"But it's the ocean past this point," Arco says. "We're at 5,000 meters. Doesn't that say 5,000 meters?" he says, pointing to something on his console.

Denison laughs. "And we'll need to drop another thousand before you'll have somewhere to park. Push on," he says, waving Arco ahead.

The ship moves forward slowly, and the tall, clear wall begins to slide away. We start advancing more slowly still —so slowly that I wonder for a second if we're actually moving at all, but Ms. Reynolt explains that this is just due to the initial push of outside water coming in to fill the last pockets of air in the chamber. "Let's go around the block. Watch your levels like we did in the simulator this morning. Less rotation, Mr. Ling. Sync with the left rig," Denison commands, and almost immediately we begin to move forward at a noticeable clip. "Check your debris field here before you pull the cork. We'll drop about a meter per second then."

My heart starts pounding at that. "How did they learn to drive this thing in one day?" I ask Ms. Reynolt under my breath.

"As your abilities in understanding yourself and others have been building, Jazwyn, so have theirs. Just look what you've been able to accomplish in a short while. Navigation and complex systems operation is in their blood. Their physical training may only amount to test runs in simulators and a few around-the-blocks, as we like to call these little outings, but they are already familiar with how it should feel down here," she explains, though, I'm still not satisfied. I want to know what's *actually* making this ship function—what does the engine look like, where are the controls that let us see into the core, and more importantly, do Avis, Pitt, Ellis, and Joss feel as unsure about operating this thing as Arco seems to?

"Can I go downstairs?" I ask. "I want to see how everything works."

"Wait until we clear threshold, then we'll be on autodescent and there will be less chance of abrupt movement."

"Threshold?"

"It will be any second now. Just listen for the bell. We need to get out far enough from the port gate before we can scan for debris—jutting rocks, anything that would interrupt our trajectory. That point is called threshold," she says patiently, just as a low-toned bell sounds. She looks ahead toward the front of the ship and nods, then looks back at me. "And there it is. You can head downstairs now if you like."

I look around my seat for a belt release so I can unclip the safety restraint, which I don't remember ever putting on in the first place. "How do I get out of this thing?" I ask, a little embarrassed.

"Just stand up—it will read your neural command and release. Remember, it's designed to work with you." I look at her in disbelief as I contemplate how ridiculous I'll look trying to stand up, but not be able to. She gives me another nod, and I try it. The belt disappears, almost seeming to disintegrate, and I look again at Ms. Reynolt, surprised. "You see? We'll join you downstairs as soon as we anchor. It shouldn't be long," she says with a smile. I nod, then slip away from the chair before it decides I need to sit back down. Myra sees my chair vacant and skitters over to talk to Ms. Reynolt as I pass Vox and try to open a channel to her.

I'm going to the core to find Dez and the others, I think, and soon hear her steps behind my own.

CHAPTER 35
Launch

The spiral staircase is narrow and winds down about 20 feet. When we reach the bottom, everything is chrome colored in the corridor that wraps around two opposite corners at the far end. I look around, but don't see Pitt or Dez, not to mention Mr. Stryker or Dame Mahgi.

"Where did they go?" I ask Vox, not really expecting an answer, but she has one.

"This way," she says walking ahead, then, veering right.

"How do you know they're that way?"

"I just do. Stow it and come on," she says, grabbing my sleeve and pulling me up to her pace. Around the corner is another short flight of stairs that leads down to a room with hundreds of flat file drawers, but no piston systems or engine blocks like I expected. It's a little warmer down here, and the light has a yellow cast as opposed to the blue cast of the upper deck. Just beyond the flat files I see Pitt standing with Mr. Stryker at the other end of the room, and then look around for Dez and Dame Mahgi, but I don't see them.

"Let's find Dez and Mahgi," I say.

Who cares where those two are? They won't be able to tell you what you want to know about what this ship can do. Vox's rudeness is even worse when it happens in my own head.

We start walking quietly toward Pitt and Mr. Stryker, and Vox suddenly stands bolt upright and turns around to face me.

"What?" I ask, surprised.

"Are you two going to be part of the core crew?" Dez says from behind me with a smile, and I nearly jump straight into Vox.

"Uh, no—but Myra is. She's going to be your nurse I guess, something like that. She's still upstairs, though. We just came to...see..." I stutter.

"We came to see what makes this ridiculous ark work," Vox says, flipping her hair out of her eyes. Dame Mahgi walks up behind Dez and raises an inky eyebrow, then looks at me.

"You want to see the reactor?" Mahgi asks, genuinely stunned, as if such a thought would be the most idiotic thing we could possibly hope to do in five lifetimes, let alone our completely insignificant one.

"Y-yes?" I say, and she closes her mouth, which she'd left hanging open. Astonished, she walks resolutely over to Pitt and Stryker with Dez, Vox, and me in tow.

"Cal, I don't think they're permitted—" Dami Mahgi says to Mr. Stryker, annoyance brimming in her voice. Stryker smiles and takes her hand to calm her indignation. "It's fine. It's just a wet run, and we'll be anchoring in a few minutes anyway," Mr. Stryker says, waving us over to him. Pitt stands behind him around a circular guard wall about the size of the one around the globe fountain back at school in Seaboard North, but there's a faint green, glowing light emanating from inside this one.

We walk up to join them and peer over the edge.

Inside the well walls, it looks like a miniature rotating planet with storms erupting all over it: tiny rips of lightning, rolling clouds that seem to scatter over the black sphere in variations of white to mottled gray.

"It's like a little planet in there," Dez says, apparently seeing it for the first time too. "I thought the medical bay was amazing, but *this*..."

"It is amazing, and yes, basically it is a little planet, Miss Spaulding," Mr. Stryker answers with a smile that says he's genuinely excited about explaining this. "It's made of iron and nickel, just like our own planet's inner core."

I raise my eyes from the little spinning sphere to Vox at this, but she's already turned her attention back to Mr. Stryker.

"How is that thing not killing everyone with radiation?" she asks, a scowl spreading across her face.

"The NIFE?" Stryker laughs. "It's not toxic like that—it just produces hydrogen, which we collect and repurpose to fuel the rest of the ship."

"So it's not a weapon? It's just a battery?" she asks, disappointment in her voice. "What's happening with the clouds? How does it even have clouds?" she adds.

"Those are the result of water vapor condensation, possibly even ice crystals—we pull water in from the sea to keep it constantly charged, and those are normal byproducts," Stryker makes a swirling gesture with his hand as he leans against the guard rail.

"So it really just runs on water?" Dez asks.

"And potassium, plus a little carbon for the iron and nickel nanocrystals to grow," Stryker adds, raising his thick, dark eyebrows and running a hand through his black, silver streaked waves.

"Why do you call it the NIFE?" I ask, since it seems like an odd name for a battery.

"Because Ni is the chemical name for Nickel, and Fe is for Iron," Avis adds, walking up behind us with Myra. I look behind him for Joss and Arco in the hopes we can start asking more questions about how this ship can gather images through to the other side of the planet like Arco had mentioned earlier, but I don't see them. I look back down into the well at the black ball and the clouds of condensation as a rip of miniature lightning streaks around it. It really could be a little planet if you just let yourself think so.

"Isn't it dangerous for lightning to be so close to it?" Myra asks, smiling stupidly at Pitt.

"It's not flammable. The static just means the vapor is getting heavy enough to fall, just like when it rains topside," Stryker explains, then angles his head toward a door about 10 feet away. "Would you like to see the moon pool? We should be anchoring any minute, and the others will be joining us."

"Oh! Come and see these little ships!" Myra says, suddenly. "Pitt was telling me about the Stingrays that are just through there."

Before I know it, she's pulling me through the doorway, then through a small corridor that opens up into a large, round room with metal finish everywhere, which is very cold in comparison to the core room. The air is damp and heavy with the smell of sea spray, and I can instantly feel it pressing in on me. A large, open square pool with a shallow lip surrounding it takes up the center of the room, and inside, dark green water laps against the interior wall. The sudden cool, heavy air, and the motion of that water make my head start to swim, and the room begins to rotate around me. I take a few steps toward the bench I see along the perimeter to try and regain my equilibrium, but before I know it the walls close in, and the room takes one final spin before everything goes black.

***

"She's OK," I hear a voice, and find myself squinting against a harsh light. "Can you hear me, Jazz? You just passed out for a few minutes." I blink a few times, and see that it's Dez and Fraya leaning over me. "It was just the nanite adjustment, but you're OK."

"Fraya?" I whisper, confused as to how she got on our ship when she's part of Jax's crew.

"We'd just anchored next to you, and Dame Mahgi arranged for me to come and help Dez...hands on training!"

And Myra nearly drowned everyone in her slobbering guilt about pulling you through here in the first place, so Reynolt had Avis take her over to green's crew before you woke up and she completely killed you dead with it, I hear Vox in my head and start laughing. Fraya's smile widens as she straightens up.

"Someone is feeling better," she says, and I nod as I try

to sit up.

"Please tell Myra that Ms. Reynolt told me to hold my breath too. I just forgot," I say, getting to my feet, then take a seat along a bench against the wall as Dez nods, then walks over to Dame Mahgi. Fraya sits next to me and touches my forehead.

"Clammy, but you'll live," she smiles. Dez comes over to me again, this time with Dame Mahgi, and hands me a cup of water. Dame Mahgi is already wearing a thin, black jumpsuit when she nods at me and starts making her way to the moon pool with the others when I see Ms. Reynolt come into the room, and this makes me wonder just how long I was out.

"Are you OK?" Ms. Reynolt asks.

"I'm OK," I say, and will a smile to stick to my face.

So which is worse, forgetting to hold your breath, or having everyone fuss over you like this? I hear Ms. Reynolt in my head, and am flooded with relief.

I think the latter, I answer. *Please tell Myra not to feel bad. I should have remembered to hold my breath.* Ms. Reynolt smiles and shakes her head at me like I'm a wet puppy.

All right, well, the others are on their way; you may want to stand before Mr. Hart sees you so green around the gills. I've played my crew swapping cards for one wet-run. She finishes the thought and smiles.

The last thing either of us needs right now is Arco worrying himself into a six-foot-two suffocation blanket, so I push up from the chair and walk slowly over to the moon pool, but then am almost immediately dizzy again.

Hold your breath. I hear Ms. Reynolt's reminder and

suck in. The dizziness starts to clear just in time for me to turn and see Arco, Mr. Stryker, and Joss come in the room together, one by one sucking in breaths. Arco looks at me, his light brown eyebrows drawing together, and I force a wide smile to offset any suspicion he might have while I slowly exhale. *Latent Receiver Empath*—thanks a lot, hypertech nanites. It was bad enough topside when he was just always paranoid something was wrong. He'll know it thanks to these stupid nanites, and he needs to concentrate on himself right now.

"What's wrong?" he says, letting his held breath out quickly as he makes his way over to me in a few strides.

"I'm fine, I just forgot to hold my breath and got a little queazy," I answer, but his expression doesn't change. "Just all those things in there rushing around or something," I add, making swirling motions with my hands over my head. "It's gone now for the most part."

"You're definitely green," he says, raising an eyebrow as his mouth quirks up in the corner. "Do you want some water?"

"No, I have—"

"Spaulding, where's the pooler down here?"

"The what?" Pitt answers.

"The pool— never mind. Dr. Denison, where's—"

"Just through there," Dame Mahgi says, pointing to the door we all just came through. "Just hold still for a moment, Miss Ripley," she says, taking my bracelet cuff and pressing down on its interior while also pressing into the pulse of my other wrist. In seconds, I feel a small prick like when we were aboard the relay sub, and then it feels like two lines of ice are being drawn up the inside of both my arms and up the sides of my neck. Once it reaches there, my nausea is gone. I blink a few times and swallow, surprised.

"It stopped. I don't feel sick any more. What was that?" I ask Dame Mahgi, who still looks as irritated as she did before.

"Just a little oxygen for your nanites. It took them hours to put you right when you first arrived, remember? If you're going to be on a ship like this regularly, Miss Ripley, you'll need to upgrade those. The ones you have now are registering as baseline technics," she says, looking at her arm panel, then, grips my shoulders and studies my face. She presses her lips together into a thin, disappointed line before she talks again. "Come to the medical bay after class, and I'll have a procedure waiting for you. I will also have a chat with Nurse Karo in the med-bay to find out how this happened," she says, patting my arms and sighing before letting me go. "Well, at least you'll sleep well tonight!" And at this, she finally smiles. I wonder if it's because she thinks whatever suffering I'm going to endure after class is what I get for spying around down here in the first place.

Of course that's what she thinks. Come on already before Arco tries to pick you up and carry you for the rest of this trip. I laugh out loud at Vox's words in my head, and Dame Mahgi's eyes go wide.

"Sorry, it just…tickles a little," I cover, flexing my hands and walking abruptly toward Vox, Avis, and the others who are taking long black bags off the walls. I look over my shoulder and smile, "...and thank you! I feel better."

Arco catches my eye and smirks, but doesn't say anything else as we head to the bags.

At the edge of the moon pool, Avis and Fraya are the first to step into the suits like Dame Mahgi's. Dr. Denison hands a bag to Arco and another one to me. "Pretty self-explanatory...unfasten the bag here and here." He unclips the top and middle of the bag and opens the flap, then lays the bag on the ground and pulls the black jumpsuit up by the shoulders and shakes it a little so the legs roll out. Each of the arms and legs has a thinly padded bumper pocket near the center. The front and back have a Y-shaped panel, and a long cord hangs from the back of the left shoulder. "Put these on, then pair up and meet us on the other side of the air lock. Each Stingray will need to have at least one trained Navigator on board or one mentor for this run."

"I'll go with you," Arco says to me. "Maybe I'll even let you drive." I roll my eyes and unclasp my bag.

"What are these? More jumpsuits?"

"They're divers," he says, and I stare at him blankly. "That's really what they're called," he laughs. "They do everything for you out there, so they might as well just be making the trip on their own—*divers*, get it?" I raise my eyebrows at him and nod as Arco shakes his head and smirks. "You used to have a sense of humor."

"You used to be funny," I smile, and his eyebrows jump higher as he laughs.

"Here—pull this and step in." He takes my suit and

turns it around for me while pointing out the cord that undoes the back. I pull it, then step in. After just a few seconds, it seems to crawl up my body, almost inflating by the time it gets to my ribcage. "Put your arms in...it's ok," Arco continues, chuckling.

Once my arms are in, the torso of the suit envelops around me. It's warm inside, almost too warm at first, but then, it's perfect.

"Can you fasten it?" I say, trying to reach again for the pull cord on the shoulder, but in all my swatting and grasping, I still can't find it. Arco suddenly belly laughs. "What? I can't reach it. Where is it?" I reach and stretch again, trying to turn to see it.

"It's...already fastened, see?" He turns around to show me that his suit is sealed and is barely able to get the words out around his laughter. "There, you're good now," he finally says, and I narrow my eyes at him.

"Very funny. Not all of us spent the morning down here, you know. And how can a diving suit be this thin? What are these little padded pockets for?"

"It's Carboderm, made by the same company that synths the atoms for the port-cloud, the same stuff that's in the Leviathan and the Stingray skins. Those pockets are life support stores: air, liquids, electrolytes. There are even toe covers that expand into a 5'x5' bubble enclosure in case you fall, or, well, if something tries to eat you," he says, nearly straight faced until he sees my horrified expression.

"You have all the jokes today, Arco. They taught you how to be funny in your underwater pilot tuhao class, huh?" I try as hard as I can to look fierce, but he's just laughing too hard, and I can't hang on. "OK, so whenever you manage to wring out, how are we not going to drown again? There's no helmet," I say, looking in the bag for one. I start to walk past him to see if it's on the ground next to where the bags were hanging, and he steps in front of me, not laughing any more. I stop just in time to avoid running face first into his chest and look up, surprised. "Wh—?"

He stares right into me, the corners of his mouth still twitching, the remnants of all that laughing still crinkling around his eyes. They're almost the color of the water in the moon pool, dark moss and amber with the light hitting it. He leans in and brings his hands over my shoulders, then lets his fingers skim my neck. Small, sharp prickles of heat run up my spine and spread first over my cheeks, then my lips as his fingers wrap around the sides of my dive collar. I try to swallow, but my throat is compromised by the pulse suddenly pounding against the heel of his hands. Waves crash in my ears, and I feel my arms raising up slowly to his wrists, out of my control like they're tied to balloons. I can't seem to move away, but when I try, I realize that I don't even want to. He pulls the edges of my collar toward him, all traces of laughing gone now. His eyes are set on mine as he lets his chin fall. His thumbs stroke my cheeks as he opens his mouth like he's going to say something, and I instinctively take a shallow breath.

Then his eyes spark like a match, and the corners of his mouth quirk the instant I hear air rushing all around me.

It starts out slowly, but builds to a steady, loud pressure, the source of which I can't find. Suddenly I feel cool instead of warm, and Arco moves his hands from my face back to my shoulders as a thin window comes down in front of my eyes and fastens to the collar just under my chin. My hands fly to my head, now completely enclosed by a helmet.

"*Arco!* Are you kidding me!?" I yell, but he taps his ear and shakes his head, his face contorting with restrained laughter again. He yanks his collar down on both sides, and his helmet appears from behind his head, then seals over his face just like mine. He takes my hand, positions my finger and thumb together, and guides them to the corner of my collar. I feel a button there that he presses his fingers over mine to squeeze, then, does the same to his own collar.

"There, now you can yell at me," I hear him say through the microphone, and he gently bumps his helmet to mine.

CHAPTER 36
Falling

Dr. Denison presses his palm to the pearlescent wall, and a port-call version of Mr. Tark appears, flickering at the edges. I grab Arco's sleeve, then pull the edge of my collar to raise my helmet. Arco raises his, and we both watch the feed.

"Mr. Tark, whenever you're ready," Denison says, standing at the edge of the moon pool with the others.

"Blue crew, I trust you're getting comfortable with your stations—some of you already went through the basic operations aboard a Leviathan this morning with our simulator program, and for those who didn't, with the accelerated algorithms of your nanites enhancing your natural abilities, I trust this run has not presented much of a learning curve for you." Tark's green jumpsuit rustles as he widens his stance and clasps his hands behind him, and if it were not for the rough edges of the transmission, I would swear he was standing there in the room with us.

"It's almost like he's right there," Arco whispers, and I raise an eyebrow, wondering if he heard me think it as well.

"Dr. Denison has likely already explained that your rate of acquisition is exponential, so you will all be experts in no time. I have conveyed as much to the Green crew—they will be your counterpart in this year's grouping, and are actually already waiting outside for you,"

Tark continues, pulling up a map labeled *American Preserve, Eastern Seaboard Floor.* It's a 3-D aerial exposure that looks like the land just drops off suddenly about a mile or so from the shore, then slopes down into three scooped out underwater areas: the Northern one labeled *Hudson Canyon,* which gives way to the second scoop labeled *Sohm Abyssal Plain,* and below these on the map, the Southern scoop is labeled *Hatteral Abyssal,* which borders the foothills of the *Bermuda Rise* on the right. "Your crew will cover the East-to-West walls your territory, which runs from the Northern edge of the Hudson Canyon to the Southern intersection of the Hatteral Abyssal and the Bermuda Rise. You will serve homesteads leading up to the Hudson Canyon divide on the Northwestern front, and the Bermuda Rise on the Eastern front."

"That has to be almost 2,000 miles if it spans two-thirds of the coast—and those foothills are just as far out from shore," Arco says, riveted in calculations.

"Your southern barrier is the intersection of the Hatteral Abyssal and the Bermuda Rise, directly west of the Bahama Islands. Any farther south and you will encounter the Puerto Rico Trench. There are no homesteads there, only research facilities, but you are not certified for physical travel that far out at this point in your training. Checkpoints are in place, and your equipment will tell you when you are approaching an unauthorized zone like this one. In case you are missing my point, ladies and gentlemen, it is systematically impossible for you to accidentally wander into these areas, so don't get any ideas. Not only will you be risking your own lives, but those of your crew as well," Tark says, scanning us all.

The map pixelates until it disappears, and another image comes up in its place: a shimmery sideways teardrop with a bulbous front window.

"That's a Stingray," Arco whispers. "The outside is like a skin. It's soft like a tadpole or something."

"*Eww,*" I say, squinting at him, and his eyes light with a smile as he chuckles to himself.

"These are the close range roamers you'll be using today—they're called Stingrays, as some of you already know, and are equipped with a hatch behind the stabilization gear, here," Tark explains, pointing to the 3-D cutaway of the craft, which just looks like a paddle boat inside—a few steering wheels, two seats, a small open area behind them, and the hatch on the bottom. *What?*

"How can that be enough protections for this deep underwater?" I ask Arco, apparently too loudly.

"Good question, Miss Ripley," Tark says. "The hull of the Stingray is made out of Carboderm, the same material as the Leviathan, and in fact, your dive suits. This is a sturdy, but flexible and porous tissue that will absorb the pressure of its environment. The internal chamber pressure will also adjust, as will your suits in conjunction with your nanites. Just think of these vessels as deep sea creatures, and you are their guts," Tark says, and closes the image. "Pair up, if you haven't already. If you have a Navigation classification, choose someone who doesn't. Spread the love, people. I'll link up with you outside."

The transmission fades out, and Denison instructs

everyone to get into the moon pool.

"The Stingray vessels are docked along the perimeter below. Once the water recedes, hop down and swim through the divider wall hatch in the floor to load up," Denison says, entering a code into the control panel just off the side of the pool. The water level immediately lowers, revealing a clear floor and crawl space door that I can now see leads to a larger, completely submerged room containing the docked Stingrays. They look like the heads of enormous silver snakes floating in place down there, the bulging eye-like window seamlessly connecting to the rest of the hull, which shimmers like a million tiny scales.

"Coming?"Arco says, already standing on the breaker wall floor of the nearly empty moon pool and extending his arm up to me.

"How did you get down there already?" I ask, incredulous.

"Jumped. Come on," he says, waving me toward him. Almost everyone else has climbed down the ladder, and Avis has already jumped through the floor door near where Arco is standing and is swimming to a Stingray beyond. "Come on...crite, I'm not going to drop you," Arco says, smiling and holding up his other arm now, waving me to him, but suddenly the air feels thick again as I'm acutely aware of the depth, the heaviness pressing down on my chest, and the water all around in every direction. I'm about to crawl into this mini fish-belly of a vessel, then drive along the bottom of the Atlantic Ocean for an outing with this class, all from the inside of a bigger fish-belly ship. How is any of this real? *I need to get out of this suit—I want to go home!*

"Jazz? Hey..." Arco says from very far away. I sit down hard, suddenly dizzy and scan the clear pool floor for Vox, feeling compelled to find her. Finally, I see her behind the control panel of one of the Stingrays as Fraya swims up through the hatch underneath, then lowers the small divider wall inside to expel the water behind her before resealing it and moving to the controls with Vox.

Jazwyn, you must compartmentalize Vox's feelings. I'm working with her now. Focus on your breathing, Ms. Reynolt says suddenly in my head.

What's wrong with her? Ms. Reynolt, where are you? I reply.

I'm just outside the Leviathan—look straight down the ramp to Mr. Tether's Stingray. Can you see me, Jazwyn? Pull your mind back from Vox's emotions. I am working with her now, and need to get back, so I need you to be strong.

"Jazz, what's happening? The nanites again?" Arco palms the deck of the moon pool and lifts himself out in one fluid movement, then kneels beside me. He brings his hands to my face, turning it side to side, but I don't have the strength to swat him away.

"I'm fine. It's Vox..." I try to tell him. I want to tell him that I feel her trying to leave, but all those words won't come out.

"What's she doing to you?" he says, turning to look for her through the exterior window, then through the clear floor of the moon pool. "She's out in the Stingray. What happened?"

Ms. Reynolt? Vox wants to leave again—she wants to go home, I think.

I know. She wants to, but she can't with Fraya there. Fraya is a projector like Myra and can't be pushed to manipulate the controls. This is why Vox is panicking. This is what you're feeling—her panic—close the door on it, breathe in and out. I need to get back to her now, Jazwyn. Please concentrate.

I close my eyes for a second and grip Arco's hands...*stop panicking.* I think, hoping to influence both of us.

"Stop panicking..." I tell him out loud and blow out a breath. After a few seconds, an excited, happy feeling begins to fall over me, and at the same time, a violent, wild resentment of it. "I feel both of them, Vox and Fraya. Vox wants to go home. She's trying to push Fraya to panic so she'll go with her, but she can't do it. She can't push her," I say in one breath.

"Is she telling you that? What's happening?" Arco says as Vox's Stingray goes down the ramp and out onto the ocean floor. I see her move past Ms. Reynolt's Stingray and then abruptly stop.

Vox, you can't go. I try to reach out to her so she stops fighting, stops emotionally thrashing to get away. I breathe in again and blow it out to push away the panic like Ms. Reynolt said, loosening my grip on Arco's hands and trying to project the sense of calm over him that I now realize Ms. Reynolt must be trying to help project over both Vox and me.

"Jazz—" Arco says firmly, his hands gripping my arms. I move mine to his and hold onto them.

*It's right there...straight up...*Vox says in my head, and I can feel her need to go like the need for air. *It's not time yet. Wait for us—you have to wait for us, and we'll all go, remember?* She doesn't answer me, but I feel the tether in my stomach let go, and the panic gives way to a feeling of grief and resignation.

"I think she's staying," I say to Arco, letting my forehead fall against his shoulder. Relief rushes through me after I exhale, and I suddenly feel a wave of cold run up my spine that makes my teeth chatter. Arco pulls me to him, and I can feel his heartbeat against my cheek, his warm, heavy breath in my hair. I blink to clear my eyes and pull back to look up at him crouched there with me at the edge of the moon pool. His hazel eyes are wide, his brows bending in, and there are too many emotions happening for me to understand what he's feeling. "Arco..." I suddenly feel compelled to tell him I'm sorry for scaring him. I have to explain, but his hands move too quickly over my face, and his mouth too quickly covers mine.

The hollow aftermath of the adrenaline rush hits me at the same time, and I feel like I would sink right into the floor if he weren't holding me against him. There's a fear, a restraint in the force of his lips pressing hard against mine, and I grip the smooth material of his dive suit, feeling it stretch over the muscles in his shoulders and gather between my fingers. He pulls me into him like I might slip, then consciously loosens the hold...I feel his fear again, fear like he might crush me. His back and forth emotions, and all the effort he's trying to put into regulating them is so endearing, yet so silly, and I'm so exhausted that I just smile uncontrollably against his lips. Then I feel relief again…his relief as he starts smiling too, pulling back and pressing his forehead against mine, both of us too afraid to move.

"I'm sorry, I just—" he starts to say, but I interrupt him.

"She was going to leave. I couldn't let her leave."

"I know, I see that now. I just felt like I couldn't get to you in time. *Again.*"

"I'm sorry, I didn't mean—" I start, but his hands move to my face as he kisses me again, softly this time, not as afraid and not as brave as before, just…sure. He's sure when his smile finds his eyes, and it occurs to me that if he has the latency classification of Empath Receiver…if he's this sure, does that mean so am I?

CHAPTER 37
Setting Out

Arco breaks the awkward silence between us with operating instructions a few minutes after we enter the Stingray, both of us darting glances and looking away when the other's composure slips into a laugh.

"Just push down for forward. We have to do it at the same time and at the same pressure, or we'll spin," Arco says, showing me how the foot pedals work. I nod, then stifle the stupid smile fighting the corners of my mouth.

"I can't believe it's this basic in here when we just came off a ship that has its own little planet inside with fully functioning thunderstorms," I answer, confused by the simplicity of this little craft. "Why don't they have some kind of drone mind control system where you can just think where you want to go?"

Arco laughs and raises his eyebrows at me. *"Drone mind control system?"*

"After everything else down here so far, it wouldn't be the splittest thing. This, though? This ship is supposed to be able to withstand the pressure of 6,000 meters of water on top of our heads? What's the point of a little toy operating system like this?"

"They're not meant to go too far…and everyone is supposed to be able to drive them, not just Nav class. You ready?"

I start pressing my foot on the pedal to move forward

down the ramp toward the seafloor, and Arco and I exchanging glances to check our sync. The lights from our Stingray and those of the others that have already made it down the ramp shine in all directions, illuminating small, rocky structures with hovering jellyfish that glow white and pink before they dart away in the light, along with a huge sea cucumber that looks like a cylindrical white pillow attached to a wide, flat fin at either end.

"Stingray seven! Nice of you to join us. Who's your second, Mr. Hart?" Mr. Tark's voice is suddenly all around us.

"Jazwyn Ripley," Arco answers.

"Welcome aboard, Miss Ripley. Mr. Hart, please set your scope to Dayrunner, channel Zephyr for comms, and try to keep up. That last part won't be too hard since we're still waiting for the rest of Green, so congratulations, you're not last out of port."

I look around, but I can't tell where Tark's voice is coming from. I scan the dashboard and notice only a few controls—a few half-moon steering columns, a hatch control, a gauge that says *climatizer,* and a light labeled *emergency* next to another clear domed light. There are a few button panels on the left side near Arco, but I can't read them from my angle, and I don't see anything that could be a speaker.

"It's a sonar wave. It came through the cap," Arco says, pointing to the window in front of us as he notices me looking around.

"Of course it did," I say, shaking my head at the irony

of having undetectable *sonar wave communication* inside the equivalent of a water scooter. We slow to a stop so Arco can adjust the communication controls that Tark just specified, and a feeling of tension squeezes my chest as I look out into the endless dark water and remember that there are people out there who need us. I take in a deep breath and try to blow it out slowly.

"Are you sure you're OK?" Arco asks, reaching over to brush my hair behind my ear with his fingers, then lets his hand rest on my shoulder. His eyes search my face for something that he can't seem to find. "I know everything was...a lot back there. And so is this," he says, angling his head toward the spread of sea before us, then strokes his thumb across my cheekbone. I turn into it before I even realize I am. His hand is warm, and I close my eyes for a second, nearly convinced that when I open them again, we'll be on the beach back home soaking up the last of the sun setting on the day. When I do open them, he's leaning his head against the back of his seat, watching me and smiling to himself. "I don't know how to say what this feels like," he says, sliding his hand down to interlace his fingers with mine as he looks down at them intertwined, the smile overtaking him.

"I think it feels *safe*, maybe?" I say, but it sounds more like a question than an answer. "I mean, everything here so far has just been anxiety, but with you now, it just feels—"

"Safe," he says, agreeing, a decided grin lighting his face. A wave of adrenaline passes over me, and then a flood of warmth that actually makes me want to giggle, but I swallow it down and study his face. Color brushes his cheeks, and I can see him fighting to keep his grin at bay as his eyes dart to the floor.

"Arco?" I say with a smile in my voice as he presses his chin to his chest, a few small laughs escaping from me like air bubbles. "Are you...*blushing?*" I say in disbelief. He laughs out loud now, then shakes his head, seeming to decide something as he lets go of my hand to hold onto the steering wheel, then begins pushing buttons on the panel to his left before he looks over at me again.

"It's just a relief to hear that I guess," he says, still grinning as he enters a final combination. "I knew it was bothering me, but I guess I didn't realize how much—the idea of not being able to keep you safe, you know?" he adds, his eyes darting to me, but then quickly moving back to his controls. For an instant, my chest constricts sharply, and I realize that the anxiety he felt from his interview has never really dissipated.

"Arco, you don't have to—" I start, but he interrupts me, stopping the trajectory of the conversation before it can really even begin.

"Anyway, the other team is finally here, so I'm just going to transmit to Tark that we're going back. Five more minutes and you'd have fallen asleep in that seat," he says, smiling to one side.

"No, it's fine, don't do that. I don't want to go back yet. Look what's out here..." I say, pressing my palm against the window next to me as three small pink and white jellyfish float by in the distance.

And just like that, the moment is gone—I want to

return to my point about the pressure he's been putting on himself to look out for me, but I don't know how to do that without also resurrecting the prickly tension that surfaces with it. I start to open my mouth to say *something,* to at least try, but the clear domed light of a moment ago suddenly turns green in the center console, and the illuminated words below it now flash *transmit ready.* Arco presses the glowing button, which makes it go out again.

"All right. Well, just press that if you want to talk to the others. They have to be within 50 yards. Go ahead, push it," he says, nodding toward the console. I press the same button, and it glows green again. "Stingray seven operational," he says, then clicks the button off.

"Copy, Stingray seven. Looks like we're all here," Tark's voice booms through our cabin. "We're going to mix it up a little now. Hart, Spaulding, Raj, Ling, and Dyer, take your pod 30 degrees south. You have one league at your disposal. Stay together, explore, and meet back here in two hours for reload and dismissal—we're going to run a little long today." Tark's voice is clear and direct, but did he just say we're going out there on our own?

"Anywhere? We can go anywhere?" I say after his voice cuts out.

"Well, within about three miles that way," Arco says, angling our Stingray abruptly left, which makes me bump into the wall on my right.

"Ow," I rub my head and try to laugh, but it comes out more like a whimper. He sucks in a breath and winces.

"Sorry..."

"Taking point, Hart?" Tieg's voice comes through the air just as he and Jax appear on our right with Avis and Myra close behind.

"Jax!" I shout, but he shakes his head at me and points to a green light on their dashboard. "Oh," I say, pressing our comms button again. "Jax, can you hear me?"

"We can all hear you, sand dollar," Vox says, pulling up on Arco's side of our Stingray with Fraya next to her.

"And now the party can begin—shall we away?" Ellis says, sidling up to Tieg's and Jax's Stingray on our right as we all move forward much more quickly than I would have expected.

"What are we supposed to be doing, just looking around?" Fraya's voice comes through, and Avis answers.

"Exploring! Can you believe we're three miles under water? Look at those stacks!" The term startles me for a second and makes me imagine our building complex back home, but then Avis shines a light on the rocks that spit out roiling, steady streams of black smoke just to the side of us.

"It might as well be a whole different planet," another voice says.

"Is that Liddick?" I ask, stretching to see past Arco and into Ellis's Stingray, which is on the other side of Vox's on our left.

"The one and only," he almost sings, and I can't help but roll my eyes.

"Try not to seduce any of the homestead natives while

we're out here, Wright. They mate for life. We may never see you again," Arco says, then smiles wryly. "On *second* thought..."

"Tempting, Hart, tempting, but then who would keep you on point?" Liddick replies, and I can just hear his smirk as our Leviathan grows smaller in the distance behind us.

"How fast are we going? The ship is so far away already," I ask, looking at our rear display.

"About 20 knots," Arco answers. "These things move a lot faster than they do in the simulator," he laughs to himself, surprised.

"Quarter-mile out so far, but we're blowing wide," Tieg says, and Arco enters something into the panel.

"Increasing left thrusters two knots," Arco says.

"Copy, adjusting for two knots," Tieg says, "Ellis, Vox, Avis, fall in. I'm reading some kind of undertow, but don't ask me how at this depth."

"Yeah, yeah," Vox says.

"Done," Ellis says, "but my scope says we've already been pulled out nearly half a league. Watch yourselves."

"How is that even possible?" Avis asks, and Arco looks down into the circular grid in the middle of our console, all five of our crafts blipping a few lines left of center, the craggy rocks on the display looking like they only get larger the farther out we go.

"There must be a gape over there somewhere. It's pulling us in," Tieg replies.

"We need to angle out—cut in 45," Arco says.

"Copy 45," Ellis answers.

"What's up there? Spaulding, can you flood it?" Arco asks, noticing something in the distance, then checking our scope.

"Where?" Vox asks.

"Up there," Fraya says as Tieg's spotlight appears to our left.

"It's just another crag," Avis says. "They're everywhere down here."

"No, I see it—look under the crag. There's an opening with light in there," Vox insists, her Stingray starting to move toward Tieg's spotlight.

"Let's go, Raj," Liddick says, his Stingray inching past us to veer off with Vox and Fraya.

"Wait," Arco protests, "you can't just rush something like that. Plus the drift. Hey!" He flips on our spotlight to keep them in sight, and Tieg slows to fall back with us.

"It's just a cave," Tieg says over the comms, still angling his light on the opening.

"But what's making it glow in there?" Jax asks.

"Can you hear that?" Arco looks over to me suddenly. "The humming? Does everyone hear that?" I look at him puzzled until I hear it too...a low frequency electrical buzz just like I heard in Ms. Plume's advisory session.

"Now I do," I say, my heart starting to pound. "Liddick, can you—" a cloud of sediment kicks up in front of us as Vox's Stingray charges forward toward the cave opening.

"Vox!" Arco yells, but she doesn't pull back.

"Follow her!" Liddick's voice sounds over the comms as his Stingray picks up speed and opens a gap between us. Arco pushes his hands through his sandy hair, then shakes his head.

"So much for protocol," he says, pushing forward toward the glowing crag opening.

"You're going in there? Are you split?" Avis asks, but is cut off by Myra.

"It's OK, come on—we need to stay together."

What are you doing? I think, focusing on Vox, but she doesn't respond. The buzzing electrical sound is stronger the closer we get to the cave opening, which is huge now that we're upon it, like a giant tear in the side of the rock face.

"It's as tall as the Leviathan," I say, craning my neck as we cross the threshold. It's wide enough for only one Stingray to go through at a time, but once we're in, it opens up into a wider, shimmering rocky space where we can all see each other again. Vox's and Liddick's vessels have stopped, and the buzzing in here is louder and lower-pitched.

Can you hear that? I think, focusing on Liddick, but he doesn't answer me either. Why isn't this telepathy working now?

"What's making the walls glow like that?" Fraya asks, excitement serving as a lid to her nerves, which I can feel simmering just below the surface.

"We need to keep moving," Liddick says, and pushes forward with Ellis as Vox pulls ahead of them.

"We shouldn't be in here," I say, looking around at the white and yellow glowing rivulets in the walls, the tops of which I can't see. "Something in here isn't right," I say as my stomach starts to sink with the buzz growing in my ears.

"It's on the grid—barely, but still on the grid—so we're not going to set off any alarms, don't worry. We should have just checked out the external structure before coming in here," Arco says, adding the last bit mainly to himself.

"Wouldn't they have closed this off if it were dangerous?" Fraya asks over the comms. "I can't imagine they'd just let us have free range of the ocean floor without checking it."

"Probably," Jax replies. "They're not just going to let the sea swallow us out here—they must have vetted it. Why else would they give us parameters?"

"I just don't like jumping in without knowing what we're getting into," Arco says as we float deeper into the cavern, the gold light ahead of us now mottled.

"Can't conquer waves from the shore, Hart," Liddick says from in front of us, just behind Vox's and Fraya's Stingray. Arco opens his mouth to respond, but is cut off by a high-pitched frequency that completely drowns out the low grade buzzing we've been hearing.

"FIVE METER WARNING, YOU ARE APPROACHING YOUR ZONE BARRIER. PLEASE RESUME APPROVED TRAJECTORY." The Stingray voice is female, but it's not Ms. Reynolt or Dame Mahgi.

"All stop and reverse," Arco says, his face contorting at the piercing sound. Tieg and Jax have backed up in the cave to make room for us to follow, but as we do, a gap opens between us and Liddick's vessel. "Back out of there, Raj," Arco commands, and the Stingray in front of us starts to spin counterclockwise.

"What's happening in there?" Myra's voice says over the comms.

"Why are we stopped?" Avis asks, and I realize they must be sitting right behind Tieg and Jax at the mouth of the cave.

"Lay off the pedal," Ellis says, evidently to Liddick, and their ship slows, but Vox's Stingray presses forward.

"Vox, *stop*—Fraya, pull off the pedal," Arco says, and almost immediately, Vox's ship starts to spin clockwise. Vox's ripped scream of frustration comes through the comms, and a wave of anger crashes over me.

"Fraya!" Jax shouts.

"Vox, we can't go through there—we're at the barrier. You heard what Tark said," I call to her.

"Pull off!" Fraya shouts. "Pull off so we can make the squealing stop. Vox, pull off!"

"She's just being obstinate—they can't go anywhere like that except in a circle," Tieg says, chuckling to himself.

"This isn't funny. We need to catch up to them. *Come on...*" Jax insists.

"No, there's no room. Stay there or you'll jam us up," Arco says.

"Vox, please; you have to pull out of there right now," I say, trying to keep my voice level until I see the huge, dark shadow passing just beyond their ship, which makes the glowing light all around cut in and out. *"What the—*Vox, there's something by you, pull off...you need to back up!"

Her Stingray drags to a stop once the momentum dies, and as the silt clears, the dim glow of the walls reflects the thick, slowly moving bulk of something much bigger than our Stingrays swimming right toward us. Fraya starts to scream.

"Vox, *damnit!*" Jax shouts.

"What's happening!" Myra yells.

"What is that? *What are those slats?!*" Fraya's voice is shrill and broken over the comms system, and I feel ice shoot down my neck. "Is it a shark?!" she cries with the last of a breath.

"We need to go. Sharks can't dive this deep. Avis make sure you're clear. Spaulding, turn six and floor it," Arco hits a series of buttons, causing a whir to start up underneath us. "Raj, fall into my wake—adjust 12 degrees, then hit the back thrusters."

"Vox, follow Ellis! We're right in front of him!" I call, but her craft doesn't move. Fraya is starting to cry. I can't let her spin out, not after seeing her after our interviews. She would flood Vox if she did, and then there would really be no chance of them pulling out. "Fraya, listen. You need to take a deep breath. You have to relax," I say, but then we begin to pull away from them. I grip Arco's forearm. "Hey! You can't leave them there," I say, and pull off the pedal I've been pressing. He crushes his lips together to catch the growl coming out as we start to spin.

"Arco, what the hell! Go back! Tieg, turn around!" Jax yells over the comms.

"No! Spaulding, hold your line or you'll crash right into us," Arco says in response, then keys a combination into his panel that straightens our trajectory.

"Don't you think I know that?" Tieg says, his voice clipped.

"You can't leave them there!" Jax yells.

"Arco!" I pull his dive suit sleeve in desperation and slam on my pedal, which must reset his button combination because we start spinning again.

"We're out and racked at the side—the mouth is clear," Avis says.

"Ellis, adjust to 45 and frog over me. I'll pick up. Jazz, let off your pedal right now, or I'll disable it for good." Arco bites off the last words as he cuts me a look that I've never seen before, then pulls off his pedal so we stop spinning, and finally, turns to me. "Listen to me—do you see that?" he says, pointing to the dark, slotted thing moving toward us in a flipping motion in the dim light of the rear console display. "If it's that big at this distance, it's going to be three times that big when it gets to us. This is not a weaponized craft, Jazz, and I'm sorry, but we have to go!"

His eyes are set, and I know he's at least right about one thing: whatever that is, it's getting bigger the closer it gets.

"We have to stay together—isn't that what Tark said?" I try not to lose control of my voice, but now that the high pitched alarm has stopped, the buzzing in my ears is getting louder. "Can't you hear that? You know what that is, Arco!"

"We can't make them come, Jazz—we have to go!"

"No! We can't leave them!"

"Arco, I swear if you pull out of there!" Jax yells over the comms again.

"I'm not doing this," Arco says flatly, and begins punching something into his panel.

"Arco! 10 yards and you'll be off my grid—you just fell off Tieg's. Hurry up!" Ellis yells as their Stingray grows smaller in the distance.

"They're all mouths!" Fraya yells over the comms. Arco's eyes are wide when he looks at me like he's desperately waiting for my permission. When I shake my head and yell again for him to go back, he pushes one more button combination, and we're suddenly moving forward again.

"Wh—?" I say, double checking to make sure my foot isn't on the pedal.

"I disabled your controls. I'm sorry, Jazz, but we have to go."

CHAPTER 38
Cave and Consequences

"We can't leave them, Arco! Go back!" I yell, but he doesn't answer. "Jax, tell him!" I look at our console to check the green light, which is on, but he doesn't answer.

"He's out of range—50 yards, remember?" The dull buzzing gets louder and louder until I can feel it in my teeth. I sink into my seat and close my eyes, focusing everything I can on Vox. I can't feel Fraya any more.

Vox, if you want to be an explorer that's on you, but Fraya doesn't know what she's doing. Bring her out! I yell in my mind, but she doesn't answer me, and now I can only see the undulating, shrinking mass in our rear display. If Vox can't hear me, maybe...*Ms. Reynolt—Vox and Fraya are stuck...Ms. Reynolt!* But there's no reply from her either. "Vox!" I yell out loud.

*I never saw it coming...*I hear in my head and begin to breathe a sigh of relief until I realize it's not Vox or Ms. Reynolt's voice. It's the marlin again—the exact same voice, the exact same fear from the port-festival, from my session with Ms. Plume.

The Stingray jumps, and I jerk against my seatbelt.

"Did you hear that?" Arco says, his face blanched as his eyebrows crash together.

"You heard it too? The marlin?" I say, shocked. "That was the marlin! I think that was my dad, Arco! Turn my controls—!" I start to shout, but a distant squeal pierces my eardrum and cuts me off.

*Going down...try...code...*I hear Vox in between the peals of high-pitched sound.

Vox! I yell to her in my mind, but the marlin responds.

*I never saw it coming before...refused...Denison's...*I squeeze my eyes shut to focus, but my concentration is broken when Liddick's voice floods our Stingray.

"Denison's *what!?*" he yells through the comms, and I press my ears closed as hard as I can to focus.

Vox! Going down to try what code? I think.

...come back...maybe vent. I will se—transmiss—ook for Liam.

Vox! I can't hear you! Vox!

But she's gone, and so is the message.

"Spaulding, how far are you from the hatch?" Arco asks over the comms.

"Closing in—10 yards."

"Copy, right behind you," Arco says, then hits the comms light so it turns off. "Jazz, listen, we—"

"Arco, it *took* them!" I yell. "It took them and it's *your* fault!" The words are out of my mouth before I realize I've said them. Arco's eyebrows pull in, and he sets his jaw before he talks again.

"What took them? How do you know?"

"She told me! They're going down in that cave!"

"All right, all right, relax...she said the marlin took them?" he asks, trying to keep his voice even.

"No! Something about a code to come back, and she's going to do something with a transmission, and something about a vent. She said Liam's name."

"She's with *Liam?*"

"I don't *know!* That's all she said because you made us pull away," I say, my heart pounding against my ribs as the Leviathan ramp comes into sight.

"OK, listen to me. Did Vox tell you they were *going* down a vent?" he asks, angling the Stingray up the hatch.

"I don't know!" I shout.

"All right, *all right.* Let's just get inside. The buzzing is gone for me—is yours gone? Jazz?" I don't answer him as we launch our helmets and seal the control panel behind us before opening the Stingray hatch and jumping into the water. We swim to the floor door of the moon pool, which is filling with milky, shimmering water. I follow Arco up the stairs and climb out, retracting my helmet. "Hold your breath, and don't let the disinfectant get into your mouth," he says, gesturing to the opaque water in the moon pool. His hands grip my waist to help lift me out at the top of the steps, then he pulls me into him. I start to push against his chest, too angry for this, and feel his heart pounding against my hand as he suddenly jerks away from me. Jax has grabbed him, and before I can scream for him to stop, he rears back and punches Arco, who falls to the ground, completely taken off guard. Jax leans down and grabs the front of his dive suit and hauls him back to his feet only to punch him again.

"Jax! Stop!" I yell, and rush to push him off.

"Ripley!" Liddick yells at Jax and rushes over with Ellis, Tieg and Avis, and it takes all four of them to pull him from Arco. Myra rushes over to me in tears.

"You left her there!" The words tear from Jax's throat

as he breaks away from the other boys and rears back for another punch. Arco rolls out of the way before Jax can hit him again and sweeps Jax's legs, making him crash to the ground. Arco gets to his feet and wipes his bleeding mouth on the back of his hand as Jax springs up, but Liddick and Tieg lock up his arms and hold him back. In our entire lives, I have never seen him this angry.

"I didn't have a *choice!"* Arco yells. "Did you want that thing to take Jazz too?"

"Where are they? Where did it take her!" Jax yells, lunging toward Arco as Liddick and Tieg continue holding him back while Avis moves in front of him and pushes back on his chest. *"Where did it take her!"*

"I don't know!" Arco yells back after wiping his mouth again.

"Jazz, did you hear it? You heard what it said?" Liddick asks, the color high in his cheeks as he struggles against Jax.

"We both heard it," Arco answers, bracing his hands on his knees and closing his eyes.

"Heard what? We didn't hear anything—*Zone, man!"* Tieg says, knocking hard against Jax's shoulder like an opposing G-ball lineman so he stops driving forward.

"Get off me!" Jax says, shuffling out from Liddick's and Tieg's grip. "What did you hear?" he shouts, his chest heaving.

"It's a long story," Arco says, spitting, then wiping his mouth on the back of his hand again.

"You have about five seconds before I start beating it out of you," Jax replies, taking a step toward Arco. I cross in front of him with a hard look as I hold up my hands.

"You need to take a breath," I say, watching the muscles in his jaw work and his dark eyes blaze, but he stops when he registers that I'm in front of him.

"They're not coming up on the sonar," Ellis says, frantically switching from one screen on the wall panel to another as Tieg and Liddick walk Jax back by the shoulders to the wall.

"Where did she go, Jazz? What did Vox say?" Liddick says over his shoulder, his palm now pressed flat to Jax's chest as Tieg brings a chair for him.

"I told you we don't know. Just give everyone a minute," Arco says, pushing off his knees to straighten.

"We don't have a minute, Hart. That thing said Denison's name!" Liddick 's voice strains with new effort to contain Jax, who throws the chair out from behind him.

"Do I look like I want to sit down?" he snarls at Tieg, then pushes Liddick out from in front of him. "What do you mean? What said something about Denison?" Jax fires at Arco through clenched teeth.

"What's going on?" Ellis asks as Tieg moves again to help Liddick with Jax, who has started advancing on Arco again. Myra wraps her arms around herself, her fear crushing my chest, and I put my arm around her.

Arco blows out a breath. "All right, but not here. Everyone else will be back any minute. Put these suits back in the bags, and we'll talk about all this in the Records room tonight."

"If you think I'm just going to—" Jax yells, trying to push toward Arco again, but Tieg shoves a broad shoulder into his chest, knocking the wind out of him to hold him in place.

"This isn't helping anything," Tieg says in a low voice close to Jax's ear, his patience fading. Jax is so angry his eyes fill with tears as he shoves Tieg with both hands, nearly knocking him down, then takes a few steps back until he turns to face the wall, bracing himself against it with his forearms as he lowers his head.

"It's complicated, and we don't have time right now. Just hang up your suit and meet in Records after dinner tonight...*please*," Arco says. Jax doesn't move at first, but then jerks the cord at his shoulder to release the torso closure of his suit. The back panel falls to his waist as he pushing his hands through his hair without turning around again, then pulls out of his sleeves. The other boys look at each other, then at Arco as they begin removing their suits, evidently having decided that Jax is no longer on a homicidal rampage. Arco turns back to me raising his eyebrows, his eyes pleading. "Jazz..."

"Don't," is all I say before I turn away from him and begin struggling to take off my own suit. Myra squeezes my shoulder with one hand, then crosses over to the suit wall with the others, giving them a wide berth. When she's clear, Arco walks up behind me and pulls the cord behind my neck, which makes the torso of my suit fall open in the back. Without turning around, I slide my arms out, letting the sleeves fall at my waist. My jumpsuit underneath is damp and sticking to me, but I don't care—my head is pounding, and I don't even know where to begin trying to understand everything that's just happened in the last hour.

"Jazz, I'm sorry about the controls, but I couldn't risk it. I had to get you out of there," Arco says, but I'm still too angry with him to reply. "All right, well, if you're going to hate me over this, you're just going to have to hate me because I would do the same thing all over again. I'm not going to lose you out here," he says, and then, almost inaudibly, "not again..."

I feel my chest squeeze so hard I can't get a breath. After a second, I turn around and see him walking over to the moon pool where he braces one hand on his hip as he brings the other to his bleeding mouth, then looks at his hand before wiping the blood on his pants. I look around for some kind of cloth, but don't see one before deciding to walk over to him.

"It looks like it hurts a lot," I say, crossing to him and bringing my fingers to his bottom lip, which is split near the left corner. His eyes soften from the narrowed glare he'd just been holding.

"Glad I got that kiss in when I did," he grins, then winces.

"We can call a medi-droid—that fixed my nose when Vox..." I say, then let the words trail off, remembering that she's gone.

"We'll find them," Arco says, putting his hand on my shoulder. I meet his eyes, and see that his left cheekbone is starting to swell.

"You need ice...how do I call the droid?" I ask out loud, trying to remember. *Do I just tell my bracelet—no, there was a button in my room.*

"It's fine. I'll deal with it later," he says, smiling to the right, then pulls his arms out of his suit. It's off and back in the bag before I can even step out of the legs of mine, and I blink hard to make sure my eyes aren't playing tricks on me.

"Is that all really part of your accelerated Coder/Navigator classification like they said earlier?" I ask, and gesture toward his bagged up suit as I hop on one leg trying to free my foot from the boot cover.

"What? Changing out of gear?" he asks, daring to let the smile start in the corner of his mouth again.

"Doing everything like you've done it a thousand times when you've only had 48 hours down here just like everyone else," I answer, finally freeing my foot and having a seat on the ground before starting on the other. "How do you just do it?"

"I don't know," he says after a second, then bends down to pick up my suit that I've finally taken off. He puts it back in the bag, then hangs both his and mine up on the wall where we first got them, Jax and the others having taken seats along the perimeter of the room to wait for the rest of the teams to come in and for class to be dismissed. "It's just there...like an instinct I guess. Maybe the same way you can feel how someone else is feeling," he says, walking back over to me and extending his arm to help me up. His eyes fix on mine like he's waiting for me to register something, to respond, and while I know acknowledgment isn't all he wants, it's all I can give him right now. I nod my head.

"Thanks," I say, taking his arm and getting to my feet,

then I brush my hands over my jumpsuit pants to straighten them.

"Meet me tonight—after all of this chaos is done for the day and we've figured out a plan," he says, catching my elbow as I start for the bench. "I just need to get my world right side up again. Just have five minutes of normal." I look at him for a second without saying anything, without really processing what he's said because everything is on this weird five-second delay, but then I agree and hear the other Stingrays beginning to dock.

It soon becomes clear that even if we'd wanted to make something up about Vox and Fraya, there's no way Liddick, Myra, or I could have hidden it from Ms. Reynolt. Before she even has the chance to see the state of Arco's face, she knows the second she comes in the moon pool bay that something is wrong as she scans the room for input.

What happened? Where are they? I hear her say in my head, and I know I have to tell her everything. I can't hide what I know from her, not even some of what I know—she'll be able to tell, and that will just make everything worse.

Something took them—and they're not the first ones. Ms. Reynolt, we need your help. Her face goes white before she nods—not a nod indicating that she will help us, but that she doesn't need to hear any more. She knows. I can only feel it for a second before she scrubs it—the guilt, the helplessness—and then any sense of her I had was gone. It's true then…everything with Liam and the others, and any lingering doubt I may have had slips away.

I will inform Dr. Denison that Vox and Fraya did not return with your pod, and we will send a team after them. Do not tell anyone about this until I have a chance to debrief you —I'll send instructions to your bracelet.

But Ms. Reynolt, we have to—

You are dismissed to your stations. Since you are already aboard and unsuited, I will advise Dr. Denison that Mr. Spaulding and Mr. Ling will take the navigation stations, Mr. Wright will take over Vox's station, and your brother will run the core with Mr. Raj for our return trip. Myra will remain in the med-bay with Dame Mahgi. I'll be up shortly.

She's cold and empty now. Can clones just turn on and turn off? Or maybe just Empath clones? She gives me a vacant look before turning to walk toward Dr. Denison. I don't know what she's telling him, and he doesn't react beyond a few nods of his own before punching something into the wall panel. Ms. Reynolt turns to look at me hard over her shoulder, and an urgency rushes over me. I take a few steps over to Arco, Avis, and Ellis. Liddick is already on his way to us with Myra, waving Jax and Tieg to him.

"We need to go," I say. "Something is going on. Ms. Reynolt wants us out of here right now," I say, and Ellis narrows his eyes.

"But what about telling Denison—" he starts to ask.

"She said they're going to send a team after them. We just need to get out of here now. Avis and Tieg are supposed to run Navigations with Arco, and you're supposed to help Jax in the core with Myra in the med-bay. Liddick is with me on the back wall," I say, and we all head for the door as inconspicuously as possible while Dr. Denison instructs Joss and Pitt to reseal their helmets and route their group back to the Green team's Leviathan.

"All right, after dinner in the Records room," Arco says to our group as we funnel out of the moon pool bay and down the corridor.

"They're sending a team, though? Right now?" Jax insists, and I nod.

"They'll find them," I say as he sets his jaw and swallows, then walks toward his station with Avis and Ellis following in his wake.

Tieg looks hard at Arco for a long minute, then looks at me like he wants to ask a question, but doesn't. He opens his mouth, then closes it again and nods, turning to follow Ellis up the stairs. Myra starts to head toward the med-bay, but Liddick asks her to wait for him before leaning in conspiratorially to Arco and me, raising his eyebrows.

"So, not to add to your problems Hart, but Mr. Universe may have caught me making out with his sister. What can I say, right?" Liddick raises his hands in feigned helplessness. I feel my eyes widen, then realize he's just trying to lighten the mood as my chest feels like it's filling with air. Arco chuckles and shakes his head.

"You and Dez...how is that adding to my problems?"

"Well, it's just a casual thing, you know," Liddick says, leaning his head to one side and smirking, "but first seeing Dez and me earlier today, then seeing you two going at it by the moon pool a little while ago...he hasn't really had a good day."

"What?" I ask, feeling heat rise in my cheeks. "People saw us?"

"He saw you through the window when we were all pulling up in the Stingrays...you should have heard him grilling Jax about it over the comms he'd just turned on during his ops check," Liddick laughs. Arco folds his arms and covers his mouth.

"Are you laughing? This isn't funny," I say, swatting Arco's arm. He moves his hand away from his bruised face and tries his best to roll in his lips, then shakes his head a few times. *"It's not!"* I insist.

"Anyway, let's get back," Liddick says, turning around with a nod and offering his arm to Myra, but I can feel that he's not done talking. Then, I hear him, and know that this break for us to talk is why he started the conversation in the first place.

Dez and me...that was just—I hear Liddick start in my head, then taper off. *Anyway, steer clear of Spaulding for a while...I wasn't stretching about him being lit. You really had him going from what I could hear over the comms, and he wants to confront you. Jax had to stop him a few times.*

Are you kidding me? How did I have him going? I just met him, and we've had exactly two conversations! I shout in my head, not sure exactly why I feel embarrassed, but I do.

You're concentrated potency, Riptide, he replies, and I can even hear his laughter in my head.

Whatever. Stow it.

Look, he just doesn't know what to do with disappointment, and he didn't plan for competition—it's nothing you did. He's a walking ego, Liddick says, and I'm starting to get angry at the idea that Tieg could possibly think I would turn into some kind of smitten lapdog just because we had a couple flirty moments. I need to change the subject back to what really matters.

Reynolt was hiding something. You felt her shift, didn't you? I ask.

I felt that wave of guilt register after you told her people were missing, and then I felt her bury it.

That's what I got too, I answer, and there was something else I couldn't place as she was pushing us out of there.

That felt like damage control—her doing the math, you know? She may not like whatever happened to everyone, but she was way too underwhelmed not to be part of it somehow.

I think you're right. And Denison didn't even flinch, I add.

Exactly. If they are sending a team out after Vox and Fraya, I doubt it's to rescue them. Something else is going on, Liddick says, looking back just as Arco puts his arm around me, but then quickly rights himself and nods at something Myra says.

Why could we feel her but nothing from the others? I wonder. *Is it because she's an Empath? Was she even a clone?*

I was thinking the same thing. I don't know, but I'll see what I can find out before dinner, he answers, then disappears around the corner to drop off Myra at the med-bay. Arco exhales audibly when we pass him.

"What's that for?" I ask as we walk up the stairs. Arco closes his eyes for a few beats and shakes his head.

"He's just exhausting lately—now all this with Jax."

"They're just worried. Aren't you? You're kind of in the same boat as they are with your si—" Arco's eyes go wide for a second, and I feel the same urgent rush I had from Ms. Reynolt. He shakes his head so slightly I almost don't see it, and I remember they could be listening, or watching, or however Arco thinks they're keeping tabs on everything. We move into our positions, and I sit alone on the back wall staring into the water and wondering where Vox and Fraya are right now, hoping that they're not terrified as Liddick comes up the stairs and meets my eyes.

This isn't over. We're going to get them back ourselves, he says in my head. I raise an eyebrow at him as Ms. Reynolt and Dr. Denison fall in behind him, and the Leviathan's engines roar to life under us.

CHAPTER 39
Rising

"The student center is right up here. Let's get a drink," Arco says once we filter back up from the docking bay. It's maddening not to be able to talk about what happened yet, but Arco insists that we can't risk being overheard.

The student center is nearly empty when we walk in, and I don't remember half of the things in there now from when we took our tour. The room is open like most of the other areas here, but this one also has several small seating groupings and three large screens floating in the air with different channels of scrolling news on each half. As we approach, one of them on the other end of the room fades, then appears closer to us.

"Whoa—" I say, startled. "Where is that?" I ask, now that I can take a closer look. The scene is from Skyboard North on the left half of the screen, and the right is of The State. "That's the Metro—that's under the dome down here."

"And that's supposed to be home?" Arco's eyebrows come together as he frowns, looking skeptically at the men on the other half of the screen.

"They're Fishers," I reply, reading the caption below the men: *Seaboard North Fisher Minority creates new baiting system—revolutionizes the trade.*

"But why are they so far inland and still hauling those

nets like that? Where are the new helocarts?"Arco asks, intently watching them carrying nets of fish as they laugh and talk. He's right—the shore is so far in the distance I almost can't make it out, but the Fishers have been hauling their catches with the hovering carts that one of the Tinkerers invented for at least a month now.

"Maybe they repurposed them somehow for this new baiting invention thing. How do we find the whole story?" I ask.

"We don't. They're just feed clips. In my Systems class this morning, they told us we won't have full access to any mainstream media our first year. Part of their immersion protocol or something," Arco says, walking us toward the stack of cups and the tall, silver dispensers on the counter that juts out from the back wall. "Looks like coffee, tea, and water."

Arco pours hot tea for me and coffee for himself, then we walk toward the narrow tables along the bowed window that stretches the length of the wall just like it does in the Records room. The same endless expanse of midnight blue unfolds in the glow of the building's exterior lights, but there's no life to be seen out there now, only The State's covered dome, hazy in the distance, and closer up, the symmetrical, undulating lines of the rest of the Gaia buildings, all of them edged in the same light on the top and the bottom.

"It looks like the outline of a huge, hilly road turned on its side out there," I say, gesturing toward the window over Arco's shoulder as he takes a seat across from me. He turns to follow my gaze and then nods, sipping his coffee.

"This whole place is on its side," he replies, turning back to face me.

"Did you think this is what it would be like here—just weird classes and serving homesteads and State personnel?" I ask, blowing on my tea.

"I guess I don't really know what I thought any more. Every perception I had about this place got swallowed up by reality as soon as they told us we got in...which seems like a lifetime ago already. What about you?"

"I thought it was the only chance we had," I say, trying to find better words somewhere in the endless water beyond the window. "I mean, I thought we'd finally be on the path we'd worked toward all these years, but now that it's gone, I guess I'm wondering what it was all for."

"We still have a path, Jazz. It's just a different one."

I look over at him and wonder how he can be so calm when we have no idea what happens to us from here on out—no promise of stability, no guarantee of any future that even remotely resembles what we've been preparing for all this time.

"How do you do that? How do you never worry about what's next?" I ask, watching his eyes warm with an immediate answer.

"I guess I'm too busy trying not to mess up right now," he says through a laugh that makes me feel lighter everywhere inside.

"I just wish I could do it," I say, smiling. "I wish I didn't feel like I had to spend every second trying to plan the future."

"Everyone tries to picture an *eventually* for themselves, at least to some degree. Before things blew up, I read a tutorial about the pod training rotation, and how when we graduate, we can keep traveling, or choose a base career...one where we can go home every night, and I wondered what I'd do, what I would want then," he says, taking a long sip of his coffee, then wraps his hands around the cup and leans in, resting his forearms on the small table between us.

"Did you decide?"

"I did today, yeah. I'd want my eventually to be a base career," he answers, then hesitates a second before looking up from his coffee to me. "I mean, I'd like to have a family at some point," he smiles as much as he can, consciously holding my eyes for a beat before looking out the window next to us.

A wave of heat hits me in the chest just as if he'd aimed a blower at it. I can feel it rushing up my neck to my cheeks as I look into my cup, then clear my throat and focus everything I can to push him *not* to ask me the same question. It's not fair to be able to feel someone else's emotions in a situation like this, especially if he doesn't even realize that I can tell his intended context is possibly a family someday *with me*—I'm not supposed to know that yet. It's too much pressure. What if I don't know what my *eventually* is? What if I don't even know what I'm doing about tomorrow in light of everything that's happened *today?* Our friends are missing, and we may have found family members who have been missing, which we didn't even realize until now. I want to say all of this, but it's not what comes out.

"Yeah," I say. "That might be nice." I bite my lip, take another sip of tea, and stare again into the expanse of nothing outside the window as I wait for the warm liquid to hit my system and tell me what to do.

After a minute, Arco reaches for my hand. I look down at his long fingers folding around mine, and something about it makes my throat close up.

"You don't always have to have a plan, Jazz," he says in a quiet voice, which makes everything at the brim in my chest spill over. I think of the marlin...that its message has actually been my *father's*, and that he's *alive*. I think about how I've been wrong about Liddick for years, and about how I don't understand this weird duality I have with Vox, who's now missing along with Fraya and the others. I think about these vacillating feelings of wanting to throttle Arco to...*this* feeling all in one afternoon, and not even knowing what this feeling is.

A hot tear starts down my cheek in my exhaustion, and I watch it dot the smooth metal finish of the table. I still can't swallow. I can't even take a decent breath, but I can sit here and let him hold my hand because I do understand that. The world won't end if I don't know anything else yet, he's right, but if I'm supposed to be able to figure out other people's feelings, I should probably start with my own.

"Arco..." I start, but lose my nerve. His fingers tighten around mine, and I take another sip, which is too fast, but at least the burning sensation on the roof of my mouth helps me steel myself enough to talk again. "Arco, what's happening? I mean, *this*, with us now? It all feels different from when we were home, even different from this morning," I finally say, the exhale lagging a few seconds after I finish the sentence. He waits before he answers, letting a smile arc along the side of his face that isn't bruising as we sit here.

"Not for me," he says into his coffee just before he takes another sip. He swallows, then swallows again, tracing his thumb over the back of my hand as he search-es my face for what to say next, then looks back down at the table with a muffled laugh. "It's funny because I always thought it was so obvious. How I was so clumsy around you all those years, all my bad jokes and awk-wardness," he says, his sandy brown waves falling over his forehead and into his eyes. I shake my head at him because none of that stood out to me as strange at all. He's always just been...*Arco*.

"I never—" I start, but he picks up my hand and brings it to his chest to stop me, folding his hand around mine.

"I know you thought that was me, and I guess it was, but it wasn't who I wanted you to see," he says.

"Arco, you're one of my best friends," I say, trying to find a way to let him know I've never thought anything but good things about him. He nods as he leans in, my hand still entwined with his, which is held so tightly against him that I can feel his heart pounding against the back of my wrist. "We've known each other since we could walk," I smile, lowering my chin to find his eyes.

"And I've probably loved you since then," he says, looking up at me warily. He takes a quick breath, exhaling almost as quickly, and I feel relief wash over me, but then a terrible sense of loss that wrestles against whatever this is that's exploding in my chest right now...which feeling is mine and which is his, or are they *both* mine? "So there it is..." he says, letting go of my hand and backing away in his seat, "...and I don't expect you to—"

I lean over the small table between us, trying to aim for the side of his mouth that isn't cut and bruised. I don't think about doing it, and am actually surprised to see myself doing it like I'm watching someone else in my skin, but I kiss him. *I* kiss *him*. It feels right, easy...I didn't plan it, and it's the one thing I'm sure about in this whole stupid place.

I rest both my forearms on the table and feel his fingertips along my jaw, his right thumb brushing my cheek as his tongue slips over mine. His fingers slide through my hair, gently pulling me closer, more deeply into the kiss, which makes my stomach feel like it's just been caught by a fast-rising hot-air balloon soaring up from the ground. Cold tingling like the oxygen dose Dame Mahgi gave me earlier spreads into my fingers and toes as I lift my right hand to touch his face. He winces for an instant, and I realize I've skimmed over his bruised cheekbone. I start to pull back, but his fingers close in more tightly around the back of my neck as he slides me out from behind the table and to my feet. I vaguely realize I'm on my tiptoes as his hand brushes over my ribs, then wraps around the back of my waist, pulling me against him while his other hand moves through my hair. The side of his thumb brushes against my jaw as he brings me closer, restrained, but firm, and I can feel his heart pounding under my hands, every muscle tensed and hard pressing against me in a surge of feeling that makes my head swim. I'm doing this to him? *Just me?*

Everything is stopped, yet spinning at the same time. His lips press against mine again in a new rhythm, this one not as slow or easy. I feel his tongue slip over mine again, and the balloon under my stomach hits a pocket of wind that sends it up in another burst of momentum. As soon as I make the conscious realization that I'm standing here kissing *Arco Hart,* the boy who used to put sand down the back of my pants, the boy who carried me up the beach with a jellyfish sting, the flailing boy on the shuttle who accidentally split *my* lip, we're still again, almost frozen in place, too afraid to move. His fingers are trembling against my throat, and I feel like I might fall through the floor again if he weren't holding me up, just like by the moon pool.

It suddenly all comes together in that moment. I see him as he really has been all these years: constant, honest, thoughtful, brave, and I'm speechless. *Almost.*

"I see you," I say against his lips. At least, I think I say it. My voice is so quiet, it could be a thought. But I must say it because he exhales quickly and abruptly like he's been holding his breath all day, and his fingers close around the back of my neck again as he angles my chin up to meet his eyes, which flicker that same green-gold color they did by the water. I feel that sense of calm again, that certainty and safety standing there folded up in him. His arms wrap around me, and I rest my cheek against his chest, which rises and falls as he takes in another deep breath and exhales, his heart still pounding. His chin touches the top of my head, and we stand like this for a minute more watching the endless dark blue water stretch out before us, which doesn't seem so empty any more.

CHAPTER 40
Truce

He holds my hand in his as we walk to the cafeteria, firmly, like any second he thinks a passing wind might blow me away from him. Everything is still spinning around inside me, but for the first time in months, I feel sure about something. I try to figure out when this all changed for me. When did I start having feelings for him like this? Just a handful of days ago, even just this morning, everything was different, but he's the same as he was then, isn't he? That can only mean I'm the one who has changed, but I'm not sure how. Maybe these nanites that are supposed to expedite our learning, our natural classifications, have sharpened other things too—blown off the dust somehow, or just shone a light?

I try not to think too much about it, but it's hard not to wonder if this is how love works...something just happens, and all you can do is watch yourself take action because everything inside you knows before you do that it's the right thing to do—that love is a sense of safety and certainty *for once* when so much else seems to be going in different directions or dependent on so many things out of your control—but whatever it is, you feel like you can trust it.

"I'm not even hungry," Arco says, grinning as we approach the cafeteria. "Are you?"

"Not even a little," I answer.

"I guess we should get something, though—it's going to be a long night," he says, scanning the room for the others. We grab a few trays and walk toward the selections, picking out some grapes and potato wedges. Jax, Ellis, Avis, Pitt, Joss, and Myra are at our table already, and tension suddenly sweeps over me. It's coming from Arco having seen Jax, or more specifically, having seen the absence of Fraya and Vox. Then reality hits me again —we've been lost in the last 45 minutes, but our friends are gone, we don't know where, and it's probable that the only people who can help us are in on it. My stomach clutches, and I swallow hard, trying to brace myself for the full effect of these feelings that I know will hit me like a tidal wave as soon as we get to the table. Jax, Avis, Myra, and Ellis weren't supposed to talk about it, but I can't imagine how they were able to keep quiet when Jax and Fraya have been inseparable for months, and Vox is one person who is definitely hard to miss. I scan the room for Liddick and Tieg, but don't see either one. Dez is sitting at a table with some other Skyboard students I don't recognize, decipherable only by their physiques at this distance.

"I don't see Liddick or Tieg. Do you think everything is OK?" Arco asks as we head toward the table.

"Liddick is probably trying to find out more about what happened earlier. I don't know about Tieg," I answer, now a little nervous about where they could be. Tieg was going to ask me something before he walked away there in the corridor, and I wish he would have. The unsettled feeling gnaws at the corner of my consciousness, and I try to push it back because the suffocation from the table has already started closing in.

Jax eyes Arco and doesn't even blink. He hasn't calmed down at all, and in fact, I think he might even be angrier now than he was earlier, though that's hard to imagine. I walk in front of Arco to try and break the line of his stare. It works, and his eyes flit to me, warming a little. I sit in the empty seat across from Jax, and Arco sits to my right, a wall of ice forming instantly between them. Arco tries to talk with Ellis about something, but I can feel his anxiety radiating off him with the obvious space for Fraya next to Jax, and the space on the other side of me for Vox.

"Hey," I say to Jax, testing the water.

"Hey," he responds flatly, then starts poking at his untouched food.

"Tieg isn't here," I say, scanning the room again. "Have you seen him?"

"He came to my room looking for Pitt, but then left again," Jax answers. "I haven't seen him since." He looks up at me, glances at Arco, then back to me, raising his eyebrows. I shake my head slightly to indicate that I'm not upset with Arco any more, and he takes a resigned deep breath, exhaling slowly. "He wasn't happy earlier," Jax continues, referring to Tieg.

"I know. Liddick told me," I say, then catch his eye again, tilting my head toward Arco.

Jax knows what he needs to do; he's just too proud to do it. I raise an eyebrow at him, then the other and angle my head toward Arco again. He rolls his eyes, then nods after a second, and I feel his ice wall start to melt. He takes another deep breath and presses his lips into a line, then swallows down the anger and pain trying to surface and explode all over Arco again. I can see him make up his mind right there, just decide to feel a different way. He's done this so many times before when things haven't gone the way he's expected—when Cora Avery broke up with him, when we thought our father died...

He suffers until he decides he's not going to any more, then just flips the switch somehow. I've always been envious of that ability. His face softens, the hard lines around his brown eyes melt away, and the ridged set of his mouth and jaw relaxes. He pushes his hands through his dark, curly hair, closes his eyes to shut off this reality so he can open them in another. When he does open them, the wall is gone. Arco must feel it too because he stops talking with Ellis and looks over to Jax, who finally looks like his best friend again.

"Ripley, I—" Arco starts, but Jax shakes his head at him.

"I know. It was the only choice you had. I would have done the same thing in your shoes," he says with a nod at Arco, then winces. "Sorry I hit you. Apparently, a lot." Arco smiles to the right, his left cheekbone starting to redden more deeply now, not to mention the cut on his lip and eyebrow.

"I'd have done the same thing," he says. Ellis looks over to us tentatively now that the others at the table have noticed Arco's face, and have realized that Vox and Fraya aren't going to show up.

"What's going on?" Joss asks, and the table falls silent

awaiting an answer from someone. I take a deep breath. There's no way we're going to be able to avoid talking about this, at least to some degree.

"You know our test drive today, the Leviathan ships and the Stingray roamers?" I ask, and Joss nods. "We were on our exploration and Vox steered off course for a minute, then disappeared. Fraya was in the Stingray with her," I continue, trying to figure out how much to hold back and how much I won't be able to, but I don't know what Ms. Reynolt expects me to say when two of our friends just don't show up for dinner, and the last place anyone saw them was with us.

"Disappeared?" he asks, his eyebrows knitting together when he sees Pitt's arm move around Myra's shoulder. "You were out there when that happened?" he asks her.

I can feel Myra's worry starting to percolate and need to stop that before it even starts, or it's going to spread like a grassfire.

"Ms. Reynolt and Dr. Denison have it all handled. They're sending a team to find them—I'm sure it will all be OK," I lie, hoping no one can tell.

"So they just went off the sonar?" Joss asks, still not quite sure this isn't a bad joke.

"We were all on our way back, and they just went a different way. That's all we know right now," Arco says, trying to squash the questioning.

"That doesn't make any sense—why would she just turn off in a different direction?" Joss presses. "Especially with Fraya on board—did anyone go after them?" he asks, and I feel the stab of regret that goes through Arco.

"We couldn't," Jax says. "It was too risky, so we came back for help."

Arco looks at Jax, surprised as Joss raises his blond eyebrows and swallows whatever he was going to say, clear disapproval on his face.

"It all went sideways pretty fast," Ellis says. "We did everything we could in the time we had." He nods to Arco, following Jax's supportive lead, which gives way to a heavy silence.

"We'll get them back," Arco says. "One way or another, we'll get them back."

CHAPTER 41
The Call

We start for the Records room after Joss and Pitt leave for the fitness room, but no one has seen Tieg or Liddick since before dinner.

"I'll go back and check our dorm—maybe Tieg is there. I only want to say all this once," Arco says.

"Maybe he went down to the fitness room too. That's the first thing Pitt wants to do whenever we have ten seconds," Jax says impatiently, then tilts his head to Ellis. "We'll go check."

Ellis nods as they head for the fitness wing, then stops and darts a glance at Arco. "Who's Liddick's roommate?" he asks all of a sudden. "Mine is Avis, yours is Tieg, Jax's is Pitt…"

"And Joss's roommate is someone named Parker," Myra adds.

"I don't think he's mentioned having one," I say. "Can you have a single room here?"

"We're talking about Liddick—he probably talked them into giving him a penthouse," Avis says, then gestures to Myra. "We'll see if he's in the Boundaries room. He was heading that way after we docked. Meet back here in what, an hour?"

"That works," Arco says. Jax nods, cutting Arco a look before he catches himself, then he and Ellis turn to follow Avis and Myra out.

"He still wants to kill me," Arco says around a forced laugh as he interlaces his fingers with mine.

"Then I guess we should go find Tieg so you can start explaining everything," I say.

He gives me a sideways look and squints. "Maybe we both shouldn't go find him..." he says, and realization dawns on me. After what Liddick said about him seeing Arco and me, it would probably be awkward if we both actually found him. I nod at Arco. "I'm sure he won't be happy if I find him, but hey, it's not like he can make this much worse, right?" Arco gestures to his face and tries to smile, and I wince at the now dark bruising.

"Does it hurt a lot?" I ask, angling his left side toward me with my fingertips.

"Nah," he lies, judging from the way his free left hand clenches into a fist as he turns his head, "but don't worry. I never saw Jax coming, if Tieg tries—" he stops abruptly and looks at me again, gripping my hand tightly in realization of what he's just said. "Jazz, that's it."

"What?" I say, not sure what I'm feeling from him right now—dread and excitement all at once.

"When Jax hit me, I never saw it coming. That's what the mar—" he stops himself again and presses his lips together like the words are still trying to come out against his will.

"Arco, *what?*"

"We'll talk about it in an hour, I promise. Are you going to go back to your room, or are you heading over to Records?"

"I don't know. I haven't thought about it. But my room

might be weird since Vox isn't..." I say, trailing off. He nods, and relaxes his grip on my hand.

"We'll find them," he says, and it's my turn to nod.

"I'm going to find Tieg. You'll be in the Records room in an hour?"

"On one condition," I say, which makes his eyes widen in surprise. He lowers his chin and cocks an eyebrow as a smile starts in the corner of his mouth.

"And what's that?"

"Call the medi-droid? It's the button on your wall by your bed. At least that's where it is in my room," I say. His smile widens as he nods.

"All right," he says, and slips his hand into my hair, his fingers folding around the back of my neck like before.

This kiss is different from the other two, not desperate like the first, not heated like the second. This one is gentle and warm, and I feel my whole body flood with it. He touches his forehead to mine like he did with our helmets earlier, the tips of our noses touching. I imagine the gagging noises Vox might make in my head if she saw us like this, and I smile for a second before I remember everything all over again. *How* do I keep forgetting the reality that she's gone?

"Hey," Arco traces his thumb over the edge of my bottom lip and smiles, which gives way to a small laugh that makes something in my chest swell.

"What?" I ask, starting to laugh myself, but he just shakes his head.

"Nothing, it's going to be OK," he says, and then I understand what it is that keeps pushing the worry and fear away…I believe him.

***

After Arco goes to find Tieg, I remember that Ms. Reynolt was supposed to talk to me at some point tonight. My heart starts pounding at the idea of it, but I have to talk to her. I have to find out what she knows. I look at my bracelet cuff for any messages, but there are none, so I decide to walk back to her room to see if she might be there. When I get there, the room is locked and the light is out. I could wait in my dorm, but I can't bring myself to go back there before I have to, not while I know that Vox is out there somewhere, and I can't even imagine poor Fraya. At least Vox knows how to survive in strange places since she's a boundary scout; didn't she say she even escaped from an underground trap once? She survived then, she can survive this. I have to believe that. But Fraya has never even been to the edge of the beach where the woods start because she's always been too afraid that Vox's people were cannibals. The irony of it all hits me, and I sigh. I have to stop thinking about it for now and remember that Vox won't let anything happen to her. I know she won't.

Before long, I'm wandering by the Boundaries room, which is just barely illuminated in that same pearlescent light that filters through everything here. It's empty when I walk in, but it doesn't feel empty, although I'm sure I don't see anyone. All the stations are turned off, but there's a low hum coming from somewhere. I look around again for the source of it, but stupidly realize I'm not going to be able to see a noise, so try to listen harder.

I close my eyes and take a step. It starts to get a little louder, so I take another step toward one of the stations, and then it fades. I readjust in the other direction and follow the trajectory, noticing that it gets even louder the closer I get to the chair where we'd found Vox sitting on Arco's lap before. The memory of that sight sends lines of fire up the sides of my throat all the way to my scalp, and I'm instantly, violently angry. The abruptness of the feelings makes me anticipate Vox's tingle in the back of my head, but of course that doesn't come. These are my feelings, and they must have been mine in the cafeteria when I saw her hanging all over him. This makes me wonder if when Liddick said *I didn't know it was like that* with Arco, did he really mean I didn't know *it was like that* for me too?

The buzzing is louder now, just like it was in Ms. Plume's office and just like it was in the cave. I have to get closer. I force myself to take the last few steps toward the station, compelled by the droning buzz that gets more and more urgent the closer I get. I squeeze my eyes until they're nearly closed trying to brace against the growing sound as I reach for the helmet, and a static crackling begins to compete with the sound in my head. For a second, I think I can hear a voice.

Vox? I push myself into the chair against the noise as if it were a solid force, the buzzing stitched with a low-pitched ringing now, and the crackling becoming more frequent. I focus as hard as I can on reaching out to Vox with my thoughts on the wild chance it could be her, but she doesn't reply. I look up at the helmet and realize it's the source of the buzzing that now turns into peals of high-pitched squealing, and I fight with myself to bring that impossible sound down directly over my ears. I reach for it, every muscle in my body protesting. I clench my jaw, squeezing my eyes closed even more tightly now against the noise that feels like it's ricocheting off my skull and into my teeth as I lock the helmet in place on my head. Then, all at once, the noise stops, leaving only the static.

Vox? I think again, hoping, but there is no reply except the crackle. I brace myself again in anticipation of the returning noise once I raise my hands to take off the helmet, and as soon as my hands touch it, I hear her.

She's OK, Vox says as clearly as if she were standing right next to me, and I can hardly believe it's really her.

Vox! Where are you? What happened? How are you making this transmission? I think.

Don't have time. Fraya is OK. Don't come through the cave —they're waiting there. There's a vent opening just past the cave that comes through to us, but I don't know if it's safe. I'll try to find another way, she replies.

Who's waiting? Vox? What's happening? Are you with Liam? I ramble, but she's gone, and so is the static. I sit in denial for another minute calling to her, but she doesn't come back. My heart pounds against my ribs as I lift the helmet, half of it physiological in preparation for the deafening buzz, which I anticipate, but never comes. I stand and press my hands to my face before turning around and jumping at the sight of Liddick standing in the doorway, his forearms hoisted up to his shoulders and braced against either side of the frame. He looks like he hasn't slept in days with his jaw set hard and his eyes almost pleading.

"Liddick?" I say, startled. "What's wrong?" But he only shakes his head. "Where were you all this time? I looked for you at dinner, but..."

"I wasn't hungry," he says abruptly. His voice is gruff, and the general exhaustion I've just felt from him turns to fear. Something has happened.

Liddick, what is it? I think, hoping he'll talk to me this way. He just looks up at me with wounded eyes, and I see the muscles working in his jaw for control. I feel like something is reaching into my chest and ripping out everything, but I don't know how to stop it—how to stop him from feeling this way. *Tell me what happened to you.* I think, starting to panic, then take several steps toward him. He doesn't budge from the doorframe, and his chin falls to his chest when I reach him. His face is pale with a thin sheen of sweat coating his skin, and he's ice cold when I reach up to angle his face so I can see his eyes.

"Liddick?" I say out loud, trying to keep my voice level.

"It's OK," he says, closing his eyes and swallowing. He releases the fist in his right hand and waves me over, his wrist propping him up against the doorframe. I raise my eyebrows, but take a few more steps until I'm perpendicular to him. "More," he says, and I move until my hip is touching his.

"Liddick, what—?" I start to ask, but he answers me by nearly collapsing onto my shoulder before I can get the rest of the words out. I catch him, my hand instinctively flying to his chest as I take a few stumbling steps forward, then back to balance us. I wrap my other arm around his waist and get him through the doorway enough to position his back against the wall inside the room. He slides down it, and I kneel beside him, taking his freezing hands in mine to try and warm them. "Liddick, what happened? I'm calling a medi-droid," I say, tapping screen after screen on my bracelet trying to find the instructions.

"No..." he answers, leaning his head back against the wall and closing his eyes. "Don't call. It'll scan me. I just need to sit here a minute," he says, swallowing again.

"You need some water. I can go to the student center and—"

"No. Stay," he says, swallowing again. I don't know what to do—even what I can do.

"You're freezing. How are you freezing and sweating at the same time?" I ask, and he shakes his head slightly from side to side.

Too hard to talk, I hear him say in my head. *Your hands are warm.*

I move closer and wrap my hand around his fingers again, bringing my other to hold against his cheek.

Liddick, what happened to you?

Port-carnate, I hear him think, and that's when everything inside me stops.

Port-carnate? Are you split? You promised you wouldn't try that!

Had to. I went to see a friend who can help us, he thinks, the color starting to come back into his cheeks as I move my hand over his face. He blinks several times, then squeezes his eyes shut for a second before reopening them. They're bloodshot, making the blue seem almost supernatural.

What's wrong? Can you see? I ask him.

You're just a little blurry, he thinks, smirking, then tries to blink a few more times.

How long have you been like this?

Just got back. Maybe 10 minutes. I was in that station where you were.

You were in here the whole time I was? Where? I think, looking around the room for somewhere I could have overlooked.

Over there. He angles his head to the opposite corner near the back of the room. *I moved to the doorway when you sat at the station. I thought I could get back to my dorm without you seeing me like this.*

"Well, I'm taking you there now. Come on," I say out loud, then wedge my shoulder under his arm. He pushes off the floor and against the wall, trying to get to his feet, which he manages after a stumble. He leans heavily on my shoulder, and I push against him as we walk a few steps before he stops to brace his hands on his knees.

"Dizzy," he breathes.

"Crite, Liddick. What did you *do* to yourself?" I ask, my pulse racing because I can't fix this—I can't do anything to repair whatever he's cooked inside himself. Port-carnate, what kind of *stupid*..."Liddick?" I say suddenly as he starts to sway, then I move to his side and put my shoulder under his arm again. "OK, we have to call a medi-droid."

"No!" he says adamantly, then drops to his hands and knees and begins to cough.

"OK, OK, let's just go to your room then. Come on. Can you get up?"

He lifts one knee off the floor and levers up on it, his arm around my shoulder for balance. We stand, and he lets his head fall back, closing his eyes and taking a long, deep breath before we take another step. When he looks forward, he opens his eyes, blinks again, and starts to walk slowly. I hold onto his wrist draping over my shoulder and lean into his ribs to help keep him upright, my fingers gripping the waist of his jumpsuit, which surprisingly makes him laugh.

You're going to give me a flosser like that, he thinks, and now I laugh too, loosening my grip on his waistband.

"Sorry," I say out loud through an exhale. We're able to pick up the pace a little as we approach the boys' corridor, and I scan for anyone who might see us. "Listen, there may be people in the hallway here." I say. He nods, and tries to straighten up as much as he can.

You'll just have to pretend to be my girl, he thinks, and I can't help but smile at his audacity, even now, feeling the way he must. I want to be fearless like he is.

You're impossible, I reply, shaking my head.

Hope Hart's not around. Or Spaulding...crite, Rip, you're breaking hearts everywhere today, he thinks, and I roll my eyes.

Tieg is split—I've only had two conversations with him, and if I would have known anyone was watching us out there...

I was watching you out there, he says in my head, and I glance up at him. His eyes are barely open, and he looks like he could pass out at any second.

Which room is yours? I ask, silently.

"27-K," he says aloud as I read the doors.

27-G...good, we're almost there.

"I laughed at first," he says deliriously and out loud again as his head falls forward.

Liddick, hang on. Just a few more doors. I think, scanning again to the end of the hallway and hoping no one appears. We get to his room, and I help him raise his bracelet cuff to the reader. The door slides open, and I walk him to his bed as the door closes behind us. "Here, just lie down," I say out loud, helping him find his way. He sits, and in one fluid motion, collapses back onto the pillow without letting go of my arms, which makes me fall on top of him. "Sorry! Are you OK?" I say, scrambling to get to my knees and push myself up, but he grips my hips and holds me in place. I'm so shocked that I momentarily freeze. He closes his eyes, but he's not asleep because I can still hear him in my head.

I laughed because I couldn't believe he finally won after all these years.

"Liddick, what are you talking about? Let me go so I can get you some water."

No water. No more water. His voice in my head trails off, and almost immediately, his hands release my hips and fall to his sides.

CHAPTER 42
The Net

"Liddick? *Liddick!*" I slide to the side of the bed and shake his arms. His eyes flutter. "Liddick, I have to get a medidroid here right now."

"No...it will scan me...will find out my nanites are wrecked," he says through another cough. "It has to be... the nanites..."

"What are you talking about?"

*They're not working. I think they're scrambled...*he continues in his thoughts. *The droid will trace the cause and report why. Can't believe I forgot... about nanites.*

"Liddick? Don't stop talking. What does scrambled mean? They can't fix themselves?"

"They're what's...doing this," he says, closing his eyes again. "Need a dose of aligned ones to... reprogram mine."

"Hey! Wake up," I say, leaning over his chest and patting his cheek, gently at first, then audibly. "Liddick, wake up." He doesn't answer, but reaches up for my hands. His are still so cold, so I wrap my fingers around them again.

*Closer...*I hear in my mind. I lean in toward him, and feel the sudden chill of his fingertips on my throat, then feel them walking behind my jaw and entwining in my hair. He pulls me in closer, and I search his face, confused.

"Liddick, can you hear me?" I ask in a whispered voice, my mouth just inches away from his. His eyes are still closed, but his heartbeat under my hands is strong. "Liddick?" I say, then focus my thoughts before he passes out completely again. *Where do I find another dose of the same nanites? Tell me how to get them for you,* I say, hoping he can still hear me.

You already have them, he says silently before bringing my mouth down over his, parting my lips in a rush of momentum and suddenly moving his tongue over mine.

It happens in slow motion, but all at once—I never saw it coming. In this moment I'm disconnected from everything I knew before, plunging into a tunnel without anything to hold onto except him. My fingers curl down into the fabric of his collar and his tighten gently in my hair as he pulls me in more firmly, his tongue passing over mine, moving in and out of my mouth until I feel dizzy. I lose all sense of up and down in this falling like we've jumped— like we had the audacity to jump when everything else said to stay, which is exactly something he would do—what I wish I could do more.

I forget to breathe and start to see white spots behind my eyelids, instinct, forcing me to pull back and gasp. It's like the first breath I've ever taken as the sudden, cool air burns my throat and lungs, but I take another and another despite the pain because I have to.

Liddick's hands are still woven through my hair, and I can feel the pressure of his fingers against the nape of my neck. I'm afraid to open my eyes, though, I don't even remember shutting them. I'm afraid to see where I really am and what really just happened because it's so nice to be in between knowing things for once—between right and wrong, after acting, but before understanding. And all at once it starts to slip away like waking up in the middle of a dream.

When I do open my eyes, his are clear and blue again, the bloodshot having faded completely. I search for words, something to put a framework of meaning around all this, but both my mind and throat lock up with the effort.

I should say that I'm sorry, but I've been waiting five years for another chance to do that right, he thinks, his trademark smirk tugging at the corner of his mouth. I swallow hard, then swallow again in an effort to get my bearings. I think it works because I become aware that my fingers are not only still gripping his collar, but are *actually* pulling some of the hairs on his chest at the bottom of four thin, reddening welts. I try to relax my hand immediately, shocked, but it's stiff like rigor mortis has set in, and my fingers ache as I try to straighten them—how hard and how long was I holding on like this?

It baffles me. The entire feeling of being alive outside of myself baffles me, and this is how he always makes me feel with his unpredictable, blind jumping, just like in the ocean that night we all sneaked away from the port festival. I never would have followed him, and I never would have gotten stung by that jellyfish if he hadn't made me feel like I could do anything.

I blink, then blink again. I should move, I should leave, but none of these thoughts make it through to the version of myself that has the power to make them happen.

You're not cold any more, is the first thought the inside version of me thinks, noticing the heat coming through his shirt as I try to straighten my fingers again.

Thanks to you, he replies. I look at him, puzzled because I realize that I have no idea how he's just suddenly better. *We have the same classification...Hybrid: Coder and Reader Empath, so we have the same nanite infrastructure.*

I must still look puzzled because he starts to chuckle until he coughs, then chuckles again. I find my voice, and with it, motor skills that help me pull back slowly. His hand falls to my shoulders, then down to my waist as I sit up beside him.

"What's funny?" I say out loud, still a little dizzy.

"The look on your face...like you're going to kill me, but you just saved me." He laughs around another cough. *I'm back because of you...because of the fluid exchange. The dose of nanites I needed to set off the chain reaction realignment was in your saliva.*

A sudden heat races up my throat and over my cheeks as my stomach stops hard and my heart begins to pound. Did he use me? Was *that* all this was?

He starts to chuckle again over broken coughs, shaking his head back and forth as adamantly as he can while sliding my hand over his heart, laying both of his on top of it.

"Whoa...whoa..." he says out loud. "Calm down, it's not like that. You just saved my life, Riptide." I feel the heat in my cheeks flare again, this time the result of conflicting feelings suddenly fighting for dominance—I want to leave right now, but part of me believes there's a reason not to, and I look away to sort it out. "Hey," he grips my hand, which he presses flat against his chest. "You can feel this and know, so don't do that," he says seriously, and this makes me look back at him.

He's quiet then as he meets my eyes without any of his standard issue flattery or charm, and I can feel his adamance pushing back at me, and underneath it, *a... loss? A fear?* No, he wouldn't just use me, I realize that now and nod as I try to understand this other feeling, but his eyes suddenly resume their normal flicker, and his mouth shifts into the smirk he wears like a favorite hat.

"Liddick, wh—" I start to ask him what he was afraid of just now, but he interrupts me.

"Though, for the record, rushing up on you like Hart did...not really my style." He closes his eyes in a long blink and shakes his head again. "Let's chalk that one up to being medically necessary," he grins, then looks at me soberly. "When I kiss you, I want you to know it's coming." I try to resurrect my question, but after hearing that, it's gone, and I realize my mouth is dry and my muscles feel weak. I try to think of something to say, but I can't. "It just hit you, didn't it?" he asks. "The fatigue?"

"Just now," I say, nodding and wishing I could lie down right here and sleep for three days.

"It's the defrag. Your nanites are essentially beating the alignment into my wrecked ones, which probably started trying to corrupt yours the second they entered your body," he says, and I look at him in surprise. "No! Don't worry," he says, chuckling around a cough again. "They're way too outnumbered. The fatigue will pass once they're repaired," he nods for emphasis, and I feel my outrage start to subside.

"And you?" I ask. "The same thing is happening in reverse inside you?"

"Essentially, but it'll take a lot longer for yours to make their way through. They're outnumbered too, but a lot stronger. Of course, we *could* expedite things if you'd like to kiss me again," he says, raising my hand to his lips, then angling his head and cocking an eyebrow at me as he kisses my fingers. And again, I can't help but smile at his stupid, reckless bravery.

"You're so impossible," I say, shaking my head and feeling order restore inside myself about him, about Arco, and about me. And then I remember...*Arco*.

"Whoa, what's wrong?" Liddick asks without missing a beat, and I scramble to downplay any uncertainty I have about what Arco's nanites might be doing to me now, or mine to him if kissing is all it takes to set off chain reactions like this.

"What happens if the nanites exchanged aren't the same?" I ask, feeling heat rise in my cheeks. Liddick smirks in understanding, and I suddenly wish I just would have looked up one of the tutorials Ellis is always going on about instead of asking.

"Nothing. They can't identify, Rip," he answers, pressing my hand to his chest again. "Nanites only see their own." He locks his eyes with mine, and I swallow hard, trying to steady the wave rising in my chest before it crashes and floods everything again. I clear my throat and move back to give him some room.

"Can you walk?" I ask, my voice sounding too loud and too high in my ears.

"I think so," he says, smiling, and after a second as he props up on his elbows. I stand, and he swings his legs over the side of the bed and braces his hand on his night-stand. He pushes up, then stands there for a few seconds to make sure he's not going to fall right back down, and when he's sure, he looks at me and nods. He takes a slow step, then another, then stumbles, and I move to help steady him.

"Are you OK?" I ask. He nods again, and I take a step back, but his arm wraps around my shoulder and pulls me back into him.

"But better safe than sorry," he grins again. Why is everything he says and does to push the limit like this so...likable? But maybe it's not. Maybe he just wants me to believe it is.

Liddick? I ask him in my thoughts. *Did you push me to feel that way? When we were...I mean, back there?* He takes in a deep breath and pulls me closer to him, then leans over and kisses my temple. He stops walking just before we open the door, turns to face me, and holds my hand to his chest again.

"Read me and see," he says, looking into my eyes, unguarded like he did before, which is too intense and makes me look away.

"I don't know how to do that. I just hadn't..."

Hadn't ever felt like that, he thinks, which pulls my eyes back to his. *I know.*

You know because you put it there? I ask, feeling the edge that would be obvious in my voice.

I know because that's how I felt too—like the whole world was right there, just one step off the edge...I know you could feel it too, and you trusted me enough to take it. That's the only way I'll ever want this, Riptide—I'll never push you, he thinks, lowering his chin to find my eyes, and I feel a comfort spread in my chest when I hear his childhood nickname for me again. He smiles wide, then pulls me into an obnoxious, sloppy hug. He's warm everywhere now, and a feeling of happiness settles over me in knowing that he's all right. Seeing him like that—fading right there in front of me...I never want to feel like that again. They say guilt is the worst feeling in the world, but it's not. It's helplessness.

"What time are we going to Records?" he asks through my hair. I maneuver my wrist cuff into sight and suck in a short gasp.

"10 minutes ago," I say, pulling back from him and turning toward the door. "Come on, they probably already started."

CHAPTER 43
Developments

Liddick walks more slowly than he normally does as we make our way to the Records room, which is fine with me because it feels like I've been hiking all day, my muscles and joints starting to stiffen in protest of any more effort I might have in mind. He doesn't put his arm back around me for support once we leave his room, and while I'm glad that he's strong enough to walk without it, I admit I also feel a little disappointed.

Maybe I'm just picking up something he's feeling, though, because as my mind clears, I know I can't be with Liddick like that. We may be a lot alike, but no matter how exciting his way of living might be, I can't go clanging around in the world like that with no rules or responsibilities. That's how people get hurt.

So we're friends, and that's it. What happened back there was just medically necessary like he said, and I'll just have to explain that to Arco, even though my stomach plummets at the thought.

"What's wrong?" Liddick asks, looking over at me. I don't know if I'll ever get used to having an internal emotional megaphone like this with him.

"I have to tell Arco," I say, looking at the ground as we walk.

"Why?" he asks, narrowing his eyes like it's the most idiotic thing he's ever heard.

"Because I can't keep a secret about something like this from him," I answer quickly, trying to disguise my growing anxiety with self-righteousness.

"It's just going to cause trouble, and we've already decided what it was back there—you saved my life, right? I hope you're not counting that as my shot," he says, raising his eyebrow and grinning.

"I know, but—"

"Unless, of course, you're feeling like a shuttle just parked on your chest because you know as well as I do that we can call it whatever we want, but it doesn't really change what it was," he slows his pace, then stops and looks at me. "And telling Hart now is the only way you think you can get that shuttle to move," he says, tucking a strand of hair behind my ear. "That's what's really bothering you about seeing him in two minutes."

I start to flare, but then realize that he's right about the time, if nothing else, and I start walking again without responding. He catches up with me, but doesn't ask me anything else before we're halfway to the Records room, where I realize I still don't know what to do. Arco will see something is wrong like he always does, which will just complicate everything now more than it already is.

"I don't know if what I think dictates what I do any more, or if what I do dictates what I think," I answer. "All I know is that I'm tired of not knowing what to expect down here."

"It's not about knowing what to expect, Riptide. It's about knowing how to keep your head above water."

I let his words hang in the air before me for a minute.

Would telling Arco just do more harm than good, and do I only worry about this because I feel like I have something to hide? I decide I have to make that decision before I can say anything, and I'm not going to be able to do that in the 30 seconds it will take to close the distance between us and the threshold of the Records room, where I can already see Jax, Tieg, Myra, Avis, Arco, and Ellis sitting around the interview station where Abe Lincoln is chattering away silently inside the projection field. Jax paces behind the couch with his arms crossed as Arco talks, and I'm a little relieved that it looks like he's explaining what happened in the Stingray without me there —I wasn't looking forward to reliving that.

Several students are scattered at the other stations tonight, some in red and some in green jumpsuits, so they must not be first years like us. We walk up to our group, and I take a seat on the couch next to Tieg, a decision I make to put a buffer between him and Liddick as I remember the tensions between them over Dez. But I clearly don't think this through as a wave of panic jogs my memory about the rest of what Liddick said—about how Tieg saw Arco kissing *me* by the moon pool and then tweaked out about it over the comms system. Tieg keeps his eyes forward and crosses his arms over his chest as I approach, and my own chest starts to clench. I make a quick scan of the available seating, but there's nowhere else to go now. I take a seat as Arco smiles at me initially, but then brings his brows together just long enough that I notice...crite. I try to smile back at him reassuringly while he continues talking, then I glance at Liddick. He already knows something is wrong, I think.

He thinks it's Tieg, but stop worrying. I'll take care of it all.

What do you mean you'll—

"Hart, hey, sorry to interrupt you, but there's something you should know," he says, and I feel ice climb up every vertebra in my spine.

Liddick, are you split? What are you doing? I'll tell him myself, but I have to think about—

"We have to go after Vox and Fraya ourselves. Tonight. Reynolt and Denison are involved somehow, and any team they send won't be on a rescue mission." Liddick continues. Arco angles his head and cocks his eyebrow.

"How do you know that?" he asks.

"Because either the Reynolt who was down there before the launch was the real one, or the Empath clones operate on a different frequency. She wasn't empty like the others at first, but when we told her what happened in the moon pool bay? That's when the ice went up. They're covering for something," he says, then angles his head at me. "Ask her."

Everyone's eyes fall on me, and I take a breath. "He's right," I say, swallowing. "I got the same impression. I could tell she knew Vox and Fraya were gone as soon as I saw her, but when I confirmed it by telling her, she just pulled a curtain. And Denison wasn't even fazed by the news. I don't trust them."

"All right, but even if that's true, how are we supposed to go after them ourselves?" Avis asks, leaning in.

"Let's just say I did a little coding of my own this afternoon—you remember when Denison and the others walked into that light field in a single file line and came out cloned? Now we can do that too. We can take a ship, and no one will know we're gone," he says, looking at me and smiling almost imperceptibly, apparently pleased with himself that he almost gave me a heart attack. Arco's eyes narrow as he processes, then quickly dart to mine, then back again to Liddick as he waits for the rest of the story. I exhale, relatively assured that this is now going in a completely different direction than I'd feared, and my heart stops trying to crash through my ribs to run down the hall.

"That's actually not a bad idea—why didn't I think of that?" Ellis asks the ground, shaking his head.

"And exactly how are we supposed to cover for a missing ship, Wright?" Arco asks, now with a strange edge in his voice.

"I'll leave that one to a core engineer. We need an Omnicoder..." Liddick says, his eyes falling on Jax.

"You said we can leave tonight? Why not right now?" Jax asks.

"Do you have an instant ship-replacement plan we can execute that I don't know about?" Liddick asks. "I thought you might need at least a few hours to make an entire vessel available, then rig the system to actually get it out of the dock and into the water without anyone seeing you. But maybe you're more talented and resourceful than I was giving you credit for?" Liddick asks with a smirk. Jax nods.

"All right. I'll figure it out if you're sure we can go after them tonight."

"We're going to need Dez," I say, and both Liddick and Tieg immediately turn to me.

Are you split? Liddick says in my head, but I don't acknowledge him.

"In case someone needs medical help," I say.

"Myra's in biodesign too," Liddick protests.

"No, no, I'm just trained as a secondary. I can help, but I can't do—I mean I would, but I—" Myra stumbles.

"It's OK, Myra. That's why we need Dez," I say, then look right at Liddick. "I don't ever want to be in a situation where I can't get someone the help they need. It's just... too hard."

Liddick inhales slowly, resigned.

"No way," Tieg says, sitting up and resting his forearms on his knees, then opens his hands as if to catch a gravity ball while he talks. "If any of you think that I'm letting her get caught up in this, you're split."

"She's already caught up in it, Tieg. We all are. Something is out there taking people. It happened to Liddick's brothers, Arco's sister, somehow my father, and now Vox and Fraya. How long do you think it will be before it takes Dez, too, or Pitt, or one of us. How long before it takes *you?*" I say, turning in my seat to face him. He looks up at me with a set jaw and hard lines around his almost glowing blue eyes, but then softens his expression when he sees that mine is imploring instead of chastising. "We need her to help us stop whatever this is, *please,*" I say. "Will you ask her?"

He looks at me for a long time before he answers, leans his head to one side, and then looks at the ground with his hands clasped in front of him. He pushes his fingers through his light brown hair as he straightens up, then interlaces them behind his head before leaning back and closing his eyes.

"All right. I'll ask her," he says, and I let out the breath I'd been holding.

"And the thing that's taking people isn't the shadow in the cave—that's just what they want us to think so we'll go back there thinking we know what to look out for," Arco says, looking at me. "It hit me earlier tonight," he adds, smirking at Jax.

"When is the next port-call scheduled?" Ellis asks.

"Not until tomorrow night, so even if this all were to come together tonight, we'd have nothing for the piggy back to ride, and if it can't ride, it can't ping back coordinates. We have to wait until then," Arco says.

"If there's no team, we need to get in that cave now," Jax says, and the memory of Vox's message hits me hard enough that I actually feel my stomach contract. I boggle at my own self-absorption—first I forget that my friends are missing after everything with Arco, and now I forget to mention I actually *just talked* with Vox after everything with Liddick. What is *happening* to me?

"I talked to Vox—" I confess, and everyone stops arguing to look at me, stunned. "Almost an hour ago. I was wandering around waiting for Arco to find Tieg, and Ellis to find Liddick, and I wound up in the Boundaries room. I heard a buzzing coming from one of the helmets just like the buzzing from the cave, so I went to it, and it was her. She was calling us," I say, feeling breathless.

You talked to Vox? Liddick thinks, Then, in that chair?

Yes, I'm sorry I didn't tell you. I was a little distracted with your whole dying right in front of me thing at the time, then, with the...um—with the not dying any more thing.

"You're just now saying this? How did you not come running in here with news like that?" Avis scolds, raising his wispy black eyebrows and letting his mouth hang open after his last word, genuinely baffled.

"Hey," Arco holds up a hand to him.

"Did she tell you anything about Fraya? Is she OK?" Jax asks, bracing his hands on the back of the couch and leaning in.

"She said Fraya was OK, and that we shouldn't go through the cave because they were already waiting there. It's like Arco said...they want us to think we know the threat, but there's another that we must not be able to see—one that we'll never see coming," I say as pieces start falling into place.

"Is that all she said?" Tieg asks.

"After that, she said she would find another way in for us, and that there was a vent just past the cave that led to them too, but she didn't know if it was safe. That's all before the feed cut out."

"That's it, then," Tieg says, extending his arms out to either side of him along the back of the couch. He flinches when he realizes his fingers brush my arm, then brings his hand up to support his head instead. I stare at him for a second in total disbelief—crite, how long is this iceberg treatment going to last? "We can't get through the cave, and even if we could, it's not like we could leave a ship that size just sitting outside…someone would see it before long, and it would be a matter of time before they caught us. There's nowhere to go until Vox gives us new coordinates, and then we won't need to ping anything," he adds.

Jax exhales hard before pushing his hands through his hair. "I can't just stand here knowing she's out there somewhere, maybe hurt, or if someone—" he says, his voice breaking off on the last word as he crosses his arms over his chest. He clears his throat and swallows, clenching his jaw, then turns around to look through the long window on the far wall.

"Jax, Vox said she's OK…we'll find her," I say to his back, but he doesn't turn around.

"If the only thing stopping us right now is needing someone to rig an unauthorized port-call without triggering alarms, like I said, we can go tonight. My friend can help with that," Liddick says to his lap, then looks up at me before meeting everyone else's expectant stares.

"Your friend can pull off an unauthorized port-call?" Arco asks, narrowing his eyes. Liddick nods.

"I just need to fix my channel so I can send up a buoy signal when we're ready, then he can port-call down here to help set up the hop."

"Oh, so your friend is *topside?*" Arco laughs and puts his hands on his hips. "Yes, please, explain how you'll be using Gaia's own mainframe to send up a buoy signal to reveal our exact coordinates to some random topsider who will then port-call *to us* and set up an outgoing hop."

Liddick takes a patient deep breath. "Because Gaia's

mainframe will never see the buoy, or the channel for the port-call, or the outgoing hop," he says, but it doesn't seem to satisfy Arco, who hasn't changed his dubious expression or his stance. "All right, you want all the how I know he'll help us? Fine," Liddick says with one more quick look at me. "We were late tonight because I had just come back from a port-carnate call," he says.

Now Arco's eyebrows shoot up as Jax turns around abruptly, and the others lean forward in their seats. "I went to see that friend I just mentioned, and came back wrecked because I didn't consider the nanites in—"

"Heh, you don't look wrecked," Tieg interrupts, laughing as he eyes Liddick up at down.

"Like I was *about* to say, that's because Jazz saw me in the Boundaries room after she talked to Vox and...helped me until it passed," Liddick replies carefully, and I feel Arco's eyes on me before I even look at him.

"Port-carnate?" Myra asks, pushing forward in her chair. "But how?"

"The night before we left Seaboard, I had to know we could get out of here if we had to, so I went to see someone I knew could help. He gave me the micro-technics I'd need, and showed me how to set up a hop point from this end back to him."

"Wait, you did all that just *in case?* We've spent our whole lives trying to get into this place—why would you even think of *just in case?"* Avis asks. Liddick sighs again, then rallies, leaning forward on his elbows with his hands held out to help him explain.

"The night before we left to come here was the first

time Jazz heard the voice that said, 'I never saw it coming,' but I'd been hearing it a lot longer," he says, working his way into the whole story about Liam and Lyden, about the scar that Liam no longer had, and about the hijacked plots he'd experienced in the virtuo-cines. I catch Jax's eyes as he realizes now, too, that all this time we'd thought Liddick just got caught up in Skyboard culture after his siblings left, but he was actually researching—collecting snippets of code, short messages, missing words, anything that might help him solve the mystery that at the time, haunted only him.

As he explains, I see him again like I did that night on the beach after the marlin when he pulled me back from an edge I hadn't foreseen, and later that night when he seemed to be fighting even the wind. He's had this whole separate nightmare for years, and none of us ever knew. I feel guilty all over again, and don't understand how I couldn't have known any of this if we're as much alike as I'm learning we are.

"*Crite...*" Ellis says, looking drained when Liddick finishes catching everyone up.

"Why didn't you tell anyone?" Jax asks.

"It was my problem, and at the time, I didn't think it affected anyone else trying to get into Gaia. It wasn't until I saw Jazz reacting to everything I was seeing and hearing with the marlin that I knew I had to build a safety net before getting on that sub."

"So this was your friend you went to see, the one from Skyboard you were talking about earlier?" Arco asks, but Liddick shakes his head.

"Same friend, but no, he's not really from Skyboard, at least, not any more," he replies. "Sorry, I had to be sure you were invested first. He's in The Badlands."

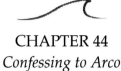

CHAPTER 44
Confessing to Arco

Everyone is speechless as Liddick's last words sink in—
The Badlands? I can't even put together a coherent
thought to ask him. He looks around at everyone's blank
faces and chuckles.

"They're not all tunnel diggers and cannibals," he says,
mocking our urban legend fears. "A lot of them are just
people who don't want to be a cog in the machine."

"And what machine is that?" Tieg asks, his eyes narrowing over the sharp cut of his cheekbone.

"All of this," Liddick says, looking around the room.
"This idea. This whole one-way track to *happiness* and
success—fame and *status.* Crite, we have an entire career
field that codes DNA just so people can look the part. A
lot of the Badlanders just don't want to be moulded into
society's version of somebody," Liddick answers, raising
his chin the way he did against the wind that night on
the beach, then darts a glance at Tieg.

"And what's wrong with creating opportunities?" Tieg
bristles, now moving to the edge of his seat like he's
going to get up. The heat coming from him and the ice
coming from Liddick meet in the middle, exactly where I
happen to be sitting, and it's anything but comfortable.

"He's not *saying* that—" I interrupt before Liddick has a
chance to stoke the fire he's just set. "He's saying that
some of them just didn't want to play the game. Our

whole lives have revolved around getting into this school, haven't they? At least ours have at Seaboard. I imagine there were similar expectations for you at Skyboard, maybe even more," I say to Tieg, and judging by the way his jaw relaxes in recognition, it must be true. "We've all felt the pressure to be what someone else has decided we should be. Probably even convinced ourselves that it's what *we* wanted too."

Tieg swallows and presses his lips together at this, and everyone looks down or away except for Liddick. He angles his head up and looks right at me, the corner of his mouth pulling back just before Jax puts everything back on course.

"Well, how's this Skyboarder supposed to help us from The Badlands when we're here under three miles of water?" he asks, tilting his head.

"He can walk me through how to launch these," Liddick says, holding out his hand to reveal two slim cylinders that together, are no bigger than a fingernail. "They're for your piggy back so you can ghost ping the messages again once you get it modified to ride an outgoing port-call."

"*Automators?* Where did you get those?" Arco asks, taking a few steps in for a closer look.

"From my friend when I ported earlier—he gave them to me after I explained how your code was going to take forever with the camouflage, but he made me promise to bring him in when we were ready to install them," Liddick explains to Arco, whose eyebrows draw together.

"Anyone can swallow automators. Why does *he* have

to do it?" Arco asks, an annoyed clip returning to his voice.

"Not him. Me. He aligned them with my bioprint just in case anyone got ideas about stealing them and leaving me behind," Liddick says, shaking his head and holding up a hand when Arco begins to protest. "I know, I told him I didn't have to worry about that, but he doesn't trust many people—you can understand why. He also insisted that he oversee the launch because apparently, these aren't your average automators. I need to find a way to fix whatever I corrupted in my channel when I came back through so I can at least send up the buoy, and then, open up a hop that can receive his port-call."

"If you can get a connection window on both ends like that, we really can just piggy back his port-call instead of waiting until tomorrow night, right?" Ellis asks, looking at Arco, who nods after a second.

"Exactly. So Ripley, you can handle the ship?" Liddick asks.

"Not yet, but I'll find a way."

"I'll help you," Ellis says. "I have an idea. Avis, we'll need you too, and also a knife or something. Myra, you should probably come with us."

Avis and Myra both agree, but exchange wary glances.

"All right, then I'll go get the clone-sim program ready. I need DNA. A hair?" Liddick says, holding out his hand. Everyone pulls out a strand of hair and passes it to him. "I'll put these in to cook after we figure out where we're going and are actually ready to board the ship. No sense in having two of us all running around here," Liddick adds.

"One of you is already too much to handle," I say, grinning at him. His eyes light with danger and promise, and a smile spreads across his face as everyone chuckles...everyone except for Arco. "Anyway, how can I help?" I ask.

"Come—"Liddick says at the same time Arco says, "Stay—"

They both look at each other, then look at me, and Arco is the first to talk again.

"You should try to get some rest, Jazz. It's been a long day, and if this works, it's going to be an even longer night, you know?"

OR, help me fix the channel and maybe we can figure out how to port-call topside before we bring my friend down...come on, Rip, I hear Liddick in my head and just barely catch myself before I look at him in astonishment.

"Yeah, maybe," I manage to say in answer to Arco, my head suddenly spinning with Liddick's proposition, and I struggle not to make eye contact with him. "When are we meeting up then?" I ask the group.

"Eleven," Liddick says, and now I turn to see his smirk deepening as I'm sure he's enjoying the dilemma he's just caused in me. "Is five hours enough for you to do something about the ship, Ripley?" he continues, turning to Jax.

"We'll still need time tonight for Tieg, Arco, Avis, and Ellis to recon and map afterward, so it'll have to be," he answers.

"All right, eleven then," Liddick says.

"I'll encode your profiles so curfew doesn't pick anyone up," Arco says, and Tieg is the first to get up.

"Tieg—don't forget to bring Dez, OK?" I ask abruptly, reaching up to grasp his forearm. He stops and looks down at me as if he's thinking of something to say again, but just nods before walking through the projection field and toward the dorm wing. Why can't I understand him as easily as the others? Is it because he's from the mountain? Have they been modified there *that* much?

"Well, if you need us, we'll be figuring out how to clone the hull of a two-ton Leviathan so we can leave it in the dock while we simultaneously steal the *real* Leviathan and get it outside of the nanite coded triple security gate —you know, just an average Coder Friday night," Ellis stands and gives us all a double thumbs up. Jax shrugs out a laugh and shakes his head.

"OK, come on," he says, slapping Avis on the back as they both follow Ellis out of the field with Myra at his side. Arco stands next to an impassioned, albeit silently lecturing Abe Lincoln as Liddick leans back in the perpendicular chair, making the tension in the air suddenly unbearable—one of them needs to leave right now, or maybe I do.

"So, Hart, I guess we're both off to make an inroad then? Both of us working on a path?" Liddick says after a minute. I feel the barbs in his tone and narrow my eyes at him. Arco angles his head and looks at him cautiously.

"If you want to call it that."

"Your job may be a *little* harder, though…what, with having to start from nothing. I just have some repair work to do," Liddick says, standing up and darting a glance at me. I squint at him in disbelief and shake my head.

What is wrong with you? Stop it, I think, but he doesn't respond. Arco looks at me quickly as understanding lights in his eyes, then turns back to Liddick and takes a step forward.

"You really think your inroad could even begin to lead somewhere?" he says, moving his hands to his hips and squaring his stance.

Liddick! Stop. Just walk away. Why are you trying to pick a fight with him tonight? I think, but he doesn't take his eyes off of Arco.

"It already is, Hart. Already is," he says dismissively with less than a foot of space between them, then turns and walks through the projection field toward the Boundaries room.

I sit motionless on the couch watching him walk away, trying to choose which question to ask him in my thoughts among the thousand fighting to get down the pipe, but I can't focus enough on just one—what was that all about? Is he trying to make Arco angry? What is he trying to prove with me sitting right here like that? Then he's out of sight, and I feel the empty place where the potential for answers used to be.

"What's he talking about?" Arco shifts his weight to one leg and his eyes to the floor, his hands still on his hips.

"About fixing his port-carnate channel for port-call while you build your code," I say, my heart starting to hammer in my chest. Arco nods, still not looking at me. "What did he mean when he said you helped him," he asks, and I suck in a breath. There it is. Now, I have to tell him.

"Arco, sit down."

"I don't want to sit down, Jazz. What did he mean?" he says, his voice restrained. His eyebrows are drawn together as he studies the floor, then shifts his weight to the other leg again and crosses his arms over himself. How this feels for him cuts into me, and I know I have to stop it. I can't let him worry like this.

"Something happened to his nanites during the port-carnate transfer. I don't know, they got misaligned somehow. I wanted to get a medi-droid, but he was sure it had to be the nanites because they weren't fixing him when he got sick, and before he got them, that never happened after a port-carnate transfer," I say all at once, waiting a second so he can process.

"Then what?" Arco says quietly, the hollow dread radiating from him and scooping whole sections out of my chest. I take in another breath and try to steel myself to jump in cold water.

"So, he needed another dose of them to realign his, and when I asked him how to get that for him, he said I already had it, and...he kissed me," I say, closing my eyes in anticipation of the explosion. It doesn't come, and when I open my eyes, I see he hasn't even moved. "Arco?" I ask softly.

"So he must be your nanite classification exactly? That's why you've been so close with him lately," he says, his eyebrows still drawn together as he tries to unravel everything. "You're *the same.*" He finally looks up at me as his jaw flexes like he's trying to keep more words behind his teeth, then swallows them down. I feel like the weight of it lands like an anchor in the bottom of my stomach, and I have to get out from under it...to just put everything on the table.

"The same classification, yes, but I don't know how to do what he does, what Vox does. I don't know how to read people, or write or fix code channels. I don't know what I am, Arco... and so yes, maybe that's why. Maybe there's something about him that tells me something about me, but it's the same with Vox," I say, fighting against the crushing feeling in my throat as it threatens to close around my words. "But you know what, none of that even matters because I just couldn't let him *die,* and there were a few times when he couldn't get up—when there was nothing I could do because he couldn't talk, he couldn't even answer with think—" I say, unable to hold off the constriction any more.

I try to swallow, to gather back the composure that's peeling away from me, and then desperately realize how tired I really am when the tears start to burn my cheeks. *That's it...*I close my eyes and take in a breath that hitches in my chest, no more energy even to wipe them away or try any more to stop them from falling.

After a minute like this, I feel Arco's hands on top of my thighs, then look up to see him kneeling in front of me. He wedges in close and slowly wraps his arm around my waist, slipping the other around my shoulders to pull me into him. All the confusion and anxiety, all the exhaustion rushes up fast like a geyser, and I hear the sobs—*my* sobs. I don't want to cry. That's actually the *last* thing I want to do right now, but I can't stop it. How can I push other people to feel anything when I can't even push myself? This idea just makes me cry harder, and Arco pulls me even more tightly against him until there's no space between us at all.

"It's OK..." he says over and over. We stay like this until I start to feel like it really is OK— his arms around me, his warm, strong body against mine, and his voice in my ear.

"Arco, I didn't mean—" I start to say into his shoulder, but he hushes me.

"Stop, I said it's OK. It wasn't your fault."

"But—"

"Jazz," he pulls back with a laugh in his voice, then brings his hands to my face and looks straight into my eyes. "It's all right. It's all going to be all right. *I love you,"* he says, the vibration of it, low and full like the bell from class echoing in my chest and causing more tears to spill into burning rivulets down my cheeks. The laugh he'd been holding in gives way, and a smile slips over his face. "Oh, you're so wrecked," he says, brushing his thumbs over my cheeks. "Come on." He helps me up, and we walk side by side, his arm around me all the way to my dorm.

When we get there, he kisses the back of my hand before turning to me, bringing his fingertips softly to my cheek again.

"Arco, I didn't mean to hurt you," I finally say, but he just shakes his head as his jaw tightens, and I know he's still upset even though he's trying not to be.

"You're totally wrung because of his jacked nanites, so stop worrying about any of that and take a nap so you get better, all right?"

He angles his chin down to catch my eyes, and I look up at him and smile as he brings my hands to his chest. I feel his heart pounding again, and something about knowing it's racing like that for *me* makes my own heart start up too.

"I'm OK," I say, feeling safe again—feeling like all of this is going to work out somehow when I see the warm smile flicker in his eyes.

"Then everything is OK for me too," he whispers, leaning in to kiss me again like he doesn't want to wake me up.

CHAPTER 45
Azeris

The drumming on my door seems to come five minutes after I close my eyes, and I startle awake. *I fixed it. Jazz, come on,* I hear in my head. As the fog clears, I realize it's not a dream, it's Liddick. He fixed his channel? I scan my bracelet along the reader, and the door slides open.

"Hey," he says, out of breath.

"Did you run down here?" I ask, rubbing my eyes. "Does Arco have the piggy back finished? And the camouflage?"

"Yes. And I don't know, but we won't need the camouflage. I found a better way just in case, so come on and I'll sh—"

"He'll get it done," I say, bringing my hands down. "He's reliable." I hear the defensive edge in my voice, and know it comes off the way it sounds when Liddick's face registers surprise. He abandons whatever he was going to say and resets, swallowing and tilting his head to one side.

"And you still don't think I am," he says, raising his chin and bracing his forearm against my doorframe, but then changes his mind and lowers his eyes to the floor, then puts his hand in his pocket.

"Liddick..." I say, letting some of the exhaustion about this old conversation linger in my voice in the hopes that he doesn't start it again.

"No, if you still think I'm unreliable, then I still have work to do, and that's all right. I'll do it," he says, drawing his dark brows together as he looks quickly to the side, and after a second more, meets my eyes again. "But Rip, you know the rest of the story now...I couldn't let you get caught up in that."

"And since I am now I'm just supposed to reconfigure everything?" I ask, squaring my shoulders and putting a hand to my hip, remembering what he did a few hours ago in front of Arco. "What were you trying to accomplish by bringing up *inroads* back there? What was the point of telling him that, especially with me *right* there?" I ask, narrowing my eyes at him. He doesn't look away this time, and doesn't try to corral the anger I know he feels from me either. Instead, he takes a step toward me.

"I brought it up so he knows what I'm coming for. So *you know* that he knows," he answers, then pushes a hand through his hair as he walks past me a few steps before turning around to face me again. "I've had enough unpleasant surprises for a lifetime, Rip, and I don't wish them on anyone. If you tell me right now that you're with him, I won't ask you for more, but you have to understand that it won't stop me from wanting more. Hell, I can't even tell you I won't still try for more. We fit, and as long as I can feel it in my *teeth* that you know it too," he says, pinching the air next to his mouth between his fingers, "I'll keep fighting for it because then...*then* it's just a matter of you trusting it eventually." I swallow hard when I hear the word *eventually* again, remembering my conversation with Arco, and the whole last 24 hours pull me under like a whirlpool. "So, are you with him?" I shake my head and blow out a long breath. "I don't know," I say, pulling my other hand to my hip as I scan the floor for an answer I don't really find, so I just give him the pieces I have. "I do have feelings for him, though, Liddick. Everything is just so wrecked here, and he's..." I search for the word that feels like a traitor who has abandoned me until it's right there, just in time. "He makes me feel *safe,*" I say, still nodding to the floor, and in the space of two beats, Liddick crashes through everything I think I know and scatters it in a hundred directions.

*"Safe...*that's not what you're built for, Riptide," he says in a slow, quiet voice. I look up at him then, something sparking low inside me like a dare, like a promise, and when I see the flicker in his eyes, the light catching behind the blue, I recognize it.

I swallow hard and pull in a deep breath against the sound of my heart pounding in my ears, but, "I— Liddick..." is all I can say. He nods after a long pause.

"Like I said, I still have work to do," he winks, cutting me loose from it, letting me step back from the heat that's too bright and too much to be mine. "Come on, I want to show you something."

"What time is it?" I say, disoriented again as I scrub my hands over my face and try to reconstruct the reality of why he's actually here.

"Almost eleven, so hurry."

"How did you even get down here? Aren't there monitors or something this late?" I ask, following him to my door.

He taps his bracelet. "Not now—they won't loop back here again until tomorrow night."

"How did you—never mind," I say, realizing I'm still too tired to process whatever Coder jargon he would wind up telling me as we go through the door. *How we have the same classification makes no sense to me,* I think to myself, shaking my head and finally dislodging the surreal feelings of a few minutes ago.

"This way," he says, leading the way down the corridor to the Boundaries room.

Everything is deserted—even the floating screens in the student center are gone. It makes me feel like we're that much more conspicuous, and that's probably the effect they're intending by having everything off like this.

In the Boundaries room, Liddick crosses to the station I sat in for Vox's transmission. He pulls up the screen and starts entering characters into the keypad.

"What are you typing in?" I ask, taking a few steps forward to watch over his shoulder.

"Just running the Trojan code and opening the channel inside it. This is why we don't need Hart's camouflage."

"Trojan? How does it work? You're sure it won't trigger the alarms Arco was talking about?" I ask.

"No, it can't. It just looks like a housekeeping program to the mainframe. They run all the time cleaning up bugs, emptying trash files that are out of date, no one monitors them."

"Liddick, how do you know all this?" I ask.

"Because...I..." he leaves a few beats in between each

of his words as he finishes typing, then takes a step back from the screen, "...know there's always a road into where I want to go," he says, turning to me with a knowing smile. I sigh and raise an eyebrow at him. "No, but really, it's years of screening cine code to find my brother's messages, and this was right there just waiting to be repurposed. I don't really know how to write more than a window channel like this, and only that thanks to my friend Azeris—whom you'll meet momentarily, if I did this right. Watch the floor there," he gestures to an area a few feet from us, radiating excitement like he's outrunning a devil.

"So, if this works, how does it work? How is your Badlander friend really coming down here?" I ask.

"I just sent a buoy signal with the Trojan anchor window, so once he gets it, he'll plug in our coordinates to open a hop on his end," Liddick says, then checks his bracelet cuff. "It's 20 to eleven now, so when he secures the anchor window and uplinks to our hop anchor, the path will run through the Trojan windows like water through a straw, and the port-call will be camouflaged—that should be any minute now."

"Liddick," I say out loud, suddenly chilled by his detailed explanation and kicking myself for prompting it with my question in the first place. *Arco doesn't know where we are, so he wouldn't have extended the privacy field again...we're not masked in here,* I think.

Liddick looks up from the transmission station and blinks at me absently.

"Have you no faith *at all* in me, Rip? I'm wounded."

"What are you talking about?" I ask as the adrenaline hits me and makes the chill even worse.

"I rerouted all that the first day I came down here to start installing the port-carnate channel. That's how I got the idea for the Trojan. They're monitoring looped feeds of the last year—the same way I looped your hallway. By the time they figure it out, we'll be long gone. Hart's field is just another layer between us and them," he says, and I feel the panic start to subside.

"All right, good."

"See? Reliable," he says, winking. I start to laugh as the nervous fear dissipates and push my hands over my face.

"OK, so this is really going to work?"

"If Hart's piggy back works, it should. After his code locks on to the port-call transmission, the Trojan will disguise it just like it's disguising Azeris's port-call... water through a straw, remember? Then the piggy back can start tracking the signature for the updated message you got. Once it does that, we'll have a map, and neither should take too long with the automators—I just won't know how to launch those until Azeris gets here..." he says all in one breath, then trails off when he sees my reactions to the flickering image beginning to appear in front of the station he's just keyed.

"Look!" I say as he turns around and laughs in satisfaction. In seconds, the rest of the image materializes, and a man about our parents' age with dark brown, messy hair wearing a battered leather vest and heavy, canvas pants appears. A leather strap runs over his shoulder and across his chest to a holster, but I can't make out what's inside it. His black boots look like the old military ones from our history imagers, and his linen shirt is marked by streaks of dirt and black grease. He's taller than Liddick, actually broader than Pitt, and I instantly want to run in the other direction when I see the hard line of his black stubbled jaw. I take a few steps back, and Liddick turns around to extend his hand.

It's OK, he's a friend, I hear him say in my head, and take his hand to step alongside him.

"Azeris!" Liddick says when the transfer completes, then drops my hand to shake the man's. Azeris looks around the room, his golden-brown eyes round and wide like a lion's. He cracks his neck and looks right at me, making the blood pound behind my ears.

"And who's this?" Azeris asks, but his voice isn't the growl I expect. It's almost happy, like I'm a pleasant surprise.

"This is Jazz, a friend. There are others coming with us. Jazz, will you get them?" Liddick asks, then turns back to Azeris. "You and I need to talk about nanites," he says, bringing his hand to Azeris's shoulder, then fishes something out of his pocket with the other. "And do I really have to swallow these things?"

***

I smile when I see Dez sitting next to Tieg on the couch in the Records room, but I didn't expect to see Pitt or Joss. I also didn't expect to see Pitt, Ellis, Avis, and my brother looking like they've just been through a war.

"What happened to your arms?" I ask as they come out from behind the couch and sit. "Why are you in bandages? And...*Joss?*"

"I needed another Omnicoder, and since Tieg and Dez were already coming, Pitt just made sense," Jax says. "Joss was in the fitness room too when we went there looking for Tieg, and after hearing what happened, he wanted to help."

"It's just not right—" Joss starts, then glances at Arco and stops himself."

"As for the bandages, we couldn't get access to the Leviathan fleet without reconfiguring some nanites for the scanner. The only place to get Coder classification nanites was here," Jax adds, raising his hands to reveal two bandaged forearms. He gestures to Pitt, Avis, and Ellis, who do the same.

"The nanites age like the rest of us, but they age in layers—so third year cadets here would have nanites with three layers in their blood, and that's the minimum security clearance to open the Leviathan dock," Ellis says.

"Are you telling us that you *fished* nanites out of your blood and stacked them up somehow?" I ask, incredulous.

"Finally, we did," Ellis says, a scowl moving over his face. "Do you have any idea how hard it is to keep them from self-destructing outside the bloodstream? This *stupid*—" he starts, indignant, then takes a deep breath and resets. "This particular nanite self-destructs if not in constant contact with blood. Needless to say, we figured that out." Everyone is wide-eyed looking at the four of them, each of us no doubt picturing them taking turns dripping blood over these tiny machines as Ellis reconfigures and stacks them. This must have taken forever. "But where did you work? How…?" I trail off, then feel compelled to look at Myra and Dez. "The med-bay. But how did you get in?"

"Arco helped mask my clearance so it wouldn't be traceable back to me. Ms. Karo will see that someone came in tonight, but when she sees the unidentified clearance, we're hoping she'll just assume it was someone above her pay grade checking up on her and let it go," she says. I nod, and then look back at the four POWs. "They'll be healed up in an hour or so—the nanites that they didn't sacrifice are knitting everything back together as we speak," Dez continues, smiling, apparently proud of her handiwork. All of the boys in bandages give her a tolerant smile.

"Where's Liddick?" Arco asks, looking around.

"He's in the Boundaries room. He fixed his channel, so his friend is in there with him," I say. Arco raises a curious eyebrow at me, and I know he's wondering how I know this if I've been sleeping all this time. "He just told me right now," I add, hoping that will assuage his concerns. His face relaxes, but only a little.

"He has a Badlander in there right *now?*" Myra asks, moving closer to Pitt, and I feel her panic rising.

"Yeah, but he's not what you'd think. I mean he looks like what you'd think, but he's Liddick's friend, so there's nothing to worry about," I add. "He just needs your piggy back code," I say to Arco. "He has something called a Trojan that he's already loaded for the port-call that brought his friend here."

"He wrote a *Trojan?*" Arco's eyes widen in surprise.

"I don't know, he said it was a housekeeping code or something."

"Oh," Arco's face relaxes into a laugh. "So he just repurposed it. He didn't write anything."

"I don't know how all that works, but his friend is in there now. What about the decoy ship?" I ask, looking at Jax and his crew.

"We only synthesized the skin after getting a scrape off one of the hulls, and Liddick helped with the cloning. Talk about running like hell before the layers could replicate right there in the classroom. We barely carried it to the dock in time for it to start fleshing out."

"How did the monitors not see you down there?" I ask.

"I replicated the Lincoln field code and uploaded it to their cuff mainframes. I'll upload it to the rest of our cuffs when we make the clones and copy our profiles to them." Arco says.

"When we do that, the real ship is outside just beyond the trench. We anchored its Stingrays outside the dock and brought in the suits," Jax adds.

"So, we have to dive to the Stingrays?" Tieg asks, obviously alarmed.

"It's the only way. We had nowhere to dock after the cloned skin replicated, and we couldn't risk a ship that big anchored just outside the gate. The skin is in the far back corner, so, way down the queue. As long as no one tries to actually go inside, we should be good," Jax explains.

"But we're diving in open water. What about currents?

What if we get blown out?" Myra asks.

"The Stingrays are anchored just outside the gate. We won't need to swim far, don't worry," Pitt says, pulling her into him.

"The plates under the ocean floor won't be volatile for another few days, so the currents won't be as bad if we can get through before that window closes," Avis adds, rubbing the back of his neck.

"All right, let's go deliver the piggy back. I'll extend the field," Arco says, turning to the panel.

"It's already OK to talk in the Boundaries room—Liddick rerouted the monitoring," I say, but Arco just nods and continues punching keys until the blue field around us turns green.

CHAPTER 46
Opening the Channel

It's 11:27 p.m. when I check my bracelet cuff on the way to the Boundaries room with the others. Azeris is laughing when we all walk in, but stops as soon as he sees us, his hand moving quickly to his holster.

"It's OK, these are the people I was telling you about," Liddick says, then turns to us. "This is Azeris, he's going to help us expedite the piggy back connection."

"*He's* going to help us?" Tieg asks, and Pitt knocks a shoulder into him. Azeris narrows his eyes at Tieg.

"You're from the hill, aren't you?" Azeris asks, letting his arm relax.

"How did you know that?" Tieg replies, some of the wind taken out of his sails. Azeris's mouth opens in what seems will be a wide grin, but instead, he taps a long finger on his top row of teeth, which he then snaps down several times against the bottom row. Dez gasps and takes a step back into Pitt.

"He's not going to eat you, Dezzie," Pitt whispers, chuckling and putting a hand on her shoulder.

"Hart, do you have it?" Liddick asks.

Arco raises his bracelet cuff. "In here. I already loaded it with the signatures," he says.

"Good, bring it," Liddick replies, then looks again at Azeris. "The mainframe is on one grid, so you can probably just access his profile and dig it out," he says as Arco keys something into his bracelet and extends his wrist.

"The soonest I can get it to populate without drawing attention is 48 hours."

"This might take 48 seconds," Azeris says, looking off of Arco's cuff, then punching something into the station panel he's standing in front of. "Still have the package?" he asks Liddick.

"Right here," he replies, then takes one of the little cylinders and swallows it just as Azeris begins to smack the side of the station.

"*Bollocks!* This is why virtuo is dead. Key in the Trojan, will you? Sim fingers are too cold to register," he says, opening and closing his hand in a fist. Liddick starts hitting keys, and the screen becomes filled with slow moving columns of code that I don't understand. "All right, now put your palm over that scrolling to launch the automator for the Trojan, and get your feet under you," he says, then looks right at me. "You—come stand next to him and think happy thoughts." I raise my eyebrows and freeze in place until Azeris waves his hand at me several times. "Come on, come on!"

"I don't know what I'm supposed to—" I start, but am cut off by the sudden pulling feeling in my stomach as Liddick puts his hand over the code, then doubles over a second later.

"Don't let him move his hand from that code until the G-force stops," Azeris says, raising his eyebrows and then darting them inward when his eyes move to Liddick, who is trying his best to stay upright.

"You...weren't kidding about...these..." he says

through clenched teeth. I wrap my arms around my stomach and try to think of something happy, but I can't get past the nausea building up in the base of my skull as my skin starts to feel clammy.

"What's happening? Automators aren't supposed to feel like that," Arco says, taking several steps toward us, but Azeris holds out a forearm and connects with his chest, abruptly stopping Arco's progression.

"You're going to contaminate the field, stretch. Back up so I don't have to put you on your butt," he says cheerfully and flutters his eyelashes. Arco squints at him, but then just shakes it off and looks at me.

"Are you all right?" he asks in a low voice, his brows drawing together. I nod quickly.

"It's just...pressure," I say, feeling like my insides are being flung against the back of my spine until I feel the sensation of Liddick's arm around me on the dune the night before we left, then see a flash of us laughing about the South American villages. I look at Liddick, whose face is much less pained than it was a minute ago.

You're remembering that? This is you? I ask him silently as the nausea recedes.

Happy thoughts. It's working, isn't it? he replies. I smile at him, then look back at Arco and Azeris.

"It's getting better," I say, and Arco's face relaxes.

"That means the automator is launched. You can pull out now," Azeris says. Liddick removes his hand and takes a deep breath.

"What was that?" Dez asks, rushing over to us.

"High speed port-tech—it harnesses your cells' ability

to replicate for a few seconds...like hitching itself to a trillion little rockets. It'll bang your drum, though. Just wait until the next one," Azeris says, clapping Liddick on the shoulder.

"So it's in there now?" Liddick asks.

"Just waiting for the cargo. Let's have the piggy back," Azeris says to Arco and holds his hand out for his bracelet. Arco raises an eyebrow, then swipes and taps at his cuff before extending his arm.

"Does she *have* to stand there?" he asks, but Azeris ignores him.

"Round two. Bottoms up," Azeris says to Liddick, who exhales, then pops the other automator into his mouth and winks at me with a bracing smile. Azeris painstakingly enters something into the panel, which appears to be working for him this time. "It's away," he says. "As soon as you see the new code generate, you know what to do. Once your guts stop spinning, you'll know your automator is launched into the port-call transmission— then we'll release the Trojan's camouflage. Got somewhere to dump the data sweep once it starts tracking those messages?" Azeris asks, and Pitt steps forward with a narrow, flat rectangle about the length of his palm.

"Is there somewhere to insert this in there?" Pitt asks. "It's the navigation relay from the Leviathan. Usually these are loaded on the dock."

"There's no receiver port for that on these stations. The maps will have to be routed to the dock system and downloaded onto the card from there. Hart, can you get into that from your mainframe and reroute the data sweep?" Liddick asks, drumming his fingers against the side of his leg, and I can feel the same adrenaline rush doing laps in my chest as we get ready to feel like we're being pulled inside-out all over again.

"I can try," Arco answers.

"Try fast. This window is pulling a lot of juice," Azeris says as Arco starts entering something into the panel, and my stomach clutches.

"How long after we get the maps until we can leave?" Ellis asks.

"We need to put our clones in place, then get into the dive suits to take the Stingrays back to the Leviathan. Clones should be almost instantaneous since I loaded the DNA an hour ago—you saw the teachers walk in and walk out. The dive may take a little longer, though," Liddick says as his eye catches the screen. "The codes are generating."

"And that's my cue..." Azeris says.

Liddick turns to him and shakes his hand. "Thanks for all your help, man."

"Someone has to watch your back, and I still owe you, so..."

"You don't owe me anything," Liddick says.

"Be careful," Azeris adds, glancing at the monitor. "If this goes how you gathered, those coordinates could come back deep. Deeper than this," he says, raising his free hand to his side and looking around the room.

"I will," Liddick says as the edges of the port-call image start to dissipate.

Azeris lifts two fingers to his forehead and nods. "You

remember how to set up that hop we talked about?" he asks.

"I got it."

"I'll see you soon then." Azeris takes a few steps back while Liddick moves the palm of his hand over the scrolling code on the monitor, which starts to speed up almost immediately. The image of Azeris starts to break apart like a tissue set on fire, holes appearing in places until the whole thing fades into wisps and is gone. A single bright green line zips from the bottom of where Azeris was standing to the ceiling, and then that also disappears.

"All right, our hop anchor is up," Liddick says, "and the one topside should pull any min—there it is..." he says, suddenly gritting his teeth, and I feel the heavy pull in my stomach again. "OK...piggy back automator... launching."

"Confirmed anchors up at both hops. The Trojan is falling in over the piggy back, camouflage deployed; it's looking good—picking up speed," Arco says, his eyes darting back and forth quickly over the code that's racing under Liddick's hand.

The stretching feeling in my stomach is much heavier this time, pulling at the small of my back like my center of gravity is somewhere around my knees. Liddick's eyes have drilled shut, and his jaw is clenched so tightly he's starting to shake.

*Happy thoughts...*I remember, and try to summon up the night before we left for Gaia again. *Liddick, remember the South American villages?* I ask, and the hard edge of his mouth breaks with a smile. In the next breath, the feeling of his hands on my face when he kissed me earlier in his room returns from nowhere—the rush of jumping in and not knowing where we might land...that grip on the one solid thing in the middle of all the fear and instability. Him.

"It starting to route—hang onto it, Wright," Arco says, looking up from the monitor to me with a question in his eyes. I nod to him to let him know everything is fine, but his face only relaxes a little as he returns his attention to the monitor.

Liddick grips my hand, and the crushing feeling in my chest lessens as flecks of heat and ice intermix and prick my skin like a million tiny pins. The spinning pressure forces my eyes closed, but soon I can feel Liddick's hands pushing through my hair again, then holding me there so tightly against his mouth—my fingers gripping the collar of his shirt in slow motion. Then I feel the sudden, sharp pain of the scratches I didn't know I'd left burning into my own skin, which causes a jolt of electricity to radiate through my stomach. In this instant, I feel like I can't get close enough to him. I gasp in the realization like I've just come up from being held underwater, then hear Arco's voice muffled from far away as I open my eyes.

"Jazz? *Jazz?* It's launched, let go. We're getting steady pings back now," Arco says, and Liddick's hand falls from the spooling code on the monitor. He leans into me for a second before getting his bearings, then lets go of my hand and braces against his knees.

"Are you OK?" Arco asks, and I nod, then look down at

Liddick.

That's how you felt earlier with me? What was that? I ask him silently as I catch my breath, my head still trying to slow the spin of the room.

You saving me again, he thinks, which causes another quickening in my stomach. He looks up at me and smiles, then pushes off his knees and turns back to Arco. "How many paths are coming back?" he asks out loud, and I look around for a chair.

"Looks like it could deliver four. Sweeping the data now," Arco says, and holds a hand out to me. I walk over to him feeling like everything inside me is bouncing off itself. He wraps his arm around my waist and shifts my weight to his leg as he sits in front of the monitor.

"Are you *really* OK?" he asks, looking up from the screen to scan my face. I nod again, then see Dez crossing to Liddick and bringing her hands to his face, and this puts me on my feet again. "It's done," Arco continues, glancing back at the monitor. "I'm routing now if you want to load the dock receiver."

"OK, Pitt, can you get that stick plugged in to receive? When you come back, we'll meet in the Interface room so we can run the clones," Liddick says, scrubbing his hand over his face and moving the other to Dez's shoulder.

"Wait, the Coders are untagged now, but I need everyone else's bracelets so I can take you off the grid too—we'll have to be invisible to the monitoring if we're all going to walk in there like this," Arco says, first programming my bracelet, then Dez's, Tieg's, and finally, Liddick's. Pitt returns completely out of breath with the navigation relay and holds it up as he crosses the threshold of the Boundaries room again.

"Loaded…looks like we have four routes for now, but that might change once we plug them into the Leviathan and run probabilities," he says, pushing a hand through his dark hair.

"Then let's get the clones and go," Liddick says, and we all head out the door.

***

When we get to the Interface classroom, everyone is gathered around the place on the floor where our teachers walked, and were then quadrupled.

"There's nothing here," Ellis says, walking back and forth over the spot.

"Not over there. Look out." Liddick trots down the steps and then climbs the next small set that leads to the lecture floor. He walks about halfway to the back wall and steps on something. A green circle of light appears in the floor, and in minutes, a thin, barely visible wavy pattern appears from the lighted area. "I put the hairs in earlier so the computer had time to process our DNA. We don't have a banked file here like the teachers, but we should still be able to walk in like they did with that sample. Go ahead," Liddick says, but no one moves. After a second, Jax takes the first steps toward the shimmering circle.

"Come on, let's just get this done. We still need to dive and get to the ship," he says, and enters the circle. Instantly, just like the teachers, another Jax follows him out the other side. I feel my mouth fall open as Arco waves them over to us.

"Give me your cuff and...uh, his," he says, extending his hand. He enters something into Jax's bracelet, then angles both Jax's and the clone's elbows upward so their bracelets touch. I walk over to the clone and raise my hand to its face.

"Jax, it even has the exact amount of stubble you do right now," I say, fascinated.

"That's great, Jazz, but we need to go," the clone says to me, and I nearly swallow my tongue as I stumble backward into Arco. Both Jaxes double over with laughter.

"I was just about to say that!" the real Jax says, laughing like a sea lion. Even Arco chuckles a little, and I shoot him a glare. He presses his lips into a hard line and swallows, smirking despite his efforts.

Let's go, Riptide. The only thing better than one of you is two, Liddick says in my head, and I roll my eyes for what has to be the tenth time at him, and that's just tonight.

"Come on," Arco says, gripping my shoulder in a half-hug. We walk toward the green circle and watch Tieg, Pitt, Ellis, Dez, and Liddick come through the other side. Arco punches whatever he punched into Jax's bracelet into theirs, then shows them how to transfer to their clones' bracelets. "Go ahead. I'm right behind you," Arco says to me.

We walk into the circle, and I hear a low frequency buzzing that I can actually feel tingling my scalp, which makes its way down over my eyes and nose, and even feels like it's resonating through the lining of my cheeks.

The sensation travels the length of my body before I make it through to the other side of the circle and walk out, and I'm afraid to turn around.

"Arco," I call out, but I don't call out alone. My heart kickstarts at the doubled sound of my own voice. "Arco!" "I'm here," he says in stereo. Ice shoots up the back of my legs and straight through to my teeth. I whip around, and see not only two of Arco, but another me as well. I hold up my hand, and she holds up hers in a perfect reflection. Our hands touch, and hers is ice cold. Our fingers interlace, and when I angle my head sideways, she does too.

"She's doing everything I do," we say in unison, and chills run up my arms. "Ok, make this stop," we say together again, and both Arcos chuckle.

"Give me your wrist," they say, and I feel like I'm crawling out of my skin. He enters the coding into my bracelet, my clone's arm extended stupidly in the air, and then he angles my elbow up like he did the others' so that our cuffs touch like they would in a reflection. He does the same to his own bracelet and his clone's, then turns to me. "There, now they won't do everything at the same time we do. They're running on the sim-corp data now like the reanimates in the Records room interview stations, so they'll just do what we'd likely do," Arco says and smiles. I look quickly over to his clone, who doesn't smile, but raises his eyebrows instead.

"What?" the other Arco says to me. "What did I do?"

"Oh, this is baked," I say, shaking my head. "Come on, let's get out of here."

"Finally, yes," Jax says.

"OK, clones, go back to our rooms, get our schedules and go to our classes, don't do anything stupid to get us kicked out," Liddick says. *Rip, see if you can talk to yours telepathically,* he continues in thought, and I nod.

Uh, hey, me? Can you hear what I'm saying? I think, focusing on my clone. To my complete surprise, she actually looks at me.

I can hear you. Don't worry, I'll handle things here.

"Crite!" I say out loud.

"What's wrong?" Arco asks, alarmed.

"I—we— can talk telepathically, like I can with Liddick and Vox," I stammer, and Arco looks at Liddick.

"Can you talk to yours?" he asks. Liddick looks at his clone, who then winks and makes a clicking sound with his mouth as he flashes a thumbs up. Arco rolls his eyes.

"Can we go now, *please?"* Jax asks, adamantly waving us on.

"Go," Liddick says to the clones, and they all head up the stairs, mine taking Arco's clone's hand.

"Did you see—?" I look up at Arco, who raises his eyebrows and opens his mouth in a wide smile, then wraps his arm around my shoulder.

"Let's go get our friends."

CHAPTER 47
Boarding

We put on the line tethers and divers that are all stacked on the deck of the last checkpoint gate to the Leviathans.

"Are you sure about this? These will work out in the open water?" Tieg asks.

"They'll work, and the Stingrays are just around the corner. You can see them from here," Pitt answers.

"When we get these on, I'm going to send a signal to the relay. The chamber in here will flood through those colored holes, and when the light turns green, I'll open the gate. We need to be completely suited before that ever happens because the water will come in like a hundred giant buckets of ice water getting thrown in our faces," Ellis says.

"Why does the water come through the smaller holes first if it's still going to rush us?" Myra asks.

"Because if some of the pressure isn't relieved in advance, it wouldn't hit us like a hundred buckets of ice water in the face, it would hit us like a shuttle in the face," Ellis replies, and Myra raises her eyebrows, then bites her bottom lip and nods.

"Avis and I showed Jax and Pitt how to navigate these things, so they can go together. Someone who's not NAV will have to come with me, and someone else can go with Tieg, Joss, Avis, or with Arco," Ellis says.

"Dez will go with me," Tieg says, which makes Liddick

give her a knowing smirk before turning to Ellis.

"Guess it's you and me, Ellie," he says.

"Don't call me that," Ellis says as his helmet comes down over his face.

"Make sure your comms are on," Arco says while everyone starts sealing their helmets, and before he seals his, he leans in and kisses me. I suddenly notice his lip is healed, and his bruising is almost gone—he *did* call the medi-droid. Knowing this makes me smile stupidly. "Stay close to me, OK?" he says, and I nod. We seal our helmets and push our comms buttons. "Everyone sound off— make sure you can all hear each other," Arco says, and a barrage of voices floods our helmets until everyone is sure they're connected before we all turn to Ellis.

"OK, roll up your suit bags and secure them to your belts. I'm going to count to three, and the colored circles will open. Hang onto something on the wall. When the water hits the threshold line, I'm going to count to three again and release the gate. If you're not holding on, you'll be jerked against your tether, so *hang on,* and make sure you're secured to the railing. Everybody copy that?" Ellis asks, and we all answer that we do. "All right, *one...* " he says, and I look over at Arco. He grabs my free hand and guides it to the railing that my other hand is holding, then stands behind me and gets a grip next to mine, pressing his forearms against my ribs. *"Two...!"* Ellis continues, and the colored circles slide open all across the front of the clear gate. *"Three!"* Water rushes in and begins pooling immediately in the reservoir just beyond the guard rail walkway where we're standing. After only a few minutes, the water is nearly to our necks, and Ellis starts talking again. "There's the green light. I'm going to release the gate!" he says, his voice raised over the roaring water, which now envelops us. "Make sure you're all holding on!" Ellis yells. "One! TWO...*Hold on!* THREE!"

He releases the gate, and a deluge of water pours in, almost immediately filling the compartment. We're all swept off our feet, and for a second, everything is upside down. I lose my grip and start to panic, but Arco is right behind me.

"I've got you," he says, and I find the railing again.

"All right—" Ellis says once the rush of the water settles, "unhook from the railing and buddy clip to two people, those on the end hooking to each other so we're in a circle, then follow me out the gate and down to the Stingrays. When we hit the floor, we can unclip and board. Copy?" he asks, and we all reply. "OK, let's go then. Clip in."

Arco unclips our tethers from the railing and secures mine to his. Jax clips his to me too, and everyone starts maneuvering. When we're all secure, Liddick is left to close the circle by clipping to Arco, and when they realize this, I feel nauseous.

Liddick — Ellis — Joss — Myra — Pitt — Dez — Tieg — Avis — Jax — me — Arco. I say everyone's names in my head as I scan each person's lineup trying to figure out how this happened, *there has to be another way,* I think.

Oh, there is, but not without looking like a giant wally about it. But I appreciate your concern, Riptide, Liddick replies in my mind, even though that particular thought of mine wasn't exactly meant for him.

Just come on, I think, and shake my head at him.

Take a deep breath, or five so you don't start roarfing in your helmet, OK? And relax, I'm not going to start anything with Hart—crite, he's clipped to you, he says, and this actually does make me feel better about the situation as we swim with our heel thrusters aiming us toward the Stingrays.

The open sea floor is a hazy white. I look down, and my suit looks puffy in the small lights coming from somewhere on my shoulder. I lift up my hand and can feel the pressure of the water around us—almost viscous. Once we're all on the sea floor, Ellis has us group together in between two of the Stingrays, then starts giving more instructions.

"The current isn't as bad as it normally is, but it's still there. Do not unclip entirely for any reason, and make sure you brace yourself against the hull of one of these Rays whenever you can as you get around to the bottom hatch. They're already open so you don't have to mess with the doors, but it's going to be a tight squeeze because the cockpits are sealed off from the water. When you get inside, you may have to maneuver to close the hatch, but when you do, you can eject the water into the reservoir chamber underneath the vessel, and then you can open the seal. OK?" Ellis asks, and we all affirm. "All right, Liddick, after we detach, we're on the end," he says, unclipping from Joss as Arco unclips Liddick's tether like he's been waiting all day to do it. "Next set, go! Strongest swimmers take the farthest Ray," Ellis says as he and Liddick swim toward the outermost ship.

Pitt unhooks from Dez, then motions for Myra to un-hook from Joss, but there's no one on Joss's other side, so she can't.

"We'll all have to go in one ship," Myra says over our helmet comms, which sends Pitt scanning. "Come on, we'll make it work," she says. Pitt finally nods to Joss, and they both swim toward the next farthest ship out on either side of Myra. This leaves everyone else tethered to their vessel partner, so Jax and Avis swim to the other side of the next farthest Stingray, while Arco and I board the one directly in front of us, and Tieg and Dez board the one we're all leaning against.

I'm first to crawl through the hatch into the half-flood-ed Stingray, and try to make as much room as I can so Arco can crawl up. He's lean, but he's so tall and broad that there's not a lot of space once he's in, and in order to shut the hatch, he has to step toward me and close the door behind him with his foot. He puts his hands on my waist and presses in against me, our helmets knocking until he cranes his neck to the side, which causes his body to shift and lean in even more. His shoulder lamp catches me in the eyes, and I squeeze them shut against the glare. Instinctively, I raise my hand to shield them, and inadvertently knock Arco's elbow, which causes his hand to land *right* on my chest. He can't feel anything with the suit glove, apparently, because he doesn't move it as he kicks back with his foot to close the hatch. I start laughing hysterically as I think of the others in this situa-tion, especially Liddick and Ellis, and how much Liddick must be cursing Tieg for partnering with Dez.

You... stow it, I imagine hearing him in my head and laugh even harder.

Arco finally shuts the door and turns to me, realizes where his hand is, and jerks it back immediately. He steps on the release button on the floor, and the water starts to drain. We retract our helmets, and I can't stop laughing picturing Jax pinned up against Avis like this, or how mortified Tieg might be pinned against Dez, let alone Pitt and Joss crammed in like sardines while Myra sings a happy song or something. I laugh so hard at this that I start crying, then coughing, and don't even realize the twelve shades of red I'm causing Arco to turn.

"I'm so sorry," he says, clearing his throat and obviously wanting to die. I can't even catch my breath long enough to explain why I'm laughing, so I just sputter and cough more.

"No... it's not....that..." I manage after a second, and he swallows hard before turning to release the cockpit seal.

"Don't take your suit off when we dock. We still need to get through the moon pool, and then come right back through it once we anchor," he says without looking at me. I feel a suffocating heaviness wash over me, which douses my hysterics, and I pull myself together.

"Sorry, I wasn't laughing at you, I promise. I was picturing Liddick and Ellis in that same position, then Jax and Avis, Dez and Tieg...oh, but Joss and Pitt crammed together with Myra trying to stay positive—that was just too much," I say, feeling giggles percolating again. He starts to chuckle at this, and I feel the blanket of his guilt lifting.

"Good. But just so you know, I couldn't feel anything. I wasn't even aware of—or I'd have—" he stumbles.

"It's OK, Arco."

"I'm just...I'm really sorry," he says again, the color crawling back up his neck and blotching his cheeks. "If I *were* going to do that, it wouldn't be like *that*, and I don't want you to think—"

"Stop, it's OK," I say again, trying to echo the same compassion he showed me earlier today. "It wasn't your fault." This brings a knowing smile to his face as he nods, then turns on the green light for the comms system.

"Everyone make it?" he asks, and each of the Stingrays answers in turn.

"We're heading down, then. Stay together," Ellis says as I notice the colored circles appearing again on the gate behind us.

"That closed fast," I say. "How long will it take for the water to drain?"

"Just a few minutes. The reservoir underneath is big. It won't take us long either—the trench where they left the Leviathan is only about half a league away," Arco says, and he's right. In minutes I see the top of the Leviathan nestled in the ravine ahead of us, and we all jet in and make our way underneath it. "You'll need your helmet again. We have to swim up through the moon pool, and the water is freezing." Arco says, and we both deploy the helmets as we pull into the Leviathan docking bay and propel up the ramp. Arco stations the Stingray alongside the right wall behind the other vessels as Dez and Tieg swim up through the moon pool, and then we seal the cockpit and make our way through the hatch.

The light reflecting off of the milky white disinfectant is obnoxiously bright when we surface, and I have to squint until it dissolves into the water. We climb out of the moon pool, and I press the retraction button for my helmet. The air in here is thick and cool like it was on the other Leviathan, and I remind myself to take a deep breath before we pass through the corridor this time.

"Hold your breath before you go through there!" I say loudly to everyone, and realize in this moment that I never did get my nanites upgraded like Dame Mahgi said I should. I try to stamp out an ember of fear that threatens to catch if I think about that too long, and hope Dez and Myra will be able to take care of it.

We pass through the core room where Jax, Ellis, and Pitt move right into their places behind that little spinning dark planet thing, a thousand knobs, screens, and little wheels strewn all over the back wall there. Dez and Myra make their way to the med-bay, and the rest of us walk up the short set of stairs to the cabin, where Joss and Avis move into the Navigator seats. Tieg and Arco look at each other, apparently not having anticipated there can be only one pilot, but seem to make a decision as Arco takes the seat, and Tieg walks to the far wall and keys something into a panel. In seconds, another seat comes out of the wall facing the front window, and a console folds down in front of it, wrapping halfway around the seat.

"Whoa, what station is that?" I ask.

"Archangel roost," Tieg says without looking away from the screens he's pulling up one after another on the console as a steering wheel like Arco's rises up from the middle.

"Which means...?" I ask, trying to keep the impatience out of my voice.

"When the pilot can't do his job, I step in," Tieg says, looking directly at me now, confidently, and without any hint of the edge he's been carrying around all day.

Arco looks up from programming his controls, and tension flares in the air between them, but neither says anything else. I nod at Tieg, who attempts a smile, then returns to his instrument panel. This leaves Liddick and me to run the back wall, and we start pulling up our screens. I look over at him and take a deep breath.

We're doing this, I think. *Can you believe we're really doing this?*

Riptide, this is only the beginning.

CHAPTER 48
Termites

"We have two solid routes coming back from this ping instead of the four we started with—one is the cave, two are otherwise improbable because the terrain is too confining, so it looks like our only option is a vent about two leagues past that crag opening," Arco says, tracing a line on the digital grid projected in front of him after we start moving through the water. "

"That's a total of about three leagues out," Avis says, pulling up the same screen.

Arco nods. "That's it, then. Scan for a camouflaging structure near the vent where we can dock."

"Aye," Avis responds.

Everything feels electric on board now, a palpable vibration in the air like the energy in a busy hallway, but without the jostle.

"Do you feel that?" I ask Liddick, who nods.

"Ms. Reynolt called it *the thrum*...everyone's feelings all at once. Makes my teeth itch, but the equipment helps to dissipate it."

"It wasn't this strong back at Gaia," I reply.

"It's because everything is amplified on these ships. Turn on your screens and you'll see."

"I'm not really sure what to do with them," I say.

"Didn't Reynolt show you?"

"Not really. I mean, we got an overview, but spent

most of it talking about Vox's adventures with carnivorous plants."

Liddick raises his eyebrows and chuffs a laugh. "All right then." He turns to his console and pulls up his main screen along with two other grids, both backlit in green. One looks like a sonar, and the other like a graph of undulating waves. "So, first, we pull up the Distance Grid and the Emotive Resonance Mapper, then set them both for the standard scan, which is three leagues—there, the two buttons left of the main grid," he points to my console. "You have pilot's lock, I have core, OK?"

I look at him like he's not finished yet, but apparently he is.

"Um…" I say.

He blinks, then looks at the floor and scratches his head, braces his forearms on his knees and clasps his hands before looking up at me again.

The Pilot's lock—you monitor Hart and his three chucklewads up there to make sure they don't fry and/or kill each other, and I monitor Pitt, your brother, Avis, and Dez downstairs. Dez monitors Myra, he says in my head.

Who monitors us? I ask, and he smirks at me.

Myra, he answers, and then laughs out loud at what must be the look of terror registering on my face. *And Dez too; they're a team. I've got your back anyway. Pull up your screens.*

I push the buttons Liddick pointed out, and two screens appear: a main screen in the middle, which is larger than the other, and displays the words *Emotive Resonance Mapper* at the top. The other has four glowing

3-D cylinders, each enclosing several wavy lines. The bottom of the cylinder on the far left reads *Left Rig,* and the next over reads *AR,* which must be Tieg's Archangel Roost. The next one over reads *Pilot,* and the one on the far right reads *Right Rig.*

"What am I supposed to monitor here?" I ask, but almost as soon as I do, I start to understand the moving lines. I feel pulled to trace the ones inside of the Left Rig with my fingertips, which are vibrating steadily, and I even hear a warm sound like a low cello note. It's strange, and makes me feel…

"Assured," Liddick says, suddenly picking up on my thoughts like he's been doing far too often lately. "These enhancement nanites choke for port-carnate, but they do make getting a read on people easier. Kind of split to be able to filter feelings through a bunch of frequency lines, right?"

"I can't believe we can read these almost like words on a page. It's not just this abstract sense I've been getting from people lately—I can actually tell that Avis is focused and that he specifically trusts Arco, not so much Tieg, but also that he's still a little bit wary about the overall plan. How can I get all that from these lines?" I ask, running my fingers over them from left to right again, amazed.

"Guess it's what we're built to do," Liddick says with a shrug before rolling his chair back over to his station and reading the lines on his screen for the crew downstairs.

"How is Jax?" I ask, moving my hand toward the third cylinder, which is Arco's.

Liddick laughs, "He's a machine—all business, no

wasted thoughts...grateful that Spaulding isn't much for chit chat."

"Oars up, locking onto course and launching in three... two...one..." Arco says just before the Leviathan pushes off. In a matter of seconds, everything outside begins moving by quickly. I imagine at this rate, it shouldn't take long to travel three leagues. *Wait...*

"How far is three leagues again?" I ask, raising my voice a little so Arco can hear me halfway across the cabin.

"About nine miles," he replies, turning over his shoulder. "Don't you have the NAV capture?" Arco asks. I stare at him blankly until Liddick answers.

"We have it," he says. Arco nods, then turns back to his controls.

"Seriously, you spent the *whole* time on plants?" Liddick asks under his breath, smirking after Arco turns around. I shake my head in disbelief at just how much I don't know about all these controls, and then remember why.

"Well, come to think of it, I *kind of* left my post just after we left port." I confess. "We went down into the core room, and not too long after that, we both got into the Stingrays."

"We?" Liddick asks.

"Vox and me," I answer, and a ball of lead drops in my chest as I sober to why we're all out here again. Liddick nods, then gestures to my main screen, no doubt to get my mind off of it.

"The capture Hart is talking about is Avis's screen. It's

basically a real-time map of where we're going. You can access it with the little blue button in the right corner of the main display."

I push that button, and a screen with a numbered grid rolls out underneath the Emotive Resonance Mapper. 3-D terrain appears on top of it, along with an actual miniaturized version of our ship moving at a steady clip.

"Wow," I say, and try to touch the rock formations, but my hand starts to feel hot and pinched, so I yank it back. When I turn around to look out the window and see the real terrain passing by in comparison, a heavy feeling pushes against me. I look around the room for an obvious cause, but don't find one.

"Check your scopes," Liddick says, apparently feeling the same shift that I do. I turn back around to face the cylinders with the wavy lines, and find that the ones in Arco's cylinder are vibrating more quickly when I touch them. A feeling of worry passes through me, or maybe it's fear? But it's more than that…the fear of something imminent…it's *dread*. I also feel pressure, like I'm running out of time to make a decision, and most surprisingly of all, on the outskirts of this is optimism.

"What?" I say out loud to myself, trying to make sense of this last bit of conflicting input. *Is this because Tieg is over Arco's shoulder in the Archangel seat? Why is Arco scrambling?* I think, not actually intending Liddick to hear.

Liddick unlocks his chair and rolls over to me again. He puts his fingers next to mine on the center-right cylinder lines, looks at Arco, then at me. He moves his fingers over the lines of the far right cylinder, Avis's data, and shakes his head at the difference.

"Rig 2 is even—focused and a little anxious like Joss on Rig 1," Liddick says, nodding to Arco's cylinder. *But he's running probabilities, and he's doing it like he has two minutes before something burns down,* he thinks.

But what's this? Why is this suppressed? I ask, guiding his fingers to the lines that shoot a feeling of paranoia and dread through me. *Does this mean he's hiding something? And this optimism here, is that him hoping something?* I ask Liddick in my mind. A corner of his mouth pulls to the side as he meets my eyes and nods again.

Seems like it, he says, letting his fingers drop away.

What do we do?

Wait. See if something changes in a few minutes I guess, see if it spreads to either of the other two rigs or the AR seat. "What's the vibration at three leagues out?" Liddick finishes out loud, angling his chin toward the Emotive Resonance Mapper overlay on the capture of Avis's screen. I have no idea how to read it, but it's easy enough to see the miniature Leviathan's proximity to the target destination, as well as where the cave is just up ahead, which is clouded in a dark red aura with wavy lines inside it on the screen.

"Hopefully not like that," I point to the lines coming from inside the colored area surrounding the cave. "There's something in there," I say, and Liddick moves his fingers to trace them.

"Something angry…" he says, and I move my fingers in as he pulls his back.

"But not angry with us," I say, surprised again that I'm able to discern anything at all from a bunch of vibrating lines on a screen. "It's not Vox or Fraya, or—"

"No, it wouldn't be any of ours," Liddick says abruptly. As we pass the cave, Arco's lines start to jump even more, and I run my fingers back over them. Whatever is making him so anxious and paranoid has compounded, and so have the scenarios he's trying to run through. The lines for Avis and Joss haven't changed at all, and I don't get any particular vibration from Tieg's. I look over at Liddick.

Can you ever get anything more than a general impression of what's going on for Tieg? I ask him in my mind.

No, which is strange, because I can read Dez a mile away. Pitt's not as easy, but he's nowhere near the vacuum his brother is.

Right, that's my impression too. Something has to be off because if he's over there with access to everything Arco has, and if Arco's levels look like this, how can his be what they are here? I ask, gesturing for Liddick to feel the lines for himself. He does, and narrows his eyes.

I'll go talk to him. My face in proximity to his fist should be enough to get something jumping, he says, smirking. *You go talk to Hart before he gives himself a seizure.*

Liddick rolls back to his station and locks his chair, then gets up to head over to Tieg. I walk down the aisle to the pilot's station and put my hand on Arco's shoulder. He flinches, and a jolt runs through me. He looks up at me, his eyes scanning and his jaw set.

"What's wrong?" he asks.

"I was about to ask you the same thing—your levels are wrecked on my readout back there," I say. His eyebrows pull together like he's going to try to protest, but then exhales, apparently realizing there's no point in trying to hide whatever this is from me. He swallows hard before punching something into his control panel and pushing the steering bar forward a few inches. The Leviathan's speed surges, and Joss and Avis quickly tap something into their consoles in response.

"Some notice next time, huh?" Joss barks without looking over.

"Sorry, but we have company," Arco says to everyone as he stands.

"There's no one else out here but us, Hart," Liddick says from a level up near Tieg. "Jazz and I would have picked it up otherwise."

"It's not a person, it's a code termite. I was trying to confirm before saying anything," he says, looking back at his screen, then slapping the back of his chair and cursing. "And there it is—already embedded."

"There can't be a termite. I scanned everything! Where did it come from?" Avis protests, scrolling through screen after screen.

"They used the Trojan code," Arco says after leaning over and reading the rest of the display, then clasps his hands behind his neck. "I caught the echo on our launch sequence right after we powered up. Once we downloaded the four routes for optimizing, it must have reconstructed the code from the initial imprint and then slipped in."

Liddick's hand pushes through his hair, and he shakes his head. "That means they knew before we ever left— they knew in the Boundaries room when I first loaded it..." he says. "They must have known the whole time."

"What's a code termite? Who knew before?" I ask Arco, then Liddick, and feel the anxiety in the room rising under my own.

"Crite, there it is!" Joss says, pulling up a second 3D screen to overlay the one displayed in the air in front of him. The glowing green lines show a small blip moving steadily over the grid, erasing the lines in its wake. Avis, increase your thrusters from 70% to 100%, or we won't make the vent before it chews through to the system override."

"Aye, but I can only hold it under glass for about five minutes in the pressurization grid," Avis replies, hitting a series of buttons. The blip begins darting all around, but can't seem to get beyond a fraction of an inch in any direction. "Locked. It's contained for now, but it won't be long before it figures out how to burrow. Patch through to core engineering for evasive measures?" he asks, then looks to Arco, whose eyes are closed as he stands there clasping his hands around the back of his head with a pensive look on his face, and doesn't seem to hear anything at all.

CHAPTER 49
Containment

"Arco!" Avis shouts, waiting for his acknowledgment. Arco's eyes snap back to his console. "Authorize! Sorry," he says, then looks over to me. "Jazz, go strap in and tell me if you see anyone—anything, near the vent once we approach. Tether, how far out are we?" he asks, resuming his seat and pressing another series of buttons before pushing his steering wheel forward another few inches. The ship surges underneath us again, and we all jostle.

"Still one league out," Joss answers.

"You trying to put everyone in the med-bay?" Tieg growls as he enters something into his console. "Activating surge stabilizers, two-second delay," he says, pushing one final button and then glaring at Arco. A low hum falls over the ship, and we seem to slow down even though the scenery outside doesn't.

"Stow it, Spaulding, we don't *need—*" Arco starts, but is interrupted as Myra and Dez appear at the top of the stairs.

"What's happening?" Dez asks, first looking at Tieg, then to me. "Your levels are everywhere, and Liddick's crashed through the floor about 10 minutes ago. What was that noise?"

"Get locked in," Arco says to them, keying in another series of buttons, which turns the light in the cabin from soft white to red. Myra takes her seat between Liddick and me, and Dez pulls the seat from the wall where Ms. Reynolt sat in our practice launch, then studies my face.

"The termite just burrowed. I can't catch it again. Trying to reroute its trajectory, but prep for hull breach and self-destruct in six minutes just in case I can't shoo it to the box...Jax, is it ready?" Avis asks over the comms, his voice straining as he frantically enters combinations on his console and flips through the floating 3-D screens in front of him.

"Five seconds, can you hold it?" Jax responds.

"That's *all* I can hold—barricades in place for medical, helm, life support, and logistics, and I've sealed the hole in the pressurization code. There should be nowhere else for this bug to go if it really is bent on a kill-all," Avis says, then raises his arm and wipes his forehead on his shoulder.

"Copy. Pitt, open the box," Jax says over the comms.

"Copy. Bait box is open," Pitt replies. "Stand by."

"There's another hole somewhere. I can't find it, but I know it's there," Arco says, desperately pushing, flipping, and sliding between screens.

"There's no hole. I just said I sealed everything," Avis insists.

"There *is* a hole! That's why it's not going to the core—see?" Arco says, pointing to Avis's screen. "Think like a bug...where is it dark..." he trails off.

"Where is it going?" Avis asks himself. "There's nowhere else it can go."

"What are they talking about?" I ask Liddick, half

through my teeth.

"Did he say, *kill-all?*" Myra asks.

"OK..." Liddick says, hitting his thighs and whirling around to his screen. "Myra, Rip, you need to help me push this thing. I'm linking your screens to the code grid so you can see what's happening—the termite code is scrolling in the middle there and moving toward critical ship systems, so we need to help Avis reroute its trajectory. He's trying to chase it to the engine room where Pitt, Jax, and Ellis can isolate it and then wipe it from the rest of the programming. See the bait box here over the moon pool decontamination system on the left, and over here on the right where he has his chaser code in place?" He touches a glowing yellow rectangle that surrounds a block of code at the lower left corner of our consoles, and then angles his chin to another glowing rectangle on the lower right corner of the screen. I feel compelled again to raise my fingers to the lines of this one, and when I do, the block of code in the lower right corner morphs into the opening and closing jaws of a shark. I pull my fingers back in surprise, and the code block of symbols and numbers returns. I move them over the unboxed scrolling lines in the middle of the screen that are disintegrating the grid lines underneath as it passes over them, and they turn into solid lines of ant-like bugs running end to end that then start crawling all over my hand. I jerk away, the scream catching in my throat.

"Wh—?!"

"Jazz! Listen," Liddick almost shouts, "emotions...fear, even panic, it's just coded data. Everything has an input and an output that resonates, a cause and effect, understand? Those aren't really bugs, the code is just acting like bugs, and it's swarming like that to push you back so you don't interfere, but we *have* to interfere. We have to overcome the code's vibration and send it in the other direction before it eats the system infrastructure—just focus. Don't let it get in your head," Liddick says, placing his hand over the code on his screen, which turns into a swarm of bugs that covers his hand in seconds. My stomach lurches, and I physically recoil at the thought of having to put my own hand over the code like that too. "Jazz, Myra, now! You know how to do this, just follow the pull. Force the bugs in the direction of the chaser code —see where the jaws are steering? Push them that way and whatever you do, don't pull back no matter what happens!" he says, now through gritted teeth.

His bugs are swarmed so thickly now that I can no longer see his hand. I suck in a sharp breath and force mine over the top code block again, which immediately floods into a pool of dark, churning legs and bodies. I bite down hard and breathe through my teeth to resist the urge to retract my hand, concentrating on moving it instead toward the left where the shark jaw is heading. From the corner of my eye I see Myra's hand shooting toward her screen, then becoming almost immediately covered in her own swarm. She starts yipping and biting off screams, which I can still hear resonating in her throat. I have to stifle my own screams as the bugs start biting, and images of the skin and muscle on my hand being ripped away in little pieces start flashing in my mind.

They're just trying to push us...they're just trying to push us! I think as loudly as I can, over and over again until I almost believe it.

"It's working!" Avis shouts. "We have ten minutes before hull breach now!"

"That's enough to make it to the vent!" Arco says. "I still can't find the hole, but we just need to cover one league. Hold it!"

Myra can't keep her screams in any longer. They tear from her throat as she yanks her hand out and frantically examines it. Dez is up and at her side in seconds, grabbing her wrist and putting both Myra's hand and her own over the termite code. The bugs swarm again, and Myra starts pleading and sobbing.

"It's not real, Myra. It's not real!" Dez repeats, her voice thick with resolve, but Myra doesn't seem to hear her.

"Slipping!" Avis says. "We're back down to six minutes! Crite, five!"

"I can't hold it!" Myra cries against the self-destruct warning tone. "I'm sorry, I can't do it!"

"Myra! *You have to!"* I yell, feeling her panic rush the room like the ocean itself has crashed in, and my vision starts to tunnel.

"I can't do it!" she yells, and pulls her hand out, collapsing in a heap of gasping tears in her chair. Dez doesn't try to grab her wrist again because she begins losing the battle with holding back her own screams. Even Liddick's voice betrays bursts of fear as he tries to tell everyone to hold on. In this surreal moment, things

become silent for me, and I realize we aren't going to be able to contain this. It really is going to win.

"One minute! Brace for hull breach!" Avis shouts, but it sounds so far away.

"We're almost there! Hold it back!" Arco yells.

"It's branched—I'm losing propellants!" Joss echoes. "The hole is in the NIFE! It's heading for the NIFE!"

I try to look away from the swarm that's now crawling up my arm to focus on the blur of Joss's hands dancing over his console, but the biting sensations that pull and prick everywhere from between my fingers to the crook of my arm claw my attention back. I turn and see that the bugs have started crawling into Dez's hair just as the last of her reserve gives way to full blown terror. She screams, but it sounds muffled with my heart pounding in my ears against the blaring alarms and rushing chaos.

"Dez!" I shout to her. My voice sounds like I'm yelling underwater, and when she turns to me in a scream, the bugs cover her neck, then begin spreading over her face and into her mouth. She lets go, falling to the floor slapping and flailing.

"Hull breach!" Avis yells as jets of water begin firing through the side walls sending pieces of metal and debris flying toward us.

"SELF-DESTRUCT INITIATED," a woman's voice says over the comms system, and the red light in the room begins flashing as a muted, beeping alarm sounds. The last thing I see is Liddick's arm, head, and half of his torso covered in writhing bugs before the black pulls me under, and I see nothing at all.

***

We should have seen it coming. It was all too easy, just stealing a two-ton sub-aquatic ship with only a day's training on how it actually works. And cloning ourselves...like they weren't still monitoring everything we did the second Fraya and Vox went missing in that cave, I hear Liddick in my head, but can only see black all around me.

"Jazz? Jazz, open your eyes. Can you hear me? We need to get off this ship. Jazz..." I hear Dez's voice, but I can't see her. I hear rushing water, feel a wet, icy sensation touch my fingertips, and blink. "She's awake! Jazz, can you hear me?" Dez asks again.

"Yeah," I say, but my voice comes out small and raspy. "Liddick was..."

"He's here. Myra, is he awake?"

"Not yet. I can't get the bleeding to stop. Aren't the nanites supposed to prevent this?" Myra's voice is desperate, and I try to get to my feet.

"You stay right there a minute," Dez's hands press my shoulders down. "Give him an accelerator—in the emergency kit in the wall. And keep the water out of that wound. What hit him?"

Liddick? I think over the roaring, a distant, sharp toned alarm, and a series of beeps and bells that all seem muffled.

Jazz! When you didn't answer me I thought...are you all right?

I think so, but water is rushing in. We have to get out of here. You're hurt? Can you move?

"It's working!" I hear Myra's voice, then see her blonde

hair flash in a blur as she turns to face us. "He's awake, and the bleeding is stopping!"

"Good, seal it and launch a disinfectant series just in case—they're in the kit too. Keep him stable until the nanites can do baseline repairs to the gashes and whatever might be bleeding inside, then we can move him. Jazz seems all right."

"Where's my brother?" I ask Dez, feeling like I've swallowed a bucket of gravel.

"He's OK. He's in the core room with Pitt and Ellis trying to slow the self-destruct sequence long enough to get us to the vent opening, but that's all I know right now."

"Dez!" I hear Arco's voice and see another blur in the distance, realizing for the first time that I'm lying on the floor.

"She's awake and talking—she'll be fine. How much farther?" Dez replies, but Arco doesn't answer. "Arco? How much farther?"

"About half a league," he finally says, sounding hollow.

"We can't make that—not at this rate of breach acceleration," Tieg's voice comes from somewhere beyond the hazy blues and flashing lights. I blink my eyes several more times trying to clear my vision, and see that water is now pouring in all around the room.

They knew we'd do this, Riptide. They knew, and they wanted us to try, I hear Liddick in my head again and look around to find him. He's sitting up against the wall about 15 feet away with Myra at his side holding a blood stained cloth to his head. I blink a few more times, and both the fog in my vision and in my understanding of what's happened up to this point start to clear.

"Let me up," I say to Dez. She moves back, and I get to my hands and knees before pulling myself to my feet. I feel like I'm watching myself count the breaks in the walls, the numbers and symbols stacking on top of each other as I focus on the force of water gushing in from everywhere, which turns into flashing clips of different ways this could end in the corners of my vision—an implosion, everyone swimming against a current, or rushing through the moon pool and loading into the Stingrays, all overlaid by the scrolling numbers. *This is what I felt Arco doing earlier,* I realize, and let my eyes close. The numbers turn into water that begins flooding from under two clear bowls turned upside down, one completely sealed, and one with a small hole in the top. The water rushes in force from the bottom of the first bowl and causes bubbles, many of which are crushed against the clear walls once it fills, and the others are pushed down to the bottom before escaping, but all the bubbles are pushed through the small hole at the top of the other bowl, and spiral upward until they disappear from view. As soon as I see this, I open my eyes and know what to do. "We have to get to the Stingrays," I say, although the voice I hear doesn't even sound like my own.

"We won't be able to get them out of dock safely without stopping, and we have to keep moving or the hull will implode—autopilot is fried, so we have to hold it manually," Arco says, his hands and Tieg's white-knuckling their steering columns.

"We don't have to launch, we just have to get inside the Stingrays."

"Jazz, there's not enough time," Tieg says, straining to maintain forward pressure.

"There is. Angle the ship so the mouth of the moon pool dock faces the vent. The implosion will spit us out—we'll be launched," I say, and Avis shakes his head violently.

"Do you know what that geometry will do to our speed? The ramp will turn into a brake rudder!"

"We aren't going to have enough speed to make it anyway. Our only resource right now is pressure!" I insist.

"Last time I checked you weren't a Nav—" Avis starts, but Arco cuts him off.

"No, but she's a coder too. That will work!" he says, nodding his head. "Where's Wright? Dez, how is he?"

"Good," Liddick says, getting to his feet and tossing away the bloodied cloth he'd been holding to his head.

"OK, Avis, Spaulding, prime the Stingrays and make sure that ramp locks out. Tether, Wright, take the girls downstairs and get everyone reloaded—tell Ellis to rig Jazz's Ray for manual controls and remind her how to drive...*stay close* to her until I catch up, do you understand?" Arco says, "Everyone go!"

Joss and Avis take Dez and Myra quickly down the stairs while Tieg and Liddick look at me, then exchange glances.

"You're split! We need to hold this speed—you can't do that on your own," Tieg protests.

"Hart, there won't be time to—"

"Crite, I swear I will beat one of you senseless *with* the other one if you don't move right now! *Go!"*

Tieg violently unclips from his station and glares at Arco as Liddick takes my shoulder, shaking his head. I struggle against him, and then manage to jerk away.

"Arco! We have enough time, come on!" I yell, but he turns his back to me.

"Get her out of here!" he yells again, and Liddick's arm wraps around my waist as he forces me backward toward the stairs. I slip out of his hold again and push back to Arco, but Tieg intercepts me, his arms closing like a vice around my hips so tightly that I can't even move my legs. I try to lever myself away from him by pushing off his shoulders with my hands, but it's no use.

Stop fighting! Can't you feel how much he hates that it's us who have to take you? Stop making it harder for him! I hear Liddick yelling in my head all the way down to the moon pool where Tieg puts me down and deploys my helmet, then, tosses me into the water. He and Liddick jump in after me. "Stop! He'll come!" Liddick says through our helmets as Tieg pulls my arm in the direction of the Stingray that Ellis is waving us toward.

"Jazz! Get in so I can lock out the ramp before this whole ocean comes down on us!" he says, and this finally halts my flailing.

"But how can he get out of there? How is the implosion not going to crush him up there?" I yell as we move to the little ship.

"His suit will deploy its impact kit when it registers the impending negative force, now get in the—" Ellis starts, but a loud scream comes through our helmet comms and cuts him off. We look around wildly for the source, and see Pitt at the mouth of the ramp engulfed in a cloud of red as he struggles to pull free from the ramp's hydraulic deployment arm.

"Pitt!" Dez yells, trying to scramble out of her Stingray.

"Dezzie, stay there!" Tieg shouts to her and pushes me against Liddick, then shoots like a bullet through the water to the ramp.

"Jazz, come on!" Ellis says, crawling up through the hatch as he sees Avis swimming over to help Tieg with Pitt, followed seconds later by Joss once he secures Myra in a Stingray. "There's no room for anyone else to help over there; we have to set up!"

"I'm almost in! Tether, hold the release and do not let go. Pitt, on three—on three, OK? Bite down!" Tieg yells.

"What's happening?" I look to Liddick as the cloud of blood surrounding Pitt gets darker and everything spins out with Myra's sobs flooding in the background, her fear and anxiety pressing down on top of my own.

"ONE!" Tieg shouts over the helmet comms.

"What's happening!?" I repeat.

"His hand is stuck—Jazz, don't look, just get in the Ray!" Liddick says, squaring my shoulders under the hatch before he follows me up. The squeeze is impossibly tight since Ellis is already inside, but then he closes the hatch and trips the drain. The barrier field comes down, and we can all move to the front of the little ship where Ellis enters a series of button combinations on the left side of the console.

"TWO!"

"All right, I just programmed the basic controls for manual, so the right side will do what you do—remember the pedals and steering with Arco? Just push down to accelerate, push forward here," Ellis says, pointing to buttons on the console and gripping the steering column.

"Are you OK?" Liddick asks, looking hard at me, and I nod.

"THREE!"

CHAPTER 50
The Bubbles

Pitt's scream rips through the helmet comms as a sudden gush of red spills into the water, and the stab of his pain cuts straight through my chest.

"Jazz, turn around!" Liddick yells, his face strained with the same feeling.

"SELF-DESTRUCT IN THREE MINUTES," the ship's announcement warns.

"OK, he's free—go to your Ray, we have to go!" Ellis shouts to Liddick, but Liddick doesn't move. "Wright! Come on!"

"She won't be able to pull in Hart on her own after this ship blows," Liddick says after a beat, and Ellis's hard expression softens. He exhales and nods.

"All right, we should only have a few hundred yards to go if this actually works. You already know how to stop, start, and steer—that's all the same, and these are the thrusters," Ellis says, pointing the two yellow buttons in the center of the console out to Liddick. "I set everything else to manual, OK? So both of you just drive and it will sync you." He looks from me to Liddick, who nods. Ellis scrambles to the other side of the barrier and deploys it, then slips out of the hatch and seals it behind him.

I look out the window and see the red cloud dissipating in the water as Tieg helps Pitt aboard someone's

Stingray, then gets into his own with Dez as the rest of us load up.

"SELF-DESTRUCT IN ONE MINUTE," the ship says, and I look around wildly to make sure I can see everyone inside a ship.

"They're all loaded, come on," Liddick says, turning our steering column and angling us toward the ramp.

"What happened? What happened to his hand?" I ask, afraid that I already know.

"It almost got him killed," Liddick says, then hits our comms button.

"—up! Line up!" Ellis is already yelling for the Stingrays to move into position in front of the ramp opening, and out of the corner of my eye, I notice Liddick's head starting to bleed again.

"Crite, what hit you?" I say, finally seeing the extent of his gash.

"I don't know. The last thing I remember was pushing the code, then a cracking sound. Things went black after that," he says, just before we topple into the side wall as the Leviathan begins to angle upward.

Everything jerks abruptly like we've been grabbed back from a full sprint as our momentum drops, and through the front window cap, I see the outer ramp straining in its locked position, then breaking off and sliding away beneath us with the force of the water pushing against it. Seconds later, a deafening crash sounds, and then we're shooting through the water end over end for several more seconds. I don't know which way is up or down as we jolt against the seat restraints over and over again until the tumbling finally begins to slow enough for me to see metallic pieces of the Leviathan shimmering everywhere, but I still don't see Arco.

"Where is he!?" I shout as soon as we get our bearings. "Ellis, where is he? You said his suit would deploy!"

"It did—it had to. Hang on, we're coming!"

"There's no register on the scan," Avis says over the comms.

"What does that mean? What does that mean there's no register?" I yell.

"There's not one *yet*, hang on!" Ellis replies.

"There he is!" Avis says and shines a spotlight at something that looks like a parachute floating in the water. "Crite, the deployment broke!"

"Let's go!" Liddick says, engaging his pedal.

My heart hammers in my chest as we speed over with the others to the material that hovers like a ghost in the water.

"Is he all right?" Ellis asks over the comms.

"He's not moving. Dez, Myra, what's your location?" Liddick asks.

"We're at…the vent," Pitt answers, coughing.

"Jax and Dez are here too," Joss follows.

"All right, it should be big enough for you to drive right in—set down and find a place to work. We'll be there soon with Hart in tow," Avis says as we pull up next to the parachute, which slips back enough for me to see Arco's face. His helmet is intact, but his eyes are closed. We anchor the Stingray, raise the seal, and open the hatch, then move toward him.

"Arco? Can you hear me?" I ask through the helmet comms as we crawl through the hatch, but he doesn't respond. Liddick and I each grab his wrists and pull him toward the Stingray, tearing away the rest of the fabric that bellows behind him like a sail. Liddick crawls back through the hatch first, then reaches down to grab Arco under the arms and hoist him up. He pulls him aboard, and I crawl up after him, helping to prop him up against the wall and fold his knees in so I can close the hatch. Liddick activates the drain and retracts the seal, and I remove Arco's helmet after mine and lift his face in my hands. "Arco? *Arco!"*

Liddick pushes a series of buttons at the helm, steers the Stingray into a sharp turn, straightens, and then we start to accelerate. In a few seconds Avis and Ellis pull alongside us as Ellis's voice comes over the comms.

"You have him? Is he OK?"

"We have him, but he's out. We need to get him to Dez and Myra. You heard they're at the vent with Pitt and Ripley—wait. Where's Tieg?"

"After he loaded Pitt, he moved Dez in with Jax and got into the Ray by himself," Ellis says.

"Where is he now?" Liddick asks as I try to hold Arco's head steady in my lap.

"We thought he came to help you," Avis answers just before he and Ellis pull up at the vent opening behind a descending Stingray.

"Jax!" I yell when I see him through the window with Dez. "He's breathing—Dez! Arco's breathing!"

"We're anchored—everyone is here. There's a short

drop, and then...wow," Joss says, trailing off.

"Hang on, Rip!" Liddick says as we maneuver into the groove, and I hold onto Arco tightly as everything around us closes in.

***

The Stingray jostles hard in the narrow passageway, and I try to brace against the side wall to keep Arco as still as possible.

"Hang on! We're almost there!" Liddick says, silhouetted by the green glow of the console screen.

"Wright! Stay on my six—Tieg found an air bell with a crag ledge!" Ellis calls through the comms as two Stingrays race forward in front of us, then, look like they disappear into the ceiling of the cave we've just entered. We follow their trajectory and break the surface of the water, the walls in here glowing an eerie blue as opposed to the white and yellow from the other cave. The refraction of the light from our Stingrays bounces off the dark water and sends dancing lines over everything as Liddick docks on the wide, glistening ledge, then helps me get Arco through the hatch. We stumble out and see Tieg and Joss kneeling with Pitt, who is sitting with his back against the rock wall as Myra finishes bandaging his left hand. Jax rushes over to help carry Arco over to Dez.

"I got him," Jax says, taking my place under Arco's arm with Liddick on the other side.

"Here, set him down," Dez says, slipping off her bag. She pulls the release cord behind Arco's shoulder and loosens the top of his dive suit, then checks his pulse as she brings a white, rounded stick about the size of her finger from the bag and waves it over his stomach, chest, neck, and finally, his head, where it turns from white to red at his eyes. She retracts it immediately to read, then exhales audibly. "He's OK, but we need to wake him up," she continues, and fishes for his bracelet cuff. When she finds it, she presses the inside of it at the same time she presses into his forearm, about six inches farther up than where Dame Mahgi had pressed my arm in the moon pool bay. A pocket of air sounds, and in a few seconds, Arco sucks in a desperate, deep breath, then coughs.

"Dez!" I shout.

"It's OK. It's just epinephrine...adrenaline to wake him up. He has—Arco, hey, look at me...you're all right— it's Dez," she says, turning his shoulders so he faces her. "Jazz is here. You have a concussion, so just try to be still while your technics work, otherwise you'll—" Arco's eyes light around the room, and after a few darting movements, he closes them tightly and brings his hands to either side of his head just before lunging to the edge of the crag ledge. "You'll get nauseous," Dez continues. "All right, you won't be able to vomit because of the suppressor in the epinephrine, so just try to be still. Sorry, I know it's awful, but it will pass. It'll help to sit up and breathe through your nose," she adds.

Arco tries to push up to his hands and knees, but can't seem to get his bearings. Liddick and Jax help him move to the wall, and I position myself behind him so that he's leaning against me, then wrap my arms around his neck and chest.

"Is he OK?" I ask.

"He'll be all right. He just needs a few minutes," Dez says through a tense smile, then rushes back to help Myra.

"You're OK...you're OK," I say into his ear, feeling my throat close up. His hand reaches up and curls around mine, and I feel tears start down my face.

"I'm OK," he echoes reassuringly, his voice low and rough. I lower my forehead to his and close my eyes, trying to will the world to stop for a second. "Pitt...was screaming?" he asks, and my eyes fly open, remembering the sound—the sight of the blood in the water. I look up wildly and see him sitting with Myra and Joss against the opposite wall holding his left hand to his chest and bleeding from his forehead. Dez moves in quickly and presses his bracelet and forearm in various places as Tieg kneels a few feet from them, then catches my eye.

"Is he all right?" I ask, my voice sounding shallow and cracked in my ears. Almost immediately, his brows draw in with worry before he catches himself, but for just an instant, his eyes soften into the same unreal blue as the glowing rivulets in the walls, and I finally see him—I finally feel something from him. It's the kind of pain that gnaws like hunger in the bottom of my stomach, then reaches up through my chest and pulls everything down...*helplessness*. "Tieg..." I trail off as he presses his lips into a hard line and sets his jaw, trying to fight the fear pressing down. When he can't, he looks away.

"What is it?" Arco says, squeezing my hand again as he tries to lift himself up.

"Stop, you have to be still," I say, pushing back on his

shoulders.

"Tieg had to sever two of his fingers to free him from the ramp's hydraulic relay," Jax says quietly, "Dez and Myra patched that up, but they couldn't get him the disinfectant series until just a few minutes ago."

"What does that mean?" I ask, turning to him.

"The spores..." Ellis says, taking a seat next to Liddick, on the other side of Jax. "They're not airborne, so everyone is all right in here, but they're already in his body."

"Hell..." Arco sighs, closing his eyes and letting his head fall back against my shoulder.

"But can't the nanites fix that? Can't they sweep them out or something?"

"They would if they could keep up. The disinfectant series suppresses the spores' rate of replication, but since he didn't get it until just now, the nanites may not be able to outpace them," Ellis continues.

"And he's starting to shiver. That's the first stage," Avis adds just as a buzzing starts in my ears. Arco grips my hand, and Liddick's eyes flash to mine before he starts scanning the room.

"We need to get out of here," he says abruptly.

"Why? What's wrong?" Myra asks, wiping her face.

"Something is coming."

"Arco needs at least ten more minutes, and Pitt..." Dez's voice trails off, her icy blue eyes wide and afraid as she looks around the cave for somewhere to go.

"How do you know that?" Tieg growls, rounding on Liddick.

"He's right! I can hear it too," I say.

"Ripley..." Arco says, extending his arm. Jax moves in and helps him to his feet as Liddick jumps back in the Stingray and pulls out a piece of the console, which then conforms to his arm when he slides it over his sleeve. I clench my teeth against the growing buzz, and see that he's doing the same.

"It's all right, Dezzie," Pitt says, trying to get to his feet. Tieg leaps over to him with Joss, and they both help him stand as Myra gathers the contents of her medical bag and straps it into place on her back. "I'm all right."

"You're feeling better?" Myra's voice pitches as she moves closer to him, her hands on his face as she studies his narrowed green eyes. He brings her forearms down to his wide chest with his good hand and smiles at her. "I'm all right," he says. "Take the sweep and give it to Arco...it has the code paths on it." He detaches the smooth, silver panel from the forearm he's holding tightly to himself, then releases it into her hands.

"You got the sweep out?" Arco asks, looking at Jax in disbelief as he brings one hand to his head.

"Pitt did. Once we went sideways, I didn't think we were going to be able to wrench it out in time, but...he did. He got it."

"Get the Nav systems, and the med and supply kits," Liddick says, angling the panel on his arm at one of the narrow crag openings. "There's a tunnel system on the other side of this wall—we'll have to squeeze through," he says, gritting his teeth against the buzzing and now, the high-pitched squealing in our heads. Arco loses his balance and bends, bracing his hand on his knee as Jax gets under his shoulder to steady him.

"We'll get the kits and the Nav units," Avis says, nodding to Ellis. They dart in and out of the Stingrays one after the other and distribute the Nav panels and bags amongst us as Myra crosses to us and gives Arco the panel from Pitt. I strap the bag Ellis gives me onto my back, then cover my ears against the almost unbearable buzzing sound as the water alongside us starts to ripple like something has been dropped into it from above. The blue light of the cave walls begins to mottle, and a dark, undulating mass appears, then disappears again just below the water's surface.

"Go!" Liddick yells, reaching for Dez, "Get her through there," he adds to Tieg, who pulls her back with him.

"Tether!" Pitt calls out in a strangled voice to Joss, who moves to his side. Pitt looks down at Myra and cups his hand along her cheek, then pulls her in and kisses her forehead. He angles her chin up and looks into her eyes. "Go with Joss," he says, bringing his ruined hand to the side of his throat.

"Are you coming!?" she cries.

"I'll be right behind you," he answers, brushing his thumb over her cheekbone. She tries to kiss him, but he holds her shoulder at bay as his eyebrows draw up. He shakes his head and runs his good hand through her hair, then darts his eyes to Joss and nods. "Go now, please," he says. Joss leads her through the opening as she protests, and when Pitt drops his hand from the side of his neck, I can see the red lesions that have already started breaking through the skin.

I yell Pitt's name, but the piercing sound in my ears drowns out my voice. The surface of the water behind us breaks, and a flat, black mass rears, revealing slatted openings that I can only partially make out in the fractured blue light. Ellis and Avis slip through the rift, and Jax ushers me toward them with Arco. Liddick is standing in front of it waving us on, and when we approach, Jax shifts Arco to him and turns back for Pitt. Liddick maneuvers Arco through the opening where Avis and Ellis intercept him, then starts pushing me through so he can go after him. I stumble on the other side, but quickly get to my hands and knees.

"Jax!" I yell through the bottom of the opening as he moves toward Pitt, who puts his hands out in front of him to stop Jax from coming any closer.

"Come on!" Jax calls to him as the writhing, dark mass inches onto the ledge from the water behind Pitt, the scattered light glinting off the needle-like teeth embedded in the slats.

"Ripley! We have to go!" Liddick grabs the back of Jax's dive suit and drags him off balance back through the fissure just in time to stop him from lunging for Pitt, whose facial contours and jawline suddenly distort beyond recognition in bursts of mangled red and white cauliflower eruptions that swell and spread. Jax must not see this yet as he continues struggling against Liddick, who finally wraps his arm around Jax's neck and shoulders and wrestles him back to the ground. I sit on his legs to help weigh him down, then grip his shoulders to make him focus on me.

"Jax, stop! It's too late! *Stop!*" I shout as the blue rivulets in the walls flash through the crag, illuminating the air bell and the shifting, breathing mass, which looks like the hatcheted underbelly of a mushroom as it pulls itself further out of the water toward Pitt.

"*Jazz!*" Arco yells, moving to us along with Ellis and Avis. "The map to the messages starts down that tunnel—we have to go now!" He motions to another opening at the other side of the cave as I tear my eyes away from Pitt stepping backward into the opening and closing mouths of the blackness that envelops him, then pulls him down.

There is only the sound of water splashing under our feet when the high-pitched keening suddenly stops, and I realize we are literally running from the esteemed Gaia Sur future we have spent our lives pursuing—a future we now know never really existed at all. In the growing darkness, it becomes clear that there is only finding my father, Liam, Lyden, and Arwyn now...there is only moving forward down a new path we never saw coming.

Are you ready to see what awaits Jazz and her friends in the caves beneath the ocean floor? Visit us below to join the Elements Series Newsletter for the latest information on TERRA: Elements Series Book Two!

www.theelementsseries.com/newsletter

Visit The Elements Series on social media!

https://www.facebook.com/TheElementsBookSeries

https://twitter.com/ElementsSeries

http://elementsseries.tumblr.com

https://instagram.com/elementsseries

Acknowledgments

Special thanks to our friend at Overdun Productions, Kyle Bainter, for your time and beautiful cinematography for the AQUA book trailer. Your ability to capture what is in plain sight, yet unseen by so many, is inspiring. Many thanks to my beta readers for your keen eyes and honest feedback, especially Kaila Brusdahl, Dayandra De Miranda-Leão, Katelynn Pittman, Margarita McClain, Tracy Ortiz, Olivia Sigsbee, Katie Sokolowski, Cassidy White, Shaun Vellucci, and of course Rachel Carpenter, whose feedback became particularly invaluable editing. Countless thanks to my writing partner and jack-of-all-trades editor Ryan Bachtel for your tireless reading and collaboration over the years, and most importantly for talking me down from all those trees along the way. To my husband, James, for your support and vision in bringing my characters to life, and for your unyielding standards. I cannot thank you enough. They have all come to be living, breathing, people for me, and because of you, now others can see them too. And, of course, Mom, thank you for always believing in me, for being in my corner no matter what, and for giving me the will to fight to the end with whatever life laces up. Finally, without the daily inspiration of the teenagers I'm lucky enough to have in my life—my own children, and my students—I couldn't have imagined Jazz's quest for purpose, Liddick's fearless drive, or Arco's selfless courage. Thank you for being indomitable, brave, resilient, impossible people. You are the stuff of stories. You are the heartbeat of us all.